Long Boat Diplomacy

Long Boat Diplomacy

Long Boat Space – Book Two

Matthew H. Ambrose- Author

Abigail Dixon – Cover Art

CONTENTS

DEDICATION

This story is for the adventurers who travel to faraway places from libraries, tree houses, out-of-the-way corners and the middle of a public square. Those who can make a throne of a mossy tree stump, and ignore the entire world while burying their nose in a good book. You are my people.

ACKNOWLEDGMENTS

This book was greatly improved by my uncompensated beta readers, James, Laura, and Bonnie. If you read the first Long Boat Story, you'll notice a marked increase in the overall quality and a decrease in typos. All in all, they made the story much better for you, the reader. Any mistakes are wholly my own.

Copyright © 2024 by Matthew H. Ambrose

All rights reserved. No part of this book may be reproduced in any manner whatsoever without written permission except in the case of brief quotations embodied in critical articles and reviews.

First Printing, 2024

FOREWORD

Long Boat Diplomacy is the second book in the Long Boat Space series, and continues the story of the Long Boat *Nai'a* and her crew. In book one, Long Boat Star Crossing the *Nai'a* completed her voyage from Sol to Tau Ceti. On the way the crew battled an enigmatic enemy determined to take or destroy the ship. Long Boat Diplomacy stands on its own as a story, but you will have a better understanding of the characters and initial situation if you have read Long Boat Star Crossing.

Chapter 1- Pay as You Exit

October 30th, AD 3187
Long Boat Nai'a - Tau Ceti Inner-System
Bridge

Captain Brelling eased back into her command chair and took a sip of coffee. It wasn't Jamaica Blue Mountain, but the local Persephone's Shadow variety was quite passable. A little over two weeks out of Tau Ceti's HAB-5, the massive, ten-kilometer-long *Nai'a* continued to slowly build velocity toward their destination in the Lalande system. They needed to keep the ship's speed down to a level manageable for the protection ships escorting them. Tau Ceti's notorious dust and debris density wasn't helping matters. The Great Prospects protection team had paid in blood to protect the *Nai'a* on the in-system passage. The captain was determined to make sure they wouldn't need to on the way out.

"Lieutenant Parks, how are we looking for the next twelve hours?" she asked the officer at the sensors station.

"Nothing but mapped objects on near and far scan, Captain, I don't anticipate any need for course changes. All these near misses aren't doing my blood pressure any favors, though."

"I'm with you, but the protection team has to save their attention and ammunition for real threats," the captain replied. "I'll be happier when we've climbed out of the plane of the ecliptic enough to shake the dust of this system off our boat."

The captain had barely finished speaking when the collision alert sounded and red light strobed through the bridge. Across the boat, the crew moved swiftly to action stations. "Steady on helm," the captain stated calmly. She punched up her direct channel to the protection team. "Eagle One, *Nai'a* Actual, advise."

"*Nai'a* Actual, Eagle One. Maintain heading, we have two bogies on scan. We can deal with them, but be ready with evasion sequence Charlie." Colonel Rai's tone was all business.

Captain Brelling resisted the urge to ask for more information, merely checking her own scan display for the bogies and verifying that Chief Nance was ready with the evasion sequence at helm. Their planned course had them boxed in to bypass three medium-large asteroids, just the right geometry for an ambush.

***

Colonel Rai watched his heads-up display as he accelerated *Harpy* toward the incoming bogies. Leftenant Wyant, his weapons officer, tagged one for *Harpy* and passed the other to *Gladius*. Rai adjusted their vector slightly for a better engagement angle. *Harpy* shuddered slightly as the missile launcher accelerated their bird out of the tube.

"Missile away," declared Wyant. "The computer assigns a .72 probability that we're dealing with ship-to-ship interceptors. Request helm control for railgun targeting."

"Aye, you have the helm."

Wyant deftly piloted *Harpy* through a tight roll, letting the targeting computer fire three short bursts from the railgun. "Returning helm control."

"Aye, I have the helm," Colonel Rai replied. He positioned the ship for another shot and watched their missile close in for the kill. With impeccable timing, the target jinked....right into the path of a cluster of railgun slugs. A brilliant flash marked the intercept.

"I think we just got lucky, sir," said Wyant, adjusting the scan and dialing up an optical feed. "We've got two large chunks of debris. My money is on separate warhead and drive sections. I've designated each."

Colonel Rai took in the vectors. "Target the warhead with the laser. If you're right, I'll buy you dinner at Six Fathoms." The optical feed flared slightly as the laser lit the target up then blanked as it detonated. "Dinner is on me. Where's the other half headed?"

"Directly at the *Nai'a*, specifically the ice shield."

"What's left of that missile probably wouldn't do much more than dent the hull but a strike on the ice shield presents an opportunity." He checked the wider scan picture and saw it was clear of bogies. "*Gladius*, report."

"Direct missile hit on our bogie sir. Minor debris from the intercept is all on a safe vector."

Captain Brelling was nearly at the toe tapping stage when Colonel Rai's voice interrupted her thoughts, "*Nai'a* Actual, we intercepted both bogies. There's no sign of a ship at either launch point. These are the same missile-based space mines we've seen before. I'm tracking a chunk of debris we believe is a missile drive section. It will impact the ice shield. Suggest you maintain course. We can learn a lot from that missile if it embeds."

"Roger, Eagle One, maintaining course and speed. We have the missile debris on scan. We'll launch the pinnace in case of a bounce." She passed the order to the pinnace crew in the boat bay.

***

Jarman Lal eased the pinnace through the boat bay doors and clear of the ship. His copilot tapped into the protection team sensor net and confirmed a clear path to the ice shield. "Run a self-check on the catcher's mitt, but don't run it out yet," Jarman told him. "I don't want to shift our center of gravity until we need to." The edge of the ice shield formed a white crescent of glare ahead of the pinnace as they slowly accelerated along the ten-kilometer length of the massive long boat. Jarman felt a surprising swell of emotion as he took in the magnificent sweep of the ship that was now his home. The emotion spiked when the pinnace cruised over a bright patch of steel amidships. The patch reminded him painfully of the inward bound attack on the *Nai'a* and its cost.

***

Captain Brelling took in the vector of missile drive section approaching the ship. She dearly wanted to capture the hardware to help the Tau Ceti government's investigation into the organization targeting the *Nai'a*. The angle was too shallow to guarantee it would embed itself in the shield, but she didn't think maneuvering would help much. It would be up to Jarman in the pinnace. She made a quick guess on the direction of the bounce and posted it to the shared scan data.

Jarman noted the flashing trace on his display and adjusted the pinnace's vector. Colonel Rai's voice reached him on the tactical net. "Eagle One maneuvering to provide scan data forward of the ice shield." Jarman held out hope for a stick, but it wasn't to be. The drive section caromed off the ice shield, heading away from the *Nai'a* with an end-over-end tumble.

"Kingfisher One maneuvering to intercept," he transmitted. Confirm my vector." The pinnace's display lit up with the strobe of three laser shots from *Harpy* in quick succession.

"This is Eagle One, your vector is clear. We'll maintain overwatch while you intercept and return."

Jarman shook his head then focused on the missile drive's trace. The vector was within five degrees of the captain's prediction so they were close on its heels. He made a slight adjustment, then accelerated for a few seconds to put them on an intercept course. "Ready on the mitt," he told his copilot. "Deploy on my mark. Three...two...one...mark!" The clunk of the catcher's mitt deploying transmitted through the hull and the pinnace crabbed sideways in space. Jarman deftly counteracted the motion with his attitude thrusters, then slowed their approach. He could see his target now, and carefully timed the tumble of the dented cylinder to impact the mitt flat and dead center. The pinnace jerked as the coated fabric of the mitt folded around the missile chunk in a perfect catch. Jarman used the induced rotation to bring the pinnace around to a return vector, carefully killed their outward momentum, and accelerated back toward the *Nai'a*. The pinnace handled like a trimaran with one hull missing, but close enough to the simulations Jarman trained on to allow him to get them headed in the right direction. "Eagle One, Kingfisher One, good capture. Confirm my return vector."

"Your return vector is clear, Kingfisher One. Don't dally, we'll be passing through a denser debris field in about five minutes. We're vectoring back to overwatch stations."

Jarman checked the numbers and bumped his velocity up to give himself a bit more margin. He approached the boat bay at the *Nai'a's* stern gingerly and confirmed that his extra package would clear the doors. Once the pinnace came to rest in its cradle, he let out a long breath. His copilot grinned at him. "I'm glad you were driving. Well done!"

"Thanks, let's hope the results are worth the effort."

Once the boat bay's atmosphere was restored, four crew members in hazmat suits approached the catcher's mitt carefully, checking the readouts and their chemical detectors. Jarman and the copilot climbed out at the all clear. "Let's get out of their way, it's going to take a while to unstick that thing from the mitt. Abishai's vacuum glue works, but it's messy."

"What's in it?"

"He didn't tell me the whole formula, but I understand breadfruit tree sap is the base with a combination of palm oils to keep it pliable. He said it yields to alcohol and patience."

***

A few hours later Captain Brelling sat down with Colonel Rai, and Commander Kevin Hartley, her first officer. "Hopefully we'll get good data from the missile drive. It looked to be in remarkably good shape considering what it's been through. How many attacks is that now on our out-bound trip?"

"Fifteen separate attacks," answered Colonel Rai. "We've taken out a total of thirty-five missiles and fifteen ballistic objects. Without your fabrication shop, we'd be running low on missiles and rail gun slugs. As it is, we're going to need to mine some raw material for slugs or order some delivered. I have contacts out this way. Most of my pilots have mining experience, so we can do it, but that takes a ship out of the protection net."

"I'll talk to Marshall Winter and have him arrange delivery along with the ice to thicken the shield," the captain answered. "He, and the Tau Ceti government, owe us that much."

Commander Hartley leaned back and folded his hands thoughtfully. "These attacks aren't doing much more than annoying us and costing us a few credits. They've actually given us enough opportunities for collision drills that our new crew members are shaping up nicely. I'm not sure what the perpetrators think they're going to accomplish."

"From what I know of these people; they're doing it purely out of spite and hoping to get lucky. One thing is certain, Marshall Winter's initial sweep missed a good chunk of the organization, or we wouldn't be getting these constant piecemeal attacks. I'm more concerned with what's going to happen when we get the cap for the ice shield delivered. We're going to be busy, and we'll have to maintain a steady course and acceleration during the installation. We'll also have several tugs in our near space. We need a plan to keep everyone safe during the operation. Kevin, I want you to spearhead the planning. Use Mr. Barboa and anyone else he suggests. See what you, he, and the protection team can come up with. I'll get with Marshall Winter and ask what assets Tau Ceti can bring to the table."

Chapter 2- Cockroaches and Other Vermin

October 30th, AD 3187
Long Boat Nai'a - Tau Ceti Inner-System
Bridge

Captain Brelling fired up the communications console in her office and put through a call to Marshall Winter back on HAB-5, Tau Ceti's commercial and governmental capital. The light speed lag would be annoying but manageable at this distance. The Marshall's face soon occupied her screen. "I see from your latest report that our friends are still giving you a hot time. "

"I'd say lukewarm. I'm grateful for their incompetence, but they *are* costing us money. Will you be able deliver the missile fuel and iron ingots I requested with the ice cap?"

"Yes, and my famously stingy government is footing the bill."

"That's good news. These miscreants are harder than cockroaches to stamp out. I believe they'll attack us when we're adding the second layer of ice to our shield. Can you provide some protection during the operation?"

"I think you're right," answered Marshall Winter. "I contacted Brigadier Tamang yesterday. Great Prospects has a team finishing up a convoy operation that can rendezvous with you a few days before the ice delivery. He said he isn't thrilled with the number of good people you lured away from him, but he isn't averse to picking up some easy credits."

"He has that trait in common with most of the people in this system, but Great Prospects has more than earned the credits we're paying." She paused.

"I have some good news for you. We captured the drive section of one of the missiles used in the latest attack. My people are going over it now. We'll get the results to you and I'll arrange transportation to HAB-5 with Great Prospects. Would you like our resident hacker to take a crack at the guidance computer?"

"Yes," he answered. "If anybody in this system can get something useful out of it, she's the one. I apologize for the continued attacks. It's obvious my initial sweep missed more of the organization than I thought possible. If we can trace the missile to its source, it may be the break I need to finally clean them out. Speaking of the enemy organization, we have a name for them, at least what they call themselves: the Restoration."

"The Restoration?" queried Captain Brelling.

"Yes," replied Marshall Winter, "we're still puzzling out what the name signifies. In any case, they're not done with the *Nai'a*."

"The protection team is keeping us safe and on schedule, but I wouldn't mind if the Restoration slacked off. The last thing I want, though, is to leave them here waiting for the next long boat. If we can help track them down by being a fat target, so be it."

"Take care, I'll be looking forward to the data from the missile. Give Colonel Rai my regards."

Captain Brelling kept her expression neutral but her heart rate jumped at the phrase. By their private code, it meant Marshall Winter would meet them with a government task force of ships during the ice shield enhancement operation. He must expect an attack even more than she did.

"You take care also, Marshall Winter. Our enemies are your enemies now." Captain Brelling answered with the acknowledgment code phrase. "*Nai'a* out."

***

Lisandra Redding looked at Abishai and Roan. They stood around the missile drive section secured to a metal bench in one of the ship's engineering workshops. "Follow my instructions and please don't get creative on me," she said. "I want the guidance computer and power source intact. Everything dangerous went with the warhead section and the ruptured fuel line, so there shouldn't be any nasty surprises. Abishai, I need you cut this rectangular section out without damaging anything underneath. Rimon claims you're an artist with a plasma cutter. Let's find out if he's right. Roan, figure out a way to secure that section so it doesn't drop. We'll want to lift it straight out by small increments once it's free."

Abishai took a pair of calipers and measured the thickness of the material. He adjusted his plasma torch, flipped down his face shield and got to work. Roan readied a metal bar with two suction cups and attached it to an overhead lift via a pair of cables.

Twenty minutes later Abishai had all but two one-centimeter sections of the rectangle cut. He stepped back to wipe sweat from his face and motioned Roan forward. Roan checked the temperature of the missile surface, then attached the suction cups and carefully tightened the cables so they would hold the section at its current height. Abishai finished his cuts. There was a slight ping as the section came loose, but it stayed steady. Lisandra carefully threaded a fiber optic cable through one end of the cut, her mouth quirking as she examined the connections inside. "Here," she said, stepping back and handing Roan and Abishai each a flat-head screwdriver. "Lever it up a half a centimeter from each end." Roan and Abishai gingerly complied. Lisandra worked a cutting tool under the edge and snipped two connections. "You can lift it about ten centimeters now, slowly." Roan worked the overhead lift controls until they had the required separation. Lisandra examined their prize carefully, then reached into her toolkit.

A few hours later she had the intact guidance computer and its dead power source separated from the missile and laid out on another bench. A pair of engineering ratings photographed both from all angles then went to work on the rest of the drive section. "No data plate, but I suppose we shouldn't expect criminals and terrorists to abide by the rules," said

Lisandra. "I recognize the design, though. It's a copy of the Sable Arms Mark X Kestrel. She looked at Roan. "Do you think you can recharge this power source? I'm going to need the guidance computer to think it's still in the missile to get anything out of it, and that starts with the power source."

"It's a micro-sandwich capacitor," Roan answered. "I don't think it's designed for recharging but I've got some tricks that might work. Can I ask how you're familiar with a Sol missile design?"

"I needed a legitimate occupation to camouflage my hacking activities. Subcontracting for General Arms and other defense companies worked nicely, and came with the added bonus of a security clearance. I want to power this back up in microgravity, but I need a few more tools. Can you meet me in shop 11B in two hours with the power supply?"

"No promises, but I'll do my best," Roan stated, rubbing his chin. "Abishai, I'll need your help." The two friends took the power supply and headed for the Section Beta hydro workshop.

Two and a half hours later when they tumbled through the door of shop 11B adjacent to the ship's spine, Lisandra had the time prominently displayed on the wall. Roan blushed, "This was trickier than I thought it would be." They activated their boot magnets to secure themselves to the floor, then unpacked and set up several small, connected electronic components. Two wires ran from the conglomeration, ending in alligator clips.

"Really?" said Lisandra, one eyebrow quirked. "Where's the power supply?"

"You're looking at a reasonable facsimile thereof," answered Roan. "The original supply wouldn't hold a charge long enough to power a flashbulb. I managed to get enough power out of it to get a read on the voltage and waveform then cobbled together a substitute power source. It emulates the original."

It took a good three seconds for Lisandra's eyebrow to un-quirk as she considered the kluged-up mess in front of her. "I can't believe you still use alligator clips, but they'll do. Go ahead and connect it up. Say a few prayers and hope we get some cooperation." Roan connected his power source to the guidance computer's power leads and stepped back. Lisandra flexed her fingers and began typing commands into her minicomp.

"Okay, my little friend," she murmured. "You're floating in space waiting for a big fat target to pass by. Be a good widget and tell Mama all about it." Roan and exchanged their own quirked eyebrows as she coaxed the guidance computer to give up its secrets.

***

A few hours later Lisandra sat down with the first officer and Colonel Rai. "Engineering confirmed via metallurgy that the missile is a local build, no surprise there," she started. "It's a fairly recent Sol-based design. Someone working for the organization attacking us no doubt brought it with them surreptitiously. Sol and the Long Boat Free Trade Syndicate have both banned its export. The radar absorbent coating is the same one used on the asteroids they attacked us with on the way in. I managed to image and copy the guidance software before the computer slagged itself. You should have seen the look on Roan's face when it popped. He probably thought we were going to die, but it was just a small thermite capsule used as an anti-tamper measure."

"You could have warned him," said Colonel Rai.

"Where's the fun in that? Anyway, the software is based loosely on the original Sable Arms package. They made several changes that violate interstellar weapons conventions. The missile was basically an autonomous mobile space mine. The attack parameters limit targeting to objects the general size and shape of a long boat. Whatever missiles are still out there shouldn't pose a hazard to in-system ships."

"Did you find anything that might help Marshall Winter track down the manufacturer?"

"The software won't help, but the engineering analysis and metallurgy should provide enough to identify the maker." She slid a data chip to each of them. "This is a copy of the software that I separated into harmless components and tagged as evidence for Marshall Winter's people. One of the many illegal mods is removal of the remote self-destruct. I was hoping to peel the self-destruct codes away and use them against the missiles, but no joy."

Colonel Rai picked up his chip and considered it. "I'll have a couple of my people look this over and see if they have any ideas. It should help our anti-missile targeting if nothing else."

"I'll have to arrange secure transport to get this to Marshall Winter," said Commander Hartley. "I don't think he'll be fading back into retirement any time soon. The rot in this system is significantly deeper than he suspected."

***

Commander Hartley and Colonel Rai briefed the captain and Mr. Barboa on the missile findings a few hours later.

"I want a surprise ready for these people when, not if, they commit to another large-scale attack," declared Captain Brelling when they were finished. "What I'm going to tell you doesn't leave this room. Marshall Winter and I set up several code phrases in case we needed to communicate in the clear. By the time we start the ice shield operation, Marshall Winter will be in an overwatch position here." She indicated the point on the holographic display, with a force of twenty ships. "I want you to figure out how to integrate his force, the additional Great Prospects ships, and our present defenses. I'm holding out hope that Marshall Winter's force will come as a shock to our attackers."

"I wish I had a better idea of just what we're facing," answered Commander Hartley.

Colonel Rai rubbed the stubble on his head. "I might be able to help. I updated my database on our competitors in the Tau Ceti. If these people want to seriously threaten the *Nai'a*, they'll need to hire a competent mercenary force. We know they tried once already. I've got a good idea of who's in position to answer the call. Only two companies have ships positioned in this part of the system, but between them, they can field a considerable force."

"Do you think they'll risk the kind of heat the Tau Ceti government will bring to bear for attacking a long boat?" asked the captain. "Your friend Ennis Elkins didn't think it was worth it."

"Ennis has more brains and morals than the average Tau Ceti mercenary commander," Colonel Rai answered. "Also, we know these people have no scruples. They'll use any kind of leverage they can get. I wouldn't be surprised if they grabbed hostages from the two companies and are holding them to ensure the cooperation of their forces. I have another worry. Even with hostages, they still have to sell the mercenaries on a survivable end game. The only leverage in this system big enough to get the government to negotiate is the *Nai'a* herself. They need possession of the ship and that means boarding and seizing control. One of the two mercenary companies, Warnicky's Wolfpack, is space infantry heavy. They have the capability to at least give it a try. How are the militia companies looking?"

Commander Hartley steepled his fingers. "We've plugged in new crew to fill the empty positions and each company has done one training rotation. Mr. Barboa says they're shaping up, but there are still some rough edges. We'll step up the drills. We aren't as good as we were on the way in to Tau Ceti, but we still field a two-battalion sized anti-boarding force equipped with powered armor."

"The way the Restoration operates, they'll keep information about our defensive capabilities from the mercenaries," said Colonel Rai. "We can use their ignorance to our advantage, but the Wolfpack has a reputation for ruthless all-out attacks. We'll need a good plan to handle them without taking major casualties. The other company is the Orca Squadron. They have at least fifty small attack vessels aboard a stealth capable carrier. Warnicky's Wolfpack has a carrier for their assault shuttles. Between the two companies, they also have thirty escort ships roughly equivalent to ours."

The captain frowned. "We're going to end up close to parity in space power. This has the potential to be a bloodbath if it's a straight up fight. I want some options to keep casualties to a minimum, priority to our side of course, but these mercenaries are likely being coerced. If we can safely preserve their companies intact, they'll be extra motivated to help stamp out this blight on the Tau Ceti system."

Chapter 3 – The Games People Play

November 2nd, AD 3187
Long Boat Nai'a - Tau Ceti Mid-System
Beta Section Armory

Abishai walked down the row of his heavy weapons squad troopers, carefully checking armor, weapons and ammo. "Swap your power pack out," he told a flechette gunner. "This one's at eighty percent. It would last for today's drill, but let's get in the habit of starting with a full-up charge every time." The trooper stepped out of line to get a fresh pack. Attention to detail was not Abishai's strong suit, but several unpleasant conversations with Mr. Barboa had given him the habit of checking everything. "Okay, you're as a ratty a bunch as I've ever seen, but you're ready. Let's show those Alpha Section slugs how a ship-rat fights! SHIP-RATS!"

"HOOAH!" the squad yelled.

"SHIP-RATS!"

"HOOAH!"

"SHIP-RATS!"

"HOOAH!"

Abishai pounded toward their initial position with the squad close behind.

Two hours later Abishai and the squad wearily cracked themselves out of their armor, then cleaned and serviced their weapons and gear. After another painstaking inspection, Abishai cleared them all to get showers and regroup for the after-action review.

Mr. Barboa took center stage as usual when they got back together. "Good job today...for a bunch of butt-dragging civilians! I don't think any of you died more than three or four times. I should make your squad leaders write simulated letters to your next of kin. Now, other than general sloppiness and tripping over our own feet, let's see how you chose to die today." He proceeded to give a scathing breakdown of several examples, mostly featuring new crew members who were still getting acclimated to moving and fighting in powered armor.

"Speed is life to you and death to your enemies, but you have to stay under control," Mr. Barboa continued. "I saw several good things today from you new chums, let's build on those." He detailed a number of instances of innovative thinking and aggressive tactics. "I believe you can get a twenty percent improvement in tactical movement speed if you'll work on the specifics I pointed out," he finished. "Get with your leaders if you have questions."

Abishai pulled one of his squad members aside after the meeting. Quester Drake was a former denizen of Tau Ceti HAB-5. His scrawny build made him the smallest member of the heavy weapons squad, but he had remarkable endurance. Abishai was pretty sure Quester's background included extra-legal activity, but so far, he had adapted better than most of the new crew. "Congratulations on avoiding Mr. Barboa's Hall of Shame this time. Let's talk about that mishap with the ammo belt, though. What happened?"

Quester hung his head, "I checked my helmet's video afterward. It was a backward feed. I know it's clearly marked, but I flipped it."

Abishai put his hand on Quester's skinny shoulder, "You aren't the first to make that mistake. Be glad it happened in a training drill. I'm sure you'll double check from now on. We learn more from what we get wrong in these drills than what we do right."

"We must be learning a lot according to Mr. Barboa," Quester said wryly. "Say, I know I'm way behind the rest of the squad. Could I get some extra powered armor time?"

Abishai rubbed his chin. "We all need to sharpen our movement skills. I have an idea about a good way for the whole squad to get more suit time. Watch your PCOM message cue."

Abishai found his wife, Shanyah, in the corridor outside the meeting room and they walked arm in arm back to their quarters. "I think we put a dent in Alpha's invincible reputation today," she said, leaning her head on his substantial shoulder.

"They were surprised by how quickly we moved," replied Abishai. "We were out of their trap and into their rear area before they could spring it. Things got ugly for them in a hurry when you took out the company commander."

"A little humility is good for them," Shanyah grinned. "How is Quester doing?"

"Much better than I was a month into training. He feels bad about reverse feeding an ammo belt, but he's coming right along. The speed and surprise we used today gave me an idea about some additional training I'd like to try. What would you say to a little competition, your squad against mine?"

"Before I answer, I'm going to need to know what kind of competition."

"I'm thinking an athletic contest in powered armor will do a lot to give the new crew confidence and improve everyone's speed," said Abishai. "A squad relay race through the maintenance spaces of all six habitat sections for a full circuit of the ship would be fun."

"I'm sure my squad is up for it," Shanyah replied "You'd better coordinate with Mr. Barboa and the section maintenance crews to clear a path. We don't want to give some poor hydro tech a heart attack."

"I want to include at least one surprise task in each leg. Mr. Barboa will have some good ideas on that score." They continued on their way, scheming as they went.

***

The next day everything was in place. Shanyah and Abishai took their places at the Beta Section start line, each grinning and ready to beat the other soundly. In less twenty-four hours the relay race had taken on a life of its own. Teams from every section were participating and half the crew was tuned in to the live feed from the participants. Mr. Barboa gave them a countdown and they were off in a gliding run on separate routes.

It didn't take long for Abishai to hit the first surprise obstacle. His route took him through the narrow gap between a massive pump and a structural beam. He knew he couldn't fit through in his armor. He quickly shucked his weapon and started the process of removing the armor and breaking it down into pieces small enough to get through the gap. With most of the ship watching, he was grateful for his full coverage under-layer. It took him close to five minutes before he was suited up again and on his way. Two minutes later he saw the next member of his squad ahead of him ready to go. He ran up and slapped the trooper on the armored shoulder, passing the virtual baton. The grenadier loped off, following the virtual route on his helmet display.

Abishai leaned over with his gauntlets on his armored knees, breathing deeply. He checked the race feed and saw that he and Shanyah had finished their relay legs in a virtual tie. It was anybody's race. The squad's stayed nearly even until Quester's leg. The newbie went over and around obstacles like a spider monkey, in spite of the bulky armor. He surprised everyone, including Mr. Barboa, by rewiring a stuck hatch control panel without removing his gauntlets. The time saved, combined with his speed, put Abishai's squad ahead by thirty seconds. They maintained the lead to the end of the course, giving the Ship Rats the win. Quester managed to survive a hearty round of back slapping when the team returned to the armory to stow their gear. They kept close track as the other squads ran the course to see if anyone beat their time.

Shanyah gave Abisha a friendly punch in the shoulder. "I suppose you had to beat me at something sooner or later. I didn't realize you had a ringer on your squad."

"I didn't realize it either, until the race," answered Abishai. I'm not sure I want to enquire where Quester picked up his hot-wiring skills."

"He made short work of the hatch control," said Shanyah. "We'll have him show us his technique during our next drill. Your squad's time will be tough to beat. I wonder if the other teams will learn from watching our runs."

Abishai shook his head, "Mr. Barboa shut all the competitors out of the race feed with Mr. Literal's help. I pity them if they try to cheat. I'm most interested in the Great Prospects commando teams. The pilots are generally Quester's size or smaller. They may have a speed advantage."

"I'm glad we decided to add them to the militia organization," Shanyah nodded. "With three-fourths of the protection ship crews off shift at any time, the commandos add a good punch to the reserve. They insisted on being part of the internal defense force for the out-system run. We all benefit from rubbing shoulders with professionals."

At the end of the day Abishai's Ship Rats won bragging rights with the fastest time. A Great Prospects commando squad came in second. Over the next week, the races became a daily part of shipboard life and a great source of entertainment for the crew. Mr. Barboa constantly shifted routes, challenges and conditions. Abishai could tell everyone in his squad was getting faster and working better with their powered armor. Increased maintenance time was the only downside he could see.

Mr. Barboa declared two days of rest and maintenance to let the militia to get their gear fully operational. After the respite, it was game on. Two days were devoted to what he called the Militia Jamboree. Day one was squad level competition and day two was individual contests culminating in the 20K race. Abishai's Ship Rats edged out Shanyah's squad for second place in the team competition.

The next day Abishai took part in the armored grappling tournament. He outclassed his competition through the first three rounds, reaching the championship bout against his friend Jarman Lal. Jarman was tall and lanky in sharp contrast to Abishai's fireplug build. They grappled together regularly, but not in powered armor. Abishai knew he had to keep a good base or Jarman would toss him around the repurposed cargo hold like a rag doll. He triggered the automatic maglocks on his boots, sacrificing agility for a better foundation.

The two men circled each other carefully, looking for an opening. Abishai feinted a low shot, then grabbed Jarman's helmet as he ducked with both hands. He tried to snap his friend's head all the way to the ground but Jarman went with the motion and pushed forward hard, catching Abishai in a double-leg takedown. As Abishai went to his back he attempted the Tawara-gaeshi rice bag throw, but couldn't get a good enough purchase on Jarman's armor. All of Jarman's weight came crashing down on top of him. Abishai thrashed like a beetle on his back until the referee declared the fall to Jarman. Jarman helped him up and they bowed to each other in the center of hold.

"I surprised you with the low shot!" Jarman said, once they took their helmets off.

"You did! It was a good counter to the head snap. I had my boots mag-locked to the deck and I couldn't sprawl fast enough. Also, note to self, Tawara-gaeshi doesn't work well in armor."

"I might manage it, but you don't have the length to get a grip," the lanky Belter replied.

"I'm just glad Shanyah decided to compete in the combat marksmanship course," said Abishai. "We'd both be looking up at first place in grappling, and I'd be getting daily reminders of her superiority."

"How did she take losing to your squad in the relays?" Jarman asked.

"Surprisingly well," said Abishai, "she's a better loser than a winner. Unfortunately, it took me seven years of marriage to win anything more significant than Monopoly against her."

"The final of the individual 20K is about to start," said Jarman. "Do you want to meet in the Star Lounge and watch it on the big display?" Abishai nodded.

Thirty minutes later they grabbed two seats together in the crowded viewing lounge. A leaded glass armor bubble provided a sparkling view of the surrounding stars, but all eyes were glued to the giant holographic display. Quester Drake of the Ship Rats and pilot Leftenant Haynes from the Great Prospects protection team were the finalists. They stood in their powered armor with a full combat load of weapons and ammunition. The pilot's armor was flat black and devoid of decoration. Quester's armor was white but his helmet was digitally painted in a snarling rat motif. Abishai made a mental note to talk to him about it. Each contestant had a hand touching bulkhead zero in the boat bay at the aft end of the *Nai'a*. The rules were simple. Get to the bow of the ship and back as quickly as possible. The spinal corridor was off limits but all other ship spaces were fair game.

The countdown reached zero and the contestants leaped for the exit to the boat bay. The black-armored pilot shot through the door with Quester close on his heels. Soon, the racers split up, using different strategies. The pilot stuck to the low gravity spaces, using his feet and hands to shoot forward in gliding spurts. Quester headed downward to the maintenance decks close to the ship's outer skin. The pilot enjoyed a substantial lead at first, but Quester settled into a loping run that ate up distance. He caught and passed his opponent when they entered the crew habitat decks amidships. The crowd gasped as the pilot leapt from a support beam to the top of the tropical dome and picked his way across the surface to slide down the other side. Abishai ground his teeth wondering if he was going to have dome repairs to conduct as a result.

Meanwhile, Quester sprinted through a different habitation section, crossing Cooper Green in seconds. He caught a quick ride on Old Speedy, the plus-velocity ring, to the next spin-ward section and shot down a wide maintenance corridor toward the bow. The star lounge was abuzz with speculation on what the contestants would do next. Quester's lead vanished when he had to divert around a pallet-load of missiles. The two racers stayed neck and neck the rest of the way to the bow. Leftenant Haynes reached the bow bulkhead just a few seconds ahead of Quester in a separate section of the ship. He bounced off the wall and immediately began retracing his route aft.

Instead of retracing his steps, Quester took a slightly different route to avoid running into the missile pallet again. When he reached the habitat sections again, he ducked into the tropical dome at the beach entrance. He pounded past a slightly startled family enjoying some beach time and dove into the water. An audible sigh went through the Star Lounge, surely the water would bog Quester down and throw the race to his opponent. The drone cameras lost track of Quester in the water and the feed switched to his helmet cam. The crowd erupted with surprised shouts as the feed showed two dolphins in ceramic armor raced through the water with Quester in tow. Abishai noted snarling rat artwork on their face shields closely matching Quester's. Seconds later, the dolphins completed the underwater run to the Six Fathoms Restaurant, launching themselves and Quester to the surface. Quester pushed off their dorsal fin armor and sailed over two tables of surprised diners to land lightly in the aisle. He wasted no time, quickly scooting for the exit trailing saltwater behind him. The dolphins raced back and forth, chittering loud encouragement through their armor's audio ports.

The Star Lounge crowd went crazy as the feed showed Quester with a substantial lead coming out of the crew habitation decks. Leftenant Haynes had a more direct route to the boat bay, but couldn't make up the time. Quester's armored hand smacked bulkhead zero before the pilot even made it to the boat bay, then he collapsed to the deck. He leaned against the bulkhead and popped his helmet off, sucking in great gasps of air. Now the spectators argued about the dolphin assist and wondered if Quester would be disqualified. They didn't have long to wait. Mr. Barboa took over the competition feed. "The winner of the individual twenty-kilometer race is Quester Drake. Well done! Your speed, skill and stamina do you and your unit credit! Recruiting the dolphins showed excellent strategy and preparation. Congratulations to Beta Company. They take the lead in the overall standings."

Leftenant Haynes congratulated Quester, giving him a slap on the armored shoulder. They were both completely spent. Together they made their way back to the Beta Section armory chatting about the race and ways to go even faster.

That evening the Beta Company militia gathered on Cooper Green to accept the trophy as the first-ever Militia Jamboree champions. Quester, Jarman, and Shanyah received medals as individual winners, leading the way for strong performances across the board. Along with the trophy, the company received a picnic catered by Passepartout's, a new ship's restaurant concession for this voyage.

Quester garnered plenty of attention and congratulations. Abishai decided to let him bask in the glory of his achievement for a while before enquiring about the rat face motif.

Rimon Barkscale, Abishai's former boss and the Beta Company commander, sat down next to Abishai. He snagged a ham and Swiss cheese croissant, took an appreciative bite and looked at the crowd around Quester. "Was the rat face on Quester's helmet your idea, squad leader?" he queried.

"No, I need to talk to him about it, but I don't want to spoil the celebration. What are your thoughts?"

"I talked to Mr. Barboa, earlier. As militia commander, he's okay with it as long as the artwork doesn't interfere with the armor's stealth capabilities. We need all the esprit de corps we can manage while we integrate the new people. We may only have a few weeks before our capabilities get a real-world test. Quester's win is a real boost and I personally like the artwork."

"The word going around," said Abishai, "is to expect an attack when we're getting the extra ice for the shield delivered and installed."

"This time," answered Rimon, "the scuttlebutt is probably accurate. I don't get why these criminals have it in for the *Nai'a* so bad, but they've shown too much persistence and resilience for my liking. They're going to have some surprises for us, and we need some better surprises for them. Quester's strategy for the race shows some promise. See if he has any ideas about how we might spoil a boarding force's day."

"I'll ask him, Rimon. Right now, I need to corral my kids and get them to eat before everything's cold." Abishai spotted Mishael and Kalei playing a game of big ball and jogged over to extract them from the gaggle of screaming kids.

Chapter 4 – Semper Paratus

November 3rd, AD 3187
Long Boat Nai'a - Tau Ceti Mid-System
Beta Section Galley

Abishai and Shanyah met Quester in the Beta Section galley for breakfast the next morning. "Are you sore from the run yesterday?" asked Abishai.

"Several places I didn't know I had muscles," he answered. "I pushed too hard a few times. It was difficult to maintain the optimum flow for working with the armor's power assist when I had all that adrenaline going through me."

"These competitions will help us all learn how to work through the natural adrenaline spike of real combat," said Shanyah. "I was keyed up for my run at the combat marksmanship course, but I have enough muscle memory from our training to channel the nerves into useful action."

"I have a few questions for you, Quester," said Abishai. First, you aren't in trouble, quite the opposite. We need the flexible thinking you showed in the race. Tell me about the helmet artwork. How did you apply it?"

"It's actually programming. The stealth suite in the armor has a lot more capability than we use. It's based on a high-end digital art platform. I used to fool around with this kind of thing back on HAB- 5 for my...uh, buddies. I used a digital sketchpad to work up the rat face, then got help getting the armor's stealth software to accept it."

"Who helped with suit software?"

"I'd rather not say." Quester examined his eggs carefully.

"I think I can guess, Lisandra Redding?" ventured Shanyah. Quester looked up and nodded. "That makes me feel better. How did you end up working with her?"

"I wasn't having any luck with a standard terminal search of the ship's data library so I tried inserting a search-bot program I wrote. Your security team confiscated all of my best stuff when I in-processed, but I can code a little." He drew a deep breath. "The next thing I knew, my terminal froze. A man's head popped up on the screen and told me I'd been a bad boy. I was so shocked I didn't even notice the door to my quarters opening to let two Ship Security officers in. They grabbed me and the terminal. Five minutes later I was sitting in Ship Security wondering if I'd just bought a ticket back to HAB-5."

"You met Mr. Literal, the artificial intelligence who serves as our data librarian," said Shayah. "He takes a dim view of monkeying around in the database."

"Lisandra told me the same thing when she showed up in Ship Security. She had me show her my search-bot program, then we spent an hour talking over mutual interests and skills. In other words, she wrang me dry and I admitted things that will get me time asteroid mining if the Tau Ceti government gets ahold of me. She and Mr. Literal were both keeping a virtual eye on me because of the programs I tried to bring on board. I agreed to run my programming ideas through her and Mr. Literal from now on. In return, she helped me with the suits. They have impressive security protocols, but she slid around them like they weren't there."

Abishai and Shanyah shared a meaningful look. "I think you found the right mentor," Abishai said. "As long as you keep your activities above board you can be a valued crew member. Tell us about the dolphins, I'm sure Shanyah wants to know how you got their cooperation."

"I've been fascinated by them ever since I came on board. We don't have any dolphins living in Tau Ceti, but the plan is to ask several pods to immigrate once Persephone is terraformed. I worked with one of the dolphin ambassadors to learn to communicate with them and asked a hundred questions. They asked as many right back and we're getting to know one another. I got the idea of taking a shortcut through their saltwater domain since it runs straight through the habitat decks. They were all for it. The dolphins want to be an active part of the ship's defenses and thought a demonstration of their capabilities would convince the powers that be to bring them fully into the militia. I wanted to give them something in thanks for the help. They chose my rat artwork for their armor. We practiced the run from the tropical dome beach to Six Fathoms at night."

"You're a disruptive influence, Quester," said Shanyah. "I mean that in a good way. The dolphins deserve a bigger role than we've allowed them. The ambassadors, me included, are acting like protective parents instead of partners. I'll talk to Mr. Barboa and Captain Brelling. If I can get them on board, we can work the dolphins into our tactical planning. Are you willing to come to the meeting with me and help convince them?"

Quester paled, but nodded. "I need to at least try."

***

Shanyah and Quester popped to their feet when the captain walked into her conference room, trailed closely by Mr. Barboa. She waved them back to their seats and took one herself across the table. Eying Quester with scant favor, she leaned back. "You've by turns impressed and alarmed your new crewmates, Mr. Drake. I've flipped back and forth between trying to turn you into a useful crew member or cutting my losses and sending you back to HAB-5 while I still can. The thing is, I don't know if they'd take you back." Quester looked like he wanted to crawl under the table. Shanyah bit her cheek to keep from laughing. "Marshall Winter has a much better dossier on you than you probably think. When he's done with his current mission, your former gang is going to be directly in his sights. He's more than glad to be rid of you. My question is this, Mr. Drake, can I trust you to put the well-being of this crew and ship ahead of your own?" She looked him directly in the eye.

Quester forced himself to return her gaze. "I can only say that I'll do my best. I left HAB-5 because my friends...my gang, was getting violent and I didn't want any part of hurting innocent people."

"I'm certain we took on at least one mole with the new crew members," the captain continued. "I'm equally certain you aren't one them. Otherwise, you would have shown more restraint and been a real danger. You may not realize it, but you're on a ship full of dangerous people. Shanyah is the best combat sharpshooter you're likely to see. She also knows several ways of incapacitating you with her bare hands. Her husband, Abishai, broke a saboteur's neck with a judo throw despite being under the influence of a debilitating drug. You've already experienced how frightening Lisandra Redding's cyber skills are. I could go on. You have the potential to be a dangerous person, Mr. Drake, but I want to be sure you're a danger to our enemies, not this ship."

Quester, having no idea what to say, wisely kept his mouth shut. Mr. Barboa decided to steer the meeting back to its original purpose. "Shanyah, you asked to meet and discuss the dolphin pod's role in ship defense. I'll admit we've been trying to keep them out of the fray against their wishes. What do you propose going forward?"

"We should work them into our defensive plans and seriously consider how they can give us an advantage in specific circumstances. Quester proved they can cooperate and provide additional mobility to armored troops. That's one angle. I want to work with them to see what options we can come up with for offensive capabilities. Being rammed by four hundred kilograms of armored dolphin will damage even combat armor, but we can do better. Quester has a few ideas, but we need some time to flesh them out. Before he goes down that rabbit trail, I want your approval. The dolphins are natural cooperative predators. In hindsight we were foolish not to take advantage of their abilities."

Captain Brelling looked back and forth between Shanyah and Quester for a few moments. "You have my tentative okay," she finally said. "Run everything by Mr. Barboa and the first officer before you commit ship's resources to it. I'm uncomfortable with the idea of involving our dolphins in combat operations, but we should let them make the choice. Mr. Barboa, what do you have to add?"

"I'll work with these two," he said, nodding. "Our conversation spurred a few ideas. If you'll lend us your conference room, captain, we can start knocking them around now."

"It's all yours for the next hour," answered Captain Brelling, "then I have a meeting with Commander Hartley and Colonel Rai. Send us all a quick summary of your ideas when you wrap up. If my guess is correct, we'll need every trick we can pull out our hats to avoid a disaster." She fixed Quester with another penetrating stare. "Don't make me regret my decision to keep you on the crew." Quester could only manage a nod. The captain quirked one eyebrow and took her leave.

Quester let out a breath he hadn't realized he was holding and slumped in his chair. Shanyah thumped him on the back and grinned, "That went well! I figured it was fifty-fifty that she would throw you in the brig until we could hand you over to the government."

"I'm glad I didn't get to experience what a bad meeting with the captain is like." Quester croaked.

Mr. Barboa shook his head. "She makes sure they go well for the ship, and usually for the individual. You did yourself a favor by keeping your comments to a minimum. Now, we want wild ideas, the wilder the better, but no going off and trying anything on your own. You have several mentors available. Keep us in the loop and we'll keep you in the captain's good graces. Show me what you've come up with so far, then I'll bounce my ideas off you." Quester pulled out his digital sketch pad and the three were soon deep in conversation about underwater weapons and tactics.

✦✦✦

Colonel Rai and Commander Hartley looked equally grim as they sat down with the captain. "I've run several simulations with my tacticians," started Colonel Rai. "They all point to a victory for our forces at a high price on both sides. In most scenarios we'll have the firepower to wipe out the attacking force but the *Nai'a* will take significant damage. If their goal is to take the ship, however, they'll be reluctant to fire on it. The danger point is when they realize their boarding force is losing. They'll likely go scorched earth and try to take the ship out. We can deal with their ships, but they can probably put enough missiles in space to overwhelm our defenses. We've got some tricks that improve the odds, but none of the outcomes are good."

The captain nodded. "Nothing I didn't expect, I appreciate your efforts. We'll keep poking at it to see what else we can do." She related her conversation with Shanyah and Quester. "You have the preliminary report. What do you think of their ideas?"

Commander Hartley's brow furrowed in concentration. "They're on the right track. Non-explosive underwater weapons won't do much to combat armor. The dolphins' big advantage is their mobility and familiarity with the environment. Anybody who gets in the water with them is going to be at their mercy. We just need an effective way for the dolphins to neutralize intruders. If they can mount an effective above-water weapon, I can see a volley of fire devastating a small force on the beach or in Six Fathoms. A big challenge we have is communicating the risks to the dolphins so they don't expose themselves to enemy fire for too long. Shanyah can do it if anyone can. I want them to keep the plans close-hold for now. We still don't know if the Restoration managed to sneak an operative on board with the new crew. Surprise will multiply whatever capabilities we can give the dolphins."

***

A week later, Leftenant Wyant led a squad of Great Prospects pilot/commandos in powered armor on a night-time training raid. They were the designated opposing force for this exercise, and he had big plans for messing up Epsilon Company's whole evening. His squad swiftly and silently entered the tropical dome through the beach portal, taking cover in the dense foliage surrounding the sandy expanse. He checked his display to see that everyone was in dispersed travel formation, then gave a double click on the com to move out. As he stood, he registered a flicker of movement from the direction of the water. His LIDAR detector immediately flashed, and he tried to hit the deck. Before he could, his armor locked up, registering two simulated hypervelocity hits, one at the vulnerable neck joint and one in the faceplate. He checked his display and every member of his eight-person squad was red.

One of his squad members managed to launch a grenade toward the water before being taken out. Wyant watched the training device hit the surface and sink. An instant later, six armored dolphins exploded out of the water. Wyant blinked as he recognized the snarling rat artwork on their face shields. They spun an intricate pattern in the air, making them hard to follow, then dropped back into the water with scarcely a splash. A few seconds later the end exercise tone sounded and his armor unlocked. Mr. Barboa walked onto the beach along with Shanyah and Quester. He called the squad down to the shore while Shanyah and Quester waded into the water to greet the dolphins.

"Take your helmets off and take a knee, folks. I want to get your impressions on what just happened," Mr. Barboa said.

"That was quick and devastating," said Leftenant Wyant. "Not to mention a complete surprise. We expected Epsilon Company militia to defend the dome, but not an attack from the water. How did they detect and target us so effectively?"

"The vibration of armored troops moving in this area easily reaches the water. The dolphins located each of you closely enough to target you with LIDAR as soon as they popped their weapons and sensor pods out of the water. We rigged the LIDAR as an extension of their natural sonar. They've been practicing."

"I can tell," said the Leftenant, wryly. "What weapon are they using?"

"Hyper velocity mini-rockets. They're recoilless, which makes them accurate for multiple shots. They don't have the punch to take out a main armor panel, but the dolphins are so accurate, they hit a weak point nearly every time. They only exposed their pods for this engagement, but I'm glad you managed to get a grenade off. The safest place for them during an underwater explosion is in the air. They reacted just right. Since the ground threat was eliminated, their jumps took them safely away from the shock of the grenade."

"What if the enemy goes into the water after them?" asked another of the Great Prospects pilots.

"We hope they're foolish enough to try," replied Mr. Barboa. "We've worked up some nasty surprises for anyone who wants to get caught with the dolphins in their natural environment. We're keeping them secret for now. Also, don't share your experience this evening with anyone. We want to make sure this capability stays a surprise. Now, put your thinking caps on. How do we best use this new capability? Most of you saw Mr. Quester demonstrate rapid, clandestine transport by dolphin tow during the militia jamboree. They can move a limited number of troops from here to Six Fathoms restaurant at the other end of Epsilon section and several points in between. You'll be the commando team we use in direct cooperation with the dolphins. Your training starts tonight." The eager looks from the team prompted an answering grin from the grizzled old hand. "Let's get to it. Shanyah and Quester will introduce you to the dolphins."

***

The next morning Mr. Barboa met with the captain, first officer and Colonel Rai. "Your pilots took right to training with the dolphins, Colonel," he started. "We practiced a variety of towing configurations. The dolphins and your people had great fun making races out of it. We also practiced some underwater neutralization. As we suspected, humans stand almost no chance in the water with dolphins without specialized equipment. Combat armor provides highly effective protection underwater because of the attenuation of both projectile and energy weapons. The dolphins' mobility advantage, however, is decisive. They can literally swim circles around a human with or without armor. We're still working on how to take full advantage of their capabilities."

Commander Hartley nodded, "We'll weave them into the defensive plans. There's a good chance we'll never need them, but I'll feel better knowing they're ready. I'm still worried about those hyper velocity mini-rockets. A stray round could go right through the tropical dome or a bulkhead and do serious damage."

"I was initially concerned as well," answered Mr. Barboa. He brought up the holographic display and started a holo recorded at the beach. Several human sized automaton targets were highlighted moving down the beach and through the nearby foliage. Six weapons pods simultaneously rose from the water. In less than a second, all ten of the automatons registered at least two hits in vulnerable places. The pods immediately sank out of sight. "That was the tactic we taught them to minimize risk. There were three misses out of six hundred rounds during the first training session, none in over five thousand since. Now, take a look at the tactic the dolphins came up with to maximize destruction."

The holo recording showed the same scene until all six armored and armed dolphins burst from the water in a dizzying array of arcs, firing as they twisted gracefully through the air. Each automaton registered at least half a dozen kill shots before the dolphins disappeared into the depths. "One hundred percent hit rate and kill rate with that tactic," said Mr. Barboa. "They've taken to the combination of LIDAR and the mini-missiles like nothing I've ever seen. Their kinesthetic sense is off the charts. They just don't miss anymore. Also, we've programmed the mini-rockets to self-destruct three meters past the range of the target."

"Impressive," said the captain leaning back. "Pass my thanks to the dolphin pod as well as Shanyah and Quester. You've all done more than I expected in a short period of time. How is Quester shaping up?"

"He picked up a number of useful skills dodging the authorities on HAB-5, so he's ahead of most of the new crew members. I can't find anything to fault since you had your talk with him. He's kept his scheming transparent so far. If we can keep him focused and busy, he'll be fine."

The captain turned her gaze on Colonel Rai. "Tell us what you've gleaned about the mercenaries we expect to face."

"As usual, there's good news and bad news," the Colonel started...

***

That evening Shanyah and Abishai put the finishing touches on a dinner of lasagna, tossed salad, and Parker House rolls. Quester entertained Mishael and Kalei with stories about growing up on HAB-5. "How are you feeling about training up the dolphins for combat?" Abishai asked Shanyah as they dodged each other artfully in the small kitchen.

"My feelings are mixed. I'm glad they have better ways to defend themselves, but I know how offensive minded they are. Straight up predators don't like sitting on the sidelines. If they have a chance to get into action, they'll take it."

"How about Quester?" asked Abishai.

"The captain put him on the straight and narrow for now. Let's keep encouraging him. He's still finding his way in a new place. Remember what it was like when we first came aboard?"

"I remember Jarman's sparkling personality," Abishai answered. "As well as his oft-stated opinion of ground hogs like us."

"We all do," said Shanyah. "It just made me more determined not to quit. He eventually came around."

"I notice a rather satisfied look on your face every time you toss him in grappling practice." Abishai opined.

"A girl can't be faulted for getting a small measure of revenge now and again. He needs a regular ego check anyway."

"I can't argue with that," replied Abishai. He turned toward the combined living/dining room of their quarters. "Hey you three, get to the table. The rolls are coming out of the oven. Get 'em while they're hot!" Once they were seated, he flipped everyone a roll then carried a basket-full to the table. Shanyah asked Mishael to give thanks for the food, then they all dug in. Quester grated a healthy portion of Pecorino Romano cheese over his lasagna then gave his salad a few scrapes as well.

"Did you really work on a ranch?" asked Mishael, opening his roll up and slathering it with a chunk of butter.

"I did. I can't actually call myself a cowboy, but one of the largest open decks on HAB-5 is called The Ranch. Really, it's a dairy farm. They're always hiring, because the pay is low and the work is hard. At the time I was in need of a job."

"What did you do?"

Quester smiled at Mishael's endless curiosity. "We're eating so I'll just say I learned my way around a short-handled shovel for several weeks. Maybe they'll have real cowboys on Persephone someday. Does the *Nai'a* have cows? You must have sheep to get authentic Romano like this."

Shanyah swallowed a bite of lasagna before answering. "We have both. There's a small herd of dairy cows, sheep, and goats on the farm in Gamma Section. The size is closely controlled by the Biome department to balance the ship's needs. Like your ranch, they're always recruiting workers. I can put a word in for you if you want to apprentice there."

Quester held up both hands. "No thanks, I've checked that box for life. I'm probably going to see if Lisandra will take me on as a cybersecurity apprentice."

"It would be a good fit," said Abishai. "You'll get a chance to qualify at several crew specialties on the way to Lalande, but it's nice to have a primary occupation. Lisandra will be an excellent mentor."

"She and your scary librarian AI are going to watch me like a hawk anyway," answered Quester. "If I'm going to stretch my hacking muscles at all, I'll have to do it on the right side of the law from now on."

Shanyah laughed, then shook her head. "Everyone has a run-in with Mr. Literal now and then. Once you get to know him and how he works, I think you'll like him."

"Is he sentient? I didn't think it was possible."

"The jury's still out. You'll have to judge for yourself. He's one of the oldest AI's you'll ever run into, and he interacts with people constantly. We may have worn off on him a bit. In any case, don't underestimate him."

"No fear of that! I plan to tread lightly and carefully in the future."

After the meal the family and Quester played a word association game that was all the rage in the Tau Ceti system. They tied in Paulene, Roan, Lisandra, and Hal, as well as Palamar and Val O'Clair, virtually to add to the fun. After the kids went to bed, Abishai and Shanyah saw Quester to the door. "Thank you for a great dinner," said Quester. "It was really nice to spend time with your family. I'm used to getting along on my own, but I can't remember having a better time."

"Being on your own isn't going to be an option on this ship," said Shanyah. "You'll learn we're all a family. Abishai and I will be here any time you need us."

Abishai clapped him on the shoulder. "Shanyah's right. This crew went through a lot together on the voyage here. We're a tightknit bunch and we want you to be one of us. I'm afraid we're facing another test soon, but I'm confident we'll pass. You have the skills to help."

Quester considered Abishai's words for a moment, then looked him in the eye. "I intend to. I've never felt part of something I could be proud of, or part of a family."

"We don't dig into peoples' past," said Abishai, "but if you ever want to talk about it, you can come to us."

Chapter 5 – Calculated Risk

November 28th, AD 3187
Long Boat Nai'a - Tau Ceti Mid-System
Beta Section Commons

Beta Section commons buzzed with friendly conversation as Abishai's church gathered for a Thanksgiving celebration. After they sang a few congregational songs, several people stood and spoke briefly about what they were thankful for this year. Beta Section head Pete Worsley wrapped up the testimonial by reading a Psalm. "I know you'll all be disappointed in the lack of a sermon today," he announced at the conclusion, garnering a smattering of chuckles. "No one volunteered, probably because they didn't want to be between you people and the food. I am grateful for all of you and the bonds of love God has blessed us with. Let's celebrate now together and give him the glory." He said a prayer of thanksgiving and dismissed everyone to the food tables.

Quester sat between Mishael and Kalei, amazed at the amount and variety of food on their plates. By the time he picked up his fork, they had both made a sizable dent in their dinner. By now he was used to the way Abishai and his progeny could tear through a meal. He casually put a forearm on each side of his plate to discourage any foraging. In spite of the precaution, he somehow only got one of the two rolls he knew he'd started with. "I've never had turkey before. Do you keep a flock on the ship?"

"No, it's vat grown," said Shanyah. "We order white and dark meat ahead of time every year. The genes are honest turkey, or so the commissary claims. Since it's the only kind of turkey I've had, I wouldn't know the difference. We raise animals on board for their milk, eggs, wool etc."

"I had the real thing a few times growing up," said Abishai. "The flavor is the same, and I don't miss the bones and gristle."

"Your fresh cranberry salad is delicious," said Quester. "I've never had anything like it. If we have cranberries in Tau Ceti, I haven't seen them."

"I'm not surprised," answered Abishai. "Apples, grapes, oranges, and pineapple were already growing on the *Nai'a* when I came on board, but coming up with cranberries was a challenge. I convinced the farm board to put in a cranberry bog by bribing them with the salad. I used up the small stock of frozen cranberries we had on the Sol – Tau Ceti run to give them a sample. They had to agree to the bog if they wanted more. The nutritional excellence of cranberries also made a convincing argument. Paulene deserves most of the credit for producing viable plants and successful harvests from our small stock of frozen seed. My punishment is hand-harvesting the cranberries every year, but I've got some helpers now." He smiled at Mishael and Kalei.

Quester finished his plate while the two children raided the dessert table with Abishai, lightening it considerably. He felt pleasantly stuffed, but decided to amble that way to see if anything caught his eye. Something labeled "White Sweet Potato Pie" looked intriguing so he cut himself a thin slice, then snagged a browned butter and chocolate chunk cookie. He caught Shanyah looking at him with a slight smile as he blissfully worked his way through a bite of pie redolent with cinnamon and nutmeg. "If I had known the food was this good, I'd have run to the Trade Syndicate's office," he said. "The only time I came close to eating this well on HAB-5 was when I worked on The Ranch. The meals almost made up for the low pay and working conditions."

"I knew the food was good from the stories I heard about the *Nai'a* growing up," said Shanyah. "It exceeded my expectations, in part, because of Abishai. He's even more of a foodie than I am. It's only fair, since he eats twice as much as most people."

As the meal wound down, several people came by to say hello and chat with Quester. He felt welcome in a way he really couldn't explain. It was a unique feeling; one he hadn't known he was missing. Thanksgiving suddenly felt significantly less trite and dated.

***

The next morning Captain Brelling steepled her fingers and looked over them at her closest advisors. "What do you think? Do we have a chance of pulling this off, or am I completely off my rocker?"

Colonel Rai frowned, "We have a chance. If it works, we'll avoid most of the bloody fight we thought was inevitable. I'm certain enough of my intelligence on the mercenaries to think it's worth the risk. We're mainly risking your vessel and crew, though, so it's your call."

"Not entirely," she answered. "I still have to convince the ship's council. I'm not going ahead without their support. This ship is as much a community as a space faring vessel. The civil and business leadership have a vote too, even if I am responsible for defense. We're going to keep the majority of the crew in the dark until the ball drops. I'm highly uncomfortable with the secrecy, but I don't see another way to maintain operational security. Thoughts?"

Her first officer, Commander Kevin Hartley, leaned forward. "We do need to keep the plan secret. I'm as certain as you are that we have a mole or two among the newcomers. After our experience with the saboteurs on the way in-system, we know how to deal with an enemy in the ranks without causing a panic. The crew knows the risk. They'll be alert for suspicious activity. They also trust us to do the right thing and protect the ship. Your plan is going to strain their trust, but I'm confident they'll go along."

"Mr. Barboa?" the captain queried.

"I may need to retire after this adventure," he said wryly. "This stunt reminds me of a certain hot shuttle pilot who couldn't resist a course through the thick of an asteroid field. Still, I think it's our best chance of getting through what's coming with a minimum of casualties all around."

"Okay, I'll put the plan to the council tonight and see what they say."

***

The ship's council chamber was sparsely populated that evening. The ship's Chief Alder, Persephone Belotic, sat on one side of the triangular table with Elder Consuela Pryachac as her advisor. Hubble Spearsley, the CEO, and his wife/deputy, Yuna Ashworth, represented the corporate leadership. The captain and first officer rounded out the gathering. "I assume from the leader and principal deputy only invitation, you're sharing protected information." Persephone Belotic stated.

"Yes," replied the captain, "and I'm going to ask for a difficult decision tonight. Don't share what we tell you with anyone outside of this room until the operation is under way, and then, only as necessary. Kevin, please lay out the tactical situation and how we intend to deal with it."

Thirty minutes later, the first officer wound up his briefing to sober looks around the table. "We rendezvous with the ice shield contractor in three days," he said. "We need to decide on our strategy now."

"I'm no tactician," said Hubble Spears, "but I can think of a dozen ways this turns into a disaster."

Consuela Pryachac gave him an appraising look, squinting through her wrinkles. "It's already a disaster," the diminutive old gardener said. "We have nothing but bad choices in front of us. It's a question of what's least bad. If we treat other's lives as less valuable than our own, we've lost our way. It's a risky plan, but I believe it would pass overwhelmingly if we put it to a vote of the crew."

Yuna Ashworth drummed her fingers on the table absently then looked up. "I'm inclined to agree with Consuela, Hubble. We don't have thousands of cold sleep passengers to protect on this run. The crew is prepared to do what the captain is asking. They take the loss of Kiko and Callie Estevez personally." The husband-wife team from Great Prospects had given their lives to save the *Nai'a* from an attack on the in-bound journey. "Given a chance to share the risk with the Great Prospects protection team, the crew would take it."

"That's my read also," said Chief Alder Belotic. "The newcomers are integrating well. Crew morale is high despite the tension. I will suggest that you figure out a way to clearly communicate your intent to the whole crew once the ball drops. You'll have a lot of highly motivated and capable people running around in combat armor. Mr. Barboa trained them to be aggressive and sneaky. They'll be more likely to destroy your plan of action than enable it if they don't know what's going on."

The captain nodded. "You're right, Persephone, the plan is guaranteed to go sideways somewhere along the way. We need everyone pulling in the same direction to have a chance of success. Kevin, put together a very succinct package of delayed orders, something a crew member can digest in 15 seconds or less. We'll leverage Lisandra Redding and Mr. Literal's capabilities to get it to everyone on time. I'll also need emergency PCOM override authorization from the council." She looked at Persephone and Hubble who both nodded. "Any other questions or concerns before we vote?"

"We can't turn a profit if we don't survive," answered Hubble. "I'm convinced."

"I have plenty of concerns," said Persephone, "but I don't object to your recommended course of action. It just means I have some work to do on the plan to protect non-combatants."

"I have a few ideas along those lines," said Commander Hartley. "If you can stay for a few minutes, I'll run them by you."

The council recorded the necessary votes and Hubble adjourned the official meeting. Commander Hartley, Persephone Belotic and Consuela Pryachac immediately began an animated conversation.

Chapter 6 – Open Doors

December 1st, AD 3187
Long Boat Nai'a - Tau Ceti Mid-System
Bridge

Three days later the tension on board ratcheted steadily up as the rendezvous and potential attack approached. Captain Brelling surveyed the bridge and tried to project a calm confidence she didn't feel. She took a deep breath and pushed a couple of tons of self-doubt firmly to the side. *The waiting really is the hardest part,* she thought. Colonel Rai commanded the space fleet, including the additional Great Prospects squadron and the Tau Ceti contingent lead by Marshall Winter. Mr. Barboa, technically Militia Colonel Barboa, though he refused to acknowledge the rank, commanded the militia battalion and attached Great Prospects commandos. Lisandra Reddick and the ship cybersecurity officer, Greer Kensing, huddled with the communications officer analyzing the traffic and readying their surprise packages. The captain suppressed a shudder at the site of Redding's mini-comp hardwired into the *Nai'a's* com system. At least Greer was keeping an eye on her. Chief Nance, their top helmsman and the real hero of the Sol – Tau Ceti Turnover sat ready at the helm, reviewing his pre-programmed maneuver options. The right people were in place and she was wise enough not to joggle anyone's elbow. The game was afoot.

Colonel Rai led ten of the fourteen original protection team ships in a sweep toward the inbound ice tugs. The six tugs were firmly coupled to a 1.1-kilometer-wide disc of ice intended to double the thickness of the *Nai'a's* interstellar dust shield for a high-speed run to Lalande. On the bridge, the officer at the sensors station noted the movement, surprised that the colonel would take over two thirds of their combat power on the sweep. The captain watched intently without comment and waited for the enemy to take advantage of the opening.

Right on cue, a host of signatures lit up the display as the enemy fleet dropped stealth and lit their drives to burn for the *Nai'a* from the direction of the inner system. The four remaining protection ships surrounding the *Nai'a* immediately burned in the opposite direction, a reasonable response to the overwhelming odds, but out of character for Great Prospects. Captain Brelling saw the looks of consternation around her and decided it was time to bring the bridge crew in on the plan. "Don't panic. We want the enemy to think the *Nai'a* is ripe for the plucking. If we can lure them into committing to a full boarding action, we'll have them right where we want them. Steady on." Several eyebrows rose at her pronouncement, but no one spoke.

"I have a fix on their frequency scheme," announced the com officer. "We're working on the encryption now. Designating the likely command ship Bogie One." The wash of red icons on the display continued inexorably toward the *Nai'a*.

***

In the Tau Ceti command ship *Judicus*, Marshall Winter held his breath. His tactical team had guessed the enemy's approach vector a little too well. The enemy fleet passed through his formation and flipped to decelerate toward the *Nai'a*, apparently without detecting his ships. By prearrangement his ships maintained stealth and radio silence, but used their cold gas propulsion systems to follow after the enemy fleet.

"The force mix appears to be what we predicted," the sensors officer announced. "The troop carrier is launching shuttles...they're vectoring for the stern. Fighters are also launching, headed for Colonel Rai's ships."

***

"My guess is they'll try for the boat bay," said the captain. Any other entry point would mean dealing with the *Nai'a's* meters-thick water jacket. It wouldn't stop them, but it would cost time to allow the water in any compartment of the jacket to spray into space. "Mr. Barboa, execute plan Broomstick Four," she sent over the tactical com.

Once again, they'd guessed the enemy's reactions correctly. The bulk of the militia was already aft, positioned between the boat bay and engineering. The other enemy objective had to be the bridge, a seven-kilometer trek through the cargo and habitation decks. The captain hoped fervently they could hold on long enough to spring their carefully prepared traps. The *Nai'a* shuddered slightly beneath her feet when the breaching charges took out the boat bay door. Soon they would find out if this plan was good enough to deal with a force of trained mercenaries.

"Lisandra, send the orders package, minus new crew," the captain ordered. Less than a second later, the PCOM of every crew member who had made the Sol – Tau Ceti crossing pinged with a priority message."

ALL VETERAN CREW, PRIORITY IS PROTECTION OF *NAI'A'S* CREW AND SHIP INTEGRITY. SECONDARY OBJECTIVE IS PRESERVATION OF THE ENEMY BOARDING FORCE. GIVE GROUND AS ORDERED AND DELAY ENEMY ADVANCE AT EVERY OPPORTUNITY.

The captain and first officer had worried long and hard over whether to include the new crew in the message. They finally decided to leave it to the veterans to pass on as they saw fit. Any delay in warning the enemy force of their intentions would work in the *Nai'a's* favor.

***

Mr. Barboa studied the enemy dispositions carefully. Thanks to the internal sensor network he knew what he was facing in detail. As expected, the enemy commander split his boarding forces, sending two-thirds forward to attempt to secure the bridge and the rest toward engineering. He ordered three companies to prepare positions in depth to protect engineering. They had trained this scenario repeatedly, so he left them to it. He took Alpha and Beta companies with him to harass and delay the force headed for the bridge.

***

Colonel Zeleski of Warnicky's Wolves muttered to himself as he waited for his sappers to clear yet another section of corridor. This operation was going much better than he had expected casualty-wise, but his progress was still slower than he preferred. Every corridor seemed to be strewn with smart anti-armor mines and covered by a heavy weapons section that quickly disengaged once his troops had a foothold. His sappers were running through explosives quickly, and half his short battalion had damaged armor. Still, he was making better progress than the detachment trying for engineering. He was halfway to bridge, and the cursed militia wouldn't be able to hem him in once he hit the habitation decks. He planned to take advantage of the wide-open space of Cooper Green to finally get ahead of the harassing forces. So far, he'd heard nothing from the Restoration's supposed spies. He strode forward as his troops cleared the next section of corridor. One more ship frame and they'd show these glorified civilians what combat speed was.

***

Mr. Barboa double checked his dispositions then jacked into the ship's data net and sent the go message to his second in command. One hundred centipede-form remote control crawlers shot from cover to assault the front and flanks of the mercenary drive toward engineering. The two-meter-long, arm-thick robots were insanely fast and nearly impossible to track as they flowed over decks, bulkheads and overhead with equal ease. The mercenaries were good. They took out nearly half of the attacking machines before they overwhelmed the front ranks and swarmed toward the rear. The centipedes carried no weapon; they were a weapon. Once close enough to attack an individual, they flowed with lightning speed around a limb or torso and applied a squeeze powerful enough to crack combat armor followed by a powerful electromagnetic pulse. Screams echoed over the tactical net as mercenaries went down left and right. A slow advance turned into a broken retreat to the boat bay.

"I don't care what they sent after you. Get your troops together and break back out of there," Colonel Zeleski told his second in command. "That was probably a last-ditch effort. Get them in a straight up fight and they'll turn tail."

"I've taken fifty percent casualties and I had to fall back to the boat bay. Every direct engagement we've had shows these people are not going to break and run," his subordinate answered. He shook his leg violently to get rid of the remnants of a centipede. It clung stubbornly until he finally shot it off with his side arm, further damaging his armor. "They have superior equipment and intelligence. I suggest you retrace your route and take them in the rear. If we can get them between us, we stand a chance of taking enough of them out to get to engineering."

"I'm too far to turn around now. I'm going for the bridge." Colonel Zeleski answered. "Your orders stay the same. Find a way to break out of there even if it's in the opposite direction. If we take the captain, they'll listen to reason. Zeleski out." He thought about his last statement and an unpleasant thought tickled the back of his conscious mind. He shook it off as his troops broke through to the habitation decks and poured out onto an empty Cooper Green, leap-frogging toward the far side. Scouts in active camouflage moved quickly toward the adjacent sections to check for flank attacks.

***

Mishael and Kalei hurried along with the rest of Mrs. Dooley's group of children, giggling quietly. She'd received word to move her twenty charges out of the path of the attack. To the kids it was an exciting game. They caught a ride to the next section on the plus-velocity ring, entered the tropical dome, and hurried toward their alternate hiding place. None of them saw the camouflaged mercenary scout observing their entry into the dome.

Marcus Pleiades wasn't here to combat children. He simply made a note of what he saw and continued to watch for militia troops in the area. The scout's sensors picked up unidentified energy signatures inside the dome, but they weren't registering as combat armor. On a ship, they could be almost anything. His chosen position was well hidden even without his flexible stealth suit. He waited for orders he didn't think would be long coming. Colonel Zeleski was determined to pass through here on the run.

***

On the bridge, Lisandra Redding gave the captain a thumbs up, and the com officer opened a channel to the captain's headpiece. Captain Brelling nodded with grim satisfaction and concentrated on the militia's tactical display.

***

Zeleski's troops fanned out over the green, maintaining combat discipline, but moving quickly by fire teams. He was in the center of the formation halfway across the green when the last of his troops cleared the entryway and joined the rest, gliding across the open space. He had hoped the militia wouldn't want to shoot up their hab decks, but this was almost too good to be true. The thought barely finished when his sniper alert system pulsed and the two mercenaries on either side of him went down hard. He hit the deck in a roll and fired at one of the indicated origins with his personal weapon. As far as he could tell, he hit nothing.

Before he could react further, his command channel crackled and an unfamiliar, unauthorized voice addressed him. "Colonel Zeleski, this is Captain Brelling. Order your mercenaries to stand down or die. I know you're in this fight against your will, but my responsibility is to my ship and crew. Brigadier Warnicky wouldn't want you to throw your people's lives away for nothing. We have the combat power to eliminate your forces. You have one chance, what is your answer?"

Zeleski was sorely tempted to tell Captain Brelling to take a flying leap. She was capable of bluffing, unfortunately he had no way of knowing whether or not she actually was. "What about Brigadier Warnicky?" he answered. "The Restoration claims they'll kill him if we don't deliver this ship."

"There's an operation underway to free him. He may not survive, but he has a better chance than the Restoration would give my crew. Order a stand down, including the troops trying to break out of the boat bay. You have five seconds."

Zeleski ground his teeth. What were his options? With one second left he opened his tactical net. "All Warnicky's Wolves, stand down. I say again, stand down. Stack arms and await further instructions."

Captain Brelling cut in. "Have everyone shed their armor and recall your scouts. Don't even start with me about keeping your dignity. You forfeited that when you decided to take the Restoration's offer, coerced or not."

***

Marcus Pleiades ignored the recall order, choosing instead to glide toward the forward entrance of the tropical dome. He didn't know why Zeleski would surrender, and he didn't trust the people on this boat. They had every reason to try him for piracy or turn him over to the Tau Ceti authorities on the same charge. The penalty was the same either way. With a hostage or two, at least he'd have some leverage.

He slid carefully through the entrance and into the mass of foliage encroaching on the sandy beach. A flicker in the corner of his eye caused him to snap his head toward the water. The motion saved his life. The first mini-missile tore through the neck of his stealth suit without detonating and just missed his throat. The second impacted his right knee with a sickening crunch. He rolled with the impact letting his suit deal with his useless right leg. He pushed himself deeper into the jungle with his hands and good leg. Pain and shock made him haze in and out of consciousness. He barely registered approaching footsteps and started to lift his weapon. A small sandalled foot came down on the compact pulse rifle with a thump. Twenty centimeters of serrated steel Hori Hori knife appeared in front of his face. The point pricked him just below the Adams apple. "Naughty, naughty," said a raspy voice. "Hold perfectly still if you want to live, mercenary. I may be old but I know which end of this cuts." Marcus looked up into Consuela Pryachac's hard black eyes and his world went dark.

***

Colonel Rai led his force of ships past the incoming ice delivery, then slipped behind the massive disc. It was a tight fit, but soon all ten ships were shielded from the sensors and weapons of the incoming enemy. The Restoration space forces were split between chasing him and covering the boarding of the *Nai'a*. He was pleased with the geometry of the situation, but success depended on timing. His weapons officer tapped into the data feed from the six tugs shepherding the ice disc. Twenty-four fighters led the enemy forces. They carried a spinal laser as their principle offensive weapon. They'd have to clear the ice before they could fire. The ships following the fighters were armed with missiles capable of maneuvering past the ice shield and attacking his ships. He expected a launch, just about...now. The trace of three dozen missiles lit his tactical display. His weapons officer let their tactical system assign targets for each of his ships. In theory, they should be able to take out four missiles apiece with this geometry, but they would only need to get three. As the missiles cleared the ice shield and burned hard to reverse course, all ten of his ships and the six tugs attached to the ice opened up with anti-missile laser batteries. The missile volley melted like snow in a warm rain. None made it to detonation range.

Knowing his enemies would shortly realize something wasn't right, the Colonel pulsed a coded signal to the six tugs that were also fully armed protection ships. Explosive charges drew straight lines of fire across the giant ice disc, splitting it into six pie-shaped wedges. Using their overpowered engines the attached ships quickly pulled the wedges apart, aided by the momentum imparted by the explosives. Colonel Rai's ships slipped through the gaps and popped massive clouds of anti-laser chaff just as the enemy fighters shot past. The fighters swiveled in space to bring their lasers to bear, but the ice and the chaff thwarted the strafing run. Colonel Rai ignored the fighters, whose momentum carried them temporarily out of the fight. His eighteen ships each fired a three-missile salvo consisting of a jammer, shotgun cannister, and capacitor-powered laser warhead. His ships also opened up with their main laser batteries. At this range, the lasers wouldn't do much to an armored hull, but they could scrag sensors and damage anti-missile mounts. The enemy ships fired back with their lasers and a missile salvo of their own.

"Execute protection plan Baker Six," ordered Colonel Rai. His ships weaved an intricate pattern designed to confuse the incoming missiles and dodge laser shots. His weapons officer activated the squadron data net and tweaked integrated defense settings for the incoming barrage. He sent one last update to their own missile wave then sat back to let the automated systems and odds have their way. The Great Prospects missile salvo bore down on the enemy formation with jammers in the lead. A split second before entering effective anti-missile laser range the jammers blazed, hashing the radar spectrum used by the anti-missile batteries. The rest of the salvo jinked to throw the enemy's targeting systems off. The enemy ships fired desperately, managing to take out two cannister missiles before final approach. The remaining cannister missiles belched a mix of tungsten shot and chaff into the enemy formation. The shot stripped away remaining sensors and laser mounts while the chaff further masked the approaching attack birds. Eighteen missiles swept through and past the enemy formation. For a moment the enemy commander thought they had gotten incredibly lucky, then eighteen capacitor pumped lasers tore through space and his formation. Fourteen of fifteen ships lost their main drives to the laser salvo. The last one turned tail and burned back toward the *Nai'a*.

***

Orca Squadron captain Julian Garrity burned hard to rejoin the rest of the Orca ships covering the boarding operation. He had no intention of continuing the attack at eighteen-to-one odds. If the fighter pilots had any sense, they would do the same. He was about to check with his commander when every green icon on the tactical display turned red. The second icy shock in the space of seconds went through him as he struggled to understand what was happening. His unwelcome passenger leaned forward in the observer's acceleration couch, examining the display intently. "We're the only effective ship left! Hit the *Nai'a* now! Full nuclear spread!" the man spat.

Lieutenant Anders, Garrity's weapons officer, started to protest that the Wolfpack troops were still aboard. The snake they were working for pulled a flechette pistol and shot Anders in the temple. Captain Garrity lashed out with his elbow, knocking the gun out of the man's hand. At the same time, he reached in under his seat and pulled a breaker switch, scramming his reactor and cutting power to every major system. The cockpit went dark as Garrity hit the quick release on his harness and launched himself at the man trying to recover his weapon. They grappled in the dark and pain lanced through Garrity as a knife blade glanced off his ribcage. Panic lent him strength as he grabbed the man's neck with his left hand and smashed him in the face repeatedly with his right elbow. He kept it up until felt the man's body go slack then pushed away, sucking in massive gulps of air. When he had his breathe again, he found the way by feel to his acceleration couch and cut on the emergency lighting. He held one hand tight against the cut on his ribs and opened the first aid kit. He dug out a self-sealing bandage and reflected on how quickly things had gone south. He knew Great Prospects' reputation and hadn't been looking forward to tangling with them. He was surprised when they opened the *Nai'a* up to attack with their sweep toward the inbound ice delivery. He wasn't surprised at all when it turned out to be a trap. He wondered if his squadron's missile salvo would do any damage.

***

Colonel Rai's weapons officer made one last adjustment to the defensive plan and prayed their intelligence was correct. The enemy's salvo was a combination of jammers and fragmentary proximity warheads. A split second after the jammers went off, every ship in Rai's formation fired anti-missile batteries and main laser banks. They targeted the probable location of each missile based on Lisandra Redding's analysis of the captured missile's computer. Half of the attack missiles exploded or careened off course from laser hits and every jammer went silent. With clean targeting data the squadron's combined laser batteries swept the remaining missiles from space before they could reach attack range. The squadron flipped to face the twenty-five fighters now burning on a reverse course and maneuvered to shelter behind the drifting ice wedges.

***

When Rai's signal reached Marshall Winter's fleet, they had immediately opened up with lasers, targeting enemy ships' drives. Thanks to their position, drifting in behind the formation, the angle was nearly perfect. In the span of two seconds, fifteen ships and twenty-five fighters around the *Nai'a* were reduced to one operational ship and a host of drifting hulks. The one "lucky" ship, sheltered by the bulk of the *Nai'a*, was met by the combined fire power of the Tau Ceti fleet when it appeared around the hull of the long boat. It managed to launch a single missile salvo, quickly blown out of space, before meeting the same fate as its sister ships. Marshall Winter hailed the two enemy carriers, calling on them to surrender and recall fighters. He carefully repositioned his forces to protect the *Nai'a* from any missile strikes. The carriers, mounting only anti-missile batteries, were a minimal threat. The Warnicky's Wolfpack assault shuttle carrier replied ten seconds later, agreeing to surrender. The Orca Squadron's carrier took a full minute to reply. A slightly harassed looking commander with blood welling from a hastily applied bandage on his temple appeared on the com and apologized. "Sorry for the delay, Marshall, I had to have a quick heart to heart with our employer. I've recalled our remaining fighters and ordered them to power their weapons down."

"Turn your employer over to me immediately. I'll send a shuttle over," the Marshall replied.

"I'm afraid he'll be in a body bag," the Wolfpack commander replied. "He objected strenuously to surrendering, but we have two of his underlings in custody. I'll be glad to hand them over. Do I have permission to launch rescue operations? We have two unarmed shuttles and a pinnace."

"Affirmative on search and rescue, coordinate with my tactical officer. Winter out." He cut the connection. "Get me Captain Brelling on com. I want to know what's happening over there."

***

Captain Brelling looked up from the split video feed of Cooper Green and the boat bay. The mercenaries, with the exception of the one scout, were cooperating. Rows of scarred and blackened armor stood testament to the intensity of the fight and the discipline of Warnicky's troops. *Nai'a* medical teams worked among the mercenaries, tending to the wounded. She activated the space forces channel. "Greetings, Marshall Winter. We persuaded the mercenaries to surrender, and we're mopping up. My scan looks much better than I anticipated. What's your situation?"

"The enemy space forces surrendered, except for one ship that was engaged with Colonel Rai's forces. It's drifting this way with weapons and active sensors down. I don't think it's a threat, but Colonel Rai detached three ships to keep an eye on it while we conduct search and rescue. The biggest problem is keeping the drifting hulks from impacting the *Nai'a*. Fortunately, most of our ships have tug grapples, and the carriers have plenty of hangar space and docking ports to handle the wrecks. Colonel Rai's force will be here in a few minutes to help. I'm allowing the carriers to use the small vessels they have left to aid search and rescue, but we're keeping them to the perimeter."

"Good," replied Captain Brelling. "I plan to keep the assault shuttles and armor from Warnicky's Wolfpack until you sort out what to do with them."

"For now, we'll leave them under your control. I need to coordinate with Colonel Rai and I'm putting government crews aboard the carriers. I didn't expect to take this number of prisoners, but it's a good problem to have. Along with search and rescue, my priority is rounding up anyone who's part of the Restoration. I know each carrier has a few of their operators aboard. We're still sorting out the rest of the ship crews."

"I probably have a few of their agents on the *Nai'a*," answered Captain Brelling. "Ship Security is doing their best to smoke them out in the wake of the battle. My medical staff is handing the mercenary casualties. By some miracle, they didn't suffer any fatalities, but more than half of them are wounded, several severely. As soon as you think it's safe, I want to transfer most of them back to their carrier. I assume they have the facilities to care for them long enough to get them to an appropriate facility."

"It shouldn't be long now," The Marshall said. "I'll have my people coordinate with yours to get it done. I confess, I thought you we're crazy to let the entire boarding force aboard the *Nai'a* without firing a shot. Congratulations, Captain! You and your crew pulled off a near miracle."

"I'm fine with calling it a real miracle. I know I put in a lot of prayer over the last few days. We couldn't have done it without your help."

***

Captain Garrity zipped the body bag with remains of his weapons officer shut and activated the cooling mechanism. He checked to make sure it was tightly secured to the deck then turned to his prisoner. With a hard expression he retightened the extra straps securing the psychopath to the observer's acceleration couch. Unfortunately, the man was unconscious so he couldn't feel the well-deserved discomfort or the pain from his battered face. Garrity winced as the motion stretched his bandaged wound. He turned to start the grim task of cleaning up his friend's blood and contemplated his situation. He was drifting slowly toward the *Nai'a* on emergency power, just waiting for a hostile knock on the hatch. He knew the Orca Squadron would pick him up, if it still existed. The *Nai'a* and her protection ships had no reason to help, except maybe the piece of human trash strapped to his observer seat. He looked at his smashed communications console, victim of an errant flechette, and wondered if it was worth the effort to try a repair. He had just about finished cleaning up when his ship lurched slightly and a series of thunks told him he had visitors.

Garrity pulled himself down the access way to the airlock and flipped open the cover of the viewing window. The suited figure in the airlock secured the outer hatch and turned locking eyes with him. They carried a short wicked-looking boarding gun of some kind. The person waved then motioned for him to back away from the lock door. He did as indicated, then floated in the passageway anchored by one hand and holding the other in plain sight. The lock cycled his visitor through. After a quick, gun-first appraisal of the situation, the figure cracked the seal on their helmet and flipped it back revealing a surprisingly youthful feminine face. "Leftenant Palamar O'Clair, Great Prospects at your service, but don't get any ideas. What's your situation?" The muzzle of her weapon stayed pointed directly at his center of mass.

"I take it your side won the fight," Garrity said, careful to appear as non-threatening as possible.

"I wouldn't call it a fight," the leftenant answered.

"I suppose not. My weapons officer is dead, murdered by the 'advisor' riding along with us when he refused to fire a nuclear salvo at the *Nai'a*."

"And the advisor?"

"I beat him unconscious. He's strapped to the observer's seat."

The leftenant took in his torn, bloody flight suit. "Do you require medical attention?"

"It can wait."

"Back down to the bridge. Keep your hands where I can see them and don't touch any controls."

Garrity pushed himself backward carefully, floating past the body bag on the deck. He eased past the unconscious Restoration operative. Sliding over the top of his acceleration couch feet first, he held himself in place with two hands on the headrest facing the Great Prospects Leftenant. Palamar O'Clair turned slowly, allowing her suit camera to take in the scene on the bridge.

"Are you getting all of this?" she asked softly into her suit com. She nodded at whatever reply she received in her earpiece. She checked the restraints on the man in the observer's seat, then opened a medkit on her belt and pulled out an injector. She carefully adjusted the injector's setting then emptied it into the man's neck. She switched her gaze to Garrity, "I gave him enough sedative to keep him out while we get where we're going. You probably realize cooperation is your best path forward. Are you going to behave yourself?" Garrity nodded. "Go ahead and strap in. Open your flight suit first so I can check that wound." She slid carefully into the weapons officer's seat next to him and loosely secured the lap belt around her suit. She worked efficiently, removing his hastily applied bandage and cleaning the wound while he tried to hold still. A light acceleration helped, pushing neatly them into their seats as the ship grappled to his maneuvered them both. She neatly applied a new bandage from his medkit, then pulled out her injector. "Just an antibiotic and mild pain killer," she said when he raised his eyebrows. She pulled his suit aside and injected his left shoulder.

"Thank you," he said as the physical pain faded into the background. "I wasn't sure you'd bother to pick us up. I should have known Great Prospects would act honorably in victory."

"You're a navigation hazard if nothing else," she replied. "Also, we're very interested in your passenger. The other two Restoration operatives on ships like yours killed the crew then committed suicide when their ship was disabled. I'm recording and broadcasting this conversation to my leadership, the *Nai'a,* and a Tau Ceti System Marshall. If you tell us everything you know about the operation, the people who are going to decide your fate will be in a better mood."

Garrity quirked his lips and nodded. "The Restoration put us in a no-win situation. From what we were told, both Brigadier Warnicky and the Orca Squadron Commander, Commodore Naismith, are prisoners. We had the choice of cooperating and helping the Restoration take the *Nai'a,* or having our commanders killed. We were offered enough money to make every one of us rich, and places in the *Nai'a's* new crew to escape Tau Ceti justice. I had no illusions about Great Prospects giving up the *Nai'a* easily, but we were supposed to have an overwhelming force advantage."

"So, you thought you'd eliminate the Great Prospects protection ships like mine, and the Wolfpack would take the *Nai'a.*" Her gaze hardened.

He didn't try to deny it. "It wouldn't have worked any other way. Great Prospects would have fought to the last ship."

"What about the nuclear missile attack on the *Nai'a*? You had to know you'd be hunted across the system for such a thing."

"I didn't know about it until our observer gave the order. I'm guessing they planned all along to destroy the *Nai'a* if they couldn't capture her, but they didn't tell us ahead of time. They told us the nukes were for the ice delivery, but that was a lie. Lieutenant Anders, back there in the body bag, died to keep the attack from happening."

"You put yourself in harm's way as well," she observed.

"Honestly, it was an instinctive reaction. He probably thought I would be intimidated into completing the launch by Patrick's death. Instead, I was angry, scared, and pumped with enough adrenaline to just barely get the better of the vile cretin. I'm glad I don't have the deaths of more than five thousand people on my conscience."

"It's a mark in your favor from my perspective," the leftenant replied. "I have a lot of friends aboard the *Nai'a,* and I'll be a crew member when the boat leaves Tau Ceti. I'm not proud of my home system right now. I envy you the satisfaction of doing the damage you did to that murderer's face. He'll get what's coming to him, but not before spending some quality time with Marshall Winter's interrogators."

Her expression grew distant as she listened to an incoming message. She gave the battered Restoration operative a wary look. "This character's partners in crime had suicide charges implanted in their heads. It's a good thing you knocked him unconscious." Garrity leaned as far away from the man as he could in the cramped bridge.

His reaction drew a chuckle from Leftenant O'Clair. "It's tiny, just enough to cause what looks like a fatal aneurism."

Garrity chuckled a bit himself and then coughed, wincing. He grabbed one of the leftover cleaning tissues and wiped his mouth. "Oh goody," he said mildly, looking at the bright red stain on the tissue.

"Just relax and breathe, Captain. Help is on the way."

Chapter 7 – Threads and Consequences

December 1st, AD 3187
Long Boat Nai'a - Tau Ceti Mid-System
Captain's Conference Room

Captain Brelling rubbed red eyes and stifled a yawn. Her people and Marshall Winter's Tau Ceti force were several hours into cleaning up the aftermath of the battle on the *Nai'a* and in space. Everyone was nearing exhaustion. To her left, Marshall Winter's hologram indicated his virtual presence at the meeting. Commander Hartley was summarizing the situation for the *Nai'a's* leadership. "At Marshall Winter's request, we allowed Warnicky's Wolfpack to withdraw their troops, minus weapons and armor, to their carrier. They took all their wounded, except the three most critical Dr. Rensaleer insisted on keeping under her care in medical. The only fatalities were four Orca Squadron crew members killed by Restoration operatives who then committed suicide or were eliminated via remote control. We still don't know which. Each carrier crew killed the lead Restoration agent on their ship and captured two more. The agent on the *Orca* wounded three bridge crew members, but the Wolfpack crew had a plan in place to deal with theirs. Between the Great Prospects ships, Marshall Winter's and the mercenary small craft, we've rounded up all the disabled ships and their crews. There's a double layer of protection ships providing sensor coverage and defense in a spherical formation around the *Nai'a*. We should be secure from external threats. I'll let Chief Bolhepp update you on the internal threat."

Ship Security Chief Bolhepp cleared his throat. "Our trap in the active cold sleep vault produced two operatives attempting to wake the prisoners bound for Lalande. From a preliminary interrogation, I believe both were in it for the money. As we agreed, I'll turn them over to Marshall Winter for prosecution. I'm not convinced those two are the only Restoration agents aboard, but we haven't had any reports of suspicious activity or sabotage. Colonel Zeleski admitted he expected intelligence from someone on the *Nai'a*, but didn't receive any. I suspect the agent saw how things were going, then decided to lay low."

"It would fit the pattern," said the captain. "Marshall, what are your plans for Orca Squadron and Warnicky's Wolfpack? I'm nervous about the crews you put aboard the carriers. They wouldn't stand much of a chance against an uprising."

"I appreciate your concern. The mercenary companies know two things down to the last troop. First, you spared their lives when you didn't have to. Second, every one of their necks is on the line depending on their behavior. I have the authority to summarily execute all of them for piracy and I have quite a reputation as a hard case. I have no intention of executing them when you risked so much to avoid loss of life, but they don't know that. I'll take them all with me back to HAB-5 so they won't have any opportunities for mischief. Most of them will get off with a fine and probation on my recommendation. The companies still have a lot of assets I'll need to deal with. In theory, the commanders of both companies are innocent of wrongdoing. If Ennis Elkins manages to free them, they'll still own a controlling interest of what's left."

"I'll happily leave the sorting of those details to you," answered the captain, "as long as they stay out of my hair. When you're ready to depart, send a Wolfpack shuttle over for their armor. Not much of it is intact and we have better. The weapons, we'll recycle."

"Fair enough," said the Marshall, "my compliments to you and your people on a job well done. You as well, Colonel Rai, Great Prospects once again showed its mettle."

"Thank you," said Colonel Rai. "It was a team effort and your crews showed real nerve letting the enemy ships pass right through their formation. The space situation is under control as Commander Hartley said, but I would like to revert to our standard defensive deployment and start rotating crew out for rest with your permission captain."

"I'm comfortable with the standard deployment now," answered the captain. "Marshall, I meant to ask about the Restoration operative the O'Clairs captured. I should probably say Captain Garrity captured him, but you know who I mean."

"I'm glad you asked. My medical team removed the suicide charge without setting it off. As soon as he's conscious I'll interrogate him. I'd like to borrow Hal Renfro for the initial session if you'll lend him to me. We make a good team."

"Good cop, bad cop?" queried the captain.

The Marshall showed his teeth in a predatory grin. "For him, it'll be bad cop, worse cop."

The captain allowed herself a small smile. "I'll send Hal right over. The last item on the agenda is the ice shield thickening operation. Do we still have ice?"

Colonel Rai nodded. "The six wedges of the disc are intact. We rounded them up and I assigned six of my ships to shepherd them until the ice contractor's tugs arrive in a few hours. The contractor's tanker has more than enough water to make up for the losses. Mr. Barboa said the installation will take longer, but it's actually an easier operation done piece by piece."

***

The next day Quester met Shanyah at the tropical dome beach to talk to the dolphins and see how they were doing. "They're disappointed they didn't get to play a bigger part in defending the ship," said Shanyah as they floated with the excited pod chittering around them. "I've expressed the captain's gratitude, and mine, for taking down the scout. Mishael, Kalei and their friends might have ended up as hostages if they hadn't. The kids are a little shaken up after hearing the shots the dolphins fired. Abishai is sticking close to them for now."

"I'm surprised the dolphins didn't accidently fire on Elder Pryachac when she captured the scout," said Quester.

"She's old friends with the pod and weighs half of what the scout does. I'm sure they recognized the vibrations of her footsteps. That's why they only fired two shots at the scout. They could tell from the scout's steps that he wasn't in full battle armor and knew the elder was nearby."

"I feel like all we did was run around like crazy people leap-frogging positions. The snipers were the only ones in Beta Company to fire a shot."

"The Great Prospects commandos feel the same way. Even though they weren't needed, they were always in the right place to make a counter-strike. The dolphins helped their movements, so they stayed busy. I'm sure every one of the pilots would've rather been out there on a protection ship, taking part in the space battle. Be happy you weren't with the companies defending aft engineering. They had a hot time of it. It was hero's work delaying the enemy then bottling them up in the boat bay. The centipedes were enough of a surprise to break the advance and send the aft force running. In spite of all the casualties the mercenaries took, they still nearly succeeded in breaking out of the boat bay later. You have to give the professionals credit for tenacity. If the mercenary commander hadn't seen reason, we would've been in the same kind of fight defending the bridge. We would've won, but the damage would be extensive and we probably would've lost people."

"Do you think the enemy will try another attack?"

"They'll need some time to regroup after this debacle. Hopefully Marshall Winter will have enough intelligence now to keep them on the run, at least until we clear the system. I heard we captured a few agents aboard the *Nai'a* to go with those on the mercenary ships. It remains to be seen whether this battle smoked them all out."

Quester looked troubled. He turned, waded out of the water and started toweling himself dry. Shanyah followed after a few more minutes with the dolphins. When she caught up, she put a hand on his shoulder. "What's bothering you, Quester?" she asked.

Quester hung his head and closed his eyes with a sigh. After a moment he looked up. "I think we'd better go see Ship Security. I know who the last Restoration agent on board is."

***

Shanyah's expression was grave as she ushered Quester into Chief Bolhepp's office. The Ship Security chief looked tired and harassed. "I hope this is important," he said, rubbing his eyes and gesturing toward a pair of chairs.

"I'm working for the Restoration," said Quester without sitting down.

Chief Bolhepp's eyes opened wide. "Let's take this down to the interrogation room. I'll need to record everything." He stood up, ushering them out the office and down the passageway. On the way he popped off a message to the first officer. "Shanyah, I would appreciate it if you would stay. You may have some valuable insight." He didn't mention that he was sure Quester would be more likely to talk in her presence.

Once they were settled at the table, Quester and Shanyah on one side and the chief on the other, Bolhepp fixed Quester with a stare. "Do you want legal representation? You aren't officially under arrest, but that may change by the time we're done. You don't have to say anything, but I assume you wouldn't have come here if you wanted to remain silent."

"I don't want a lawyer. I'll tell you all I know," said Quester. "I'd like Shanyah to stay."

"We're in agreement on that. We'll start when the first officer arrives. Just start at the beginning and tell us everything you know. Any detail you remember could be important."

A moment later the door opened admitting Commander Hartley. "Quester here says he's working for the Restoration," stated the chief. The first officer's eyebrows rose.

"I didn't see that coming," he said sitting down. "I'm glad you turned yourself in, Quester, it's never comfortable having an enemy in our midst, and I imagine you've been pretty nervous yourself."

Questor swallowed, nodded then forged ahead. "Yesterday made me realize this is all a lot more serious than I thought. I could have caused a lot of people, a lot of friends, to die.

"The chief said to start at the beginning, so here goes. About a year ago, a woman I didn't know named Helen started recruiting me for the Restoration. I didn't know what she was after at first. She talked about the Long Boat Free Trade Syndicate and its lock on interstellar trade. Her favorite tirade was about how hypocritical the 'Free Trade' part of the syndicate's name supposedly is. She'd go on about how the trade syndicate steals star system sovereignty and wealth that rightfully belongs to the systems who built the long boats in the first place. It all sounded quite logical, but my hogwash detector is well honed.

"I did some of my own research and found most of her arguments didn't stand up to facts. Every long boat in the trade syndicate paid off its investors or bought itself free of government ownership with money put up by the crew. It's a requirement of membership, but I suppose you know that better than I do. I also looked at the system gross product records for Tau Ceti over the last 500 years. Nearly every long boat visit to this system correlated with an acceleration in economic activity and wealth. Also, by last count, there were twenty-two long boats still under government or corporate ownership and two or three under construction in the Sol system. If a company or star system government wants to own a long boat, the only thing stopping them is time and money.

"I shortly realized she was a fanatic trying to recruit me for her 'side'. Since the only side I've ever been on is my own, I played along. I've been a good actor ever since I can remember, so I think she bought my enthusiasm. I figured her organization's blind fanaticism would give me an opening to take advantage of down the line. She was also well funded and I wasn't in a position to refuse cash.

"A few months ago, she ramped up the pressure, giving me a few extra-legal tasks to test my loyalty to the cause. It was all stuff I'd done before, some minor hacking and looking into personal records. She never said what she did with the data. When the *Nai'a* changed destinations from Sol to Lalande, she told me to apply for a crew position. This would be my chance to help the cause. I almost balked, but things were heating up with my gang. It looked like an opportunity to escape that way of life with my skin intact. As it was, I had to ghost the gang for a week before reporting aboard so they wouldn't find out. Helen helped with a safe apartment."

Quester dug into a pocket and pulled out a data chip. He slid it across to Chief Bolhepp. "This has the address of the apartment plus the place I think she lived, several places she frequented, and a few pictures. I'm sure she's burned the identity by now, but it wouldn't hurt to check."

"Did she give you any idea of their goals beyond taking over the *Nai'a*?" Chief Bolhepp asked. "We already know they have it in for the Tau Ceti government and the Long Boat Free Trade Syndicate."

"They want to restore ownership of all long boats to the government. By government, they mean a Sol-based central government of all human inhabited systems. They want to turn the clock back six hundred years and reestablish the colonial system. They call themselves the Restoration because they want to restore 'order' to the human expansion. They're smart enough to realize controlling the long boats is the only way they have a prayer of controlling the other systems from Sol. Step one is taking direct control of any long boats they can and setting the star systems and trade syndicate at each other's throats to muddy the waters. I still think they're off their collective rockers. Short of someone inventing faster than light travel, there's no way to control a system that's a twenty-year voyage away. I was careful to go along and act like a true believer, though.

"A few days before I reported aboard, Helen gave me a sketchy outline of their plan to take the *Nai'a*. She wanted me to gather all the information I could about troop dispositions and give the Wolfpack commander intelligence during the fight. She taught me how to program my PCOM so I could communicate with them. I memorized several code phrases with primary and back up frequencies. You may not believe me, but I intended to use the channel to give them false information. When the captain sent the delayed orders out, I gave up on the idea. I didn't want to risk messing up the plan. I thought my silence would discourage and confuse the mercenary commander more than any false information I could think of."

"For the record, you made the right call," said Commander Hartley. "If Colonel Zeleski thought he had better intelligence, he would have been more likely to continue the attack. Also for the record, I believe you intended to give them false information. What made you decide to switch sides?"

"I was never on their side," replied Quester. "I was just using them the way they wanted to use me. Honestly, I wasn't on the *Nai'a's* side either in the beginning. I wanted to see which way the chips would fall before I made my play. After a few weeks aboard, though, Shanyah and the rest of the Beta Sections crew had me feeling like a family member. I couldn't see doing anything to hurt the crew or the ship. I should have come clean when we went to see the captain about the dolphins, but I froze up. The fight, and the reality that the Restoration was willing to kill everyone on this ship, brought things into focus. I suppose I've punched my ticket to one of Marshall Winter's detention cells, but I'm sick of carrying on with the deception."

"Legally, you're still a crew member of the *Nai'a* until your case is resolved by our judicial system," said Chief Bolhepp. "Because you're in a probationary status as new crew, it would be pretty simple to terminate your contract and hand you over to the Marshall. I doubt the captain will do that, though, and you'll get at least a hearing before anything is decided. Whether you like it or not, I'm going to assign you an attorney to explain your options. In the meantime, tell us more about this operative Helen, and what you know about other agents aboard the *Nai'a*."

Two hours later, Quester felt like a wrung-out dishrag. He'd told them every significant thing he could think of and a lot that wasn't. His feelings were a swirling mix of dread toward the future, relief at finally coming clean, and euphoria from the victory over the Restoration. Shanyah and Chief Bolhepp walked him to the brig. "Can't you release him to me?" asked Shanyah. "You know he's not a flight risk."

"Not with the charges he has hanging over his head," answered Chief Bolhepp. "Some time in the brig will help sort him out. You can visit later if you want to."

"Okay, we'll bring him supper. Nothing against the galley, but Abishai's cooking is better." She gave Quester a hug and turned away before he could see her tears welling up.

Quester spent the next hour staring at the ceiling from the surprisingly comfortable bunk. He had expected bare ship steel, but it was well padded with something that had a vaguely organic feel to it. He'd been in a lock-up or two and had to admit the *Nai'a's* brig was the nicest he could remember. The hour of introspection wasn't going anywhere, so the clang of his door opening provided a welcome distraction. A Ship Security guard ushered in a tall middle-aged looking woman with pixie-cut brown hair and a professional manner. Quester got up from the cot and faced the two. "I'm Lisa Gallred, your appointed attorney if you'll have me," the woman said, by way of introduction, and put her hand out.

"Quester Drake," he returned, shaking her hand, "glad to make your acquaintance. I could certainly use a lawyer right now."

The guard looked questioningly at the attorney. "I'll be fine. I'll let you know when we're done." He locked the door behind her. "Have a seat on the bunk," she told Quester, then toed an unseen switch and stood back. A small table and stool unfolded from the floor, taking up most of the rest of the cell. "Not the most comfortable seat on the ship, but it's better than standing up," she said, sitting down opposite Quester and pulling up some documents on her digital legal pad. "Your situation is complex. We're going to have deal with the captain's chain of authority, the civil side of ship government, and the *Nai'a's* business entity that holds your contract. Also, they haven't finalized the charges against you. Anything up to mutiny and conspiracy to mutiny are possible. Once you're formally charged, we'll need to decide whether you want a civil-criminal trial or court-martial. They could forego all of that, terminate your probationary crew contract, and turn you over to the Tau Ceti authorities after a formal hearing. In any event, we'll have a chance to state your case. My question is, where do you want to spend your future?"

"Where?" queried Quester.

"You have a chance, not a great one, but a chance, of staying on board the *Nai'a*. If you'd rather remain in Tau Ceti, I'll try to get what guarantees I can, but you'll need a local lawyer. We'll know more once the Marshall sorts out the mercenaries and the Restoration operatives. I watched the recording of your interview. In the future, don't do that without your lawyer present. Do you have anything to add that might help me argue your case?"

"Nothing I can think of," answered Quester. "I'll cooperate any way I can. My preference is to remain aboard the *Nai'a* as long as the captain's not going to put me out an airlock."

Lisa quirked an eyebrow. "I know she can be intimidating, but she's not going to space you. First, she's actually been meticulously fair in every dealing I've had with her and she's never had anyone executed. Second, I'm a better lawyer than that. Since you're cooperating, we can probably negotiate a plea deal. For now, try to keep your spirits up and see what else you can remember about your dealings with the Restoration."

"What about the agents that tried to free the cold sleep prisoners?" Quester asked.

"They were in quite a rush to waive their right to a hearing. We turned them over to the Tau Ceti authorities. Apparently, they're even more intimidated by the captain than you are. I don't think they ever intended to stay aboard once their work was done." As she finished speaking, the door opened again.

The guard poked his head in. "Dinner delivery. You're not allowed visitors yet, other than your lawyer. Abishai dropped this off." He brought a paper bag over and set it in front of Quester with a thump.

Lisa stood and shook Quester's hand. "I'll be back when I have news. It may not be until tomorrow morning." Once she and the guard were gone. Quester opened the bag and breathed in the rich aroma of basil and garlic mixed with the yeasty smell of fresh bread. The appetite he'd lacked came roaring back as he realized he hadn't eaten since breakfast. There was a large portion of mushroom and sausage stuffed manicotti accompanied by three soft puffy breadsticks. A salad of romaine lettuce with cucumbers and halved cherry tomatoes and a couple of peanut butter cookies rounded out the feast. At the bottom of the bag Quester found a worn physical copy of the Bible he recognized as Abishai's. He put it aside carefully, picked up the bamboo spork, and dug into the meal.

Chapter 8 – Layered Shield

December 2nd, AD 3187
Long Boat Nai'a - Tau Ceti Mid-System
Captain's Conference Room

Captain Brelling's sense of déjà vu kicked in well before the caffeine from her coffee. She'd managed four hours of sleep and wasn't completely exhausted. The meeting participants were exactly the same as the previous day. "Marshall Winter, please get us started," she said.

"I'm confident I have all the living Restoration operatives directly involved in the attack in custody. The two you sent over were happy to turn state's evidence for a plea agreement with a reduced sentence. Unfortunately, they didn't help us much. I believe their Restoration contact was the same woman who recruited Quester Drake. We're making some headway with the financial trail from their up-front payments. They weren't recruited for the Restoration cause, but the promised final payment for getting the prisoners out of cold sleep was substantial." He furrowed his brow slightly.

"The observer from Captain Garrity's ship is a bigger fish, but he isn't cooperating. We managed to get enough out of him to determine he's a leader in the local Restoration organization. We found his true identity. He's a citizen of Tau Ceti so we'll deal with him.

"I have better news from Ennis Elkins. His operation to free the mercenary commanders was successful. Both brigadiers are alive, if a little banged up. Better yet, Ennis bagged the Restoration leader that originally tried to recruit him. I think he's another Lalande import. Once we squeeze him dry and positively identify him, I'll let you know if he's a candidate to join your group of prisoners in cold sleep."

"What are you going to do with the Warnicky and the Orca Squadron commander?" asked Colonel Rai.

"They'll join me back at HAB-5 if they want to recover their equipment and people," the Marshall answered. "I suspect we'll negotiate a settlement that leaves them owing the government a substantial sum. I'm going to need some muscle to pursue the leads we have on the Restoration. I'll put the two companies to work while I've got them on a short leash. Part of what they owe will be for repairs to the *Nai'a*. Be sure to send me a bill."

"I'm working on an itemized list with engineering now," said Hubble Spears. "Do you need anything else?"

"The only other thing I want from the *Nai'a* is one Quester Drake. I don't suppose you've sorted out his status yet?"

Captain Brelling quirked her lips. "His crew retention hearing is this morning. If the board terminates his contract, he's yours to deal with. If the board decides to retain him, we'll see what route he decides to take in disposing of the charges against him, but he'll remain on the ship as crew. That's not negotiable. Our agreement with your government doesn't require me to turn a crew member over to you short of a capital murder charge."

"I understand. Can I at least get a face-to-face interview?" asked Marshall Winter.

"He's already said he's willing. If you have time to pay us a visit, I'll have Chief Bolhepp make the arrangements," Captain Brelling answered. She turned to the protection force commander. "Colonel Rai, any issues with space defense?"

"Nothing major," answered the colonel. "We'll be back to a normal rotation in the next few hours. All my ships are rearmed and refueled. We haven't had any unusual sensor contacts since the battle. My boss authorized me to let you know he'll arrive in twenty-four hours with an offer from the Dust Miners Alliance."

"What does the DMA want with the *Nai'a*?" asked the captain. She gave Marshall Winter's hologram a glance, but he looked equally puzzled.

"Brigadier Tamang didn't give me any details," answered Colonel Rai. "He just told me not to be alarmed at the armada coming behind him. He also requested an audience with Marshall Winter."

The Marshall steepled his fingers in thought. "I think you, Brigadier Tamang, and I need to sit down together, Captain. I want to talk to Quester anyway, so I'll shuttle over tomorrow with your permission."

"I agree. Whatever the DMA is up to I want a Tau Ceti government representative to be here when we talk," answered the captain. She turned to her militia commander. "Mr. Barboa, I know you'd rather be supervising preparations for the ice shield operation. Give us a quick summary of what to expect."

"Mr. Lal is more than capable of standing in for me," Barboa answered. "Today the team is laying a thermal grid over the front of the shield in six pie-shaped sections. They'll be finished in about 48 hours, then we can start fitting the pieces to the shield. Our .001G acceleration, along with some edge plates driven into the ice, will hold each piece temporarily in place. We'll heat the grid for that section and melt enough ice to between the new and old ice to form a bond as it refreezes. The first chunk will be the trickiest. Colonel Rai tells me the contractor's tug pilots are the best. We'll see if they live up to the hype. Once all the pieces are bonded, we'll bring the tanker in to fill in any gaps between them. I expect each piece to take eight hours, so we're looking at a three-day operation including filling the gaps. We'll have a significant imbalance while we have an odd number of pieces in place. The bearings on the free-rotating ring are rated for it. Chief Nance wrote a program to handle the helm adjustments. We're going to go through quite a bit of thruster fuel. Chief Nance also wrote a training simulation for manual helm control. The *Nai'a* doesn't dodge well at the best of times, but during this operation, we'll need to maintain a steady course."

The captain nodded, "That's exactly why I'm happy they jumped the gun and started their attack before we were deep into the operation. Thanks for the rundown, Mr. Barboa. Does anyone have anything to add?" No one spoke up. "Alright, I know everyone here has things to do. We'll call the meeting adjourned."

***

Quester Drake marched into the Beta Section galley followed closely by a Ship Security guard and his attorney, Lisa Gallred. He was thankful they had allowed him to change into a standard ship suit and he wasn't required to wear restraints. He came to attention in front of a long table with six crew members seated at it. He recognized Pete Worsley in the middle; the others weren't familiar. "Have a seat, Mr. Drake," Pete Worsley said, indicating a small table with two chairs between them. "This is a formal hearing, but it's not a military proceeding. The retention board is here to decide if you will remain on the *Nai'a* as a crew member." Quester swallowed, then joined his attorney at the table. Only then did he notice that several of his Beta Section crewmates were seated around the room.

Lisa Gallred's advice on the hearing had been simple. "Keep your ears open and your mouth shut as much as possible. Answer any questions openly and honestly. Don't make excuses." He knew the board members had seen his interview with Chief Bolhepp because he'd signed a document allowing them access.

A severe-looking woman on the left end of the table started the questioning. "In your own words, Quester Drake, tell us why you want to remain a crew member on the *Nai'a*."

Quester wiped sweaty palms on his ship suit, considering the unexpected question for a moment, then looked the woman in the eye. "I have three main reasons. First, I don't want to face Tau Ceti justice for what I've done. I'd rather pay my debt to the crew. Second, several violently inclined people are waiting to hammer me if I show my face on HAB-5 again. Third, this crew is the only good thing I've ever been a part of. I don't want to lose being part of you." Uncharacteristic emotion gripped him as he realized the truth of his own words. The woman returned his gaze forthrightly when he finished, her mouth slightly pursed. He knew he was being weighed in a fine balance.

Pete Worsley spoke next. "We're all aware of Mr. Drake's actions, both positive and negative since joining the crew. Does anyone wish to speak for him?"

Abishai stood up and walked in front of the board. "I'll speak for Quester. You know his public exploits. He went against the Restoration's orders and helped make our defenses stronger. I want to talk about how he treats people, specifically my children. You can tell a lot about someone's character by the way they act toward those they don't stand to gain anything from. He spends time with Mishael and Kalei telling them stories and listening to them. He's been consistently patient and kind. Shanyah can tell you he's the same with our dolphin family. He admits his motivations for joining the crew are questionable. How many of us can say our own motives are completely pure? I believe Quester will be a good crew member. He needs us and we need him." Abishai returned to his seat and one of Quester's heavy weapons squad mates replaced him, reading a short statement praising his consistent effort to improve. One by one several crewmates spoke on his behalf. Even Leftenant Haynes, who he'd beaten in the combat armor race, spoke for him. Quester had to blink back moisture from his eyes. He'd been aboard less than two months. How could he come to mean this much to so many people in such a short time? How could they mean so much to him?

Everyone who wanted to speak had a turn, and Quester thought they were finished when Shanyah came breathlessly through the door. "Sorry I'm late. May I speak for Quester on behalf of the dolphins?" Pete nodded. Shanyah pulled a rolled-up sheet of plastic from her pocket and opened it.

"The dolphins had quite a bit to say. I'll give you my best condensed translation. 'Quester was brought to us by the star tides and currents. He knows the boundary of water and air. He is a member of our pod now. His heart will not depart from us even if you send his body away.' They feel very strongly that we should keep Quester on the crew. I hope you will consider their wishes." The board exchanged meaningful looks as Shanyah joined Abishai.

Pete Worsley waited a moment to see if anyone else would speak, then asked, "does anyone wish to speak against Mr. Drake?" When no one came forward, he looked at the other board members. "We can begin deliberations then. Two minutes each for opening statements then we'll open the floor for discussion." Quester was surprised they allowed him, and anyone else who wanted to stay, sit through the discussions. The panel members made valid arguments both for and against keeping him on the crew. Although it was disconcerting to hear them discussing his merits and shortcomings, he was glad to witness the process. Waiting out the decision somewhere else would have been nerve-wracking. Occasionally they asked him questions. He tried to heed Lisa's advice, paying close attention to the discussion and keeping his answers to the point. After about twenty minutes, the discussion wound down and Pete Worsley called for a vote. To Quester's surprise it was unanimous in favor of keeping him on the crew. His crewmates clapped loudly at the announcement and gathered around him. He got so many hugs and slaps on the back that he didn't know who was who half the time. Pete came over and shook his hand. "You've earned a new start. I'm confident you'll be a good member of the Beta Section crew. Any time you want to talk, come find me. Abishai can tell you where I usually conduct office hours."

Quester turned to his lawyer. "I wasn't expecting it to go as well as it did. I'm not sure what I was expecting."

"I was fairly confident they would keep you," Lisa replied. "This crew doesn't mind a challenge if they think you can be salvaged. Next up is deciding what to do about the charges against you. I have the full list now. The most serious is conspiracy to commit mutiny. That one is going to be hard to fight and carries a lengthy sentence of confinement at hard labor. I don't have a plea offer from the civil prosecutor. I'm sure he thinks he can get a conviction and make an example of you. He's probably right. The captain, however, is willing to take care of the charges at a captain's mast and impose non-judicial punishment."

"What does that mean?" asked Quester.

"It means, while the charges and subsequent punishment will go on your record, you won't have criminal convictions. Also, non-judicial punishment is typically extra duty, you wouldn't be in the brig, but the tasks the chief of boat assigns for extra duty won't be fun. You can ask Abishai about what to expect." Quester looked at Abishai in surprise. He couldn't imagine him getting in trouble with the captain.

"It's a long story," said Abishai. "I'll fill you in later. Just pray no sludge tanks are due for cleaning."

"Bottom line, Quester," said his lawyer. "I recommend taking the deal from the captain. The consequences will be much less than a conviction by the ship's civilian judiciary. Your own testimony is enough to guarantee we'd lose in court."

Quester looked at Shanyah and Abishai. "What do you two think? I admit, I'm not looking forward to facing the captain again."

"I know it doesn't feel like it, but the captain is already on your side," said Abishai. "She wouldn't have offered you a captain's mast if she wanted to throw the book at you. I'm not going to lie; I stood in front of her with two dozen other crew members at the same kind of proceeding. I was scared out of my wits, but I got through it and you will too. Your lawyer's advice is sound. Unless you're actually innocent, you're always better going the non-judicial route."

"I can't claim innocence after spilling my guts," said Quester. He turned to Lisa. "You can tell them I'll accept the captain's mast."

"Good, it's set for 1400 hours today in the ship's council chamber," his lawyer answered.

"Wait a minute! How did they know I'd take it?"

"They didn't, but the captain was sure enough you'd do the smart thing to put it on the ship's schedule."

Quester snorted. "Yeah, smart, that's me."

Lisa looked at Shanyah. "Will you take responsibility for him until the captain's mast?" Quester looked around quickly to find the Ship Security guard nowhere in sight. "He has to be escorted by a crew member for the time being, but he doesn't need to go back to the brig."

"We'll take him back to our quarters and get a good lunch in him," Shanyah answered.

Quester didn't see how he was going to have an appetite, but changed his mind quickly when Abishai put a bowl of home-made chicken soup in front of him with hot cheese biscuits on the side.

After he was comfortably full and seated on the couch, with Lionel purring in his lap, Mishael and Kalei peppered him with questions. He shot a beseeching look at Shanyah. "Hiding anything from them is next to impossible," she said with a grin. "We gave up trying on anything but surprises like birthday presents. Just tell them the truth." The subsequent two-barreled interrogation effectively kept him from dwelling on the pending captain's mast.

***

Quester did his best to keep his knees from shaking as he stood at attention waiting for the captain to enter the council chamber. The only other person present was the chief of boat. This was as private a proceeding as the retention board had been public. The captain entered, dressed in the same service uniform that Quester had donned for the first time today. She took her seat and regarded Quester with a serious expression. "Quester Drake, you stand accused of conspiracy to commit mutiny and a number of lesser charges. You requested a captain's mast to resolve these issues. The captain's mast is now in session. In view of your admitted actions and mitigating circumstances, I impose a punishment of ten hours of extra duty per week for one standard year. Further, you will forfeit one tenth of your standard crew share for the voyage to Lalande. Do you have any questions?"

Quester blinked, taken aback by the speed of events. He had expected a lengthy dressing down. He swallowed and managed to croak out, "no Ma'am."

"Very well. This captain's mast is concluded. You're dismissed." Quester saluted, did an about face and marched out of the chamber. He was standing in the corridor trying to absorb what had just happened when the chief of boat caught up with him.

"I'll send you your extra duty schedule some time this evening," the COB said. "For today, report to the Farm in Gamma Section at 1830 for two hours of work. They're perpetually short on short-handled shovel experts." Quester was too stunned to muster an answer, but wondered how the COB knew about his shoveling skills.

As he walked back to Beta Section quarters, he was too lost in thought to notice a furry cream and gray assassin stalking him. One moment he was walking along, and the next his feet were tangled with 10 kilograms of wiry muscle and bone wrapped in fur. He sprawled in an unkempt heap, finally rolling to his back. Lionel jumped on his chest, bleeking merrily in triumph. "You win, Lionel," Quester laughed. He lifted the cat up with both hands, rose to his feet and perched the Maine Coon on his shoulder. "That seals it, I'm an official crewmember now."

***

The next day the Great Prospects company CEO and commander, Brigadier Jason Tamang, and his wife, Esther, arrived aboard the *Nai'a*. Captain Brelling and Marshall Winter greeted them in the functional, but still under repair, boat bay. "It's hard to believe it was a bit more than six months ago when I welcomed you aboard for the first time," said the captain as she shook the brigadier's hand. Esther grabbed her for a hug she didn't know she needed until she felt the persistent tension in her spine relax and a weight lift from her heart. Heaven knew, no one else on this ship would dare give her a hug.

"It seems much longer for us as well," Esther said. "It's been a busy half year. It's so good to see you again! I know you've had a difficult time the last few days, but we're glad you came through it relatively unscathed." She looked around at the scorch marks and fresh repairs evident throughout the bay.

"Thanks in large part to your reinforcements and Marshall Winter's. Without both, I wouldn't have risked trapping the boarding force on the *Nai'a*."

"You shouldn't have needed to fight your way into and out of Tau Ceti," said the Brigadier. "I'm here to see if we can find a way to make the rest of your exit uneventful."

"I'm all for a boring trip from here on," replied the captain. "Let's get to my conference room. I'm pretty sure the steward finagled some fresh Kouign-amann pastries and the last of the Terran coffee beans for our consumption. Let's not keep them waiting."

Soon they were all settled in enjoying the coffee and pastries. The Brigadier took an appreciative sip of the smooth brew and looked up, "Kona?" he asked the captain.

"Yes, we have contacts."

"It lives up to the hype. As much as I hate to get down to business, I should. There's a force of ships inbound. I'm here to ensure you that they're friends. The Dust Miners Alliance finally found something we can all agree on. We want the *Nai'a* protected. Unfortunately, we arrived too late to head off the latest attack."

"How many ships?" asked the captain.

"One hundred and fifty-four at last count. I expect the number to climb significantly as we cross through DMA space. Most of the habitats out this way are lending ships to the cause. No offense, Marshall, but you know the government can't effectively protect the *Nai'a* out to heliopause. The DMA is happy to do the honors."

"You'll get no argument from me," answered the Marshall. "It's no secret that we don't operate much in DMA territory. I would appreciate being included in the planning, though. I imagine that's why you invited me to the meeting."

"Yes, and I wanted to make sure no one started shooting when the ships show up. It's going to be a nightmare coordinating ship assignments as it is. I'm here to do the job, at no cost to the *Nai'a*."

"As much as I appreciate it, aren't you going to lose your DMA guild card if you don't charge me something?" asked the captain. She hid a smile behind her cup.

"We're already charging you our usual exorbitant rates for the protection team," he answered. "The DMA is footing the bill for the armada's expenses. What I need is an operations center with a communications suite capable of handling the traffic. I'd operate from one of the supply ships, but the *Nai'a* is going to be at the center of the layered defense. It would be best to operate from here. Besides, the food is much better." He licked a stray flake of Kouign-amann from his upper lip.

"Amen to that," said Esther Tamang eyeing another pastry. "I'd better stop if I want to fit my ship suit. Those things are heavenly. Could we borrow Jarman Lal and Mr. Barboa to help us set up?"

"You'll have to wait until they finish the ice shield operation," said the captain. "I can't spare them until then, but I'll have the first officer get you set up in the auxiliary bridge. It has a complete coms suite and probably most of what you'll need. Who is this armada of rugged individualists going to answer to?"

"I'll be in command with Esther as my executive officer," answered Tamang, "but we'll be working for you. Esther worked up an amendment to our current contract to establish the business relationship if you agree. We plan to deploy the ships in a multi-layered shell with survey ships out front. They have the best long-range sensors. The fleet includes six mother ships to service the other vessels and provide quarters for off-duty crew. You won't need to make room on the *Nai'a*."

"I imagine some of the DMA crews would like to visit us," said the captain. "We'd be rude to keep them at arm's length. I have no problem hosting visitors from the fleet, subject to the usual security and medical scans. Commander Hartley will make the arrangements."

"Part of me wants to advise you against it for security reasons," the brigadier answered, "but keeping morale up while we crawl to the heliopause is going to be difficult. Off time on the *Nai'a* will help a lot. There's something else we need to discuss, but I need Marshall Winter's permission to broach the subject." He looked at the Marshall. "You know the geometry is going to out the secret anyway."

Marshall Winter's expression tightened, but he nodded. "I have the authority to release the information to Captain Brelling, and you're correct, they're going to pass close enough to see the *Wanderer* with optical sensors." He turned to the captain. "Tau Ceti has a long boat under construction, the same basic design as the *Nai'a*. The *Wanderer* will be complete and ready to sail in less than a year. Half the system has a stake in the boat through individual or company shares. We intend to use the ship for dedicated runs to Sol, then use the proceeds to build a second vessel to explore and possibly colonize a nearby system."

Captain Brelling drummed her fingers on the table for a few moments, frowning slightly. "I would ask why the secrecy, but the Restoration's repeated attempts to steal my ship answer that question. If most of the people in this system know about it, you can bet they do. They're probably just waiting for you to complete the *Wanderer* before they try to take it."

"I agree," said the Marshall. "With the dent we just put in their organization and the leads we have to follow up on, I'm optimistic we'll eliminate the threat. The DMA fleet will set my mind at ease about the

Nai'a so I can focus on dismantling the remaining Restoration organization in Tau Ceti.

"There's another reason for our secrecy. The powers that be in the Sol system don't like former colonies having their own long boats. We want to apply for associate membership in the Long Boat Free Trade Syndicate when the *Wanderer* reaches Sol on its first voyage. The trade syndicate has a big enough stick to keep the boat from being embargoed or harassed."

"Sounds like another reason for the Restoration to drive a wedge between Tau Ceti and the trade syndicate," said the captain. "You know the price of associate membership is a clear path to self-ownership for the boat."

"We planned to set it up that way from the beginning," the Marshall answered. "Once the boat pays off its investors, it will be as free as the *Nai'a*."

"If the *Nai'a* were really free, I wouldn't be burning for Lalande," said the captain with a hint of bitterness, then shook her head. "Never mind, we all have responsibilities thrust on us we'd rather not shoulder. It's the price of the freedom we do enjoy. Jason, please thank the DMA on my behalf. I'll breathe easier with the extended defensive shell in place."

"I'll pass on your thanks. If you can see your way to doing some additional trading as you pass through, it will bolster the goodwill the *Nai'a* already enjoys. The small habitats out here are always keen on new entertainment and food crop strains. The biome department on the Great Prospects habitat turned back flips over your gift of the seed vault."

"Trade, entertainment, and plants are all in our wheel house," nodded the captain. "Hubble and the crew will be happy to oblige."

"I have a meeting with Quester Drake in a few minutes," said Marshall Winter. "I'll send over the *Wanderer's* specifications on. We'd appreciate a look from your engineering team to let us know if they have any suggestions for improvement. Let me know if there's anything you need from me before I head back in-system." He stood up and shook hands with everyone before departing.

***

Marshall Winter found Abishai waiting for him in the corridor. He'd expected a Ship Security officer. He recognized Abishai as the crewman who'd taken down the saboteur on the inbound voyage shortly after Turnover. He put his hand out, "Marshall Winter, you're Abishai Bonaparte', right?"

Abishai shook the proffered hand. "Yes, it's good to meet you. If you come with me, Quester is waiting in our quarters. I thought this talk might go better over lunch."

The Marshall quirked an eyebrow, "It's not what I expected, but I'm not going to refuse the offer of a meal. Lead on." As they made their way toward Abishai's quarters, Marshall Winter peppered Abishai with questions about the original sabotage and the recent battle. He found the view from troops in the field useful in filling out the picture of a complex situation. Abishai answered everything good naturedly, glad to help the Marshall's investigation any way he could.

Soon they reached Beta Section quarters, joining Abishai's family and Quester around the dining table. Abishai said a blessing and they all passed around bowls of cucumber-tomato salad, hot rolls, and rigatoni in a creamy sauce redolent with garlic. A block of Pecorino Romano cheese and a grater made the rounds as well. The Marshall noticed Mishael and Kalei grating cheese on everything, so he did the same. He joined in the light banter when his mouth wasn't full, choosing to wait until Quester was ready to talk.

Quester went through his food like a combine through a wheat field, casting glances Winter's way. Finally, he wiped sauce off his chin and leaned back. "Go ahead, sir, and don't mind the kids. They know more than you do about me. They're natural born investigators." Mishael and Kalei giggled.

"You're not what your dossier led me to expect," the Marshall began. "Regardless, what I need from you is any light you can shed on the Restoration's organization."

"I've changed since coming aboard the *Nai'a*," Quester returned. "Coming from one of the lower rungs on the HAB-5 social ladder to a place on this crew was an eye-opener."

"I can imagine," said Winter. "Believe it or not, I started on about the same rung. A cop who decided to care about me helped put me on another path. I won't ask you to betray your gang. After you left, they became a lot smaller and a lot less dangerous. Have you remembered anything more about the operative who recruited you? Did she ever mention anyone else in the organization?"

"One thing comes to mind," said Quester thoughtfully. "She had excellent self-control, but it slipped a time or two when she mentioned the people she hired to raid the cold sleep vaults. She seemed anxious about the operation. It's just a guess, but I think she cares a great deal about at least one of the prisoners. I don't know what she'll do when she hears the operation failed, but it might be a chance to flush her into the open."

The Marshall's eyes narrowed. "The agents who attempted to free the cold sleep passengers are in my custody. They've been singing loud and long to save their own hides, but I don't really trust anything they say. This brings up some intriguing possibilities. Anything else? I'm fine with informed speculation."

"I can't think of anything Chief Bolhepp didn't pump out of me already. I assume he passed along the data from the chip I gave him."

"Yes, I have my people working on some discreet surveillance based on the photos and addresses. We might get lucky. I'm sure she'll go to ground and change identities once the word of the failed attack gets out."

Shanyah set a cup of coffee in front of the Marshall while Abishai set a plate of warm oatmeal cookies with chocolate-chips and walnuts in the middle of the table. The Marshall took a big bite of chewy-crunchy cookie and sighed contentedly as he chewed. "I'm sorely tempted to sign on and leave Tau Ceti far behind myself," he said. "Unfortunately, duty beckons. I'm going to chase down every bit of the Restoration I can find. The future of this system depends on it."

"I wouldn't trade places with you, Marshall, but we'll certainly pray for your success," said Abishai. "I know firsthand how fanatical these people can be."

"You pulled the first thread loose when you tossed Nicholas Withers, AKA Gerald Minnick, face first into a bulkhead," the Marshall answered. "It's my job to unravel the rest of the organization."

"I'm glad I helped, even if that isn't a good memory for me," said Abishai."

Shanyah stepped to Abishai's side, sliding an arm around his broad shoulders. "I know it was a traumatic experience, but I can't regret that it brought the two of us together."

"And replaced the feud between Jarman and me with a lasting friendship," said Abishai, shaking his head. "I hope we're done with fighting them on the ship."

"I'm certain the Restoration has a few more tricks up its sleeve," said the Marshall, "but your new escort should keep them off your back until the *Nai'a* is out of range. I think the only agents you have on board now are safely ensconced in cold sleep." He stood, looked longingly at the plate of cookies then shook hands with Abishai, Shanyah and Quester. "I'm due back at my command ship in two hours to depart for HAB-5 I wish you and the rest of the *Nai'a's* crew an uneventful journey to Lalande."

Shanyah pulled a bag of cookies from behind her back and handed them to the Marshall. "To stave off starvation on the way," she said with a smile.

After the Marshall left, Quester said, "thanks for bringing him here for the interview. I've seen all of the inside of Ship Security that I ever want to. I'm going to my quarters to change for a few hours of extra duty on the Farm." He gave the kids a hug.

Mishael and Kalei huddled together quickly, then grabbed Quester by the ship suit sleeves to keep him from leaving. "Can we go with Quester?" asked Mishael plaintively. "We want to help!"

"Hmm," said Abishai, looking a question at Quester, who nodded. "I'll message Mr. Clement and see if he'll allow a couple of uninvited guests to come along. Go change into some older clothes and Quester will drop by on his way if the answer is yes." The kids ran shrieking to their rooms, determined to be the first one changed and ready.

Mr. Clement quickly replied to Abishai's message saying he would enjoy having a couple of extra workers. When Quester showed back up in a faded ship suit with the sleeves cut off, Kalei and Mishael each grabbed a hand and drug him off toward the Farm. Shanyah watched them go with a smile then grabbed Abishai before he could start cleaning up from lunch. She gave him a long kiss, then a longer hug. "You know," she murmured in his ear. "Sponsoring Quester is turning out to have some unexpected benefits."

***

Mr. Clement met Quester and the children with a large shovel in one hand, and a small shovel in the other. He wore a straw hat and denim overalls. He gave Quester the large shovel and handed Mishael the smaller one. "You two can start on the cow stalls while Kalei and I plant some snap peas." He pulled small clear bag of soaked peas from on pocket and gave them to Kalei.

An hour later Mishael and Kalei had both tired of real farm work and been released to play in the small brook that ran along one side of the farm space. Mr. Clement grabbed a shovel and helped Quester finish up the stalls. When the two dumped the last wheelbarrow load, Mr. Clement leaned on his shovel and pulled a red print handkerchief out of a pocket to wipe his brow. Quester grinned at the deliberately anachronistic image the farmer portrayed, and took a drink of cold water from a canteen hung on a convenient peg. Clement grinned back. "I don't get a lot of volunteers for this work," he said. "I was delighted when the COB sent you my way. You're better with a shovel than I expected."

Quester quickly recounted his experience at the Ranch on Hab-5. "In spite of the smelly hard work and low pay, those are honestly some of my best memories of HAB-5. I didn't have any serious worries on the Ranch and they fed you really well. Why did you volunteer for this job?"

"It's actually highly sought after, for much the same reason you have good memories of the Ranch. The work is hard, but mostly non-technical and a lot of people enjoy working with animals more than machines or people. It requires a master qualification in biome management, but that side mostly manages itself. In its own way, it's the most mentally relaxing berth on the ship."

"I can't disagree," said Quester feeding one of the goats a carrot top as he leaned his back against the fenced in cow pasture. "I don't think I'm the farming type, but doing some honest work gives you a good feeling." As he finished speaking, he nearly jumped out of his skin as something warm and wet ran up the back of his neck and into this hair. "GHAAA!" He yelled jumping away from the fence. One of the dairy cows had just licked his neck like it was a fudgsicle. Mr. Clement had dropped his shovel and was holding his sides, trying not to fall on the ground in laughter. "THAT'S! not the feeling I was referring to," declared Quester, grabbing part of an old towel and rubbing cow spit from his neck and hair.

It took Mr. Clement a minute to find his voice, "Sorry, sorry," he said, holding one hand up "The look on your face, though, I couldn't help myself. I'd be laughing with you, if you were laughing. I've lost count of the times Henrietta's slimed me like that. She thinks sweaty humans make a fine salt lick."

"I can see I'll need to be on my toes around her," said Quester, giving Henrietta the side eye. "Much as I'm enjoying our time with you, I need to get Mishael and Kalei back to their parents. I'll see you tomorrow if the COB doesn't change the schedule."

"I'll look forward to it. I have a number of tasks that go better with an extra pair of hands. I'll have a list ready when you show up and we'll start working them off."

"No more shoveling manure?"

"Well, we have a machine to cover ninety-five percent of our shoveling needs," the farmer answered with a grin, "but the COB wanted me to give you the full treatment."

Quester shook his head and laughed, "I did wonder why a ship as modern as the *Nai'a* wasn't more up to date on agricultural equipment."

"Don't worry, I'll work you just as hard, but the tasks will be less smelly."

Quester called Mishael and Kalei over from their miniature dam-building project. Mr. Clement handed each of them a small sweetgrass basket of vegetables to take home. "Send the baskets back with Quester and I just might refill them," he told them with a smile.

***

While Quester was busy on the farm, Captain Brelling walked with Marshall Winter to the boat bay to see him off. Walking to the aft bay wasn't necessary. The *Nai'a's* small vacuum tram system would have whisked them the five kilometers in a few minutes. She hadn't had the opportunity for much exercise, though, so she suggested the stroll. "I won't be able to walk twenty meters without coming back to where I started in my command ship," the Marshall's answered. "A long walk will do me good."

"I feel a slightly bad about leaving you with this mess," the captain said. "We don't make any money sitting still, though, and we're needed in Lalande as soon as possible."

"It's not your mess," he replied, "and you've given me enough of a start to be optimistic about finally cleaning it up. I received personal messages from both mercenary commanders. They're understandably peeved at the Restoration. I won't need to motivate them to lend their best efforts to helping me break up what's left of the organization in Tau Ceti. They're also both very grateful to us, especially you, for not just playing it safe and blowing their people to dust bunnies. I would be surprised if they don't both find a tangible way to express their thanks before you exit the system."

The captain quirked an eyebrow at that, "I can't imagine what they'll come up with, but I'll look forward to sharing it with my people. I still need to formally thank the crew and hand out several well-deserved awards. I always have confidence in my people, but they consistently exceed my expectations."

"You and your crew have a great deal to be proud of." He waved at one of several repair patches in the corridor. "You'll carry the reminders of this battle with you. I'll keep you updated until you're out of communications range. I'm sure the government will foot the bill for a message to Lalande, so you'll get an update when you arrive. Do you know where your bound from there?"

"Most likely Sol," Brelling said. "I'll know more once we untangle the Restoration's roots in Lalande, but there's no way they could have bankrolled the kind of operations we've seen without support from the home system. The tech trail leads there as well. I'm hoping the trade syndicate will figure out that end long before we get there."

The Marshall considered that. "I don't think you should feel too bad about leaving me with situation in here Tau Ceti," he said. You've got plenty on your plate." Soon enough they found themselves at the boat bay. "All the best to you and your crew, Captain," said Marshall Winter at the boarding hatch of his shuttle. He shook her hand firmly. "Tau Ceti owes you all more than we can repay. I hope the *Nai'a* comes back our way in my lifetime so we can reminisce."

"By the time we get back here, you and I will both be entitled to some reminiscence if we're still kicking," she replied. "Good hunting! We'll all rest easier when you've cleaned the Restoration out of this system." She clapped him on the shoulder, then stood back. Once the hatch closed, she quickly exited the boat bay and headed for the vacuum tram. She used the overhead grab bar to pop herself into the front seat of the two-person capsule, fastened the acceleration harness, then pulled the hatch down and sealed it. She punched in the frame number needed to get her back to the bridge and sat back to enjoy the ride. The front of the capsule was completely clear. Some design engineer in centuries past had decided a shuttle ride should at least be a small thrill. Rings of light flashed by faster and faster as shuttle the accelerated, ultimately blurring into an extended flash. When the flash cleared, she appeared to be traveling through a dense starfield. *It's too bad we haven't cracked the code for faster than light travel, or maybe it isn't,* she thought. *The tyrants of the universe would probably use it to make something like the Restoration's goals a reality.* After a few minutes of coasting, the tram pod decelerated and the light show played in reverse as the pod dropped out of "hyperspace" and came to a stop with a thunk. She couldn't help but grin as she popped the hatch and swung herself over to the deck. You never knew what the light show would be on the tram, but it was always fun. She straightened her uniform and headed for the bridge.

Chapter 9 – Sister Ship

December 8th, AD 3187
Long Boat Nai'a - Tau Ceti Mid-System
Captain's Conference Room

The captain nodded to Mr. Barboa who brought up a feed from one of the contractor's tugs on the holographic display. It showed the full 1.1-kilometer diameter of the massive ice shield, now twice its normal thickness. "We placed the final section two days ago and everything looks good. We're conducting a final inspection with the contractor, but I don't anticipate any issues."

"How are the bearings on the ring mount handling the extra load?" the first officer inquired.

"At our current low acceleration," Chief of Engineering Owen Halsey answered, "the load isn't stressing the bearings at all. We had an anxious moment when the first section was in place. The imbalance created stress points we hadn't anticipated, but the bearings and Chief Nance were up to the task. He adjusted the thruster program to cancel the wobble. I'd like to run up to our full acceleration for a few hours while the contractor is still on hand in case we need any adjustments. It will also help me baseline the engines for the interstellar run to Tau Ceti with our current mass load."

"The area we're traveling through has a low density of debris by Tau Ceti standards," said the first officer. "I think we can run it up to .1G without causing any problems. Colonel Rai, will the protection team have any issues clearing the path?"

"I checked with Brigadier Tamang before I came here. His outer pickets and the forward DMA ships will plow the road for us. My ships probably won't need to do anything. It's not a problem as far as debris goes. Moving the schedule up will help throw off any attack attempts as well."

"Let's do it then," said the captain. "Will engineering be ready by 1400?"

"Engineering will be ready," answered Owen. "What about the inspection, Mr. Barboa?"

"We should be complete in the next hour," answered Mr. Barboa. "Let me check on Jarman." He zoomed the view in on a speck barely visible on the face of the ice shield. The speck resolved into a figure in a vacuum suit gliding slowly across the shield along one of the seams between sections. "It looks like he'll be done on schedule." The figure bounced slightly as Jarman used his fingertips to gently propel himself forward. "I'm glad we have Mr. Lal. Moving across a hard surface in .01G isn't a common skill, but he makes it look easy."

***

Captain Brelling checked her displays carefully, then nodded to Chief Nance at the helm. "Ahead .1 gravity helm."

"Roger, ahead point one," he replied sliding the throttle control. The background hum of the ship ramped subtly upward as three mighty fusion engines propelled the massive bulk of the *Nai'a* forward. ".1G and holding."

"Engineering?" queried Brelling.

"All systems green, captain," Commander Halsey said from the engineering watch station. Normally he would be in aft engineering, but on this occasion, he preferred the bridge. "Load readings on the bearings are nominal. Temperature also looks good. We'll continue to monitor everything for the two-hour burn."

"*Nai'a* One, *Nai'a* Actual, how are we looking out there?" the captain called over the com.

"*Nai'a* Actual, *Nai'a* One," Jarman replied from the pinnace. "Nothing to report, the shield and support structure are functioning nominally."

The captain checked the video feed from the pinnace on her display and nodded in satisfaction. "Thank you *Nai'a* One, *Nai'a* Actual out." She checked a few more readouts, then turned to her chief engineer. "While we're waiting, Owen, update me the battle damage repairs."

"We've drafted everyone with an apprentice machinist rating and above to help, and we're working through the priorities," he replied. All damage to secondary and tertiary power and data runs is repaired, and you saw that the boat bay is back in business. Most of what we have left is physical patching and repair of hatches, decks, and bulkheads. There's so much minor damage that I estimate we'll be at it for another week at least.

"What concerns me most is our supply of ship steel stock. I've given Esther Tamang samples and the metallurgy analysis of our original supply. She turned them over to a company that claims they can match it from raw materials on hand. We'll see if their samples measure up. I'm most worried about corrosion if they can't match our alloy."

"That's good news, Owen!" said the captain with a satisfied nod. "I thought we'd be even longer getting the ship back to one hundred percent. I'll leave the ship steel restock in your hands, but let me know if there's anything I can do to expedite the process."

"It should work out, but I'll keep you and the first officer in the loop. Since everything looks good with the shield, with your permission, I'll shift to aft engineering and check on the engines. I want to see how they're handling the load at full acceleration."

"That's fine with me. Mr. Bloom can handle the engineering watch here." She nodded at the senior rating standing by to take over. The captain leaned back, content to let her people do their jobs, and contemplated their next steps. This afternoon she had meetings scheduled with Persephone Belotic and Brigadier Tamang. She wasn't sure when it happened, but the persistent knot of worry she'd been carrying around had finally eased. If she'd been under tension, the crew had to be feeling it too. It was time to do something about it.

***

Persephone Belotic and Yuna Ashworth were chatting amiably when Captain Brelling and Commander Hartley walked into the captain's conference room. Yuna stood to give the commander, her former deputy, a quick hug. Once they were all seated, the captain got down to business. "Crew morale is still very good, but we've been under constant threat and stress, practically since leaving HAB-5. We need a little Christmas, to quote an ancient song. Have you made any plans, Persephone?"

The Chief Alder smiled. "We absolutely need a little Christmas and we'll have it. We would under any circumstances. However, with Yuna's help, I think you'll find this one extra special. Even with the hectic training and now repair schedule our people have practiced in small groups. The ship chorale will have a concert ready. We also have something special in the works that I'm keeping secret for now. Yuna?"

Yuna Ashworth grinned, rubbing her hands together. The captain, astonished at the expression from the normally stern woman, tried to keep a look of surprise from her face. "Our crew morale fund was in great shape when we parked at HAB-5, so I took the liberty of laying in some special supplies for the season. The ship is going to look very festive for the week of Christmas. Also, the galleys and restaurants are stocked with seasonal items from several different cultures."

"Thank you, ladies, for taking the initiative," said the captain. "I should've known you'd have preparations well in hand. Is there anything the first officer and I can do to help?"

"Don't go poking around and trying to learn our secrets," said Persephone. "I promise you'll enjoy them more if they come as a surprise."

"Hmph," said the captain. "I enjoy surprises like I enjoy a toothache, but I'll play along. Do you think your preparations can stand another two or three hundred guests? I'm thinking of inviting the DMA fleet to visit and attend the concerts. I'm assuming we'll be able to put on more than one performance."

"We can absorb that many easily," said Persephone, "but I'll need to let the food providers know. If we can get ball park numbers and dates, it will help. We already planned for at least three concert dates so everyone has a chance to attend."

"I'll coordinate with Brigadier Tamang," said the first officer. "I'm sure he'll welcome the opportunity to rotate crews through for some holiday-flavored R&R." The meeting lasted another twenty minutes as they hammered out the details needing coordination.

When Brigadier Tamang and his wife/XO, Esther, showed up they looked more than a bit harassed. "Forgive me, but you two look like this is a bad time," said the captain. "Would you like to postpone the meeting?"

"No, no," said the brigadier plopping down in the chair opposite her after seating his wife. "There isn't going to be a good time and my staff needs to learn to handle minor scuffles without one of us to bail them out."

"You can always tell a dust miner, but you can't tell them much," said Esther wryly. "Everyone wants to be out front, and every assignment from us that isn't is taken as a personal insult. It's like dealing with a bunch of twelve-year-olds."

The captain chuckled. "I don't envy you the task. I have a proposition for you. By the week of Christmas, we'll have our repairs well in hand. We'll be ready for visitors and we have several concerts planned. I'd like to invite the fleet to visit if you can work out a rotation that makes sense with your defensive deployment."

"I'd like to stuff two thirds of them upside down in a barrel rather than rewarding them," answered the Brigadier, "but I know they're all champing at the bit to visit the *Nai'a*. Maybe the threat of being disinvited will keep the rowdies in line."

"I'm sure it will help," said Esther. "It just so happens the timing should work out for another group to visit the *Nai'a*, and they would appreciate a visit from you. We'll be in shuttle range of the *Wanderer*. The construction crew would love to get a look at the ship theirs is patterned after. I think the Marshall told you we're using the *Nai'a's* base design. The engineers over there are salivating at the chance to compare the ships and bend the ears of your experts."

"How many more people are we talking about?" asked Commander Hartley.

"If they all come, it's about seven hundred," said the Brigadier. "Of course, they would come in three or four shifts. It won't be all at once."

"As long as my chief engineer and his minions have a chance to visit the *Wanderer*, it's a go," said the captain. "I wouldn't mind seeing the ship myself."

"I was told to give you and your crew an open invitation to visit. The best window is over the next month or so."

The captain looked at the first officer. "You have a lot on your plate already, Kevin. Can you handle coordination of the reciprocal visits to the *Wanderer*?"

"I can feel significant delegation coming on, Captain. Consider it handled."

***

Three days later Jarman Lal piloted the *Nai'a's* pinnace for a quick trip to the *Wanderer*. Half of the engineering department had already made the trip and were crawling all over the new ship with their counterparts. This load was focused on Biome and water management. Abishai, Shanyah, and their kids were aboard, shepherding seedlings and soil from the tropical dome. Quester's farm time paid off when Mr. Clement decided against the trip. Instead, he deputized Quester to deliver the *Nai'a's* gifts of seed, soil, and compost samples from the Farm. Roan and Paulene were also in the delegation to lend their expertise. As they approached, Jarman pulled up a video feed for the passengers in the pinnace. The shiny ship looked to be a near-perfect match for the *Nai'a* minus the ice shield. It was already spinning to generate .5G in the habitation sections.

Their counterparts met them in the *Wanderer*'s boat bay. In no time, everyone was chatting excitedly over the gifts. Abishai and his family went with the team working on the *Wanderer*'s tropical dome. The dome was complete, but nearly empty inside. "You still have that new ship smell," said Abishai to Chuck Dumas, the project lead.

"Your gifts will help us toward a more tropical aroma," he replied with a smile. "We'll need to revise our plans to incorporate the additional varieties, but it's a good problem to have. We just started working up our soil last month so this will be a great time to add your samples in and give our micro-organisms a big boost."

Abishai looked at the floor of the dome. Half of the familiar French drain system was exposed, and he bent down to inspect a nearby section. Mishael and Kalei took the opportunity to use it as a balance beam. He stood up and reached into his backpack to pull out a rather odd-looking cylindrical machine with very sharp cutting teeth on one end. He handed the machine to Chuck.

"Your crew will thank you for this in the future. One of my tasks on the *Nai'a* was cleaning out the French drains when they were completely clogged with roots. My buddy, Roan, came up with this solution. The operating manual and plans for building more are included in the onboard software."

Chuck turned the machine around in his hands, inspecting it closely. "I wondered about cleaning those once everything is covered in soil."

Abishai handed him a data chip. "Roan and I worked up a program for tracking changes to the watering system. You'll find the original design, matching what you have now, and the changes I made to eliminate potential leaks and other problems."

"I hope our future crew appreciates the trouble you're saving them," said Chuck, tucking the chip into a pocket. "I know I do. Any other suggestions?"

"The data chip also includes accumulated wisdom from the leader of the tropical gang on the *Nai'a*," answered Abishai. "You'll have to forgive Elder Pryachac's bluntness. She always has a point, and usually a pungent way to make it."

"Pungent?"

"You'll understand when you watch the interviews I did on the chip. Fortunately, most tropical fruit juice washes out."

"What Abishai is carefully not saying," interjected Shanyah, "is that Consuela Pryachac's favorite way to deal with annoying people who call her 'Elder' is to pelt them with overripe fruit. Abishai managed to annoy her more than once during the interviews."

"She sounds interesting. Just how old is she?" asked Chuck.

"She steadfastly refuses to tell," Shanyah answered. "I've done some digging and I'd estimate she's approaching four hundred. She's a real testament to living in .5G your whole life, Doc's gene therapy, and the health of the biome on the *Nai'a*."

"Between you me and the deck plate," said Chuck, "I think there are a number of citizens that old in Tau Ceti. For some reason, they get very cagy about it when they pass two-hundred."

"For good reason I suppose," Shanyah said. "When you're that old, you don't want it rubbed in your face, which is why Consuela pelts people who call her 'Elder' with fruit. On the plus side, extended life spans help retain knowledge needed in a long boat crew. We don't have to keep relearning lessons if we pay attention to our elders and extensive historical database. I'll leave you and Abishai to kibitz about all things tropical. The kids and I want to see how Quester is doing."

When Shanyah, Mishael, and Kalei arrived in the hab section occupied by the *Wanderer*'s farm in progress, Quester was deep in conversation with a blonde woman about his height, but twice as wide. Both of them gestured, indicating heights, widths, and depths of the various food and feed crops planned for the space. Quester looked up as they approached. "This is Marlene Lantel," he said, indicating his counterpart. "Meet Shanyah and the dynamic duo, Mishael and Kalei."

"Pleased to meet you all!" said Marlene, shaking hands all around after a quick wipe on her ship suit. "The *Nai'a* is something of a legend with us. I expected someone 3-meters tall and got Quester, a skinny Tau Cetan." She grinned, giving Quester a friendly shove.

"He may not be 3-meters tall, but he's cut quite a swath since he came on board," answered Shanyah. "Right now, he's somewhere between beloved and notorious, depending on who you talk to. For now, he's working on keeping his head down." Quester turned slightly pink, but kept his mouth closed.

"I'm glad he's here in any case," replied Marlene. "These gifts from the *Nai'a* are priceless in more ways than one. We'll be carrying forward part of the tradition of a proud ship, and one that won't be forgotten in Tau Ceti any time soon."

Shanyah's expression grew serious, "Quester, could you give these two a tour while Marlene and I talk?" She waved toward Mishael and Kalei. Quester gave her a curious look, but took the kids to see the work in progress on the stream. Shanyah looked Marlene in the eye. "I'm worried about the *Wanderer*'s security. I'm not sure what your arrangements are, but if the Restoration targeted the *Nai'a*, they'll try for you if they can. Do you have measures in place in case they try to take over the ship?"

Marlene shook her head. "A number of us feel the same way, but we're much more a construction crew than a ship's crew. Administrator Noland doesn't think the threat out here in Dust Miner territory is serious enough to even plan for. We don't have weapons or anyone trained to use them beyond a three-person security department. We do have a four-ship space patrol, but their main concern is incoming rocks. The leadership is more focused on construction timelines than anything else."

"I'll talk to Captain Brelling," said Shanyah. "We're still in coms range of Marshall Winter's ships. The local government knows enough to start providing better security, but he may not be aware just how little you have."

"You can talk to your captain, just like that?" Marlene asked, eyebrows raised.

"Believe me, no one bothers her with trivial matters," Shanyah answered, "but she's willing to listen to anyone if they think she should know something."

"I'd breathe easier if we had better protection here. I feel like a sitting duck."

"I'll see what we can do while we're close enough. I doubt I'm the only crew member from the *Nai'a* who's concerned."

***

On the return trip, Abishai and Shanyah talked over the situation. "Marshall Winter is well aware of how big the threat from the Restoration is," said Shanyah. "Unless he gets ahead of them, you know they'll try to steal the *Wanderer*. I'm scratching my head trying to figure out why their security is so light. One assault shuttle could take that ship right now."

"It's at least a year from being finished," replied Abishai. "They only have one fusion plant installed and no engines. They could take it, but they wouldn't be going anywhere. The threat will be greater when the ship is complete."

"With the resources and ingenuity the Restoration showed in its attacks on us, I wouldn't count the ship safe, even in its current condition."

"I don't disagree. I can see why the administrator might have his focus elsewhere, though."

"I'm going to provide some focus on security, one way or another," said Shayah, with quiet determination.

Abishai nodded, "I'll back you one-hundred percent. I'm not the only one either. Let's make it clear the concerns come from *Nai'a* crew members. I don't want to get anyone on the construction crew in trouble."

Shanyah patted his knee and leaned her head on his shoulder. "I don't want to be a trouble maker, but those people deserve more than tissue-thin security while they're building a key component of the system's future."

Chapter 10 – Nativity

December 24th, AD 3187
Long Boat Nai'a - Tau Ceti Mid-Outer-System
Cooper Green

Roan and Paulene along with the O'Clairs, rode herd on Mishael and Kalei while they dashed from booth to booth at the market. Each booth along the edge of Cooper Green was decorated appropriately for Christmas in a different culture and time period. Traditional Christmas food, small hand-made trinkets, and smiles abounded. Pete Worsley, dressed as the fourth century bishop, St. Nicholas, strode through the crowd, greeting everyone and surreptitiously bestowing small gifts on young and old alike. Roan discovered a tiny set of two interlocked silver filigree rings sitting on his shoulder. Paulene couldn't help a laugh when Roan cast a baleful glance at the saint's retreating back. Pete was never too subtle with his hints. Mishael later found a beautifully painted wooden top in his pocket. Kalei found a small fabric pouch with a carved wooden lamb inside.

The group sampled Swedish rosette cookies, figgy pudding, pavlova, Polish mazurka and babka, eventually running out of appetite for sweets. "We'd better find our seats," announced Paulene. "The concert starts in five minutes." The green was filled to capacity for the final of three concerts organized by the crew. Dust Miner fleet crews and construction workers from the *Wanderer* made up a good portion of the audience. The choir filed onto a raised platform at one end of the green while a twelve-piece orchestra played a medley of Christmas songs. Soon the choir launched into "Angels We have Heard on High," weaving a beautiful harmony on the chorus. They followed with additional Christmas carols cheered on loudly by the appreciative audience. A small group, dressed in Renaissance garb, sang Carols of the Bells in madrigal style. Next came a group of musicians marching onto the stage with a variety of instruments and drums, tossing the melody of the "Little Drummer Boy" from one instrument to another.

The final song was an a cappella version of "Silent Night". During the song, a giant hologram showed a live portrayal of the nativity scene from Bethlehem with Mary, Joseph, and the baby Jesus set on the Farm. Shepherds, villagers, cows, and sheep gathered round the little family and the hay-filled manger. Soft lantern light revealed faces turned as one toward the sleeping baby.

Roan leaned over to Paulene. "Is that Shepherd on the left, Quester?"

"Yes, and those two village children are Mishael and Kalei," she answered. "They snuck out during "Little Drummer Boy" to take their places."

Silence descended with the last note of the choir and held for a heartbeat before the audience erupted in applause. Pete Worsley, still dressed as St. Nicholas, invited everyone to continue enjoying the market and make a trip to the Farm to see the nativity scene in person.

***

Abishai, Shanyah, Mishael, and Kalei shared their Christmas morning celebration with Quester. They all slept in and Abishai baked his family's traditional Christmas bread filled with nuts and dried fruit for breakfast. Quester arrived in time to exchange gifts while the bread cooled. "That smells like a dream," he said taking a moment to peak under the cloth covering the wreath-shaped loaf.

"Let it be for now," said Shanyah. "It's time to read the Christmas story. Would you do the honors, Quester?" She handed him a Bible open to the second chapter of Luke. When Quester finished reading, he handed the Bible thoughtfully back to Shanyah. Abishai prayed and thanked God for the unspeakable gift of His Son, for the blessings of his family and their new friend Quester. They chatted for a little while about their parts in the concert and nativity, the positive reactions from the visitors, and the wonderful market.

"It's time for gifts!" said Abishai. "Kalei gets to go first, since she's the youngest." Kalei ran off and returned with a small lumpy sack. The four-year-old fished inside and pulled out something circular and flat, wrapped in equal parts colorful tissue paper and tape. She handed the package to Mishael and clapped her hands in excitement as he opened it. Inside was bright green flying disc emblazoned with a gold dragon.

"It's an ancient mold called a Fastback!" she exclaimed. "Mr. Roan and I made it!"

Mishael gave his sister a big hug. "Thanks sis! I can't wait to throw it with you on the green!"

Kalei pulled another package out of her sack, a similarly wrapped flat rectangle and handed it to Quester. The object he unwrapped appeared to be wood, banded in various shades of brown and tan. It was about two-centimeters thick, rounded at the corners and very smooth. He quirked an eyebrow in question at Kalei. "It's a cutting board, silly. I'm not supposed to say who helped me make it."

"Thank you, Kalei, I'll have to get your dad to show me how to use it. I have no cooking skills, but it's time I learned."

"It might help you attract a wife." Abishai winked at him. Quester's eyes went wide and everyone laughed at his expression.

A kukui nut necklace for Shanyah followed, and a teakwood spoon for Abishai, then Mishael jumped up to haul out his sack of gifts. Once everyone finished giving presents, they gathered around the table for big chunks of warm Christmas bread with butter. "I can't wait to see what St. Nicholas put in my sock," said Kalei with her mouth half full. "Did Mr. Worsley come while we were sleeping?"

"Someone kept the tradition of St. Nicholas alive from the shape of that stocking," replied Abishai. "We'll get to those soon enough. Finish your milk." Kalei downed the last of her cup, hesitated for a moment, then grabbed another chunk of bread.

Quester took an appreciative sip of coffee, took in the scene around him, and smiled. "I can't recall a better Christmas. Thank you all for inviting me and for all the presents!" Somehow, everything he'd received was cooking related, and all of it handmade. "Give me a year or so and I might be able to turn out an edible sandwich."

Abishai clapped him on the shoulder. "Have some faith, young man. I'll have you whipping up tasty meals in no time. You like to eat! You can start on the foods you enjoy most."

"If you keep inviting me over, I won't have much incentive to learn for myself."

"The galley is good enough to keep you satisfied," said Shanyah. "Banning you from our quarters won't really help. We'll just have to figure out another way to get you motivated."

Quester just laughed. "You two are about as subtle as meter-long spanner upside the head."

Abishai held up a finger. "Don't tempt me. I know exactly where to get one of those."

***

Two days later the *Nai'a* was mostly back to normal. The flood of visitors slowed to a trickle, and everyone was in some semblance of their normal routine. Captain Brelling invited Administrator Noland to visit the *Nai'a*, and he was due in a couple of hours. She'd also sent an inquiry about the *Wanderer*'s security situation to Marshall Winter. She sat now in her cabin trying to come up with a diplomatic way of addressing the danger with the administrator. All indications were that he didn't perceive the Restoration as a serious threat.

She greeted the administrator, escorted by Hubble Spears, in her conference room. Brigadier Tamang and Commander Hartley rounded out the meeting. Perry Noland was a medium-height round fellow with a shaved head and dark brown eyes that looked like they would normally twinkle. At the moment, though, his expression was serious. "Thanks for the invitation, Captain Brelling. I spent the trip over reviewing a report on your latest battle with the Restoration. My compliments to Commander Hartley on a thorough analysis of the events and repercussions."

"Please have a seat, Administrator Noland. You've probably figured out those repercussions are the reason I wanted to see you." The captain poured coffee all around, then sat down and steepled her fingers. "My people enjoyed seeing your work on the *Wanderer*. She's shaping into a fine ship. Of course, we're a bit biased since you're using largely the same design as the *Nai'a*. Nearly all our crew members, however, expressed concerns about the lack of security for the ship. We're acutely aware of how serious the threat from the Restoration is. I would like your take on the situation. Perhaps there's some way we can help."

The administrator nodded. "I'll confess my expertise is project management. Although security is a part of every project, I don't think we've done a good job of assessing the threat. Technically, I and the rest of my construction crew, are employees of the joint venture put together to construct the *Wanderer*. My direction is to get the ship done on time, within budget, to the contracted performance specifications. Among cost, schedule, and performance, I was told to focus on schedule. I fear my focus blinded me to things I should have paid closer attention to. The truth is, I don't have the resources to hire the kind of security that could stand off a dedicated attack like the *Nai'a* just experienced. I'll have to run the numbers, but my guess is I would need to delay our schedule by six months to free up the money in the short term, and the overall budget would go up. Without help from the board and a cash infusion, I'm going to have to live with the risk. I'm not comfortable with ignoring the threat, but I don't see a solution."

The captain pursed her lips thoughtfully. "I do think you have some time to work out a better situation. My reading of the Restoration says they will wait at least until the ship's engines and fusion plants are on line. Your original budget is insufficient for the current circumstances. We had a similar situation when we needed to stand up our militia. Fortunately, Hubble and our board agreed with the necessary expenditures. Your board will need to acknowledge the facts and find funds to secure the ship properly. I think this is a case of everyone doing their jobs, but missing where they need to be integrated. Brigadier Tamang, your thoughts?"

"You hit it on the head, Captain. I have authority to protect the *Nai'a*, but not the *Wanderer*. Marshall Winter's warrant gives him full authority to pursue the Restoration, but doesn't mention the *Wanderer*. We need to get our collective acts together, but we all work for different authorities. I'll petition the DMA for permission to split off a squadron for space patrol around the *Wanderer* in the short term. Whoever gets tagged for that is going to moan, but I'm used to it."

"I'm grateful for anything you can spare," said Perry, "but won't you be thinning the *Nai'a's* defenses?

"Trust me," answered Tamang wryly, "they need thinning. What we have now is seriously overkill. Your thoughts, Captain?"

"I'll defer to your judgment," the captain said. "Marshall Winter is now aware of the situation. He promised to confer with the government and the board of the joint venture building the *Wanderer* to get a coordinated plan together."

"My crew will be happy to have an effective space patrol," said the administrator. "I'll do my best to improve internal security between now and the time we have full-up power and engines."

"If you ask for volunteers," said Brigadier Tamang. "I'm certain you can stand up a militia platoon patterned after the *Nai'a's* troops. Equipping them is another matter. As you said, your budget doesn't cover a larger security force. Even one combat platoon would make stealing the *Wanderer* a much more difficult proposition."

The captain drummed her fingers on the table in contemplation. "We can spare a platoon's worth of powered armor and weapons since we didn't have much battle damage. If you want light personal armor and weapons we can supply as many as you can use. Mr. Barboa is expecting your request. I suggest you have your security detachment confer with him so we can make the transfer. Hubble, can you handle the business end?"

"No problem," he answered. "we'll make it a rental contract with option to buy and bill the government for now. The Marshall has enough discretionary budget to cover it."

After the meeting, the captain took Administrator Noland on a tour of the *Nai'a*. "Your ship seems so much more alive than the *Wanderer*," he commented as they made their way to the boat bay for his departure.

"We have a fully functional biome and a full crew," she replied. "I suspect those make the difference. The crew is the life of the ship and the most important part of a successful vessel. I know most of your construction crew won't sail with the *Wanderer*, but the more they identify with the ship, the better off you'll be."

"I think most of them feel that way already," he replied. "They've invested a lot of themselves into making her a reality."

"If they do feel that way, you won't have any problems getting militia volunteers. You'll probably find out some of your people have skills you never knew about."

"No doubt," he replied. When they reached his shuttle, he shook the captain's hand. "I can't thank you enough for all the assistance, Captain."

"We're happy to help! Everyone here is excited about a sister ship sailing the courses between the stars soon. Perhaps we'll cross paths down the line."

"I hope you do! I won't be along for the ride. I like it here in Tau Ceti too much, but the *Wanderer* will be hard to leave after so many years building her."

Back in her office the captain was surprised by a visit from Dr. Rensaleer, the ship's chief physician. "What brings you so far from Medical?" asked the captain.

"We need to talk about one of my patients," the doctor answered. "I think you know who. He's been asking about his status and in another few days, I won't have any reason to keep him. His partially collapsed lung is nearly healed."

"I'll come back to medical with you now," agreed the captain. "I don't have anything on the calendar for the next hour. It's past time I paid Captain Garrity a visit."

When they arrived, Julian Garrity was finishing a lunch of ricotta-stuffed shells in a rich Bolognese sauce with soft garlic bread sticks and a tossed salad. When he saw the captain, he looked like he wanted to stand but she waved him back down.

"I feel like I'm taking advantage of your hospitality, Captain," he said. "I could easily get used to the food here, though." He motioned at the remains of his meal.

"Don't stop eating on my account," she answered, pulling up a chair. "Dr. Rensaleer uses appetite as one of her release criteria, and I'm sure you'd like to get out of here in spite of the hospitality."

Garrity used the last of a breadstick to sop up the flavorful sauce and chewed appreciatively. Captain Brelling let him finish while she gathered her own thoughts.

"I apologize for keeping you in suspense about your status," she said "It's a bit complicated. We should have turned you over to Marshall Winter to face the music with the rest of Orca Squadron. However, I feel we owe you better options. You probably saved everyone in this ship at great peril to yourself. We don't forget when someone does that, and we don't toss them aside."

"Are you forgetting I was part of the force trying to take your ship from you in the first place?" he asked, unable to keep the skepticism from his tone.

"Nevertheless, you could have let the Restoration operative launch those missiles and kill us all, but you didn't," answered Captain Brelling. "I'm sorry about Lieutenant Anders."

"Me too, I've written a letter to his parents three times now. I can't seem to find the right words. He's the real reason I took on that...person." His face grew red with the memory and unresolved anger.

"Still, you did the right thing in the moment. I made a deal with Marshall Winter. He's dropped all charges in your case. I also took the liberty of securing a release from your Orca Squadron contract. I hope you don't mind?"

Julian's mouth quirked. "My resignation letter is in my outbox, ready to send. That one I didn't have any trouble writing. I don't like the way they do business."

"Both mercenary companies will be on a short leash working directly for Marshall Winter now," the captain said, "but you have choices. One of those choices is joining the crew of the *Nai'a*. You were a Tau Ceti security officer before getting caught in a 'right-sizing' personnel cut, and you're a highly qualified pilot. We would be happy to add you to the crew. Alternately, you can stay here in Tau Ceti. Brigadier Tamang has positions open in the Great Prospects squadron that will secure the *Wanderer* for the immediate future. If none of those options appeal to you, we'll pay your passage to any destination in the system. Feel free to take some time to think it over. Your net access will be restored today, and we'll get you settled in temporary quarters as soon as the doctor releases you."

Garrity shook his head. "That's a lot to absorb, Captain, and a much better outlook than I expected. The usual penalty for what we did is a quick execution." He shook his head a bit then looked her in the eye. "Thank you!"

"You're welcome, take a few days and get know the ship and crew. Have you had any visitors?

"The O'Clairs have been by several times and an older gentleman who said his name was Pete. I recognized him on the live stream of the Christmas celebrations playing St. Nicholas. Who is he really?"

"Among other things, he's the section head of Beta Section. Civilian governance of the ship is organized by the six habitat sections. The section heads are also called alders and report to the chief alder. They run the day-to-day business of the ship at their level so I don't have to employ a huge staff on the command side."

"So, he's part of the ship leadership?"

"In more ways than just his position. He'd deny it, but he's a large part of the beating heart of the *Nai'a*. He's also accumulated a great deal of wisdom. If you're smart, you'll look him up before making your decision. The O'Clairs can help you find him. Do you have any questions for me before I get back to digging through a mountain of reports?"

"No, Captain, you've given me plenty to think about, thanks again. I don't deserve any of what you've offered, but I'm grateful for the opportunity to come out of this alive with a chance for a decent future."

"We all get blessed with undeserved breaks in life now and then. When it happens to me, I try to use the opportunity to pass on the blessing to others. You might say that's what I'm doing here today." She left Captain Garrity deep in thought.

Chapter 11 – Farewell

January 10th, AD 3188
Long Boat Nai'a - Tau Ceti Mid-System
Six Fathoms Restaurant

Captain Brelling, the Tamangs, Colonel Rai, and Commander Hartley enjoyed an appetizer of onion rings and fried green tomatoes while the conversation buzzed around them. The ship was approaching TAU Ceti Heliopause and it was time to bid farewell to the Great Prospects protection team. They'd chosen Six Fathoms for the sendoff celebration so the dolphins could participate. The off-duty flight crews had formed quite a friendship with the pod, especially the commando force. The DMA fleet had departed over a week ago to return to their normal business activities. The brigadier and his wife decided to stay on and travel back with the protection team so they could enjoy a few more days on the *Nai'a* and better security for the flight home.

The brigadier stood up raising his glass and his voice. "A toast to the mighty *Nai'a* and her crew. Safe passage and following winds!" The crowd in the restaurant responded enthusiastically.

Captain Brelling stood and raised her glass. "A toast to Great Prospects, the finest protection team in the space-ways. Blessings on you all and confusion to your enemies!" The dolphin pod exploded from the water in perfect formation, completing a triple flip and slipping back into the water with just a little spray on the party goers closest to the tank.

The wait staff started serving main dishes, and the noise abated while everyone enjoyed the food. Shanyah, Abishai, and Quester occupied a table with the O'Clairs and one of the Great Prospects pilot teams heading back in-system. Shanyah kept a repeater from the tank's hydrophone next to her in case she needed to translate for the dolphin pod, but they were currently engaged with their own seafood treat. "Last chance to bail," said Abishai to the O'Clairs. "Are you sure you want to leave everything behind?"

"Sure enough," replied Palamar, nodding her head. "We want to get started on a family. The trip to Lalande will give us the space to be the kind of parents we want to be. Our own parents are less than thrilled, but they understand our reasons. They were gone enough during our childhood to sympathize with the decision."

"We'll miss our friends on the protection team," said Val, nodding at their dinner companions. "We've been through a lot together. Colonel Rai made a last-minute appeal. He's losing a third of his pilot teams to the *Nai'a*. Palamar and I may have a little trepidation, but we don't have any doubts. This is what we want to do."

"We'll be over-staffed with pilots. Do you know where you'll be slotted in?" asked Quester.

"I've been working on my medical degree," answered Palamar. "I'm going to take a technician slot in Medical for now and see if I can work my way to an internship under Dr. Rensaleer."

"I've got a position on the bottom rung of Biome," said Val. "I understand I'll be doing a lot of system check routes and filter cleaning. Frankly, it's way too much like honest work for a pilot, but at least I'll feel useful."

***

Julian Garrity consulted his PCOM's map and made his way along a meandering stream until he saw Pete Worsley sitting on a bench. The section head was holding a cane pole attached to a long string with red and white bobber at the end. He was shoeless and dressed in an old T-shirt and shorts. A straw hat topped off the ensemble. He looked up and nodded toward the other end of the bench. "Have a seat, Mr. Garrity. I have the makings to rig another pole if you want to try your luck."

Garrity just shook his head. "No thanks, I might catch something and I wouldn't know what to do."

"Not likely, the fish and I have an understanding. They steal my bait occasionally to give me a thrill, and I use a dull hook. I've been praying for you to have wisdom. Have you come to a decision?"

"No, but I need to. The Great Prospects squadron leaves tomorrow. It's the last ride out of here if I want to stay in Tau Ceti. I've thought long and hard about our earlier conversations, but I'm still torn. Every crew member I've met has been friendly with the exception of Jarman, and even he was polite and supportive. I don't think he does friendly."

"He didn't do polite and supportive until nearly dying on the trip here, but that's his story to tell."

"I still cringe when someone thanks me for saving the ship," said Julian. "I was here to do the opposite."

"You still kept us from being blown out of space," answered Pete. "I'm sure most of the crew has forgiven your part in the initial attack. The question is, will you accept being forgiven?"

Julian nodded. "That's the thing I'm having trouble getting past, along with losing Lieutenant Anders."

Pete twitched his line a bit. "It's a good sign those things still bother you. You don't need to forget Lieutenant Anders or those events, but time will help you heal the wounds they caused. You'll carry those with you whether you stay or go. If you're the kind of man I think you are, you'll want to be where you can do the most good. Where do you think that is?"

Julian leaned his chin on a fist, contemplating the ripples in the brook. "I'm not eager to join another mercenary outfit, even one as good as Great Prospects. I don't think the security service will have me back with my record. Anything else in Tau Ceti would be entry level. Security work was my favorite job, one where I felt I was serving a greater cause. I have the offer to take a position with Ship Security on the *Nai'a*. Sorry for the stream of consciousness."

"No worries," said Pete, "it doesn't strain the old noodle much to sit here and listen. I'm happy to be a sounding board. If you'll forgive me, you sound like you already know what you should do. Is there anything keeping you in Tau Ceti?"

"Not really. I have a sister on HAB-5. From her last message, she'll be happy to see me gone. Orca Squadron has a black reputation right now. Anyway, thanks for listening. It looks like you've got a bite!"

Pete's bobber dipped, bounced, then went completely under. His pole bent as he engaged in a brief tug-of-war, then the bobber and empty hook came flying out of the water. "See!" he said, holding the shiny hook up. "Nothing but bait stealers in here." Julian just laughed, nearly bending double when a shiny fish jumped clear of the water and landed with a resounding splash.

When he recovered his composure, he wiped his eyes. "I talked to Hal Renfro as you suggested. He had good things to say about Ship Security. His wife Lisandra's story is quite a tale."

"She's a valued member of the crew now," Pete said, eyeing his empty hook. "I know you will be too if you sign on.

"I have my own bias. I don't mind saying I hope you stay. For your own sake though, listen to your heart some. For all its warts, Tau Ceti is your home. You know all the pro and con arguments. Which path is calling you?"

Pete rigged another mealworm on the hook and put his line back in the water. They sat in comfortable silence for a time while Julian watched the water flow and listened to the music of the brook and birds.

Finally, Julian stood and reached over to shake Pete's hand. "Thanks again, I have some people to talk to and a message to compose. I'll be seeing you."

* * *

"The *Nai'a* feels like a second home," said Esther Tamang, "but it's time we get back to the company habitat." She gave Captain Brelling a hug.

"We'll miss you," replied the captain. "The *Nai'a* and Great Prospects are forever connected. You have a blank check with us and with the Long Boat Free Trade Syndicate as far as my influence reaches."

"You have an important mission in Lalande and Sol, I suspect, afterward," said Brigadier Tamang. "Humanity's place in the stars will be a lot more secure if you can put a stop to the Restoration and their aspirations."

"That's my goal, but I'll need a lot of help," said the captain shaking his hand. "God bless both of you and protect you on your way home." She watched them climb into their executive yacht, blinking back unwanted moisture from her eyes. She would truly miss them. Having someone to talk to who wasn't part of her crew had been a rare outlet. It was time, though, to get on with the job and get this ship on the long trip to Lalande.

***

The Starlight Lounge wasn't crowded, but all of the Great Prospects spacers now joining the *Nai'a's* crew were there to sign the articles. Julian Garrity, having made his decision, tagged onto the end of the line. Once everyone had signed and been sworn in as ship's crew, they gathered with their friends for a celebration. The lounge staff provided a buffet of finger foods and took drink orders. The O'Clairs each took one of Julian's elbows and chivied him over to the table where Abishai, his family, and close friends huddled. "You all know Julian Garrity, I think," said Palamar. "We invited him to join us. He's going to be living in Beta Section with us and working Ship Security as his primary specialty."

"How about taking a turn with me in water management?" said Roan, "You'll need a secondary specialty and I'm short an apprentice." Julian looked a bit uncertain.

"If you take his offer, make sure he doesn't talk you into carrying the 'Big Ole Wrench' everywhere," said Abishai grinning. "That's why my shoulders are this wide."

"Hey!" said Roan, "Don't spoil all my fun. You've got to keep newbies on their toes."

Julian smiled at their banter. "I'll consider it. I'm supposed to get an orientation to each department over the next couple of weeks. After that, I'll make a decision or have one made for me. Ship's needs come first, or so the articles say."

"True enough," said Hal Renfro. "You'll find the leadership works hard to put people in positions they want to be in, though. They'll also move you every couple of years on your first crossing. Most of us enjoy the variety and it never hurts to pick up new skills. How did you get mixed up with these two?" He nodded at the O'Clairs.

"Palamar is the reason I'm alive. They docked with my ship and rescued me after I scrammed my reactor and brought my fists to a knife fight. Truthfully, I was more afraid of her than the guy with the knife, she's much more professional. I knew it would go badly for me if I didn't cooperate. Thankfully, she's also merciful."

"You were already having a bad day," said Palamar. "It's a good thing for everyone on this ship that you stopped the missile launch."

"I'm glad about that part of it, anyway," Julian replied. "The rest of my choices leading up to the moment, not as much."

"I understand impossible choices," said Jarman Lal, shaking his hand. "You were put in a really bad position. Something these Restoration people seem to specialize in. There's no depth they won't sink to for an advantage."

Julian grimaced, "They are a special brand of evil in the universe. The opportunity to help deal with them in Lalande was a selling point for signing on."

"Everyone on this crew has a personal stake in seeing them brought to justice," replied Jarman. Abishai and I both could tell you some stories."

An announcement over the lounge speakers urged everyone to watch the display beginning outside the ship. One by one the Great Prospects protection ships, full running lights aglow, lined up in a diamond formation, expertly keeping pace with the *Nai'a's* rotation. When the formation was complete, the ships blinked their running lights three times in perfect synchronization, then lit their engines and raced toward home. Val and Palamar hugged each other in the ensuing silence, watching their friends and family depart.

Slowly, the party wound back up. Julian observed the friendly banter of the group, participating occasionally and wondering if anyone harbored ill feelings toward him. Lisandra Redding caught his attention. "I know what you're thinking. I've been there," she told him. "I had a hard time for a long while believing they would forgive me for what I'd done. It took me longer to trust my feelings than it took them to trust me. Give yourself time and get to know your crewmates. They're some great people."

***

Captain Brelling settled into her office chair and brought up her message que. At the top was an encoded priority recording from Marshall Winter. She input the passcode for decryption and waited for it to process. The lag on lightspeed communications made a two-way conversation impossible, but they sent each other updates regularly. A minute later, Winter's face popped up on her screen. "Greetings from the inner system," he began. "I imagine this message will catch you departing Tau Ceti jurisdiction. I hate to see you go, but I'm sure it's a relief to be beyond the reach of certain criminal elements. Speaking of those, we've rounded up another good-sized chunk of their organization, including the operative who recruited Quester. Enough of them turned informant to give us a shot at dismantling the rest of the organization in the next few months. I've underestimated them before, so I'm not going to discount the threat they still pose to the *Wanderer*. Thanks to the *Nai'a*, the *Wanderer* now has a platoon of powered armor militia training up, along with two platoons of light militia. Everyone on the construction crew has weapons and the training to use them on the Swiss model. I lent them a security service veteran to help with training, organization, and planning. Great Prospects picked up the space patrol contract long term. They may regret the choice if a bunch of their crews sign on to the *Wanderer* the way they did the *Nai'a*. Replacements aren't a problem for the Tamangs, though. Their company has the best reputation of any protection outfit in the system. That's all for now. I'll be able to send updates until you're about a year out of Tau Ceti. Safe journey!"

Captain Brelling closed the message and started a recording of her own in reply. Once she had it canned and on the way, she headed to the bridge. "As you were," she responded to the captain-on-deck announcement. Commander Hartley had the bridge watch. She crossed over to the command chair to confer with him. "Have we acquired the syndicate buoy?"

"Aye Captain, acquired and locked with a whisker laser connection," he answered.

"Execute the data drop."

"Communications, execute data drop, Tau Ceti final," ordered Hartley

"Aye, data drop in process," replied the coms officer.

The Long Boat Free Trade Syndicate maintained multiple space buoys in all inhabited systems. They were stealthy, and only LBFTS ships knew the locations and security protocols to use them. Tampering with the buoys was on the short list of offenses bad enough to merit a system interdiction by the syndicate. The next syndicate member long boat in Tau Ceti would get a comprehensive report on the *Nai'a's* experience in the system from the buoys when it arrived.

Chapter 12 – Long March

January 11th, AD 3189
Long Boat Nai'a – One Year Out of Tau Ceti
Cooper Green

Mishael eyed the flight of the flying disc launched by his sister. For a five-year-old girl, she had an impressive arm, but her accuracy was spotty. He took three steps and launched himself into the air, whooping as he snagged the disc at the top of his leap. He quickly located their friend Belle and launched a soft toss to her before Quester could get between them. Quester quickly reversed direction, trying to get in Belle's throwing lane but she snuck a worm-burner past him a foot off the deck to Kalei. Quester collapsed to the ground, feigning exhaustion, and all three kids piled on top of him shouting "We win! We win!"

"You win!" agreed Quester with a groan. "I need a rest and food." He put Mishael in a head lock as he stood and gave him a mild noogie. Mishael grabbed his arm with both hands and dropped to the deck, taking Quester with him. Mishael tried to swing his legs around for an arm bar, but Quester was wise to the move and shook him off. Spinning to his feet, Quester sprinted for the picnic tables with the kids in hot pursuit.

"I ought to charge by the hour," he told Abishai. "Those three don't know how to get tired."

"They do, but even with your stamina, it takes more than one adult to wear them out," answered Abishai. "It's time to eat anyway." He looked over to the next table where several adults were gaga over the O'Clairs' new baby. The girl was beautiful in the way only newborns can be. It didn't hurt that she had strikingly attractive parents. Abishai noticed Paulene pulling Roan aside and whispering something in his ear that made him blush bright pink. Abishai shook his head. Roan better wise up before Paulene found some other eligible bachelor to start a family with. "Come and get it before the kids eat it all!" he hollered, uncovering the last of the food dishes. Slowly, the adults trickled over to load up plates. Abishai stood back with remarkable restraint, not wanting to let his appetite devastate the spread before anyone else got a chance. Giving in when there was a gap, he snagged a pickled daikon spear from the relish tray to tide him over. Quester winked at Abishai as he piled his plate with several half-sandwiches, cucumber-tomato salad with feta, and half a sliced mango.

"Your self-control is improving," Quester said.

"Not really," Abishai answered. "Shanyah threatened to volunteer me for the next sludge tank cleaning if I didn't let everyone else go first. I can still taste the air in my memory." He shuddered slightly.

"Taste the air?"

"You have to experience it to understand," said Abishai. "As an appetite suppressant, it works wonders. Just be happy you got through your extra duty without landing that task."

"I don't know what to do with myself with all this free time," Quester replied.

"You can volunteer," said Abishai. "Did you notice nearly every extra duty assignment you pulled is normally covered by volunteers?"

"I did," Quester answered. "Most of the time a volunteer showed me what to do when I was getting started."

"What was your favorite duty?"

"Strangely," answered Quester, "it was the retired spacers community. Most of what I did was listen to the residents talk, between helping them with activities and meals. I felt like I was in long boat *Nai'a* history class."

"Most of them did a lot of training and teaching at the end of their careers," said Abishai. "Some of them still take a turn. They especially enjoy the younger children."

"One of the residents asked when you were coming by to sing," said Quester. "Geneva Green, I think it was. I hadn't realized you were a regular there."

"Once a week I try to spend my lunch hour singing old sacred songs or whatever they want for whoever will put up with me. Shanyah taught me enough ukulele to accompany myself with basic chords. I've even been known to sing a space shanty or two. It's probably the only time you'll hear me singing solo except in the shower. Geneva's favorite is 'In the Garden'. The folks there are the most appreciative audience in the known galaxy."

"I know what you mean. I've never received so many 'thank you's' in my life, and for doing not much of anything."

"You gave your time and attention," said Abishai. "Nothing's more precious to them. You don't have to stop. The community welcomes visitors and volunteers. I'm taking Kalei, Mishael and Belle, with me tomorrow if you want to join us."

"I will," Quester replied. "I'm missing my friends there already."

***

Captain Brelling gathered her thoughts while she waited for the rest of the ship's council and their deputies to arrive. Council meetings had been blessedly rare in the year since leaving the Tau Ceti system, but it was time to catch everyone up and focus on the next destination. Once they were all seated and supplied with their beverage of choice, she asked the first officer to cover the state of the ship.

"Physically, the *Nai'a* is ship shape," Commander Hartley started. "Repairs to the battle damage are complete and double checked. We reestablished full triple redundancy on all essential systems. The engines are handling the acceleration load without a problem. Biome reports a consistent microorganism ecology in good health. All six section environments are in equilibrium.

"There were some biome spikes and valleys with all of the new people and visitors aboard in Tau Ceti, but they've smoothed out. From a department standpoint, the new crew members are fitting in and doing well. We don't have any personnel shortages. My only concern there will be cold sleep technicians for our next leg to Sol. We'll need to make sure we have enough qualified people to handle the passenger load from Lalande."

"Historically, long boats pick up a capacity load of cold sleep passengers for the Lalande - Sol run," said Hubble Spears. "Yuna is helping with a plan to rotate people through for refresher training when the time comes.

"On the business side, we did very well in Tau Ceti in spite of some extra expenses from the various attacks. The government reimbursed us for most of those. Also, the *Wanderer* joint venture bought a slew of data and biological material beyond what we offered as a gift. They paid us back already for the combat armor and weapons. Their CEO took my suggestion and offered another round of stock, which sold immediately. We bought a block for the *Nai'a* and a good number of crew members made personal investments. Bottom line, the crew share for the Sol -Tau Ceti run is enough to make most of the veterans independently wealthy. A few adventurers will probably decide to put down roots in Lalande and make a go of it there."

"That's a good segue into crew morale," said Chief Alder, Persephone Belotic. "I'm glad to report a happy crew. We're also experiencing a minor baby boom. Most of the couples from Great Prospects decided to start families, and more than a few of the other couples on board took surviving Tau Ceti as a sign to expand their own families. We have plenty of capacity so everyone was approved that applied. Those babies will be acquiring their first specialty ratings by the time we get to Lalande. They might even help solve the cold sleep technician shortage, if we have one. We've adjusted work schedules, and Hubble graciously authorized overtime for people working extra hours to cover for time off for the new parents. Fortunately, there are precedents for this situation and Mr. Literal helped with a few successful strategies used by past crews. As problems go, this is my favorite kind to have. Probably because of my new grandson."

"Congratulations!" said the captain. "We'll need extra educational capacity as this generation matures, but I know you're already planning for it. I have good news from Marshall Winter. This will likely be the last data packet we get from Tau Ceti. Anything critical will be waiting for us in Lalande. His campaign against the Tau Ceti branch of the Restoration went well. He's wrapping things up and handing the investigation to a younger successor so he can get back to whatever he was doing in retirement. Lisandra Redding's hacking tools and a lot of hard work exposed a clandestine financial network. Taking the network apart helped Marshall Winter round up most of the major players left in system. He's also given us an evidence packet implicating every one of the prisoners we have in cold sleep. One of them, Stephen Owens, was the leader of Restoration in Tau Ceti. When we get to Lalande, there will be a reckoning for all of them. The long boat we'll meet there is flying into a mess. I'm hoping they'll have most of it sorted before we arrive, but I'm not counting on it."

"I recommend we continue militia training at a reduced frequency," said Commander Hartley. "With all the unknowns heading into Lalande, I'll be a lot more comfortable with a capable internal defense. Also, the militia jamboree was a huge hit with the crew. We should make it an annual event."

"I agree on both counts," said Persephone. "The militia training and competition will help the new crew members integrate."

"I included militia expenses in the budget for this run," said Hubble. "We've also initiated an arts program to buy original art and entertainment from crew members who don't want to manage their own content. You wouldn't believe the profit the holo production company turned on the combined episodes of 'Galactic Galahad'. We bought up a large library of local holo shows, books, and music to sell in Lalande and our future destinations."

The meeting continued with more mundane matters. By the end, Captain Brelling was satisfied with her ship's condition inside and out. They had a long trip to Lalande ahead and she was more hopeful than she'd felt in a long time.

***

That evening Paulene and Roan showed up unannounced at Abishai's door. He invited them in and looked a question at Roan. Mishael and Kalei were listening to Shanyah read a Pippi Longstocking book. "We won't be long and the kids are welcome to hear this," Roan said with a blush. Shanyah finished the chapter while Roan and Paulene took seats.

Abishai managed not to laugh at Roan's obvious case of nerves. "Okay you two, out with it," said Shanyah.

Roan hung his head for a moment then looked up. "I finally asked Paulene to marry me," he choked out.

Paulene rolled her eyes. "I accepted, fool that I am." She gave Roan a kiss on the cheek. Shanyah grabbed Paulene up in a big hug while Abishai pounded Roan on the back.

"I thought you'd never come to your senses, numbskull!" Abishai declared. "What did the trick?"

"Partly the glances Paulene keeps throwing at Julian Garrity, but mostly these two," he waved at the kids, also Belle, and the O'Clairs' new little princess. "We both want a family and we both want it with each other. It was time to quit stalling."

"I can see where Julian could give you a run for your money," said Abishai. "He's a lot better looking for one thing." He dug an elbow into Roan's ribs.

"He's a great guy, for another," said Roan punching Abishai lightly on the arm. "He's a lot better apprentice than you ever were, even part time. Fortunately, Paulene said yes. I'll happily run with her to the altar."

"When is the big day?" asked Shanyah.

"We're having a small ceremony officiated by Pete Worsley during lunch tomorrow at his 'office'," answered Paulene. "I'm not wasting any time getting this nailed down!"

"You do move fast, girl!" declared Shanyah with a laugh. "Are we invited?"

"Of course! Other than Pete, you're the first ones to know, but I'll send an invitation to our other friends tonight. There's plenty of room on the creek bank."

***

At the wedding, everyone wore their ship suits, but Paulene stood out with a crown of flowers woven by Shanyah. Mishael, Kalei, and Belle threw flower petals all along the path to Pete's bench on the creek. The ceremony was quick and to the point. Pete read a passage from the second chapter of Genesis and the couple's vows from an ancient-looking book of prayer. At the end, Shanyah and Abishai sang 'Walk Hand in Hand with Me' and the couple fled to raucous cheers from their friends and showers of flower petals.

Julian Garrity walked with Abishai afterward. Abishai was finally caught up with his work in the tropical dome, and volunteered to cover Roan's duties for the afternoon. "You seem to be getting along well, Julian," said Abishai. "It doesn't seem that long ago when I was in your shoes, new crew and Roan's apprentice."

"I have my rough moments, but I know how bad things could be. I do miss Tau Ceti, but the things I miss were mostly lost to me anyway. Every day I'm a little more a part of the crew. Things like this ceremony help."

"We're all rooting for you," said Abishai. Have you talked to Jarman Lal? He's been through some difficult things and there's enough distance for both of you to work through them with someone else."

"I've mostly come to terms with what I did," Julian answered, "but I wouldn't mind getting his perspective. He's not the most approachable person on the boat."

"He and I were antagonists from day one out of Sol," said Abishai nodding, "but we've since become friends. I didn't realize the burden he was carrying and he was, frankly, a jerk. We both had our attitudes adjusted when saboteurs attacked the ship and crew. I know he respects you."

Julian glanced over. "I've heard stories about the sabotage. You wouldn't care to give me your account, would you?"

"I just reacted to the situation I was forced into," Abishai answered, "but I suppose there's enough distance now for me too. I'll tell you my story if you'll tell me yours."

"It's a deal."

Over the course of their work shift, Abishai related the events of the Sol-Tau Ceti Turnover sabotage and his part in saving the ship from crippling damage. Julian listened, asking questions now and then.

"The Restoration has a type, doesn't it?" mused Julian.

"If you mean people who are willing to inflict any amount of pain, suffering, and death to achieve their ends," said Abishai, "I agree."

"They seem to view everyone, even their own ranks, as expendable," said Julian. "That attitude gives them a lot of freedom of action, but I have to believe it causes morale problems internally."

"Marshall Winter used that weakness to turn a number of their agents," said Abishai. "Not many of their operatives are true to any cause, other than their own greed."

Julian cranked the last nut tight on a pump casing. "It's something to keep in mind when we get to Lalande. Put nothing past them and look to exploit the fragility of their morale. It's funny how many morale issues are cause by a lack of morals. My own experience with that left a bitter taste."

"I understand," answered Abishai. "I imagine you still feel betrayed by the Orca Squadron leadership. Letting go of that isn't easy, but it would be step forward."

Julian grimaced. "Even a year later I'm still angry with them. You're probably right. I need to focus on the future. Let me put a good torque on this, and we can call it a day." He pulled the Big Ole Wrench out of his work pack and snugged down the massive mounting nut on the pump.

Abishai waved at the meter long spanner. "I thought I warned you about carrying that thing."

"I kind of like it," said Julian. "It keeps me anchored to the deck, and when I'm holding it, Roan is less inclined to make me the butt of one of his lame jokes."

"From what I hear, you give as good as you get," said Abishai. "It doesn't hurt that you're also a Ship Security officer. Roan needs to settle down a little now that he's married. He'll never stop ribbing you, though. It's his way of showing that he likes you."

"We'll see if Paulene has any mellowing influence on him. I don't want to haul him in, but he'd better keep his pranks within bounds."

"He's better than he used to be. I think he would get himself in scrapes just to see if the authorities cared enough to rein him in. Say, why don't you come to dinner at our quarters tonight? Jarman will be there."

"Thanks, I'd enjoy a change from the galley," said Julian. The two reached Beta Section maintenance, stowed their gear, and headed their respective ways.

***

The Nai'a continued to accelerate into the void between stars for another seven years. Her mighty engines pushed her ever faster until she reached just over 83 percent of the speed of light. She would coast at this tremendous velocity for several more years until it was time to flip the boat and decelerate for eight years to reach her destination in the Lalande system.

Chapter 13 – Maximum Velocity

January 15th, AD 3196
Long Boat Nai'a – Eight Years Out of Tau Ceti
Bridge of the Nai'a

"Main engine cut off in five...four...three...two...one...main engine cutoff," Chief Nance announced from the helm. Captain Brelling felt the apparent gravity shift slightly forward. The *Nai'a* coasted now, at a significantly higher than normal velocity.

"Sensors, talk to me," ordered the captain.

"Near space hydrogen density is normal. Far space probes one through four indicate clear sailing ahead."

"Thank you, engineering?"

"All systems green," the engineering watch officer reported. "We've steadily narrowed the electrostatic scoop to account for our velocity. Hydrogen flow numbers are nominal. The ice shield is showing expected wear. We're at 99% of original thickness. All stations are manned for habitation deck reconfiguration."

"Let's hold off for an hour," said the captain. "We've never pushed the ship to this velocity. I want a feel for how she sails before we commit to coast configuration."

The watch continued uneventfully for about thirty minutes until a red indicator flashed on the sensors console. "We've lost coms to far space probe four," announced the watch stander. "Probe three is down...probe two is down..." The tension on the bridge ratcheted up and a few seconds later an extended hiss, like the grandmother of all snakes, translated through the ship's structure. The captain felt an icy chill run up her spine. The sound was far from new now, but it gave her the heebie-jeebies every time.

"Engineering?" she queried.

"No damage reports so far. Whatever that was, the ice shield did its job. We'll get a remote out for a fly-over of the shield."

"Sensors?"

"The final data from the lost probes indicates a small cloud of interstellar molecular matter. Probe one punched through the hole created by the first three. I'm processing the data to see if we can fine-tune the robe sensors and spot the next one with more warning."

"More warning would be good," said the captain, "but it's not as if we can dodge. We'll have to trust the shield to hold. Let's get some replacement probes out."

An hour later sensors had new far-space probes in place, and engineering gave a thumbs up on the ice shield. "Commence habitat deck reconfiguration," ordered the captain, gritting her teeth. The subsequent grinding noises and booms translating through the deck were an unfortunate by-product of slowly swiveling habitation decks from a nine-degree angle for acceleration, back to perpendicular for coast mode. Soon everything would feel straight up and down again, but moving that much metal came with a price.

***

Abishai, Roan, and Julian Garrity watched with trepidation as the massive Beta section main deck plate slid on equally massive rollers overhead, praying that none of them would bind. Roan and Julian had spent the last month lubricating rollers and contact points. All power, air, water, and data conduits from the habitation decks to the maintenance spaces were disconnected and sealed. The three men wore hearing protection, wincing whenever the inevitable squeal of metal on metal pierced the background rumble of the rollers. At last, the plate slid into place with a mighty boom and the rumble ceased. Julian looked at Roan wide eyed. Roan returned the look with eyes just as wide, then bent over in laughter. Abishai clapped Julian on the shoulder. "Reconfiguration isn't for the faint of heart. Nothing stuck, though, so we're looking good. Come on, Roan, we've got a slew of connections to make." Each of them consulted their PCOMs and went in different directions to work off their part of the list.

Abishai completed his list within a couple of hours. When he finished, he found Julian struggling with a water main valve. Abishai tapped him on the shoulder, slid the Big Ole Wrench out of Julian's work pack, and motioned him to one side. "One of the reasons I like this hunk of metal is the nifty hole at the end of the handle. If you slip it over the hub of the of the valve wheel, the handle fits between the lugs on the rim and you can use all this leverage to convince Mr. Valve to open." He grunted with effort, loosening the valve wheel a quarter turn, then stood back to let Julian finish the job. Together, they worked off the rest of the list, restoring connections and inspecting for leaks and other problems. Roan met them back in Beta Section maintenance where Rimon Barkscale monitored the section maintenance console.

"I assume you didn't run into any major problems," the supervisor said. "You're back early and I'm showing good connections across Beta Section."

"Having a third person helped," replied Roan. "We need to keep an eye on the water connections for the next week or so, but everything looks good."

"Thanks for helping out, Abishai," said Rimon. "I'm surprised you didn't want to keep an eye on the tropical dome systems."

"I was probably safer in the maintenance spaces," replied Abishai. "The last time we reconfigured, a couple of hundred kilos of fruit and coconuts came raining down. The kids set up a tropical smoothy stand for a week with the excess."

"Not that I don't value each of you and enjoy your company, but my office will smell better if you all knock off and get a shower," said Rimon.

Dinner is on me at Nolen's tonight. Bring Shanyah, Mishael, and Kelai. I haven't seen them lately. They can tell me if you're behaving. The same goes for Paulene."

"Paulene would never snitch on me," said Roan. "I'm the picture of responsibility these days anyway." He winked broadly, and the three companions started toward Beta Section quarters to get ready for the evening.

***

Captain Brelling surveyed her readouts then quirked an eyebrow at her chief engineer who was standing behind the engineering station. "Everything looks to be under control, Captain," Commander Owen Halsey said. "We've got a few water leaks and intermittent connection issues to fix but they're all on secondary or tertiary systems. We should have all those cleared up within the day." The captain nodded then turned the bridge over to the scheduled watch stander. She motioned to Commander Halsey to follow her and headed to her office.

The first officer met them in the small space and they all took seats. "It's not too late to rethink our strategy of making this run at high velocity," the captain said, looking them both in the eye. "The double-thick shield is holding and should be sufficient to protect us for the rest of the voyage. However, I'm not as confident about it as I'd like to be. We could conduct Turnover in the near future and decelerate to a more moderate speed. It would cost us some years on the voyage. I want to be on time in Lalande, but I don't want the schedule to drive a bad decision. Thoughts?"

"Turnover will be our point of greatest vulnerability," said the first officer. "It's been long enough since the last long boat passage between these systems that we don't have great data on the possibility of interstellar matter shoals or other hazards. We do know none were encountered on any of the previous runs between Tau Ceti and Lalande. We also know we've encountered enough matter to cause concern recently. My recommendation is to stay the course, at least until we get a good read on the frequency of impacts."

"Kevin has a point," Halsey said. "I know the vibration induced by molecular particles hitting the shield is unpleasant. I'm starting to realize how pre-space submariners felt when they could hear the engines of an enemy destroyer. My best analysis, however, says the shield can take it, even if the frequency of impacts increases significantly. Even micro-meteoroids are survivable as long as we don't take several in the same spot."

"You put your finger on my concern," said the captain. "We've got several years of travel in these conditions ahead of us. I suppose we'll just have to get used to the sound effects. Meanwhile, I want some ideas on how to push our probes out farther and get a better warning than the lead probes going dead."

"We're still dialing in the best way to communicate at this velocity," answered the engineer. "The conditions are stretching our equipment to the limit. I have some ideas, though, and it's my department's top priority. We'll figure something out."

"I'm confident you will," the captain said. "Meanwhile, Kevin, I'm concerned about the crew. If the impact vibrations are wearing on us, we can't be the only ones. Ask Persephone to take an informal poll of the section heads and see how people are coping. I've tried ignoring it, and it's not working for me."

***

"Dad?" Mishael asked looking down at his father. "What's causing those awful hisses through the ship? I asked Quester and he said it's interstellar flatulence. I had to look the word up. I think he's putting me on."

"Quester? Putting you on? Say it isn't so!" Abishai said, looking up with a grin. At fifteen, Mishael topped him by five gangly centimeters. He didn't want to think about just how tall the young man was going to get, or how big once he filled out. "Quester's almost right. It's mostly interstellar gas with a smattering of micro particles of cosmic dust. When the ice shield plows through them, the vibration of the impact transmits through the mounting ring into the hull."

"It makes sense, but I get a really bad feeling every time I hear that sound. I can feel it in my bones."

"Your ancestors probably sailed from Tahiti to Hawaii in outrigger canoes with nothing but what they could carry and the stars to guide them," Abishai answered. He put one arm around Mishael's shoulders. "Be of good courage. I trust in God to keep us safe. We're in a good ship, with a skilled captain and crewmates." Mishael nodded, but the look of concern remained on his face.

"The sound is putting the dolphins on edge too," said Shanyah, "It resembles something they call ocean fire. I think it's the noise hot lava makes when it contacts water. I can understand their anxiety. Quester and I are trying to find a way to insulate them from the vibrations, but water conducts sound too well. I passed the concern up through engineering channels. Hopefully someone will think of a way to at least take the edge off."

***

Commander Owen Halsey pinched the bridge of his nose hard, trying to ward off an incipient headache. He wasn't sure if it was a direct or indirect result of what everyone was calling 'The Serpent's Call', but he was sure it was related. The shear randomness of the dust strikes added to everyone's misery. There had been three in the last hour. He looked around the small meeting space adjacent to forward engineering. Chief of Boat Oswald, Jarman Lal, Mr. Barboa, and two of his junior engineering officers were gathered to figure out how to deal with the problem. "Let's talk about the probe issue first," he started. "Any ideas on how to increase survivability and communications range? I'd like a probe at least five light minutes out so we can get a useful warning."

"I've tested an Extra-Low Frequency transceiver that has promise," said Jarman. "ELF should penetrate the ice shield without much attenuation and give us the range we need." Dark circles under his eyes testified to Jarman's semi-exhausted condition.

"You don't look so great," said Owen. "Are you sure you don't want to knock off and get some rest?"

Jarman raised both hands. "I'll survive. I'm having trouble sleeping when I do try to rest. Bad memories, and no, I don't want to talk about it."

One of the junior engineers raised his hand. Owen nodded at him. "Why don't we take a page from the *Nai'a* and equip each probe with an ice shield?" he said. "A couple of meters of ice, backed by a carbon nanotube shell, should extend their survivability quite a bit. I can adjust the guidance software to account for the extra mass."

Owen scratched his chin for a moment. "I like it," he stated. "We'll get both of those ideas in motion when we're done. What about our thornier issue of the vibrations? Any ideas there?"

Mr. Barboa frowned and shook his head. "I can think of a couple of different kinds of bearings that might dampen the noise better than what we have. Unfortunately, we don't have the means to refit them in flight. It would take the resources of a major ship yard, and we'd have to stop the spin."

"I haven't had time," said COB Oswald, "but I want to consult with Mr. Literal to see if we have records of other boats traveling at this velocity. We may be overlooking something obvious, or there might be a brilliant solution. If we can learn from history, it might save us some skull sweat."

"Okay," said the chief engineer, "Let me know what you find out. The rest of us will work on the new probes."

***

COB Oswald sat in front of the data terminal in his office and mentally connected his PCOM to the device. "Mr. Literal, COB Oswald here. Do you have a few minutes?"

"Good afternoon, Chief of Boat Oswald," the ship's AI data librarian answered immediately. Today the AI's avatar sported a bowtie, vest, and top hat. "How may I be of assistance?"

COB Oswald blinked at the get-up, but didn't comment. "I need a search on problems caused by high velocity passages and their solutions, please."

"Your search yielded five hundred thousand, eight hundred and twenty-three results," the AI replied immediately. "Would you like those downloaded to your terminal?"

"No, thank you, please filter to results from voyages with coast velocities of over .75 C and including the terms 'sound' or 'ice shield'."

"Your request generated two hundred and thirteen results. May I suggest sharing the purpose of your search? I have a new subroutine designed to prioritize results based on narrative. I would appreciate a chance to give it a real test."

Knowing Mr. Literal was capable of reading expressions, COB Oswald carefully kept the surprise he felt off of his features. "I'm happy to give your new subroutine a try. Will the prioritized list still contain all of the original results?"

"Certainly!"

"Okay, there are two main problems we need to solve..." The COB went on to describe the sounds, the rapid loss of probes, and the ideas in play so far.

Mr. Literal took all of two seconds to digest the information and reply. "I've identified two high probability results dealing with probe range extension and protection, and one high probability result on shield noise mitigation. They'll be at the top of the prioritized list. Would you like those downloaded now?"

"Yes, and please send copies to Owen Halsey, Mr. Barboa, and Jarman Lal. Thanks for your help, Mr. Literal."

"My pleasure," answered the AI, with a tip of his bowler.

COB Oswald cut the connection and allowed his eyebrows to go up a couple of millimeters. Mr. Literal's subroutines were getting better and his wardrobe was getting stranger. He shook his head and dove into the data. His eyes went wide as he read the opening paragraph of the noise mitigation entry.

***

The chief engineer was still shaking his head when he met with the captain and first officer a few hours later. "The answer was right in front of us. After smacking myself in the forehead a couple of times, I ran the numbers and it looks doable. The best sound insulator in the universe is a vacuum. It's back to the moldy old saw the goes 'no one can hear you scream in space'. We'll be coasting for the next several years so there's no overriding reason to keep the shield attached directly to the ship. We'll need to mount a few sets of thrusters to the shield frame for station keeping. We have the schematics and software package for those in the data the COB dug up. He and Mr. Literal also gave us a leg up on mini-shields and ELF communications suites for the probes. I keep kicking myself for not digging into the historical data sooner."

"We're all going to learn a lot on this voyage," replied the captain. "Hopefully not the hard way. We detach the shield every time we hit turnover, or prepare for system departure. This won't be much different. How soon can you execute?"

"Mr. Barboa is preparing a team to conduct a spacewalk between the shield and ship to attach the thruster packages. Once the team is back on board, we can detach the shield. I estimate we'll be ready about three hours from now. I'm planning for a five-meter separation to give the station keeping program time and space to make corrections."

Another cosmic-sized hiss set the captain's teeth on edge before she replied. "We all eagerly await separation from those," she said with a grimace. "We'll be standing by if you need anything. I want to be on the bridge for this."

True to his word, Commander Halsey showed up on the bridge three hours later to report readiness for shield separation. "We've deployed a single example of the shielded probe to five light minutes ahead. So far, it's surviving and giving us almost a minute's warning on incoming molecular matter strikes. The data will help the station keeping package on the shield. We're ready to conduct separation on your order, Captain."

"Execute separation."

"Shield separation in three...two...one...we have separation," announced the chief engineer. "The ice shield is free of the ship...now at one meter...two...three...four...five meters and holding. Station keeping program initiated. Shield is in position and holding steady."

"Probe indicates a minor dust strike impacting in sixty seconds," announced the sensors tech.

The captain carefully did not hold her breath waiting for another nails-on-chalkboard vibration to pass through the ship. The minute came and went with no detectable hiss. "I don't know why I didn't believe it would work, but it sounds like it did. Commander Halsey, well done!"

"Thank you, Captain. It was a team effort. The strike had almost no effect on the shield's position in relation to the ship. I estimate it will take several more before the guidance package will need to use the station-keeping thrusters. I'll keep watch over the next few hours to make sure everything is working as it should." pulled up a customized 3D display showing impact vibrations in the shield, position data, and thruster fuel levels.

Chapter 14 – Making H2O

January 18th, AD 3196
Long Boat Nai'a – Eight Years Out of Tau Ceti
Frame 56 of the Nai'a

Mishael and Kalei followed Roan's directions to a little-used hatch just aft of the Beta Section habitation deck. They climbed down a ladder and went through another hatch to where Roan was working on a low four-wheeled vehicle. As they watched, he filled a tank on the contraption from a pressurized bottle. His precociously freckled son waved a greeting and grinned. "Bet you can't guess what this is," he declared, hopping up and down with excitement.

"I'm not even going to try," replied Kalei. "Out with it!"

"Dad built us a go-cart!" said Grady. "Isn't it great!"

"Maybe," she replied. "What's a go-cart?"

"A go-cart, young lady," said Roan with a grin matching Grady's, "is a millennium-plus old invention that is the bane of parents and joy of children everywhere in the populated universe. This one is a present to myself to celebrate surviving my recent space-walk."

"Wait, aren't you a parent?" asked Mishael.

"Yes," answered Roan, "but you know I'm a kid at heart. Remember floating the central corridor with me? We'll have to give that another go, now that we're in coast mode. One other benefit of coast mode is that the frame fifty-six passageway is exposed and completely free of obstacles all the way around the ship." He waved in both directions. "We've got the perfect three-plus kilometer track to run this baby down and hydrogen to spare."

"I have a feeling I'm going to regret this," said Mishael. "What's the hydrogen for?"

"Another great invention, the rotary internal combustion engine."

Roan had Mishael help him set the go-cart in the middle of the corridor, then motioned everyone to stand back. He gave a hard pull on the starter chord and the engine roared to life. Roan's grin got wider. He sat in the vehicle, strapped himself in, and donned an antique looking white helmet and goggles. "Wait here and stay clear of the corridor!" he yelled. "I'll be back through in a jiffy!" He stomped on the throttle pedal and the cart shot down the corridor with Roan whooping at the top of his lungs. The kids laughed and slapped each other on the back.

Less than three minutes later Roan roared past them at full speed, waving and yelling, "Yeeee...Haaaaaw...." After another two trips, he brought the cart to a halt and looked up. "Who's next?"

***

Captain Brelling set a heavily loaded lunch tray on the table across from Jarman and sat down with a sigh. "I was really hoping this would be a quiet, boring passage. At least we're done with the Serpent's Call. Commander Halsey's fix worked and the shield is keeping position just fine."

"I'm as glad as anyone," replied Jarman. "I'm finally getting some sleep again."

"You look better," the captain said around a mouth full of fresh papaya with lemon juice. "I'm guessing the Serpent's Call ripped the scab off an old wound."

"It did," answered Jarman. "I thought I was over Hygeia III. Now I don't know if I ever will be. Those faces keep coming back to me in my dreams, especially my uncle's."

"You don't need to forget, but you do need to make your peace with those ghosts. I'm sure your uncle would want you to."

"I should take friendly advice and talk it through with someone. Abishai suggested Julian Garrity. I'll see if he's willing to rehash old emotional baggage."

The captain nodded. "You'd both benefit. I need you sharp and ready. You and Mr. Barboa are the only people on this boat I trust to lead a spacewalk in these conditions. I hope we don't need to conduct another, but I'm not counting on it."

"Our teams did the job," Jarman answered, "but all of us were feeling vulnerable out there. Something about the extra velocity keeps me looking over my shoulder. The radiation count wasn't any worse than we experienced with the ice repair operation on the last passage, though."

***

Mishael and Kalei were still bubbling over with excitement when they returned to their quarters for lunch. Abishai bustled around in the kitchen area, getting tomato soup with cheese, crackers, and a fruit platter together. "What is Roan up to?" he asked grating yellow cheddar cheese and sprinkling fresh chopped basil onto the bowls of soup.

The two looked at each other, then shrugged. Kalei described Roan's go-cart and the fun they'd had taking turns zooming all the way around frame fifty-six. "Grady set the record time since he masses half of what any of the rest of us do. You wouldn't believe what a rush it is zipping along that dark corridor at sixty kilometers-per-hour when you're practically sitting on the deck. It looks like an infinite tunnel in the headlights."

"What will my old buddy think of next?" said Abishai setting out the food. "Roan wouldn't put any of you in serious danger, but the COB is going to eat him for lunch if you get caught."

"We're sworn to secrecy," said Mishael, "but he knew we would have to tell you if you asked."

"You're both old enough to make some of your own decisions about taking risks. I'll just warn you; your mother and I are not saving you from any consequences if you do get caught. Remember what happened the last time Roan got you mixed up with the COB?" They both nodded solemnly. "Enough said, lets pray and eat before the soup gets cold."

Later, Abishai tracked Roan down in Beta Section maintenance. "Are you going to show me your go-cart, or am I going to turn you in to Paulene?"

"Paulene's riding it right now!" Roan said with a laugh. "Let's go! We just have to stay off the track because she does not slow down." He grabbed a pressurized flask of hydrogen and set off.

Abishai peeked carefully out of the side corridor as the go-cart went roaring by with Paulene at the wheel, an ear-to-ear grin splitting her face. Grady, dressed in a bright blue jumpsuit with at least a dozen colorful patches, stood by with a tool kit, a smudge or two of grease on his face authenticating the look. Paulene braked to a halt on her next pass and climbed carefully out. "Tighten the clutch a quarter turn," she said to Grady, patting him on the head. "It was slipping a bit." Grady pulled a screwdriver out of the toolkit and quickly bent to the task.

"That's quite the seven-year-old mechanic you have," said Abishai, watching Grady work.

"He helped me with every step of the build!" answered Roan proudly. "He managed to keep it a secret too. I'd call that a near miracle for a boy his age."

"He definitely enjoys all things mechanical," said Paulene. "There's no doubt he's his father's son. There's a helmet that should fit you in that locker, Abishai."

"Do you think that contraption can handle my mass?" Abishai said doubtfully.

"It's over engineered, no worries," answered Roan. "Just don't turn it around. Spin-ward travel only on this track or you may take a flyer. You can't steer floating through the air." He hooked up the hydrogen bottle and topped off the fuel while Grady drained the water capture tank at the end of the exhaust.

Abishai carefully settled his frame into the seat and strapped in. Grady pulled the starter chord and the engine roared to life. Abishai tentatively pressed the throttle pedal forward until the RPMs caused the clutch to engage and propel him forward. He whooped and leaned into the motion as Roan yelled, "Let 'er eat!"

***

A few days later Captain Brelling invited Chief of Boat Oswald into her office for a cup of coffee. "There's something I'm wondering if I should officially notice or not," she opened. "Do you know what I'm talking about?"

The COB took a slow sip of coffee before answering. "There might be a go-cart track operating on the frame fifty-six passageway, but I'm not paying it much attention."

"I see, what don't you know about it?"

"It's very popular with the crew, especially the former Great Prospects spacers. They have at least two carts operating now, but no accidents or injuries sufficient to need medical attention."

"Should I notice it?"

"I'd leave it be for now," said the COB. "The operators aren't charging anything. Unless it becomes a safety issue, it's a good way for people to blow off some steam. We have plenty built up from the Serpent's Call."

"Alright, I'll hold off for a few days, but I want the operation brought into the open eventually."

***

Two days later Roan was doing a brisk business. He had three carts running, never more than two at one time spaced evenly to avoid collisions. The corridor wasn't wide enough to pass, so races weren't an option except against the clock. Grady still held pride of place with the fastest time. Roan was thinking of creating mass categories to make the competition fair. He watched with a smile as his pit crew efficiently refueled, dehydrated and checked over the idle cart. Mishael and Kalei graciously deferred to Grady's expertise in spite of the age difference, letting him boss the crew.

Abishai stood out of the way watching for the next cart to go zooming by. Quester sped through without stopping. A tiny pair of goggles peered over his right shoulder and a furry ringed tail streamed behind the go-cart. Lionel let out a long yowl to voice his approval of their breakneck speed. Abishai shook his head. Lionel and Quester were two of a kind, there wasn't much they wouldn't attempt.

Abishai turned to Roan. "Where did you get goggles to fit a cat?" he asked. "I'm still surprised he's willing to wear them."

"Mr. Literal found a design in his database we could use a printer on," answered Roan. "Who knows how it got in there. Quester convinced Lionel to wear the goggles, but it took some doing. He drew the line at the helmet, though." Roan held up a diminutive white crash helmet with cutouts for a cat's ears. He heard the hatch behind him open and turned to come face to face with the captain. Roan's features blanched and his mouth opened and closed like a fish as he fought for something to say. The COB's appearance behind the captain didn't help a bit.

The captain managed not to laugh at Roan's discomfort, keeping a stern expression. "Well?" she said, "are you going to stand there catching flies or hand me a helmet?" She let her expression slide into a grin when Roan scrambled to find one her size in the locker. The pit crew's eyes were wide but they quickly set the captain's cart up in the passageway and helped her strap in. She took off howling like a banshee at the go signal. The COB pulled Roan aside and soon they were deep in conversation about his now public enterprise.

Chapter 15 – Careers and Careening

February 18th, AD 3196
Long Boat Nai'a – Eight Years Out of Tau Ceti
Beta Section Quarters

Quester and Mishael leaned over the Boorlong's Revenge board, carefully calculating their next moves. Kalei pounded away on the virtual keyboard of her PCOM, working her way through the final scene of a short story for school. Shanyah walked up behind Abishai as he took in the tableau and put him in a light choke-hold. "A penny for your thoughts," she murmured in his ear.

"Or you'll make me tap?" asked Abishai. He thought he might be able to throw her with a drop Seo Nagi, but she would land in the middle of the game. Their quarters weren't big enough for unarmed combat practice.

"No, but I will give you the noogie of your life if you don't tell me what you're thinking."

"I've been noogied by experts, but I won't tempt you. I was thinking about our two precocious progeny and the career choices in front of them. Living on the *Nai'a* imposes certain limitations."

"You used up your quota of three syllable words for the day," mused Shanyah. "The limitations on the ship aren't too restrictive. Look at all the specialties you have qualifications in, and you haven't touched half of what's available. The skills they gain here will mostly translate to any large habitat. Both of them inherited your eclectic tastes. I'm looking forward to seeing what they choose."

"I was thinking more in terms of them being stuck on the ship for this long passage," said Abishai. "It seems crazy, but they could both be married and starting families before we get to Lalande. We made the decision, and now they have no choice. You and I both left home at an age they'll reach about the time we hit turnover"

"The *Nai'a* is their home," answered Shanyah. "I'm comfortable with the stability the ship provides. Lalande is wide open if they want to strike out on their own, and we'll likely travel to Sol afterward. In a way they'll have more opportunity than most people get in a lifetime."

Abishai nodded in agreement. "Neither of them is chafing at our enforced small-town isolation yet. The sheer size of the ship helps, and Roan's hijinks add some fun and variety."

"Speaking of variety, are you still planning to perform in the variety show next month?" asked Shanyah.

"My quartet is working up a few songs and I'm still working on a spiritual to sing with my ukulele. How about you?"

"The members of the Pacific Islanders Heritage Club are working on a traditional dance medley. The men could use extra bodies for the Māori haka. You'd look wild in a full set of tattoos."

"Not even temporary tats, thank you very much," replied Abishai. "I have enough hair on my chest to look like a bear as it is."

"Quester is participating. Are you going to let him show you up?" prodded Shanyah with a grin.

"He shows me up regularly at militia drill these days. We each have our own talents."

"Okay, I can tell your mind is made up. At least be in the audience for our performance."

"I wouldn't miss it. In fact, I'm going to insist you give me a private dress rehearsal."

"Hmmm...I can arrange for that. It will cost you though."

"Cost me?" said Abishai, eyebrows rising.

"I'll think of something appropriate," Shanyah replied with conspiratorial wink.

"Did you hear the snow slope is open in Gamma Section?" Abishai asked, changing the subject.

"You're not going to try snowboarding again?"

"No, I learned my lesson from spending four weeks in a knee brace last year. I just thought it would be fun to schedule some family sledding time."

"I know Mishael and Kalei will enjoy it," Shanyah replied. "They'll probably ditch our toboggan for skis, though. How about inviting the O'Clairs? They would have a blast tobogganing with us."

"Great idea! I'll ping Val and coordinate a time for reservations."

***

Abishai looked back to make sure everyone was aboard the toboggan and hanging on. He was the designated pilot because no one wanted him landing on them if they crashed. Behind him Shanyah, Val, Palamar, Lana, and Yuki made a full load for the flat-bottomed sled. "Here we go!" he yelled. "Everybody push with your hands, one, two, three, GO!!"

The toboggan inched forward with each push then gained momentum as the slope steepened. Abishai steered as best he could, but physics had more control than he did. Half way down he yelled "BUMP!!" as they plowed over a small mogul and caught a few seconds of air. Screams of laughter came from the back of the toboggan as they slammed back to the snow. The run quickly flattened out, and the sled bumped to a halt. Abishai stood up and looked back, realizing he was short a passenger. "Yuki?" He yelled. He looked up the slope and spotted a figure in a bright orange snowsuit still sliding toward them, arms and legs akimbo. Palamar rushed over as her younger daughter slid to a halt. She pulled the girl to her feet to make sure she was okay. Yuki was laughing so hard she could barely stand up.

"I fell off the back!" she finally managed to say. "It's hard to hang on with mittens." Palamar dusted the snow off Yuki's suit and patted her on the back with a grin.

"Watch the aerials ramp," Val said. "Quester promised to give us a show." The group turned to look.

Quester whooped as he flew down the near-vertical slope toward the ramp. He was carrying a lot of speed and his momentum shot him up into the air. On his third flip he saw he was going to overshoot the landing area. Flailing his arms in a momentary panic, he tried to get his board back under him but misjudged the rotation, plunging head first into a soft pile of snow. Val O'Clair leaned over the Abishai. "He stuck the landing."

"Too easy," Abishai replied shaking his head. He trotted over, grabbed Quester's ankles and pulled him out of the artificial drift. Quester flailed and sputtered, pulling his clogged goggles off and spitting out a mouthful of snow. "Maybe start at the recommended drop point instead of the top next time?" Abishai said. "Are you okay?" Quester just gave him a weak thumbs up, then leaned over and put his hands on his knees to catch his breath.

Kalei and Mishael whooshed up and slid to a stop on their skis, spraying Quester with a fine mist of snow. "I'll give that a one out of ten," laughed Kalei. "I hope they got it on the cameras." Her observation earned her a baleful look from Quester. The teen-agers helped him dust the rest of the snow from his outfit and the three headed for the lift.

"Who's up for another toboggan run?" called Abishai.

"I'm driving this time," said Shanyah.

"And Yuki is going between us," declared Palamar.

Abishai raised both hands in surrender and hooked the toboggan up to the tow line. The rest of the group made their way up the stairs on the sledding side of the slope.

***

Abishai and Mishael found Pete Worsley on his usual creek-side bench. This time he was wearing jeans and a jacket appropriate to the "winter temperate climate" temperature in Beta Section. "Have a seat," he welcomed them. "Business or social call?"

"Some of each," answered Abishai. "We haven't talked recently, and Mishael wants to get your perspective on a few things."

"Fishing's no good at this temperature," Pete replied. "I'm all ears."

"I took one of those interest & aptitude tests," Mishael started. "Most people's results show peaks and valleys. Mine's more like a mesa, flat as a pancake. I'm having trouble deciding what to apprentice in because everything interests me. I know I have to concentrate somewhere to develop useful skills. I feel pulled in a dozen directions."

"Have you prayed about it?" Pete asked.

"Dad said you were going to ask me that. Yes, I have prayed, every morning for the last month at least. God's answer seems to be wait, but I need to make a decision soon. I'm coming to the end of the work along program. I've enjoyed every job and everyone I've worked with. Some were obviously trying to sell me on their specialty and others were actively testing me to see if I would get discouraged. Both approaches motivated me to dig in and learn. It's like coming to a loaded table with a teeny-tiny plate."

"I can tell you're frustrated," Pete replied with a hand on Mishael's shoulder, "but it's a blessing, in a way, to have wide interests. The downside is a lifetime of difficult choices. I'll tell you the same thing I told your father when we had a similar discussion on the way out of Sol. Think in terms of how you can best be a blessing to others. It doesn't have to be immediately tangible. Every job on the ship helps keep us alive and thriving as a community. The real question is, how can your talents be used to bless others both on the job and off?"

"I hadn't looked at it from that perspective," Mishael said with a furrowed brow. "It's been all about what I want. Now I feel selfish."

"You should pay attention to your heart's desires as well. When you know they are God given, those are also a guide. Read Psalm 37, and study on verse 4. I believe God gives us desires that are in his will when we seek his will, and that he fulfills them. There are some additional words of encouragement in the passage about patience and a promise or two that should help settle your mind. On a related subject, people who are knowledgeable in many areas make good leaders. Captain Brelling has more qualifications than almost anyone on the ship. I think you would do well in the ship's officer corps. I told your father the same thing, but he's chosen to lead from where he is."

Abishai smiled, remembering the conversation. "I just didn't have the confidence to try the officer route. Looking back, it was for the best. I'd rather be the guy with the shovel, than the three standing around telling him what to do."

"You'll notice the captain, and most of the officers, don't hesitate to pick up a shovel if it's needed," said Pete, "but someone has to focus on the big picture as well. It's a team effort. We've been blessed to have the right people in the right places most of the time on the *Nai'a*. Enough pontificating! What do you think, Mishael? Is any of this helping?"

Mishael nodded. "It is. I've got a lot to think about, but I have a better focus now. I want to fit into the crew in a way that strengthens all of us, even if I'm the weakest link."

Pete eyes widened a bit. He clapped Mishael on the shoulder. "I wish my perspective had been that mature when I was fifteen! You'll be fine. Also, as many years as we're all living these days, you can have several careers if you want to."

"I'm curious," said Abishai. "I know Elder Pryachac's age is a closely guarded secret. Just how long are people living with the benefits of personal biome management, gene therapy, and lower gravity?"

Pete looked thoughtful. "I do my best to forget how old I am, but I know a few retired spacers aboard who are well into their fourth century by an Earth clock. We all have fewer subjective years on us because of the time dilation on our voyages, but there's no doubt we're living much longer and heathier lives. I don't know what the upper limit is, but at a guess I would say it's about a four-fold increase. I know the captain, Chief Alder Belotic and Dr. Rensaleer have regular discussions about the impact on younger folks like Mishael, here, and Kalei. We need to make sure they have opportunities, both aboard ship and off."

"I agree," said Abishai. "I'm glad we picked up some new people here in Tau Ceti. A regular infusion of new blood is probably good for the crew, and those that left the ship show the kids they're not stuck here forever if they don't want to be." The light began to wane and the trio rose to walk back to the quarters area together. "Join us for supper?" Abishai asked. "Shanyah's grilling mahi-mahi."

"You got me by the tastebuds!" answered Pete. "I'll just swing by my quarters and grab some cider to go with the meal."

***

As the Nai'a coasted at high velocity through the interstellar medium toward Lalande, the crew worked to keep the ship and each other in top form. Babies were born, children grew, and people learned new skills. In the back of everyone's mind was the upcoming Turnover. On the last run, flipping the boat had set off a flurry of sabotage and life changing events. This time their velocity and interstellar dust were the enemy. The crew prepared the ship using every best practice they could glean from nearly a millennium of long boat voyages.

Chapter 16 – Turnover

May 7th, AD 3201
Long Boat Nai'a – Turnover, Eight Years' Travel from Lalande
Bridge

The sensors officer studied her displays with careful concentration. "Interstellar medium density is trending down, captain," she announced. "The model predicts a low in ten minutes."

"Thank you," answered Captain Brelling. She switched her com panel to all hands and opened the channel. "All hands, this is the captain, Turnover will commence in eight minutes. I say again Turnover will commence in eight minutes. You are ready and the ship is ready. Stay frosty and we'll put the old girl on the ball to Lalande. You have my full confidence. Captain out."

At the helm, Chief Nance brought up the automated astrogation program that would tumble the *Nai'a* end for end, assuming everything went to plan. On the previous voyage, nothing had gone to plan. Then working as a Restoration agent, Lisandra Redding had hacked the automated navigation program and shut it down just as the maneuver commenced. The chief had expertly completed the flip using manual helm control, but he was fervently hoping his skills wouldn't be tested this time. He adjusted the 3D vector graphic hologram representing the ship's current attitude and the intercept course to Lalande, then tried to relax.

The sensors officer monitored input from fifteen probes. For this event, triple redundancy felt like barely enough. The lieutenant junior-grade at the engineering station waited until the countdown reached five minutes, then pressed a button on his display. "Ice shield maneuver initiated," he said.

One minute later he pressed a second button. "Ice shield maneuver complete. Holding steady at seventy-five meters clearance." Captain Brelling nodded. With the ice shield already detached and capable of self-maneuver, the sequence for Turnover was slightly altered from the usual.

"Sensors?" queried the captain.

"Approaching minimum density in the interstellar medium as predicted."

"Aye, Helm, you have the call. Execute Turnover on your mark."

Chief Nance consulted the interstellar flux readings model for a minute then opened the all-hands com channel. "Commencing Turnover in one minute on my mark. Three...two...one...mark."

All over the ship, Turnover station displays showed the countdown in large red numbers. Captain Brelling projected a calm confidence she didn't feel. She wondered if the memory of their last Turnover was weighing on the crew as well. So far, only minor internal rigging issues, quickly corrected by the crew, had cropped up.

***

Abishai stood behind Julian Garrity at the Beta Section Hydro monitoring panel with memories of his own making his palms sweaty. "Everything is in the green," Julian said. "After the stories you and Rimon told about the last Turnover, I was half expecting utter chaos."

"It was well-managed chaos, I'll have you know," answered Abishai. "Count your blessings. I'll take uneventful anytime. Our biggest challenge will likely be chasing down leaks when we rig for deceleration. I'm getting ahead of myself though. Let's both say a prayer for a safe Turnover."

"Amen," Julian replied.

***

Chief Nance consulted his readouts as the number edged toward zero. "Commencing Turnover maneuver on my mark. Three...two...one...mark." The *Nai'a* shuddered slightly as powerful bow and stern maneuvering thrusters fired in sequence, sending the ship into a sedate end-for-end tumble. Captain Brelling grimaced as the ship's spin, combined with the maneuver, did unkind things to her inner ear.

"Ninety degrees," announced Nance when they hit the halfway point. The ship was now flying sideways through space at over eighty percent of the speed of light. Most of the ship was unprotected by the ice shield at this angle.

Turnover continued without incident until the ship was within twenty degrees of course alignment. "Multiple dust strikes on forward probes," announced the sensors officer. "Impact predicted in fifteen seconds."

Chief Nance's fingers were already dancing across the helm panel as he went to manual control. He used the maneuvering thrusters to speed their rotation in an attempt to get the ship fully behind the shield before impact. He almost made it. An unholy shriek like a giant band saw echoed through the ship.

Chief Nance deftly brought the tumble to a halt as the bridge crew assessed the ship's condition. He made two small adjustments then announced, "Turnover complete, alignment for Lalande verified. We are on course."

"Engineering?" queried the captain.

"One bow compartment lost pressure," the officer reported. "No casualties. Forward engineering has a team on the way to assess the damage. All critical systems are green. Permission to bring the shield in and rig for deceleration?"

"Permission granted." They would bring the shield to the ship's stern slip-ring and run the engine pylons out to start slowing their flight.

The captain keyed in aft engineering on her com and got her chief engineer on the line. "Any reason not to run the engines out and start the burn?" she asked.

"Everything looks good," he replied. "We lost some sensor panels and hull plate up front, but nothing we can't repair. We're ready to rig the engines for deceleration on your command."

"I'll wait for the initial damage assessment from forward engineering," said the captain. "Go ahead and re-attach the ice shield while we're waiting. We'll see if your work on the slip ring bearings helps tone down the Serpent's Call."

"Aye, Ma'am we'll start the process now. Aft engineering out."

Guided by optical sensors, the ring of the ice shield support structure slid smoothly into the re-engineered aft slip ring mount with just a muffled thump. The new magnetic bearings supported the ring, allowing the shield to remain steady while the ship continued to spin. Like a maglev train, the bearings would theoretically maintain a small gap between the ring and the mount, even under deceleration. Commander Halsey checked the readouts closely for several minutes then nodded in satisfaction. "We've got a positive capture and the gap is as predicted," he announced. "We'll see how she does when we kick in the engines."

Back on the bridge the engineering officer indicated that the damage control team had a report. The captain motioned for him to put it on speaker. "Midshipman Bonaparte' reporting," a nervous voice sounded. The captain's eyes widened a little, but she didn't say anything. "We've patched the hull breach temporarily until an external repair can be completed. The compartment is repressurized and the team is restoring a severed cable run. The run is the only damage other than the hull."

"Any reason on your end to delay deceleration?" queried the engineering officer.

"Negative," the midshipman responded.

"Bridge out."

"Signal aft engineering to rig engines for deceleration'" said the captain.

"Aye Ma'am, rigging main engines for deceleration."

A series of vibrations and thumps accompanied the deployment of the three engine pylons to clear the edges of the ice shield. Within a minute the fusion engine telltales glowed green. "Engines rigged for deceleration and set to helm control," announced the engineering officer.

"Helm, slow and steady, bring engines to .1G," ordered the captain.

"Aye, bringing engines to .1G," Chief Nance answered. The ship gained a low background hum as the mighty engines used fusion power to begin slowing the *Nai'a's* bulk. Nance continued to apply power in steady increments, adjusting with maneuvering thrusters when needed. Within a few minutes he had the thrust at a steady .1G. "Engines holding steady at .1G," he announced.

"Astrogation, how is our course?" the captain asked.

"We are on the ball for a Lalande intercept, Ma'am," came the reply.

"Well done!" said the captain. She opened the all-hands channel. "All hands, this is the captain, congratulations on another successful Turnover! This one was less eventful than the last, thank goodness. You performed admirably and we took only minor damage from a last-second dust strike. I know you have several hours of work to rig the hab decks for deceleration, but the party tonight is on me!"

Chapter 17 – Celebration

May 7th, AD 3201
Long Boat Nai'a – Turnover, Eight Years' Travel from Lalande
Cooper Green

Abishai gathered with his friends and family, fresh from a shower and not a little tired. After chasing down leaks in Beta Section hydro, he and the family had pitched in with the tropical dome gang gathering fallen fruit and coconuts. Mishael's description of the damage in the forward compartment had been harrowing, and the pictures from a hull crawler remote even more so. It looked like someone had taken several strokes with a giant hacksaw to the bow, slicing into the damaged compartment. Fortunately, it was a storage space for forward engineering, and they hadn't lost anything essential.

The crowd on Cooper Green was upbeat and excited for the show to come. Food booths of many varieties lined two sides of the green. Abishai headed for one with a banner advertising champignons and halb-hahnchen with his son in tow. Mishael had learned to follow his fathers' instinct for food at these big events. When they arrived at the booth, Rimon Barkscale, dressed in lederhosen, was stirring a giant skillet containing a fragrant combination of mushrooms, onions, and bacon. Abishai took a long moment to appreciate the heady scent. Vat-grown chicken halves turned on several spits in a roaster behind Rimon. Abishai ordered a half-chicken and a serving of the mushroom mixture for each of them. Rimon spooned a generous portion of the savory champignons into two cardboard dishes, adding a dollop of sour cream and half a slice of bread per tradition. "I wish you'd do this more often," said Abishai. "Champignons are delicious, and I can never get them quite the same on the stove top."

"Something about this big old pan and the open air works magic," answered Rimon. "If I made them every month, they wouldn't be special. Also, cleaning this thing is a bear. Lucky for you, the captain specifically requested German fest food for the Turnover party so I couldn't refuse. If you want to ensure the champignons come back soon, you'll help me clean the pan."

"Gladly!" replied Abishai dipping his bread in the delicious sauce. "Just let me know when and Mishael and I will be there." Mishael shot him a look, but soon lost himself in his own portion of the food. The midshipman now out-massed his father by a good twenty kilos and could work his way through calories like a starving tiger.

"How about some pomme frites?" Rimon asked.

"I need to save room for the nineteen other booths I want to visit," Abishai replied, but Mishael grabbed a cone of the fried potatoes and added a squirt of mayonnaise on top. Abishai just shook his head. He didn't even try to keep up anymore. He spotted a fresh-squeezed lemonade stand and joined the line with Mishael. The stand had three servers, each crewing their own citrus smasher, so the line went quickly. "I can't think of anything I'd rather drink," said Abishai. "it's hard to improve on fresh squeezed lemon juice, cold water, and simple syrup."

Mishael nodded as he sipped his appreciatively. "It goes down easy. What's next?"

Abishai looked around, sniffing the air. "Over there," he pointed. "SSambap, Korean lettuce wraps, and maybe some Yaki Mandu." Thin sliced seasoned 'beef' and several vegetables were sizzling on a grill. The proprietor grinned and handed Abishai a lettuce leaf.

"Keep up if you can!" he declared then started spooning food onto his leaf from over a dozen dishes set into the counter between them. There was steaming hot beef, several types of kimchee, fresh vegetables, and sauces. In less than a minute he gave the leaf an expert fold and handed it to Mishael on a plate. Abishai couldn't match the pace but soon had his own leaf loaded and folded.

"What is all this stuff? asked Mishael, eyeing the leaf wrap and ingredients with equal suspicion.

"It's all good for you, and delicious," replied his father. "Take a bite and see."

Mishael shrugged, took a big bite, and chewed. His eyes closed in gustatory bliss as the flavors did a dance on his taste buds. Fresh, salty, sweet, savory, tart crunchiness, with a spicy bite had him going in quickly for a second large mouthful. Abishai devoured his at a similar pace, earning a big smile from the chef.

Shanyah and Kalei conducted their own gourmet odyssey on the other side of the green in company with the O'Clairs. When everyone was loaded up, they grabbed empty seats at a table. "Are you ready for your apprenticeship in Medical?" Palamar O'Clair asked Kalei.

"Definitely," she answered around a mouthful of Chicago dog. "I've had enough schooling for now. I want to do something practical for a change."

"I remember my first few months being practical alright," Palamar said with a wicked grin, "practically everything everyone else didn't want to do. I think you'll do fine. You've been focused on Medical since you were five. You'll know soon enough if it's your true calling."

"You managed to qualify quickly," Kalei replied, "considering your background as a pilot."

"To be fair, I already had a pre-med degree under my belt before joining the *Nai'a*," Palamar said. "I worked on it in parallel. Most pilots train for a secondary occupation. You never know when time or an accident might catch up with you."

Abishai and Mishael joined them at the table, each balancing a near-impossible load of victuals. Shanyah snagged a mini-doughnut from one of

Abishai's plates and popped it in her mouth. "Dessert tax," she said when she finished chewing.

Abishai settled thick forearms around his food and tried to watch for other tax collectors as he ate. Despite his vigilance, he was certain a couple thousand calories went missing. Mishael didn't bother, sharing freely with Lana and Yuki O'Clair before wandering off to find more dessert.

"The show starts in 15 minutes," said Val. "I think I'll go grab some ice cream. Who's with me?" Everyone except Shanyah and Abishai followed him toward the Big Scoops booth.

Shanyah finished the last bite of cheesecake on her plate and leaned back with a sigh. "I'm glad this Turnover was less eventful. The aftermath of the last one brought us together, though, a shiny silver lining to a very dark cloud."

Abishai leaned over and gave her a kiss. "Mishael did well leading the damage control party. He said he mainly tried to keep from tripping over his own feet and took his cues from Chief Carter."

"I wondered if some 'adventure' might convince him to try a different track, but he seems determined to stick it out and make ensign. His marks and ratings are top notch. It's good to see him focus on something."

"So far, so good. He's got the temperament for it. I don't think I ever did."

"You do pretty well in the moment, Love," answered Shanyah. "Fighting through literal panic isn't something many people can do."

"I can only pray I never face a test like that again," said Abishai with feeling. "I wouldn't wish it on anyone. As you said though, it brought us together. I'm eternally grateful for discovering you!" This time it was Shanyah who leaned over for a kiss.

***

Decelerating at .1G, the Nai'a made her way toward Lalande. The crew and captain counted the largely uneventful years as a blessing.

Chapter 18 – One Year to Lalande

May 10th, AD 3208
Long Boat Nai'a – One Year of Travel from Lalande
Captain's Conference Room

"We've had a good run since Turnover," said Captain Brelling to the assembled boat leadership. "We're in communications range of the Lalande system so it's time to assess our status and make plans for system approach. Commander Halsey, give us your rundown."

"All systems are in good shape," he answered. "Our new vacuum-rated fabricator restored full hull integrity in the damaged bow section. The only item of concern is the ice shield. If we hadn't doubled the thickness, I doubt we would've survived the high-speed transit. We took a couple of hits to the stern on blow-throughs, but none were serious enough to cause a hull breach. The shield itself is extensively cratered and will need to be completely refurbished before our next crossing. We're safe enough at this velocity, though, and Lalande is a much cleaner system than Tau Ceti. We shouldn't need a protection team to deal with space debris. The pinnace and our remotes will be up to the task."

The captain's lips formed a thin line. "I agree for passive threats. It's the active ones I'm concerned about. I have to assume the Restoration has a well-established organization in place in Lalande. The question is whether the long boat *Kilimanjaro* from Sol managed to deal with them while we were in transit. We'll see what comes from the system as we approach. The first communications package should be inbound but we're too far out for a meaningful two-way conversation."

The first officer leaned forward. "Jarman Lal and some of the former Great Prospects pilots have a few ideas about dealing with active threats. We may not have the option of hiring a trusted team in Lalande, but we have the pilots and resources to give ourselves a degree of protection, especially if we're willing to commit resources to building our own defensive fleet."

"I'm aware of our cabal of pilots and their bent toward paranoia," said the captain. "In this case, the universe may really be out to get us, at least in the Lalande system. Have you discussed the business case with the CEO?"

"They have," answered Hubble Spears. "Our fabrication facilities can handle the modular small ship design they propose and we have the resources. A dozen of those stinger boats will take our ship steel reserve down to twenty percent of capacity. Overall, the cost will take a few percentage points off of the profit for this run. Most of the loss we can offset by selling the ships when we leave the system. There should be a good market since the design is easily converted for mining exploration. I recommend working up and testing a prototype now. We can go ahead with the rest, or cancel the project based on what we hear from Lalande."

"I agree," said the captain. "Do you have any objections, Persephone?" she asked.

"None," answered the Chief Alder. "Morale is good, thanks to militia competitions and a number of creative home-grown recreational opportunities. We've got another year of travel, though, and preparing to defend ourselves on arrival will help keep everyone busy and give them a sense of control. On a separate note, Yuna is doing wonders working up a core cadre of cold sleep physicians and technicians. We'll likely have a significant passenger load if we head back to Sol."

"We're still very much up in the air on the actual situation in Lalande," said the captain. "For now, we'll prepare as we discussed. Any other topics?"

"I'd like to ramp up militia training again," the first officer said. "The extra drill served us well in Tau Ceti and we've worked up a few new tricks and systems I want to get everyone to be familiar with."

"We already planned for increased training," answered the captain. "Is there anything the militia needs?"

"Mr. Barboa has everything well in hand. As we train up, he'll hand over command of the militia battalion to someone else. He doesn't want to admit it, but he can't throw himself and other people around the way he used to."

"If it comes down to Mr. Barboa throwing someone around, we're in serious trouble," answered the captain. "I know he likes to prove himself to his troops, but it's his tactical sense that makes him valuable."

"He knows it, but old habits die hard."

"I'm satisfied with where we are and the immediate plans," said the captain. "When we hear from Lalande, we'll get back together and refine our preparations."

***

Abishai approached Mishael carefully, keeping his center of gravity low and looking for an opening. His son was as broad as he was now, and significantly taller. Thanks to a lifetime of grappling practice, he also had the core strength of a lowland gorilla and the kinesthetic sense of a person born and raised in .5G. The combination made him a very difficult opponent. Abishai had long since used up his bag of tricks. He waited for Mishael's left foot to come down, then shot low for an ankle pick. Mishael jerked the ankle back while grabbing the collar of Abishai's judo gi and pulling him forward. He used the leverage to pull himself into a twisting flip that landed him on Abishai's back. He tried to snake an arm around his father's neck while sinking hooks in with both legs, but Abishai caught the wrist and bucked hard. Mishael sailed across the mat, then tucked into a roll and came up on his feet. His father was in hot pursuit, looking to take advantage before Mishael could get set. Abishai hit him low, like a 130-kilo wrecking ball. Mishael didn't even try to stop him. He bent double, reached over Abishai's back, wrapped his long arms around his father's waist and tossed him like a bag of rice. Abishai's flying form ran out of dojo space and thumped into the padded wall feet first. He managed a twisting half-flip to land on his feet but held both hands up in surrender. "I'll concede that round." He bent over and put his hands on his knees to catch his breath. "You're getting harder and harder to fool," he said. "You should compete in the unarmed combat all-ship tournament."

Mishael shook his head. "What if I come up against you or Mom?" he answered.

"You'll probably thump me like you've been doing two out three times. Your mother is another story. You don't have as much height advantage on her and she's sneaky. We're about even in every-day practice, but something about the tournament makes her kick it up a notch. I'd be more worried about your sister, though. You out-mass her, but she's scary fast and knows all your strengths and weaknesses."

"I might have to enter just to take her down a notch," said Mishael. "She's bound to be out of practice after all those hours in Medical on her internship." His rivalry with his sister was all the more real for being friendly.

"Well, you know better than to underestimate her," Abishai answered. "If she enters, she'll be in it to win. If she can take you down along the way it will be icing on the cake." He thought about his daughter with a momentary flash of parental pride. She'd grown from a lanky, awkward teenager with boundless energy into a beautiful, compassionate, woman, driven to be the best at everything she did. She was a taller reflection of her mother, too focused on her medical career to notice the attention of most of the eligible young men on the *Nai'a*. She was also rapidly becoming the favorite doctor of the ship's children.

He was just as proud of Mishael, recently promoted to lieutenant. The discipline of military training had helped him focus and given him a solid sense of purpose. Promotion opportunities could be rare, but ship's officers often took a break from service in the chain of command to return to a technical specialty. Mishael had high scores in simulated helm competitions, and his size and strength made him a natural at damage control. Abishai wasn't keen on the idea of his son piloting one of the rumored new sting ships, but he knew it wasn't his decision.

"What's Mom cooking for supper?" asked Mishael. Even though he had his own quarters now he took half his evening meals with his parents and sister.

"Something that smells like curry has been simmering in the slow cooker since this morning, and I have instructions to make a batch of basmati rice when I get home," Abishai answered. "Don't be late or we'll start without you."

***

Three weeks later, Jarman Lal, Julian Garrity, Val O'Clair, and several other pilots gathered in the aft boat bay to check over the sting ship prototype. The ten-meter vessel was built around a recoilless rail gun and coaxial laser. The pilot would literally sit on top of the weapon housing and put feet on either side of it. The hexagonal hull had external hard points for up to six missiles, fuel tanks, or high-density capacitors to charge the rail gun and laser. A typical load-out would be a mix of ordnance based on the threat environment.

"It's a lot of punch in a small package," said Val, running his hand along the hull. "I'm sure she'll be nimble, but it's not going to take much damage to put her out of the fight."

"We're counting on agility and a low radar signature for survivability," said Jarman. "Most missiles won't be optimized to track something this small. Random jinks will make targeting with other weapons difficult. Our best information on Lalande says they won't be expecting anything like these ships, so we'll have surprise on our side initially. Julian has the most time in small fighters so he's our test pilot. Val will pilot the pinnace while

I man the sensor suite. The rest of you clear the bay and we'll see what she can do."

Julian strapped himself into the cramped space, pulled the clear canopy down, and sealed it. He checked his flight suit and helmet seals as well. The ship would maintain a breathable atmosphere in the cockpit, but he wasn't going to trust it on the first test flight. He flipped the main power bus and ran through the flight pre-checks. Once he was satisfied that all systems were green, he opened a com channel. "Sting One ready for launch."

"*Nai'a* One ready for launch," Val echoed from the pinnace. "Boat bay control, proceed with launch sequence."

"Roger, evacuation commencing now, two minutes to doors open."

Julian double checked his readouts and the oxygen connection to his flight suit while he waited. He felt a minor rumble as the boat bay doors slid fully open.

"Releasing docking clamp on Stinger One, now," said boat bay control. Julian felt and heard the click as the *Nai'a* turned his little sting ship free. He checked his clearance and feathered his thrusters to raise the ship off the deck and compensate for the momentum imparted by the *Nai'a's* rotation and .1G of thrust. The combination could be tricky, but Julian had more launches than he could count under his belt. He flew the sting ship out into the black then maneuvered carefully to clear the ice shield supports and the shield itself. At a kilometer clearance he flipped the little ship and matched the *Nai'a's* course, waiting for the pinnace.

Val soon pulled the pinnace into a matching course a few hundred meters away. "Sting One, we have you visually and on sensors, you are cleared to proceed with the test profile."

"Roger *Nai'a* One," Julian answered. He gripped his controls lightly and accelerated away, gradually pushing the ship up to a full 10G thrust. His flight suit and training helped him compensate and keep from passing out. He spun the ship in a wide spiraling arc to head back toward the *Nai'a*. He was surprised by how small the massive ship had grown, and his face split with a grin. The thrust to weight ratio of the sting ship made it a hot rocket indeed. He pointed the nose at a spot just beyond the pinnace. "*Nai'a* One, stand by for a full thrust pass," he called.

He flashed by the pinnace, then flipped the ship and burned at full thrust again to kill his momentum. He put the sting ship through a series of maneuvers until he was confident in the handling. He nodded to himself in satisfaction then sped away from the *Nai'a* and pinnace until he was twenty kilometers distant. "*Nai'a* One, Sting One, ready for laser tag when you are."

Two hours later Jarman, Val, Julian and the rest of pilots gathered in the aft engineering meeting room to go over the numbers. "I knew from the simulations the sting ship would be nimble, but I didn't really believe it until I felt it in my bones," said Julian. "Nothing I've flown could match it in a dogfight."

"Based on our attempts to track and tag you with the pinnace's laser I believe it," answered Jarman. "We couldn't get any significant dwell time. I also believe we're incredibly fortunate to have your services as a pilot. I've never seen anyone dance a ship around the way you did. We had zero damaging hits to, let's see...twenty four out of thirty for you. Val is a top-notch pilot and nothing in the Lalande system is likely to be any more agile than the pinnace. Did you have any technical issues?"

"None," answered Julian. "All systems were rock solid. We'll want to do some live fire to stress the rail gun and laser. If we have any problems, I expect it to be with those systems. Assuming the main weapons are what we hope, we'll have a lot of tactical options." The group spent the next few hours enthusiastically discussing the possibilities.

***

"I don't like it, Kevin," said the captain. "We should have received the first communications package four weeks ago and three more since then."

"I agree," answered the first officer. "Mr. Barboa and I and the coms officer have been over the equipment multiple times. We even ran the pinnace out and sent a simulated signal at the expected strength. The coms array picked it up fine. Our daily high-power pings are going out on schedule. I don't have an answer."

The captain's PCOM beeped the tone of a bridge alert. She raised one eyebrow and tapped it to open the channel. "Captain here."

"We received the first burst of data from Lalande, captain. Integrity, thirty percent." Captain Brelling knew the burst would repeat every ten minutes for the next twenty-four hours. They should be able to resolve a clean copy within a few hours.

"Roger, transfer what you have to a data chip and have it delivered to my office." She closed the connection and put through a quick message to Lisandra Redding. She drummed her fingers on the desk. "I still have a bad feeling about this. There's no reason to delay the communication packets four weeks. At least we know the problem isn't on our end. I'll schedule a ship's council meeting for tomorrow."

***

The next day, Captain Brelling filled coffee cups around the table then took a sip of her own. "We've all had time to go over the messages in the data packet. I've asked Lisandra to give us a report on the cybersecurity side."

The hacker used her mini-comp, hardwired into the room's data jack as usual, to pull up a set of statistics on the wall display. "Mr. Literal and I both analyzed the data set on a sand-boxed system. Bottom line, it's nothing but the text files. Only one of them was encrypted, addressed to the captain. With the low bandwidth at this distance, the risk of malware is low. Mr. Literal did note, the packet is forty percent smaller than the historic average for Lalande. You also know it's four weeks late. I would expect a late package to be larger than average, but I don't know if those data points are actually cause for concern."

"Thank you, Lisandra," said the captain. "The encrypted message I have purports to be from the chief of the Long Boat Free Trade Syndicate

Lalande office. The encryption protocol is out of date, but valid. The message itself is a short welcome to the system, but devoid of useful information. We also received a standard navigational update and communications protocols. My overall impression is we're getting the bare minimum of information from the system. Did anyone else find anything unusual?"

Hubble Spears frowned thoughtfully. "The business messages seem innocuous enough. If anything, I'm surprised there's nothing in there to address. Usually at least a few companies go out of business, or change hands, and I'd have some instructions for the syndicate office to set up alternatives. This time all our delivery contracts still have valid customers so there's no need. Like your message set, it's basically a nothing-burger. It contains all the right forms but it's about as useful as a one-legged stool. I also expected a summary of trade opportunities from the syndicate office, but there's nothing."

The Chief Alder spoke up next. "I'm sensing a pattern. I normally get a list of leave possibilities and an estimate of cold sleep passenger numbers. Instead, I got a short welcome like you, Captain. I'm no investigator, but someone sanitized that package of most of its useful information, if it was ever there to begin with."

The captain nodded; her expression grim. "I agree, Persephone, I wanted to make sure you all had the same impression. Someone is trying to convince us everything is just fine in an unconvincing fashion. The clincher is no message from the *Kilimanjaro*. The captain would send me an encrypted summary of the progress of their investigation even if was over and done. From the message, you wouldn't know a long boat had been in system. We need to ramp up preparations for a hostile environment. It's possible the *Kilimanjaro* ran into a problem during the crossing, but I doubt it."

The first officer raised his hand. "I gave the fabrication team the go ahead to start manufacturing sting ships. The Initial tests exceeded expectations. With a few small tweaks, the design will be solid. Based on our last update on Lalande, no one operates a large carrier or small ships like these. They should come as a surprise if anyone attacks us."

"We can't and won't fight an entire star system," replied the captain, "but we'll prepare to defend ourselves. We need to come up with options for the most likely scenarios. My first priority is the safety of this ship and crew. If the Lalande government won't cooperate, we won't even stop in system, but we have an obligation to find out the status of the *Kilimanjaro*. We hold a big hammer in the form of interdiction, and Lalande knows from experience what that means. There are bound to be bad actors in Lalande, but I doubt the people as a whole want another three-hundred years of economic isolation."

She pursed her lips thoughtfully. "How dumb do we want to play it? I could ask for explanations, but they would know we're wise to their games."

"What do we know about the current government?" asked Persephone. "I know they replaced the dictatorship that earned them the first interdiction, but that was centuries ago."

"What we have is about fifty years out of date," answered Commander Hartley. "The government is a constitutional monarchy established by the House of Bancroft. The hereditary monarch wields actual power as head of state, but legislature and laws are the business of a three-house parliament: the House of Lords, the House of Merchants, and the House of Workers. Uriah Bancroft successfully petitioned to have the interdiction lifted after establishing and stabilizing the system of government. His descendants have ruled, with varying levels of personal power, ever since. It sounds like a complete mess to me, but they make it work. The chaos of the interdiction years left a lot of hard feelings toward the Long Boat Free Trade Syndicate. It's not too surprising the Restoration found fertile ground here. Still, the government has been very careful to maintain a good relationship with the syndicate ever since."

"I have personal experience dealing with the Lalande government," said the captain. "More years ago than I want to admit, we were nearly sabotaged with a bio agent while in the Lalande system. The system authorities took swift action against the perpetrators. They can be prickly to deal with, but I have no complaints about the way they cleaned up the mess. Unfortunately, my part in thwarting the attack resulted in a personal vendetta. Nicholas Withers, AKA 'Gerald Minnick', nearly killed us all on the trip to Tau Ceti, as you all know. His father spent years in prison for the bio agent attack. Now Nicholas faces the same thing along with his Restoration cronies in cold sleep.

"The Bancroft in power back then was sincerely apologetic. He gave our captain an audience to apologize in person, and provided security out of the Crown Guards for the rest of our time in system. They were exceedingly professional and capable. By now, it's likely one of his descendants has succeeded him. The rules of succession are somewhat murky to me, but it's supposed to be 'most capable' rather than simply next in line."

Hubble Spears nodded. "I remember the incident. Another interesting thing about Lalande is their terraforming efforts. By an accident of cosmic positioning, they started further ahead than any other populated system. New Dawn will likely be the first truly colonized planet outside of Sol because of its position and water content. The terraforming efforts continued even during interdiction. It's a point of pride with them."

Captain Brelling drummed her fingers on the table. "What we know doesn't match up to the information in the packet. Until we know more, I don't want to tip our hand. We'll send an equally bland reply and see how things develop. We'll ramp up preparations now and refine our strategy as we go. I don't think we'll get a true read on the situation until we can talk to our people in Lalande."

Chapter 19 – Heliopause

February 15th, AD 3208
Long Boat Nai'a – Lalande System Heliopause
Bridge

Captain Brelling checked her display. Nothing showed this far out. Lalande was a remarkably clean system compared to Tau Ceti. Also, industry and habitation were concentrated in the inner system, especially around New Dawn. Official communications were still frustratingly bland, but she hoped to do something about it shortly. She looked over at the coms officer expectantly, but the Lieutenant Carlson continued to work, head down. After an interminable few minutes, the Lieutenant looked up. "No return signal from the buoy, Ma'am," he said. "I'm not even getting a reflection of our own tight beam."

"Keep trying," she replied. She switched her display to repeat the coms console. After another thirty minutes of trying, they still didn't have a reply from the syndicate buoy. She suspected it was no longer there.

"Ma'am, I have an incoming laser carrier signal," said the coms officer. "It's not from the buoy, but something in-system from us. Do you want me to open the channel?"

"Sensors, do we have a ship on scan in that direction?" asked the captain.

"Nothing on passive or active, Ma'am. Should I try a high-power pulse?"

"Negative, let's see what they have to say first. Coms, open the channel, audio only to my console. Keep it segregated from our data net and keep the beam low power. I don't want anything leaking through to the inner system."

The channel opened with a pop. "Long Boat *Nai'a*, this is special envoy of The Bancroft, Rolland Dunleavy," a professional voice stated. "I'm transmitting my bona fides and need to speak with your captain, over."

The captain's eyebrows tried to rise but she schooled her expression and hit her transmit button. "Mr. Dunleavy, this is Captain Brelling. Is it possible you used to be Lieutenant Dunleavy of the Crown Guards, over?"

There was a brief pause. "It is, if old memories serve me. You've come up in the world since we last met, Captain. I recall meeting a brash and skilled shuttle pilot by the name of Ensign Brelling when I held that title."

Captain Brelling muted her pickup. "Do the bona fides check out?" she asked the comms officer who nodded. "Open the video channel." Rolland Dunleavy's face soon filled her screen and he smiled. The years had changed him into a lean and world-worn version of the fresh-faced lieutenant she remembered.

"You look well, Rolland. I can't say I expected to run into you this far from New Dawn orbit."

"At least you didn't say I haven't changed. You bear your own years remarkably well. Of course, you've experienced fewer than I have at the speeds you travel. I'll use that as my excuse for looking older."

The captain shook her head slightly, remembering Rolland's silver tongue, but wanting to keep the conversation professional. "What brings you our way?" she asked. We aren't picking up your vessel on normal scan."

"I count that as good news," he answered. "The pod I'm in is designed for stealth and I'm on a ballistic trajectory. I'm going to have to beg the favor of being picked up. I have no maneuvering capability and limited environmental capacity, so it's a matter of some urgency. I assume you have my course and speed from your com laser."

The captain's eyebrows did go up this time. The man didn't lack for courage. "What were you going to do if we didn't pick you up?"

"Fortunately, it's an academic matter now. I'll fill you in when we can talk in person. I'll just say that things are not as they seem in the Lalande system. I'm sure you already figured that out, but I have some details for you which should be helpful."

"Very well," said the captain. "I'll sign off now to get the rescue mission in motion. Transmit the specifications of your pod. Do you have a space suit?"

"Negative," he answered, "and I don't have an airlock either. Sorry to be a pain, but we put this mission together in a rush."

"I have an overabundance of pilots and smart engineers. We'll figure it out."

***

As it turned out the answer was straight-forward. A few tweaks to the pinnace's catcher's mitt allowed Jarman to snag Dunleavy's pod after matching vectors in the pinnace. They touched down in the aft boat bay a few hours later. The three-meter pod was dead black and covered in radar absorbent material with the exception of a communications array and a small set of sensors. Several minutes later, *Nai'a* engineers were obliged to literally break the seal on the lone entry hatch, and extract Envoy Dunleavy.

Jarman and an engineer hauled him out into the light gravity of the boat bay, and he thanked each of them. His plain black ship suit had wrinkles on its wrinkles. The first officer was standing by and stuck out his hand. "Welcome aboard, Envoy Dunleavy. Captain Brelling asked me to escort you to guest quarters where you can freshen up -- unless your business is too urgent?"

"Please just call me Rolland," the compactly muscular, graying man replied. "I'll accept your offer. I know I'm overripe. The pod's facilities are, in a word, rudimentary. My business is urgent, but there's time to get cleaned up."

They made their way forward, chatting about the *Nai'a* and Dunleavy's memories of her last visit to Lalande.

***

Two hours later, Commander Hartley escorted a fresher, but slightly unsteady, Envoy Dunleavy to the captain's conference room. Captain Brelling surprised everyone in the room, including herself, by greeting the envoy with a long hug. Rolland returned it after a moment's hesitation. The strength in her arms surprised and pleased him. His legs were wobbly after ten days in free-fall, and she was rock steady. "Sorry if I embarrassed you, Rolland," the captain said after releasing him and making introductions. "I must remember you even more fondly than I thought."

"I can stand a little embarrassment at your hands," he replied with a wink. Jarman, the first officer, Mr. Barboa, Julian Garrity, and Chief Engineer Owen Halsey observed the byplay with varying degrees of shock. A side of their captain most of them wouldn't have dreamed of was showing.

"Much as I would enjoy reminiscing, Rolland, it will have to wait," said the captain. "What can you tell us about the situation in the system?"

The envoy frowned in concentration as he thought about where to begin. "I'll catch you up on the political situation, then we can talk about recent events. The Bancroft you met long since abdicated and we've been through two more since. One was assassinated and the other also abdicated to pursue other interests. The Bancroft now in office is Wallace the Third. I represent The Bancroft and have the authority to enter into agreements with foreign powers on his behalf. Parliament and The Bancroft generally get along well. That said, we've never lacked for dissident factions. Two of the last three Bancrofts living long enough to retire is an anomaly. Until the long boat *Kilimanjaro* arrived fifteen years ago, things were relatively quiet in the system.

"It came as a shock when the captain of the *Kilimanjaro* told us several Lalande citizens were accused of terrorism and attacking a long boat in the Tau Ceti system. When he revealed the *Nai'a* was the target and on the way here with prisoners, we started making connections. The Withers family vehemently denies any involvement, but can't or won't account for the location of several members. Unfortunately, our best efforts to ferret out any real evidence of a connection to the attacks came up empty. The *Kilimanjaro* stayed for a year but she had to return to Sol to honor her contracts. There's a small team of investigators they left with the Long Boat Free Trade Syndicate office. The team's been chipping away, but haven't come up with much of anything either.

"The Bancroft and I both thought it was much ado about nothing until your incoming signal reached us. We were expecting the *Nai'a*, but you're a couple of years ahead of schedule. We *weren't* expecting the attempted coup that followed the news of your impending arrival. I believe you caught the rebels off guard and forced them to move before they were ready. Regardless, they came within a whisker of killing The Bancroft and seized control of several major habitats. It's been a running fight since then, with forces loyal to the crown slowly gaining the upper hand. It's still a mess, but most of the people who were duped or blackmailed into helping the rebels are now fighting on our side.

"There was an ugly incident a month ago. The rebels took control of New Dawn dome Epsilon early in the coup attempt. The locals didn't take kindly to the action and put together a plan to take the dome back. When the rebels realized they were losing, they collapsed the dome and took out the main power grid before attempting to escape in a shuttle. They were shot down by the local militia. Twenty percent of the dome population died. Fortunately, the site was originally all underground and most of the people were below when the dome collapsed. When word got out to the rest of the system, the rebels found themselves dealing with insurrections of their own on every habitat they've taken."

Captain Brelling grimaced. "Unfortunately, we're all too familiar with the lengths these people will go to. What you've told us explains a lot about the lack of information we've received on the way in. I assume the rebels captured the long-distance communications facilities immediately."

Rolland nodded. "We've mostly cleaned them out of the New Dawn orbit habitats, but they still have a good foothold in the outer system and they still control the outer communications arrays."

"They've been feeding us a whole lot of nothing and we've returned the favor," stated the captain. "I'm sure they're smart enough to know their accomplices failed to take the *Nai'a* and we're not here to lend them a hand. I need to fill you in on what we learned about the organization behind the attacks on us and, we believe, your insurrection."

She proceeded give the envoy a detailed rundown of the Restoration's actions in Tau Ceti and goals as far as they could be discerned. By the time she was finished Rolland was nodding thoughtfully.

"It fits," he said. "The Bancroft would never go along with dismantling the Long Boat Free Trade Syndicate. The honor of his house would be forfeit. The rebels seized the *Nessie*, our government owned long boat, early on and burned out of system on a course for Sol. We had nothing in place to stop them. We doubt most of the crew was part of the rebellion so we wouldn't have shot at the ship in any case."

"I imagine you came here to both warn us and coordinate action against the Restoration rebels?" asked the captain.

"Aye, that I did. We're ready to make a push against the rebels in the outer system. The Bancroft sent me to rendezvous with you knowing the *Nai'a* will be a lightning rod. The rebels will have to concentrate their space combat power to try to take the ship. It will give us an opportunity to deal their mobile forces a decisive defeat." He slid a data chip across to the captain. "This contains everything we know about their ships and people. It also lists the forces The Bancroft has at his disposal. He's called in every personal favor, and used every ounce of goodwill he has to scrape together enough ships to give us a force advantage. Still, it's going to be a hard fight. With the *Nai'a* in the middle of it, we can't guarantee your safety."

Captain Brelling passed the chip to her first officer. "My people will analyze this while you get a meal and some rest," she said. "I'll walk you to one of our restaurants and you can tell me the story of how you ended up in a life pod on a ballistic trajectory to nowhere.”

“Do you still have the fish and chips place?”

“Absolutely!” She took his arm and led him from the room.

Commander Hartley looked at his compatriots with a slight smile. “Lisandra Reddick and Greer Kensing will do bad things to me if I don’t let them clear this chip before we read it. Lisandra’s on the way up. If she’s her usual efficient self, we’ll be in business shortly.”

***

Rolland Dunleavy dipped a perfectly fried chip in tartar sauce, took a bite and chewed appreciatively. “It’s hard to believe twelve hours ago I was floating toward infinity wondering if I would make contact,” he said.

“I’m not sure I want to know this, but what were you going to do if you didn’t?” asked Captain Brelling.

“It wasn’t quite a suicide mission, but close,” he answered. “The pod has an emergency low-power cold sleep capability. In theory, I would have hooked myself up to three different IVs and a few other uncomfortable connections, hit the go button, and gone under. I had enough power to keep me alive in that state for about six months. Hopefully, long enough for The Bancroft to regain control of the outer system and send a rescue ship. It’s a new process with technology just in from Sol. They say the survival rate is better than fifty percent.”

The captain swallowed a tasty bite of breaded cod and shook her head. “You took a big chance and we appreciate it. Without your intel, we’d be flying blind into a very sticky situation. How did you get the pod headed our way with the rebels watching?”

“We have a hush-hush base on one of the minor moons of the outermost planet, Kojin,” he replied. “I took a stealthy courier there with the pod and they realigned a linear accelerator to sling shot me around Kojin and toward the *Nai’a*. It was a ride I won’t soon forget. It looked like I could have reached out and touched the cloud tops on the way by. If Kojin hadn't been in the right place, we couldn't have pulled it off."

"Maybe you can set up a business and sell gas giant thrill rides when this is all over."

"I will happily return to teaching at New Leeds, thank you. I thought my adventuring days were long past, but when The Bancroft calls, you answer."

"I'm not familiar with an emergency cold sleep protocol," said Captain Brelling. "I'm sure our cold sleep department will be interested."

"You're welcome to the pod and everything in it," answered Rolland. I never want to see it again. The cold sleep protocol is public domain, so you can pull all the specifications and instructions from the module in the pod. It's designed as a last-ditch chance to survive a ship disaster."

"It might be worth the space and weight to outfit the pinnace with a kit," the captain mused. "You should get some rest, and I need to get back and see what my tactical experts have come up with. It's been good to see you again, Rolland. Promise me another date before you have to leave us?"

He grinned. "This is a date?"

"As close to one as I've had in a long time."

"I promise you a real date, one that most people would recognize as one, soon."

"I'll hold you to that."

***

The first officer had The Bancroft's deployments and the known rebel forces depicted on the holographic display when Captain Brelling returned to the conference room. "Give me the tour, Kevin, she said, taking her seat.

"The general situation is just what the envoy said. Rebel forces are converging on our course to gain control of the *Nai'a* and add it to the Restoration fleet. They shouldn't be aware of our defensive capabilities. The Restoration operates between thirty and forty ships of various types.

The most capable are five Lalande Security Force corvettes that went over to the enemy side. Those ships have missile and laser armament. They also carry an assault shuttle and a heavy squad of marines. How loyal the crews are to the rebel/Restoration cause is an open question. The rest of the ships are repurposed mining or cargo vessels with cobbled together armament. Based on what the Restoration put together in Tau Ceti, we don't want to underestimate their effectiveness.

"The Bancroft has thirty-two ships, including eight corvettes, sortieing to attack the rebels when they concentrate to take the *Nai'a*. The Bancroft's other ships are a mix of personal security craft and armed courier vessels. In general, his ships are higher quality and more heavily armed. His tacticians recommend that we play dumb as long as we can, and even appear to cooperate with the hijacking if possible. They'll look for an opportune moment to jump the rebel force."

"What's your opinion of their chances?" the captain asked Mr. Barboa.

"With what they have on the board," Barboa answered, "The Bancroft's force will likely take heavy casualties, but win. The problem with the way they want to go about it, is they're the hammer and we're the anvil. The *Nai'a* is going to take a lot of damage if we're just passive. Also, remember the nuclear attack Julian Garrity stopped back in Tau Ceti. You can bet your life at least two of the enemy ships will be tasked with destroying the *Nai'a* if they start to lose."

"I hope you big brains have some better options," said the captain. "We haven't been working up a squadron of sting ships and all our other surprises so we can sit idly by waiting for the Bancroft to save us. Also, I have no intention of letting these people board the ship like we did in Tau Ceti. They're the type who have no qualms about using bio-agents, and I'm not risking our people again."

Mr. Barboa nodded. "A lot will depend on how good The Bancroft's fleet commander is. I don't think we should risk trying to contact them before we get the ball rolling. They'll need to be flexible enough to see what's happening and react properly. If we get it right, what's coming will be a big surprise to both forces. Our best chance will be to hit them when the whole force is still in-system from us. We'll only have the inward arc to defend. If we let them in close, the geometry gets much more complex."

"Show me some possibilities then," she answered. "I want to brief the envoy on at least three courses of action and get his opinion. He was a brilliant tactician back in the day."

***

The next morning after a breakfast of fresh strawberry waffles in the Alpha Section galley with the tactical team, Rolland Dunleavy gathered with them again in the captain's conference room. Mr. Barboa first described the sting ship squadron and its capabilities. "Those must have been the tarp-covered lumps I saw in the boat bay," said the envoy. "I wondered what you were hiding."

"We weren't sure you were a friend just yet," said Mr. Barboa. "If we want to survive the coming fight intact, those ships need to come as a shock to our adversaries." He went on to describe the other preparations and possible ways to use the new capabilities against the rebels. Rolland asked several insightful questions and made suggestions as the morning wore on.

When the session wound down, Rolland Dunleavy leaned back and nodded thoughtfully. "You've put yourselves on a much better footing than I would have imagined," he said. "I like the idea of engaging the enemy before they can flank you. It simplifies both targeting and defense. It also takes full advantage of the shadow of your massive ice shield to protect the *Nai'a*. I hope the enemy commander is as ignorant as I was of your offensive capability, but I think you're safe there. It's been centuries since anyone thought of a long boat as a military threat. As for the commander of The Bancroft's fleet, I trained him in tactics myself. I think he'll adapt quickly to the situation and take full advantage. Aggression is one of the hallmarks of The Bancroft Himself after all."

"The Bancroft Himself is commanding the fleet?" said the first officer incredulously.

"Desperate times call for desperate measures. The Bancroft's hold on this system is tenuous and he didn't trust anyone else with this command. His participation is a state secret, but sooner or later he'll be missed and everyone with a functioning brain will draw the correct conclusion. I tried to advise him against it, but he really is the best fleet commander in the system. Before he became the Bancroft, he commanded a fleet that cleaned out a pirate nest based in the moons of Kojin. That's how we obtained the base I launched from. When you attack, I have confidence he'll follow up with everything he has. For the sake of redundancy though, I have a set of brevity codes we can use to quickly communicate the general situation to him. If we transmit just after your first salvo, you'll retain the element of surprise."

"It's going to be a matter of timing and targeting," said Mr. Barboa. "It's time we deployed the sensor array we've been working on. We'll suspend it from the ice shield frame using a combination of power and data cables. The array is an order of magnitude more capable than our probes, even in passive mode. The information you gave us on the corvettes' signature and the kluged-together nature of their other ships should allow us to discriminate targets and concentrate on the most capable with our first salvo. Something I'm concerned about is hitting The Bancroft's fleet by accident. Some of the enemy ships are going to dodge the sting ships' rail gun rounds. They could be hazardous to our friends if they're following in the enemy's course."

"From what we know of the current geometry," said Jarman gesturing to the display. "The Bancroft's force should be arriving at enough of an angle to keep them safe. A lot can change in the next few days. It really depends on what the rebel fleet does."

"All the more reason to get the array in place," said the captain. "The timing and targeting depend on knowing the enemy dispositions. I don't expect anything but the corvettes to be particularly stealthy. We should pick up heat signatures within the next few days."

***

Mishael trudged wearily through the maintenance corridor between frames seventy-three and seventy-four. He was regretting the decision to make the five-kilometer walk to his quarters after a long twelve-hour shift of maintenance and training in the boat bay. Sensors in the dark passageway noted his presence and lights turned on as he went. He checked manual readouts at several monitoring points along the way, a habit instilled in him during his stints in engineering and the Biome department. He was making a notation on his PCOM about a low voltage reading when something like wet sandpaper rasped across the back of his neck and something heavy landed on his shoulders. Mishael's high-pitched scream echoed down the corridor as he grabbed at his neck and danced an impromptu jig. His hands just grazed soft fur, but Lionel was off down the corridor like a shot before he could catch hold. "You're going to use up one of your nine lives scaring me like that!" Mishael yelled at Lionel's departing tail. He bent over and put his hands on his knees while his heart rate returned to normal. Suddenly he felt wide awake again. He kept a sharp lookout on his surroundings the rest of the way to his quarters.

Chapter 20 – Bag of Tricks

February 20th, AD 3208
Long Boat Nai'a – Outer Lalande System
Aft Boat Bay

Shanyah carefully torqued the last bolt on the sting ship's capacitor pack and ran a check on the super conductor connections. Everything looked good, so she gave her son a thumbs up and packed up her tool kit. Boat bay officer Lieutenant Mishael Bonaparte' nodded gravely and made a quick annotation on his data pad. He'd wanted desperately to pilot one of the lethal little ships, but neither his reflexes nor his size allowed it. His size and strength did, however, make him a perfect boat bay officer and he took to the job with typical determination. Having his mother work for him as a sting ship technician felt decidedly weird, but they were both enjoying the time together. Boat bay officer was a new position. Normally a rating would run the bay, but the sting ship squadron required rapid rearming and refueling by a large team of technicians. It all required enough people and coordination that the captain decided to put Mishael in charge.

Tension on the ship was ramping up. Everyone knew a confrontation was coming. Mishael rechecked his screen and nodded in satisfaction. The ships were fully loaded with the most probable weapon mix, and ready to launch at the captain's command.

The pilots waited in a nearby compartment outfitted as a ready room. Mr. Barboa regularly visited them in person with updates and advice. In between, they strapped themselves into simulation pods and rehearsed tactical scenarios.

Today, Captain Brelling showed up in the ready room and the pilots all popped to attention. "At ease," the captain said with a wave. "Everyone take your seats. I know from experience waiting is the hardest part. I'm sorry you haven't been able to take the ships out for exercises lately, but you understand the need for secrecy. You're going to be a nasty surprise for these Restoration vermin, but only if we can keep your capabilities under wraps.

"We've been tracking the enemy force through a combination of sloppy radio discipline and heat signatures. About an hour ago they executed a burn to put them on a reciprocal course to ours. I don't have to tell you what a favor they're doing us by coming right down our throats like this. In addition, they're concentrated, which is smart for defense, but limits their offensive options." She activated the room's tactical display repeater.

"Mr. Barboa and Envoy Dunleavy both believe they will flip and execute a burn designed to match our trajectory approximately here. I'm tempted to let them get that close and get up-the-kilt shots, but it would put the engagement zone closer to the ship than I'm comfortable with. If the situation develops as expected, we'll engage them approximately here." She indicated the position on the display. "They'll hit that zone in about eighteen hours. Steward Holcomb is on her way with a hot meal, then I expect you to get a good eight hours' sleep. You know the mental exercises for inducing slumber, use them. Well rested pilots have better reaction times. I want you at your best. I know many of you are combat veterans. That, and your tactical simulation scores, give me great confidence in your abilities. I'll be praying for all of you. God Bless!"

After the captain left the room, Commander Julian Garrity stood up and looked around at his pilots. "Everything she said goes double for me. We stand between this ship and destruction. Trust your training and rehearsals, and trust each other. We'll meet for a preflight briefing here in twelve hours. Dismissed!"

Steward Holcomb rolled a cart through the door and the pilots quickly reconfigured the room for chow. Stuffed shells with garlic bread sticks and

Caeser salad were soon the focus of attention, between friendly insults and speculation on the rebels' capabilities.

***

Though it wasn't technically her watch, Captain Brelling sat in the bridge's command chair projecting her typical calm. Inside, her pancreas was having a battle with her latest cup of coffee and losing. So far, the enemy force was cooperating, which made her even more nervous. The surprises she and the crew of the *Nai'a* were ready to unleash couldn't make the battle entirely one-sided. The Restoration had proved themselves both resilient and resourceful. Overconfidence was a rat poison she refused to indulge in.

Chief Nance looked up from the new tactical console on the bridge. "The enemy force will enter the engagement zone in five minutes. I estimate optimal execution of engagement plan three in approximately eight minutes. Targets are resolving, designating corvettes as bogies one through five."

Individual ships began to populate the main display. First, the corvettes in a diamond pattern of four ships surrounded what was likely the command vessel. Next, various ships winked into existence around them. "We have firm targeting solutions on nineteen ships, tentative on twelve more. We're likely missing a few in the sensor shadow of the forward ships. Engagement plan three is still the optimal attack sequence," Chief Nance announced.

"Confirm engagement plan three," answered the captain. "Sting ship squadron is ready. You have the call on execution, chief." A few more ship icons popped up on the display. All of them were within the expected zone.

"Sensors, any sign of force Bancroft?" queried the captain.

"We have a cluster of faint heat signatures on this vector." An emerald green line appeared on the display, slightly offset from the enemy formation.

The captain relaxed fractionally. There wasn't any way to know if the range would work out in their favor, but at least they wouldn't be firing into The Bancroft's formation. Her thoughts were interrupted by the coms officer. "Ma'am, I have an incoming request from someone claiming to be Commodore Yates of the Free Lalande Space Force."

Captain Brelling took a moment, pursing her lips. "I suppose it's less suspicious to take the call than ignore it. Chief Nance, execute engagement plan three as we discussed, regardless of my conversation. Coms, open the channel to my console, tight video feed of my face only." While the com officer made the connection, she reflected on the decision to have Chief Nance start the ball and control the ship's defenses. He was consistently the best in the simulated war games at timing a strike. He had an intuitive feel for time and space relationships. Now that she was going to be busy distracting the enemy commander, the decision looked better than ever. She almost snorted to herself when she thought about Chief Nance taking her role and talking to the commodore. Knowing Nance, he'd probably brazen it out. The connection light on her console went green and she smoothed her features.

Commodore Yates was an older slightly-pudgy man in a black uniform heavily decorated with gold braid and several rows of medals. Given the recent genesis of the "Lalande Freedom Space Force" Captain Brelling wondered exactly what combat actions the man had earned the decorations in. At the moment, he had what he probably thought was a friendly smile on his face. Rolland Dunleavy leaned close from his jump seat and whispered, "Benjamin Yates, he's as sincere as a backhand compliment and very direct in his tactics."

Captain Brelling put on her own friendly but professional face and opened her end of the channel. "Commodore Yates, I'm Captain Brelling of the Long Boat *Nai'a*. We didn't expect a greeting party quite this far out. All the system communication indicated a fairly quiet arrival."

Commodore Yates' smile grew slightly wider. "I'm afraid the situation in the system is actually unstable at the moment. I've been tasked with escorting the *Nai'a* in-system to prevent any unfortunate incidents. My ships will take up station around the *Nai'a* and match your course. With your permission, I'd like to pay you a visit in my corvette's shuttle."

"We appreciate the escort. Once your ships are in position, we'll welcome you properly," answered the captain. She kicked herself mentally for coming too close to the truth. The count-down clock to engagement plan three read thirty seconds. "I look forward to learning more about the current situation," she continued, studying her adversary.

"I'll have my staff give you a full update," the commodore said, nodding agreeably. His eyes flicked suddenly to the left. After a moment's pause his expression abruptly changed. "Our scans indicate an anomaly in front of your ice shield, explain."

Captain Brelling had no problem producing a chuckle. "We thickened our ice shield for a fast passage so I'm sure we picked up all manner of interstellar debris. Perhaps that's what your sensors are picking up." The countdown reached zero as she finished. The commodore hadn't looked convinced, but before he could make any more demands, the com channel cut out. Captain Brelling said a silent prayer for her pilots as she watched engagement plan three unfold on the tactical plot.

***

When the tactical countdown hit zero, several things happened at once. Chief Nance's execution signal reached eight stealthed mines dropped behind the decelerating *Nai'a*. As one, they pulsed the enemy formation with wide spectrum jamming, spending their capacitors in a two second maelstrom that blinded nearly every sensor in the fleet. At the same time twelve sting ships slid from behind the *Nai'a's* ice shield and fired. Their first laser shots were timed perfectly to arrive with the wave of jamming. Twelve enemy ships, including the five corvettes, spewed molten metal and atmosphere. Each sting ship followed up their lasers with two rapid rail gun shots and a two-missile salvo. Using the real-time feed from the *Nai'a's* now active sensor array, they targeted the five corvettes with another railgun shot each, then spread the rest of their ordnance across the remaining ships. With their ammunition and capacitors spent, eight of the sting ships flipped and headed for the *Nai'a*. Four snugged into rapid recharging hard points. The other four entered the open boat bay to rearm. Mishael, and his crews in hard suits jumped to the task.

Julian Garrity took station in his sting ship just outside the ice shield. His ship and three others were outfitted with pods of six small anti-missile guided rockets each. He watched his plot for incoming fire, jinking to a new position every second or so.

Even as the sting ships were taking their initial shots, the *Nai'a* rang like a bell. Sixteen spring-loaded launchers kicked capital ship missiles out and away from the ship. Chief Nance fed the missiles targeting updates as their drives kicked in and they sped toward the enemy.

***

The 'Free Lalande Space Force' corvette *Pellucidar* jerked hard enough to throw Commander Don Bollicks against his shock harness and make him bite his lip. Atmosphere whistled out of the bridge as he slammed his helmet down and activated the seal. Half the lights on the engineering station were red, but somehow his ship's sensors were still operable. He watched in horror as their formation came apart on the tactical plot. The flagship icon was blood red and appeared to be drifting on a ballistic course. "Helm!" he shouted, "evasive action now and watch the other ships." His helmsman struggled to cancel the beginnings of a tumble and change course. Something slammed the ship again, adding to his problems. Bollicks ignored everything but the tactical plot. He realized he was probably the senior officer with an effective ship left in the fleet. The other four corvettes were out of action. Several other ships were drifting hulks, and the survivors were scattering to avoid a salvo of missiles bearing down from the *Nai'a*. He keyed the feet channel, "All captains, this is Commander Bollicks. Engage the *Nai'a* and any ship in her vicinity with everything you've got. Fire as soon as you have a solution!"

He released the transmit button. "Weapons, what do we have?"

"Spinal laser and enough charge for two shots. Everything else is gone. We'll need helm to line us up for a shot."

"Helm?"

"Still killing our rotation, sir. Forward attitude thrusters are gone. I'm down to one amidships and three of four aft."

"Just get us lined up with that cursed long boat. Guns, fire as you bear."

As the helmsman struggled to line them up for a shot a voice came over the fleet channel. "All rebel ships, this is The Bancroft commanding the Lalande Security fleet. Indicate your surrender by cutting your engines and strobing running lights or you'll be destroyed. We have every remaining ship of your formation targeted with multiple systems. I have no control over the missile salvo bearing down on you from the *Nai'a*, but perhaps they'll show mercy. You have two seconds. The Bancroft out."

"Take the shot!" Bollicks ground out as his rotating ship aligned on the *Nai'a*. A blaze of coherent light shot from the bow, vaporizing a jammed weapon port along the way. A moment later a section of the *Nai'a's* ice shield vaporized, sending ice shards and superheated steam in all directions. Before Bollicks could celebrate, the *Pellucidar* vanished in a blinding flash, struck by no less than six main battle lasers from the Bancroft's fleet.

***

Julian Garrity grimaced as a momentary flash caused his cockpit windows to darken. A split second later, a blast of ice and steam from a giant divot in the ice shield kicked his little ship end for end. He shook his head to clear it, then quickly corrected his tumble and got the sting ship pointed toward the enemy.

His heads-up display showed a trio of incoming missiles. He noted the targeting of the three other sting ships providing defense and snapped off a salvo of rockets at the missile he had the best angle on. A second later the hostile missile icons vanished and a swarm of green ship designators appeared beyond what was left of the enemy formation.

***

Captain Brelling relaxed her grip on the arms of the command chair when the final hostile missile icons disappeared from the display. "Safe the capital missiles," she ordered Chief Nance.

He quickly complied before they went into terminal attack mode. He ensured none were headed for the friendly force then cut their drives and activated the recovery beacons. "Roger, missiles safed," he reported. "All remaining enemy ships have cut main engines. Force Bancroft is maintaining beam range."

"Damage report?" she queried.

"No damage to the ship," replied the engineering officer. "The ice shield took a few laser hits and the sensor array is down twenty percent on active sensors. We're still assessing ice shield integrity."

"Coms, open a tight beam channel to The Bancroft's flagship per the envoy's protocol," the captain ordered. "Put it on the main screen." Within a minute the display came to life filled with an ornate coat of arms that faded to reveal a fit looking man in a plain, dark-grey ship suit adorned only with the single star of a commodore. He had piercing blue eyes and graying red hair cut in a space-practical flat top. A dusting of freckles across the bridge of his nose did nothing to alter the seriousness of his expression.

"Captain Brelling, I presume?" he began.

She nodded.

"I am The Bancroft, Wallace the Third. Please allow me to apologize for the welcome you received to the Lalande system. I congratulate you on your readiness to fend off the rebel attack. We would have had words about the firepower you're carrying under other circumstances, but I think both my government and the trade syndicate will overlook a little stretching of the long boat protocols in this instance. On balance, I'm grateful you came loaded for bear. You left us without much to do but mop up."

"I'm grateful you came to our assistance, Your Highness," the captain said gravely. "I doubt we would have emerged practically unscathed without your help."

"That's true for my forces as well," he answered. "I had little doubt of victory, but the cost..." He shook his head. "We did do you the favor of taking out the last few holdouts and a large cargo ship trailing the formation. It had enough capital missiles in box launchers to throw a thirty-missile salvo."

"We probably wouldn't have survived if they had launched," said the captain gratefully. "Is there anything we can assist you or your fleet with? We have a pinnace and a shuttle capable of search and rescue operations. We also have a first-class trauma team and probably more medical capacity than your fleet."

"Your help with SAR and the wounded is welcome. Thanks to you, we have an abundance of drifting hulks to check. I have prize crews for the few intact ships. It hurts to lose five corvettes from my security forces, but we were never realistically going to get those back. The flag captain's executive officer will handle SAR coordination. May I pay you a visit when the situation is under control?"

"The Bancroft is always welcome aboard the *Nai'a*," she answered. "Doubly so today, Your Highness, I'll look forward to it."

"I see over your shoulder that my envoy is alive and well. Don't let him put you to sleep with old war stories. The Bancroft out." The screen showed the coat of arms again then blanked.

Captain Brelling opened the all-hands channel. "This is the captain. Well done shipmates! Aside from minor damage to the ice shield and sensors, we survived the attack unscathed. Your vigilance and expertise once again carried the day. The situation here in Lalande is still fluid, but we have friendly forces nearby to assist. I'm proud of all of you, Brelling out."

She switched off the channel and looked up at Chief Nance. "That goes double for you, Chief, your timing couldn't have been better. I almost went cross-eyed trying to talk with the 'commodore' and watch the tactical display at the same time."

"They accommodated us by coming in with a tight formation," answered Nance. "They didn't expect us to have teeth, or factor in the need to shoot around the ice shield."

"I, for one," said the captain, "am thankful they weren't more tactically competent. The Bancroft was also surprised, but he didn't hesitate to follow up on our success. Now, we have to help with the cleanup."

Chapter 21 – Spinning in the Void

February 20th, AD 3208
Long Boat Nai'a – Outer Lalande System
Aft Boat Bay

Mishael squatted, putting the shoulder of his hard suit against the misaligned sting ship. He straightened with a grunt, shoving it by brute force into position. He quickly secured the locking collars and stepped back.

"With you around, who needs a ship hoist?" his mother said.

"I like to lend a hand where I can," said Mishael with a grin. "I'm not much good at standing around watching people work."

Mishael looked around the controlled chaos of the boat bay. Crews were refueling and rearming four of the sting ships. Another four fully loaded fighters were out on space patrol under the leadership of Lieutenant Commander Val O'Clair.

Julian Garrity herded his flight of pilots into an out-of-the-way corner then walked over to Mishael. "We've been tasked with aiding The Bancroft's fleet on search and rescue," he said. "As we've rehearsed, you'll lead the team in the pinnace with Jarman as pilot, and Shanyah will lead the team in the shuttle. The med techs will be here shortly. Val O'Clair will provide overwatch with his wingman and leave two ships here for space patrol. Priority is the safety of your people. We know the Restoration is a bunch of fanatics. Don't take any chances. Use the protocols you've learned. Stabilize the wounded and get them back here where the trauma team can deal with them."

Mishael nodded. He quickly joined his mother in swapping out his suit's environmental unit for a fresh pack and grabbed a boarding shotgun. He clipped an ammunition pack to a hard point, slung a tungsten-headed cutter mattock and a wrecking bar over his back and headed for the pinnace. Jarman was finishing up pre-flight checks as he formed his team up outside the pinnace. In addition to the med-tech, two engineering ratings joined him with a heavy plasma cutter and a hydraulic device the called the can-opener. Between the three of them, they should be able to cut, pry and hammer their way through most wreckage to get to survivors. He looked across the bay before boarding and saw his sister setting up a triage station by the lock. He gave her a smile and a thumbs up. She gave him an uncertain wave in return and went back to her task.

***

Jarman executed the flight to the approaching debris field expertly. He carefully conserved fuel and slotted them into the spot assigned by the Bancroft's flagship. During the flight, the Bancroft's staff had sorted assignments and told them to hold outside the field until they could give Jarman a clear flight-path to the target. The shuttle, with a greater litter capacity, would await patients and ferry them back to the *Nai'a* when full.

The two sting ships hovered, watching for any sign of hostile activity. Eventually, they were assigned the remains of a converted mining craft. Jarman took them carefully along the indicated clear path to match course with the drifting hulk. He felt a jolt of adrenaline as he recognized the design of the stricken ship. It was a common model used throughout inhabited space for mining survey, especially in asteroid belts. It was also the type of ship his mother and father had gone mining in back in the Sol system, and never returned.

Shoving his emotions to one side, Jarman feathered his controls until the top of the pinnace was pointed at the slowly tumbling hulk. He opened a PCOM-to-PCOM channel with Mishael. "This is a modified GN 230 design, Mishael. I'm transmitting the interior layout to your PCOM. Let me know when your team is ready to go. Remember, the clock is ticking on our return flight."

"Roger," Mishael replied. "I have the file. We're ready."

Jarman activated the warning light in the aft compartment, waited three seconds, then pressed the button to open the clam shell doors. Mishael and his teammates looked up as the opening gave them a view of the wrecked ship. The front of the cockpit was slagged from a head-on laser hit. A railgun round had nearly severed the main engine from the rest of the craft, and there were no lights showing. Three box launchers of missiles, hastily welded to the exterior of the ship's hold, appeared intact and unfired. Mishael spotted the airlock on the second spin. It appeared undamaged.

"We'll split up. Doc, you come with me. We'll try the airlock and check the quarters section. Ponder and Kent, you get started with the plasma cutter on the cockpit." He squatted slightly and released his boots' maglock. The med-tech followed suit.

"Nice and easy on my mark." He watched the ruined ship, carefully timing the jump." Three...two...one...Go!"

He and the med-tech pushed off together, tucking and flipping to make their approach to the ship feet first. By skill or luck, Mishael's feet contacted the hull close beside the airlock hatch. He bent his knees deeply to absorb his momentum, activating the maglocks at the same time. The med tech bounced awkwardly off an antenna, nearly floating away into the void before Mishael grabbed her ankle and pulled her down to the hull.

Mishael slapped the wide-eyed tech on the shoulder and started the standard emergency-power-only sequence on the airlock. He deliberately ignored the way the universe was spinning around him, relying on the maglocks to keep him glued to the hull. Once the lock's pressure gauge hit zero, he undogged the hatch and carefully swung it open. He grabbed a handhold inside the lock and pulled himself in. He locked his boots to the deck inside the airlock then reached out to help the med-tech. Between

Mishael's considerable bulk and his hard suit, there was barely room for her in the lock. Together they closed the hatch and dogged it in place.

Mishael peered through the small viewing window, but didn't see anything in the dimly lit corridor beyond. Through his boots he could the feel the thumps as his engineering ratings locked their tools to the twisted metal of the cockpit. The pressure gauge in the interior hatch indicated normal pressure in the corridor, so he started the cycling sequence. The lock batteries should be good for four or five cycles without ship power.

Once the interior and exterior pressure equalized, he opened the inner hatch and pulled himself through, motioning the med-tech to stay put. He activated his suit's exterior audio pickup and microphone, listening for any sign of life in the ship. He locked his boots to the deck of the corridor and turned on his helmet light. According to Jarman's schematic, the cockpit should be to the left of the intersection in front of him, and the living quarters to the right.

Moving one step at a time, he approached the intersection. A quick glance to the left showed the emergency hatch to the cockpit had slammed shut when it lost pressure. As he turned to the right, something punched the chest of his suit hard, knocking him into the bulkhead. The barrel of a slug carbine came into his vision as it aligned with his faceplate. Without thinking he slapped the weapon to the side with his left hand, grabbing the barrel and pulling its owner toward him. The man's eyes opened wide as he was yanked forward. Mishael kept his grip on the weapon, grabbing the man's collar with his other hand and bouncing his skull off the bulkhead. The man shook his head to clear it and tried to yank the gun away. Mishael slammed him into the unyielding bulkhead a few more times until he went limp.

Mishael held the man at arm's length while checking his suit's integrity. Fortunately, the round hadn't penetrated, merely gouging the armored chest plate as it struck a glancing blow. His captive's faded grey ship suit was worn and stained. His face sported a patchy five-day growth of beard.

Mishael was reasonably sure he hadn't bathed or brushed his teeth in a while. He zip-tied the man's wrists together behind him, then used three magnet-headed bungee cords to secure him to the bulkhead.

He motioned the med tech to come ahead and check the prisoner's condition, then started up the corridor he'd come from. There were sleeping cabins on either side followed by a refresher on the left and a galley on the right, according to the schematic. He checked the sleeping cabin on the right. It was unkempt, but deserted. Various clothing items and empty food containers floated and bumped into one another with the ship's motion. Judging by his appearance, the man who'd attacked him had probably come from there. The other sleeping cabin was neat, with both bunks made up and everything secured, but also unoccupied. Mishael decided to check the galley. His helmet light caught the skinny occupant in the face and she screamed, holding a large kitchen knife in front of her. Mishael hastily backed out and motioned to the med tech. His suit said the atmosphere was good so he cracked opened his faceplate.

"There's a young girl in the galley," he told the med tech once she removed her soft suit's helmet and stowed it on her belt. "She's got a knife and I probably scared her out of three years' growth in this hard suit. See if you can reason with her. How's the prisoner?"

"Likely concussed, but he'll be okay," the med answered. "I wonder what the story is here. I didn't expect kids."

"I'm with you, but let's do what we can for her. She may be able to fill us in."

The med tech peered slowly into the galley, shining a flashlight carefully to the side to better illuminate the space. "Hi in there, I'm Sadie, a med tech from the *Nai'a*. We're here to help." This time the girl didn't scream but stared at her round-eyed, her knuckles white where they still gripped the knife.

"How do I know you're not one of them?!" the girl shouted, wiping a tear away with the back of her sleeve.

"My shipmates just fought a battle with 'them', but I suppose you'll have to take my word for it," Sadie answered. "We need to get you off this ship. It's not safe. I promise you we'll do our best to protect you."

"I'm not going anywhere without Dad!" the girl said. "Where's Roach?"

"Would Roach be a smelly man with a bad beard?"

"Yes."

"He's unconscious and tied to the wall down the corridor," Sadie told her, motioning back that way. "He tried to shoot my team leader and got a little beat up."

"You should have beaten him to a pulp," stated the girl. "He's smacked me around enough the last few weeks."

"Where's your dad?" asked Sadie.

"In the cockpit."

Sadie gestured toward the table and benches bolted to the deck. "Why don't we belt ourselves in and you can tell me about it."

The girl nodded, then carefully put the knife in a drawer where kitchen tools were neatly arrayed on a magnetic strip. She gripped the table edge, slid on to one bench and belted herself in with the ease of long practice. She looked to be eleven or twelve with dark curly hair and an olive complexion. The variable light pseudo-gravity induced by the ship's spin didn't seem to bother her. Sadie did her best to emulate the girl, but made a more awkward job of getting settled on the opposite bench in her soft suit. "What's your name?" she asked.

"Anthea Driscoll," the girl answered. "Where's your team leader?"

"Just outside the door. I think you've already met."

"Tell him he can come in," said Anthea. "I'm sorry about screaming at him, but he startled me, and he's huge."

"He is big," Sadie nodded, "even without the hard suit."

Mishael poked his head in the door and smiled at the girl through his open faceplate. "I'm Lieutenant Mishael Bonaparte' of the long boat *Nai'a*. Sorry about scaring you. I would have screamed too, in your place."

"I doubt it," said the girl studying his face carefully. "You don't look like anything would scare you."

"You might be surprised. One of our ship's cats, Lionel, scared me silly not long ago in a dark corridor. I hate to admit it, but I probably sounded a lot like you did when I startled you. If we take you back to the *Nai'a*, I'll introduce you."

Anthea squinted skeptically at him. "He made you scream like a little girl? I really need to meet him. I guess the *Suncatcher* is too far gone to stay here."

"From what I saw, she'll probably be scrapped," said Mishael honestly, pulling himself into the room. "Can you tell us how you and your dad ended up here?"

"I don't know where here is," answered Anthea, "but we were prospecting in the outer belt a month ago when we were ordered to heave to by a big corvette and boarded. They took Mom to another ship and forced Dad to work on modifying the *Suncatcher* to launch missiles. They said we'd never see her again if we didn't cooperate. Schultz and his crony Roach have been riding with us and bossing Dad around ever since. Dad says Mom is piloting one of the other ships. He thinks he knows which one from the com traffic and her style."

"Was Schultz also in the cockpit?" asked Sadie.

"Yes, a few hours ago he told us to secure everything back here and stay out of their way. Dad looked worried and just nodded at me. I was strapped into my bunk while we were under acceleration, but something big hit the ship and we lost power. We've been drifting ever since. The cockpit hatch is sealed and jammed. I was afraid of what Roach might do. I came in here and grabbed the knife in case he tried something."

"Roach is literally tied up," said Mishael. "I guarantee he won't bother you again." He could make out a fading bruise on the girl's cheekbone. "We have a pinnace holding station just a few meters away. Is your ship suit space-worthy?"

"Yes," Anthea answered. "I just need my helmet and gloves from the cabin."

Mishael backed out of the way and checked on the still unconscious Roach while Sadie and Anthea went to collect her gear and two space-rated duffle bags of the family's possessions. He crossed to the other cabin and managed to find Roach's helmet among the swirling detritus. He returned to where the man was bungee-corded to the wall, put the helmet over his head, and activated the neck seal. He wasn't confident the patched ship suit would resist vacuum, but he didn't see an alternative. Anthea's suit showed some wear, but was obviously well maintained.

"Okay," Mishael said when Anthea and Sadie were ready. "You two go through the lock, then I'll follow with Roach. Once we're all on the hull, I'll help you cross over, then I need to help the rest of the team."

Two lock cycles and four emergency patches hastily applied to Roach's suit later, the four of them were on the hull and ready to cross. Sadie went first, timing her jump perfectly and sticking the landing. She detached her safety line and Mishael quickly reeled it back in. He attached the line to Anthea's suit then reached to grab her by the belt and collar. She shook her head and motioned for him to bend down and touch helmets. "You don't need to toss me over like a bag of rice. I can do this," she said.

"Okay, remember to detach the safety line when you're secure," he answered and stood back.

Anthea crouched slightly taking a grip on an antenna mount. She unlocked her boots and waited for the rotation to line them up with the pinnace. With a gentle push, she launched herself through space doing a graceful forward flip to land knees-bent in the back of the pinnace. She detached the safety line before Sadie could react, and Mishael gave her two thumbs-up before reeling it back in.

Mishael looked at Roach's limp form and grimaced. He detached the line securing the hijacker to the hull, then grabbed him by the belt. This time he didn't bother with the safety line, giving Roach a casual heave toward the pinnace. Roach sailed through space and thumped into the deck of the pinnace beside Sadie. She caught him on the bounce and secured him to a litter with several straps. Mishael took considerably more care with the two duffle bags, tossing them gently into Sadie's waiting arms.

Mishael used his mag boots and hand holds to make his way forward to the cockpit. Ponder and Kent were just bending back a section of slagged metal to gain access to the space. "It looks like we've got one injured and one dead," reported Ponder over the team channel.

Mishael peered into the cockpit. One of the occupants had a hand gun still gripped in his lifeless fist. Half his faceplate was gone and his eyes bulged in a combination of surprise and vacuum exposure. It was an ugly way to go, but Mishael couldn't dredge up any sympathy for the criminal. The pilot, Anthea's father, if Mishael was any judge of family resemblance, was unconscious. His helmet was cracked but patched and his suit seemed to be maintaining atmosphere. Mishael backed out and motioned Ponder forward. The smaller man would have a better chance of extricating the pilot from the tight quarters of the cockpit.

"See if you can get him loose from the seat harness," said Mishael. "I'm worried about his legs. The console is bent downward." Ponder removed a cutting tool from his belt pouch and got to work. Five minutes later, he backed out of the cockpit.

"I've got the webbing loose but his legs are pinned under the console. It's not a job for the plasma cutter with him in there and I don't see a way to get at it with the can opener," Ponder said.

Mishael reached for his two-meter wrecking bar and stuck his head back into the cockpit. He examined the situation carefully then managed to get the curved end of bar under the lip of the console next to the pilot. He braced his feet on the hull, knees bent and heaved on other end of the bar will all his strength. Metal bent and tore with a shriek. The bar came loose and Mishael nearly went flying, but one boot held. Kent grabbed his other leg and pulled it back down to the hull. Ponder slid back into the cockpit and worked to get the pilot free. Within a minute, Mishael was helping pull the man out. His legs were bent at an unnatural angle. Ponder and Kent applied-auto splints to each leg after checking for suit leaks.

"Sadie, we've got the pilot free," Mishael called on the team net. "He's got injuries to both lower legs. Ponder and Kent will jump him across shortly."

"Roger," she answered. "I have a litter prepped and ready."

Mishael admired the teamwork and agility Ponder and Kent showed getting the pilot across the void and into the pinnace. He quickly followed, landing next to Anthea and quickly strapping himself into a web seat beside her. The girl clutched his arm anxiously as she watched the medic secure the pilot to a litter. Mishael felt Anthes's reaction in her grip as she realized her father was alive.

"We're all back sir," Mishael called to Jarman, patting the girl's gloved hand. "Button us up." The clamshell doors closed and the pumps kicked in to restore the atmosphere.

"All secure in the aft compartment?" queried Jarman.

"Aye sir!" Mishael answered. The aye was barely out of his mouth when acceleration kicked in and he felt the pinnace gyrate through a series of maneuvers.

"Sorry for the rough ride," Jarman transmitted. "Local space is crowded with uncontrolled objects and I had to dodge. It's a good thing you finished up when you did."

Sadie was strapped into a moveable seat next to the pilot, running a scanner over his injured legs. When the atmosphere indicator turned green, she quickly doffed her helmet and unsealed her patient's. She secured the helmet nearby and felt for the pilot's pulse at his neck. Nodding in satisfaction she secured a tourniquet over his suit above each knee but did not activate them. She attached a micro-monitor to his neck, then dialed a setting on her injector and gave him a shot. Within a few seconds, the man's vital signs were displayed on a small screen above his litter.

Anthea had her helmet off, watching wide eyed as the med-tech worked. Mishael kept a worried eye on her, but she had enough wisdom not to interfere. After one more pass of the scanner over her patient's legs, Sadie leaned back and studied his vital signs. Satisfied, she turned to Anthea. "Is this your dad?" Anthea blinked furiously and nodded. "I'm going to be straight with you. He's got serious leg injuries, multiple fractures, but he's stable. His suit has some built-in trauma capability that's keeping him from bleeding so I don't need the tourniquets. Otherwise, he's just got some minor bruises from being thrown around in his harness. We won't know about his legs until we get him back to the *Nai'a*. We've got a couple of top-notch surgeons and I know they'll do their best for him. Would you like to sit with your dad?" Anthea gulped and nodded. Mishael quickly checked with Jarman to make sure he was done maneuvering for the next few minutes then nodded agreement. Anthea unwebbed herself without help and traded places with Sadie. She held her father's hand between hers and studied his face. It was the first time she'd seen him without a look of worry since they'd been hijacked. Her lower lip trembled and she took it between her teeth to get it to behave.

Jarman was more than glad to put the wrecked ship behind him. Debris from the space battle kept his full attention as he threaded the pinnace out of the danger zone. Val O'Clair soon joined up with the pinnace in his sting ship. "*Nai'a* One, this is Scorpion Two," he transmitted. "The shuttle and my wingman are matching courses with the *Nai'a* now. They have a full load of emergency medical cases. The Bancroft fleet's space control has our return course clear."

"Roger, Scorpion Two," Jarman answered. "We'll burn for home in thirty seconds."

***

When the boat bay finished repressurizing around the shuttle, the pilot dropped the rear cargo door and the med-techs began moving litter patients to the triage station. Kalei went from patient to patient, directing the med-techs to move them quickly to Medical if they were stable. One patient went into cardiac arrest as she was examining him. She used power cutters to open the chest of his ship suit, quickly placed the pads of an automated external defibrillator, and stood back. The AED shocked the patient and his heart began beating again. She applied a pressure bandage to a wound in his side and ran a hand scanner over his abdomen. After checking his heart beat again, she motioned the med- tech to move him out of the triage station and get him to Dr. Rensaleer.

Shanyah brought the last litter from the shuttle. The figure on it was pathetically small. Kalei guessed the boy to be five or six years old. His right arm was in an auto splint, and Shanyah was monitoring a torniquet just below his shoulder. Kalei quickly checked him over. The boy's face was pale and his eyes were wide. Kalei could tell he was on the verge of shock. Her scan showed a displaced fracture and arterial bleeding in his arm. The medical monitor showed he'd been given a mild painkiller. She took his other hand in hers and smiled. "I'm Doctor Kalei. I'm going to take care of you. Do you understand me?" The boy nodded, his mop of light brown hair waving in the low gravity.

"What's your name, sweetie?"

"Brin," he croaked.

"I need to operate on your arm, Brin. I'm going to give you something to make you sleep. Think about your favorite place. I'll see you when you wake up. Okay?" He nodded weakly. She estimated his mass then dialed up a general anesthetic and a broad-spectrum antibiotic and injected his neck. With her mother's help, she transferred him gently to the triage station operating table and activated the temporary enclosure that would help maintain a sterile environment. "Keep monitoring that tourniquet," she told her mother. "I'm going to need you to assist." All of the med-techs were enroute to Medical with other patients. She quickly donned a fresh set of gloves and used her cutters to remove the boy's ship suit from his chest and left arm. She started an IV drip then carefully tackled the job of removing the sleeve from his broken arm, leaving the tourniquet in place. Her mother watched, face grim as Kalei sanitized the area and began to work on the boy's arm. "Ease the tourniquet pressure slightly," she ordered. Blood spurted until Kaei could clamp the bleeder. She continued to work swiftly, bringing the arm bones back into alignment and fusing them together with artificial bone grafts that would dissolve over time. Once she was satisfied, she checked for other damage, cleaned the wound, and closed up. She had Shanyah remove the tourniquet, then replaced the emergency splint with a better sized inflatable cast. She checked Brin's vital signs then nodded at her mother and tapped the button to retract the temporary enclosure. One of the med-techs was back so she transferred Brin to the litter and sent him on his way to Medical.

A claxon warned them that the boat bay would depressurize shortly. She and Shanyah passed through the lock to the *Nai'a's* interior and entered a compartment outfitted as a break room. Shanyah grabbed two cold drinks from cooler and passed one to Kalei. "Drink," she said, "before you fall over from dehydration. I know you and how you forget your own body's needs when you're focusing." Kalei nodded drained the container in one long draught and reached for another.

"Right as usual, Mom," she said, wiping her brow. "I didn't realize how thirsty I was." She shook her head. "I knew this could be ugly but I didn't expect kids."

"From what I saw and heard, the Restoration rebels built part of their fleet from hijacked mining ships," said Shanyah. "A lot of prospectors take their families with them. The rebels split them up to force the parents to cooperate."

"Your stories about these slimeballs don't do the reality justice. Who takes kids into space combat on purpose?" Kalei shook her head in disgust.

"The Restoration, they're not strong on basic decency. We did take you and Mishael along with the entire ship into a battle when you were kids, though."

"That wasn't the captain's choice. The Restoration forced the confrontation."

"True enough, come here." Shanyah enveloped her grown daughter in a big hug. Kalei sighed and sagged against her mother, absorbing her solid strength. "You're still my girl. Not so little anymore, but you've been through a wringer and the day's not over. I'm proud of you."

A med-tech poked his head in the compartment. "The pinnace is in the boat bay and they're repressurizing now. They have one patient with major injuries." Kalei gave her mom one last return squeeze then straightened.

"Duty calls," she said. "Thanks for standing in during the operation. I have enough of my crew back to help me now."

"I'll go in with you anyway," Shanyah said patting her on the back. "I may be able to help and the sting ships will need attention afterward."

The pinnace's clam shell doors were opening when they glide-stepped into the boat bay. Mishael handled the litter with one of his teammates, while Sadie monitored their patient. Anthea hovered nearby. Mishael secured the litter to one of the triage station pedestals and stepped back, bending down to talk to Anthea as Sadie and Kalei conferred. "That tall lady doctor is my sister," Mishael told Anthea. "She's really good." About then, Shanyah made her way to them and squatted down to Anthea's height.

"I see you have a new friend, Mishael, do you want to introduce us?" Shanyah asked with a broad smile.

"Anthea, this is my mom, Shanyah," Mishal answered. "Anthea was on the ship we were assigned. The patient is her father. She's had a rough month and a pretty awful day, but she's been a trooper."

Anthea solemnly shook Shanyah's hand, studying her face. "You look alike. Are you sure you're not his sister?"

Shanyah laughed. "I'm one hundred percent certain," she said. "How are you feeling?"

"I'm okay, I guess. I think Dad will make it, but I'm worried about Mom. Can you find out anything out about her? The rebels took her to pilot one of the other ships."

"I'll see what I can find out. What's her name?"

"Crinea Driscoll."

Shanyah quickly composed an inquiry with her PCOM and sent it high-priority up the chain of command. "Our people will work on contacting your mother, "she said. "I'm sure she's worried about you too. Let's go see about your dad." Kalei was checking Anthea's father over carefully. She'd cut away the top of his ship suit and placed additional micro-monitors. After a checking his vitals, she caught sight of Anthea. Shanyah introduced them.

"Your dad's going to be okay," she said, looking Anthea in the eye as she shook her hand. "Sadie did a great job stabilizing him. He needs surgery on his legs so we're going to get him to Medical as quickly as we can. Is it okay if I check you over?"

Anthea nodded, then reached over to squeeze her father's hand before Sadie wheeled him off. Kalei whisked a privacy curtain around them. She quickly assessed the girl's condition then stood back and smiled. "A few bumps and bruises and you're a little dehydrated, but in good shape overall. I prescribe a shower, a good meal with my mother, here, plenty of fluids, and a nap. When you've completed those, you should be able to visit your dad. How does that sound?"

"Pretty good," Anthea nodded. She followed Shanyah out of the boat bay and they stopped in the break room to get the girl a drink. She chose a triple berry fizz, downed half of it immediately then surprised a laugh out of Shanyah with a loud burp. "Sorry," she said blushing.

"No worries," replied Shanyah. "A fizz will do that to you every time. Have you ever had a vacuum tram ride?" Anthea shook her head. "You're in for a treat."

When they reached Shanyah's quarters, she pulled up a holo-projection of a recent family picture so she could show Anthea what Abishai looked like.

"Your family runs big," the girl stated.

Shanyah laughed again, "Yes, we do. My husband Abishai makes up in width what he lacks in height. Mishael is just big in all directions. I didn't want you to be startled if Abishai comes in while you're here. She rummaged in a storage area and came up with a ship suit that should fit Anthea well enough, if a bit loosely. "This was Kalei's when she was about your age. I should have recycled it ages ago, but I couldn't bear to let it go." The suit was powder pink with at least two dozen butterfly appliques distributed randomly across its surface. Anthea's face split in a big grin. She grabbed the suit and held it at arm's length to admire the bright colors. Shanyah grabbed a package of underthings recently delivered by the chandlery then showed Anthea the shower controls and how to lock the bathroom door. Thirty minutes later the girl emerged, looking freshly scrubbed. She twirled once so Shanyah could properly admire her colorful attire. Shanyah clapped and showed her how to cycle her own clothes through the sanitizer. Anthea was delighted by the array of scents available, choosing bergamot-lime.

Shanyah had a lunch of chicken noodle soup and herbed cheddar biscuits ready on the kitchen table. Anthea dove right in. Shanyah silently gave thanks and prayed for the young girl and her family before she followed suit. Within a few minutes, Anthea soaked up the last of the chicken broth with a bite of biscuit and wiped her chin with a napkin. "I was hungrier than I realized," she said. "Your noodles are the best I've ever tasted, sort of chewy, and thicker than I'm used to."

"I have to give credit to Abishai. I can make them, but he's the expert. It's an old family recipe. If you ask him nicely when he's in the right mood, he'll teach you how it's done. He's surprisingly cagey about cooking techniques for a man who loves to cook and eat. I'd offer you more soup and another biscuit, but we finished off the left-overs. Also, you should probably slow down and give your stomach a chance to decide if it's full. I have some mandarin-pineapple popsicles if you'd like to try one?"

"Yes, please," Anthea replied. She rubbed her stomach. "Thank you for lunch."

"You're welcome," Shanyah said with a smile. "I'm glad you enjoyed it. This family likes its food, but it can be frightening to watch Abishai and Mishael tear through a meal. Both of them eat enough for two."

She retrieved two popsicles from the freezer, peeled the cellulose wrappers off, and handed one to Anthea. The girl made short work of the treat, then looked around for somewhere to put the pressed bamboo stick. Shanyah took it, rinsing them both and leaving them in the sink. "Why don't we go sit on the couch and I'll pull up my messages to see if there's any news about your mother."

They sat down, Anthea drawing her knees up to her chest with a furrowed brow. Shanyah checked her PCOM messages, but found nothing about the Driscolls. "No news yet. Honey, you really should take a nap, remember doctor's orders."

Anthea scrunched up her features. "I don't think I can sleep. What if Mom died in the battle? What about Dad's legs?" Tears began to leak down her face and she rubbed her eyes with balled fists, trying to get rid of them.

Shanyah scootched over and gathered the girl in her arms. Anthea collapsed against her and let the tears flow. Shanyah patted her back, resting her chin lightly on the girl's dark curls. "I know, I know, child. You don't have to hold it in," she murmured.

***

Captain Brelling decided to greet The Bancroft in the boat bay. The system sovereign rated special treatment on any day. Today, he had earned her regard by his actions. Envoy Rolland Dunleavy, stood by her side. Two understatedly lethal-looking crown guards exited the shuttle and took up positions on either side of the hatch. The Bancroft Himself glided down the ramp next, handling the low gravity of the boat bay like an old space hand. Captain Brelling gave him a formal bow as he approached and Rolland went down on one knee. "Get up, you old pirate," said the Bancroft to Rolland, extending his hand to the captain for a firm handshake. "I'm not here to test your flexibility and we can save formalities for the throne room."

"Welcome aboard the *Nai'a*, Your Highness," said Captain Brelling. The Bancroft was impressive in person. Of average height and build, he exuded an intensity that made him seem larger. He still wore the dark grey uniform of the Lalande System Security Forces. Two more crown guards followed him from the shuttle.

"Please call me Wallace," The Bancroft said, "You're not one of my subjects and it will make conversation simpler."

Captain Brelling smiled, "Very well, Wallace, if you'll call me Anne. Few people call a captain by her first name. It will be a refreshing change."

"So let it be done, Anne," The Bancroft said formally, bowing slightly.

"Follow me, please," replied the captain. "We'll take the vacuum tram if that's acceptable? Your crown guards are welcome to accompany us."

"I'm afraid they wouldn't have it any other way."

A few minutes later the captain was making introductions in the ship's council chamber. She wanted the rest the *Nai'a's* leadership to hear what Wallace had to say first hand. The Bancroft filled them in on the current situation, which was largely unchanged from what Rolland had told them.

"We're consolidating our hold on the majority of the system infrastructure," Wallace told them. "I just detached a six-ship squadron to retake the long-distance communications facilities on this side of the system. Since the rebels are getting no cooperation and outright resistance from most Lalande citizens, they're doomed in the long run. I have you to thank for moving their timetable up. I don't like to think what would have happened if they hadn't been rushed by your early arrival."

The captain briefed him on the *Nai'a's* multiple run-ins with the Restoration and what they knew of the organization's goals. "They use people without regard to any form of morality," she said in closing. "I didn't have trouble choosing sides once Rolland briefed me.

"I would appreciate your help reuniting a family swept up in their operation against the *Nai'a*. The Driscolls were deliberately separated, and I want to do what we can for them. I suspect there are others."

The Bancroft nodded; his expression serious. "Your suspicions are correct. My staff is working to reunite several family members. Unfortunately, we had civilian casualties from both the battle and Restoration rebels taking their frustration out once they realized the battle was lost. It wasn't all one-sided though. The miners out here are tough, resourceful people. We've got several medical cases, both on your ship and in our fleet, to identify."

Captain Brelling's eyes narrowed. "Another item is the Long Boat Free Trade Syndicate's buoy on this side of the system. It's been destroyed in direct violation of our free trade agreement with your government. I don't have to remind you of the penalty for tampering with a syndicate buoy."

The Bancroft paled. Interdiction was too much a part of Lalande system history and the reason for his family's rise to power. "You have my pledge as The Bancroft to do everything in my power to identify the parties responsible and render them due justice," he said formally. "I am confident no one loyal to my government perpetrated such a thing."

The captain's lips quirked, "The trade syndicate itself was penetrated and so was your government. Between the two of us we need to find out how it happened so we can prevent any unpleasant events in the future. You'll find in my bona fides that I'm empowered by the trade syndicate as both an investigator and plenipotentiary with full diplomatic authority." The announcement caused a few surprised looks around the table. "We didn't expect to encounter a full-on rebellion. However, I can't blame the system government for the acts of terrorists likely backed by the Restoration. I believe they are one and the same."

"The pieces fit together," said Wallace the Third, rubbing his chin. "My intelligence people, including Rolland, are starting to connect the dots between the rebellion and outside backers with deep pockets. Unfortunately, these people are devilishly good at covering their tracks in our financial system."

Captain Brelling grinned a wicked grin. "If you allow us access, I have just the person for uncovering those tracks."

***

Anthea was sleeping peacefully on the couch and Shanyah had drifted off herself in a chair when she received a PCOM call from Kalei. "Hi Mom, good news," Kalei said. "Anthea's father is going to be fine. His legs will take a few months to heal, but the surgery went well and we expect a full recovery. He should be awake and able to take visitors in about an hour. Seeing Anthea will be really good for him if she can make it."

"She's asleep right now, but I'll wake her in time to be there for him."

"How is she?" asked Kalei.

"Quite pleased with your old pink ship suit and eating like your father. She's also very scared and alone, but she had a good cry before dropping off. How are you? You sound tired."

"Exhausted," Kalei answered, "I'm going to go fall down for four hours on Dr. Rensaleer's orders. I'm not sure what's keeping her on her feet, but I'm not going to argue. We have everyone stable and the med techs are working out their own sleep schedule. We ended up overflowing into the cold sleep prep clinic to have enough beds. I think I'm babbling. Am I babbling?"

"Yes, dear," Shayah said with a smile. "Go get some sleep and your brain will work better." Shanyah closed the connection and finished cleaning up from the meal. Abishai came in looking exhausted himself. Shanyah put a finger to her lips then gave him a hug and kiss. "The visitor I messaged you about is asleep on the couch. I'm going to wake her up soon so she can visit her father in medical. You look like you've been through a wringer."

Abishai nodded wearily. "Roan, Quester, and I have been reloading missiles. They're both better at EV operations, but it's a brute force job and we're still figuring out the best procedures. I've hand-cranked four launch springs back into place in the last two hours. It's a good thing we didn't have to fight an extended battle."

"We had more time to work on the sting ship procedures," replied Shanyah. "Mishael's team has the rearm and refuel rotation down. Let me wake up our guest and introduce you two."

Shanyah shook Anthea's shoulder gently and the girl's eyes blinked open. She sat up, then stretched and yawned. Shanyah moved out of the way so she could see Abishai. "This is my sweaty husband, Abishai. Abishai, meet Anthea Driscoll. With you, she's now met the whole family."

Anthea smiled shyly, then put out her hand. "You look even bigger in person," she said, as her hand disappeared into his.

"I grew up on Earth," Abishai replied with a grin. "I was wider than most people even there. I'm glad to meet you, Anthea. I hope we'll have time to get to know each other."

"Earth? Wow, I've never met an earthling. Will you tell me about it?"

Abishai laughed. "Shanyah is an earthling too, and there are several more of us on the crew. I'll tell you what, when we have time, I'll swap you some stories. You tell me about Lalande, and I'll tell you about earth."

"It's a deal," agreed Anthea

"Your father is going to be awake from surgery soon," said Shanyah. "Do you want to go to Medical with me? We'll get the added bonus of not smelling my husband." Anthea nodded. Abishai thumbed his nose at Shanyah, said goodbye to Anthea, and headed to the shower.

"What does this mean?" asked Anthea once he disappeared. She put her thumb to the tip of her nose and waggled her fingers.

Shanyah chuckled. "It means Abishai can't handle the truth. Let's get to medical."

A ten-minute walk later they passed through the entrance to Medical, and Dr. Rensaleer met them. "Is this the intrepid young lady Kalei told me about?" she asked.

"This is Anthea Driscoll in the flesh, Shanyah answered. "Can we see her father?"

"Absolutely!" Dr. Rensaleer declared. "He should be conscious soon. He'll be a little groggy, but I imagine he'd much rather see Anthea's face than mine when he wakes."

Anthea and Shanyah followed the doctor to one of the patient rooms. "We've had to double up so we have another patient here," said Dr. Rensaleer. "We don't know who he is yet, but he won't be awake." Anthea's father was on the left side of the room. She walked over quickly and took his hand. He stirred at the touch and his eyes opened. After a few moments he focused on her face.

"My star," he said lifting his hand to her face with a weak smile. She pressed her face against his palm, then leaned down to kiss his cheek.

"I'm here, Papa," she said, blinking back tears.

Dr. Rensaleer stepped to Anthea's side and introduced herself and Shanyah.

"Please call me Alexander," he replied.

The doctor spent the next few minutes updating Mr. Driscoll on his condition. "We're going to keep you here on the *Nai'a* until you've fully recovered," she finished.

"Anthea can stay with us while you heal up," said Shanyah. "We're trying to locate your wife. The Bancroft's fleet is still cleaning up, but they've promised to let us know if they find her."

Alexander nodded. "Thank you. I think she was piloting the *Plucky Penguin*, but I could be wrong. It's old Sinterman's ship."

"I'm passing the information along now," said Shanyah.

"I know you surprised the rebels with your attack," said Alexander, looking at Shanyah. "If The Bancroft's fleet is here and you're cooperating with them, I assume you won?"

"Yes, all the ships in the rebel fleet were destroyed or surrendered," answered Shanyah. "We picked you up in the search and rescue operation."

Alexander looked at his daughter. "What happened to Roach?" he asked.

"He's enjoying the hospitality of our brig," answered Shanyah. "My son Mishael had to bounce him off a bulkhead a few times, but he survived both that and a leaky suit."

"There's a reason he's called Roach," said Alexander. "Tell your son thank you for me. I'm going to want to hear that story. Thank you for taking care of Anthea." Anthea spent a few minutes filling her father in on the details of the rescue and her time with Shanyah.

The door to the room opened and a med tech came in. "You've got a call you're going to want to take," he told Alexander, handing him a video-com terminal and pressing the button to connect the call.

Alexander held the terminal so Anthea could see and would be in the pickup. A beautiful dark-eyed woman's face filled the screen. "Mama!" the girl shouted, hugging her father around the neck. Dr. Rensaleer, the med-tech, and Shanyah quietly left the room to give them privacy.

"Oh, my baby!" Crinea Driscoll took a moment to find her voice again. "It's so good to see both of you alive. I've prayed every spare minute for this. How are you?"

"We're both doing fine, now," answered Alexander. "Anthea is better than I am. I had both legs broken in the battle, but the doctors here on the *Nai'a* fixed me up. They tell me I'll make a full recovery in a few months if I don't do anything stupid. The crew has been good to both of us. They rescued us off the *Suncatcher*. What about you?"

"I'm fine too," she answered. "I got knocked around a little when the *Plucky Penguin* took a hit, but I timed a bathroom break just right and the two terrorists riding with me got the worst of it. The *Penguin* is a write-off. A shuttle from The Bancroft's fleet pulled me off and brought me to the corvette I'm on now. I can't tell you which one for security reasons. What kind of shape is the *Suncatcher* in?"

Alexander grimaced. "From what they told me, the old girl is beat to scrap. Given the trajectories, I don't even know if they'll bother to salvage her. The crew that rescued us was thoughtful enough to bring a couple of bags full of our personal items, so we didn't lose everything. Anthea helped pack."

"Other than you two," she answered, "there wasn't anything I'll miss all that much. The security force people have been very vague about what they intend to do with me. I think they believed my story, but I was still aboard a ship of the enemy fleet. At least they haven't thrown me in their brig and they let me make this call. I'm hopeful they'll get us all back together."

"If we can make that happen, I'll be happy," said Alexander. "The whole system may be in turmoil, but we'll land on our feet."

Crinea smiled. "That's my Alexander, ever the optimist, even with two broken legs. The com officer is giving me the times-up sign. They have other people who need to make calls. I love you both!"

"Love you too!" Alexander and Anthea chorused before the feed cut out.

***

Captain Brelling, The Bancroft, and Rolland Dunleavy retired to her small conference room after the ship's council meeting. "I hope you don't mind the stance I'm taking," Captain Brelling said once they were seated and supplied with coffee and cookies. "I want you to be aware of my duty to both this ship and the trade syndicate. While I value a good relationship with your government, those come first."

"On the contrary," answered The Bancroft, "I prefer plain speaking. I need to know your priorities more than I need my ego massaged. I'm well aware of the trade syndicate's status as a de facto sovereign nation. Our painful mutual history saw to that. I have a favor, several actually, but one in particular, to ask. Can you take in the displaced crews and families for the in-system run? I can't guarantee their loyalties are in the right place, but they won't have any love for the rebels. My ships are overcrowded, and I know they would be more comfortable on the *Nai'a*."

"I spoke to the council about the people swept up by the rebels. We all agreed to give them passage as far as New Dawn. There are, however, conditions. We won't ask for compensation. Hubble's benevolence fund will cover it as we do for all distressed spacers. Assuming your courts clear them of aiding the enemy, how will you compensate them for their lost ships?"

Wallace frowned. "I've been looking for a way to do it, but my government is already operating in the red. Constitutionally I can only operate at a deficit for the length of the emergency plus one year. Unfortunately, my government's credit rating is trash right now. The exchequer can't even secure a loan from any of the Sol-based banks. They refuse to take on the risk. They don't seem to realize the rebels will likely freeze all their assets if they win."

"I wonder," said Rolland with a wrinkled brow. "The banks are risk averse, but they should still be willing to loan at an interest rate commensurate with the risk. I don't have any evidence, but I think they've been warned off and some of them may be backing the Restoration. We badly need to trace the money trail."

"Did you get anything from the systems of the commodore's corvette?" asked the captain. "As I mentioned earlier, I have someone uniquely qualified to parse digital systems and trace money."

"Sounds like the hacker that caused you so much trouble on your last voyage," said The Bancroft flatly.

"The very one," answered the captain without apology. "You'll also recall she was one of the reasons we survived the attacks in Tau Ceti. She was badly used by the Restoration and she's firmly on our side now."

"I'm not sure I want someone with those skills poking around in our financial systems, friendly or not," Wallace answered. "It's a moot point at the moment. We're too far out for a secure link. We didn't get anything useful from the corvette, but we did recover 'Commodore' Yates's body."

"If you're willing to bring it here," said Captain Brelling, "we might be able to get something from his PCOM."

"I thought PCOMs were nearly impossible to hack," said Wallace.

"Nearly impossible and impossible aren't the same thing," returned the captain.

"Under the joint agreement we'll be signing," Wallace considered, "my government will pledge full cooperation with your investigation. We can hand Yates over to you under that agreement as long as you agree to share all of your findings with us."

"Rolland can be present and part of the forensic team, if that will help," said the captain. Wallace nodded. "I also have good news on the money front. The *Nai'a* carries portable currency in the form of electronic bearer bonds drawn on the Bank of Sol for emergencies. We can extend you a loan on behalf of the trade syndicate to get you through the current situation with reasonable repayment terms."

The Bancroft grimaced and rubbed his flat top. "As much as I hate to look a gift horse in the mouth, why is the Long Boat Free Trade Syndicate sticking its neck out to help my government?"

"Two reasons," answered Captain Brelling. "First, we can't safely make a profit trading with a system in the middle of a civil war. Second, the Restoration is making war on the syndicate. If we don't stop them, the syndicate, and free trade among the inhabited stars, will cease to exist. Your enemies are our enemies. Mounting evidence points to Lalande and Sol as the joint epicenters of the Restoration."

Wallace looked at Captain Brelling intently for a few heartbeats, then seemed to come to a decision. "For either of us to survive the next few months we're going to have to trust one another. I have a clandestine plan to build a Lalande system-owned long boat every five years. I don't want to be in the position we were in when the syndicate interdicted us. I know it sounds like exactly what the Restoration is shooting for, but I promise you, interfering with syndicate long boats was never on the table. We'd be cutting our economic lifeblood to a trickle.

Captain Brelling smiled wryly and shook her head. "I don't know where the notion came from, but the syndicate has no problem with government and commercial enterprises building long boats to compete with the free traders. Our only stipulation has always been that the owners provide a reasonable path for the crew to buy their independence if they wish to. Competition is good for us. We compete with one another. The truth is, most new boats operate at a disadvantage because of a lack of experience and the shared database the syndicate has built over the centuries. Even with the disadvantage of inexperience, the constant demand for moving people and data makes any reasonably run long boat a profitable enterprise. I wish you all the best with your long boat fleet.

"If you can tolerate some advice, I'll even lend you our crew's expertise while we're in system to help you get started. We also have a non-proprietary starter database we can give you. We have a vested interest in long boats succeeding and eventually joining the syndicate."

"All of what you say makes sense intellectually," answered Wallace, spreading his hands. "Our unpleasant mutual history has, perhaps, clouded my judgment. I can only say thank you and gladly accept the help offered."

Rolland leaned back in his chair and stared at the ceiling; lips pursed. He popped upright suddenly with a gleam in his eye. "All of the generosity has been one-sided up to now, but I think we have a way to balance the equation somewhat. What would you say the admiralty court will find on the salvaged and surrendered ships from the battle, Your Highness?"

"Twenty percent goes to the crown chest," answered The Bancroft, "but an honest review of the battle, will award most of the prize money to the *Nai'a*. She did the vast majority of the damage to the rebel fleet."

Captain Brelling smiled as the pieces clicked together for her guests. "I've already checked with our legal department and corporate board," she said. "Prize money goes fifty-fifty to the corporation and crew personal accounts. The board has agreed to put the corporate half toward getting the local spacers hijacked by the rebels back on their feet."

"I'm once again in your debt," said Wallace, looking down thoughtfully. "This time a debt of honor. It's not a feeling I like, but I'd better get used to setting my pride aside. I'm glad we're allies, Anne. I've seen what you do to your enemies. With you and your crew on our side, we may come out of this as a whole star nation again."

"It's better business to get along with everyone, but we've learned some people have no interest in a cordial relationship," answered the captain. "For those, you need as big a stick as you can lay your hands on."

"You brought a bigger stick than the Restoration was ready for," Wallace replied. "Your sting ships pack a wallop for small vessels and I know they didn't expect capital ship missiles from a long boat."

"I'll have to explain both of those when we return to Sol. The syndicate is very sensitive about any long boat appearing to be a military threat.

Interstellar conquest of anything but a brand-new colony is so impractical it's a joke. Still, there are appearances we need to maintain."

"If it will help," said Wallace, "I'll send my full endorsement of your armament precautions with you to Sol. I might even send an envoy to deliver them." He glanced pointedly at Rolland.

Captain Brelling managed to stifle a laugh at The Bancroft's insight into her feelings. She didn't think she and Rolland had given anything away, but Wallace and the envoy were obviously very close. She stomped firmly on the spike of hope welling up in her heart and got back to business. "It will help. I still expect some of the powers that be to 'view with alarm' our weapons and actions. I can live with that because we're still alive to be viewed."

"Aye, it's a good thing for us you are," Wallace replied. "The mess we'd be in if we had both the Restoration and the free trade syndicate at our throats doesn't bear thinking on."

Chapter 22 – Predictable Consequences

February 25th, AD 3208
Long Boat Nai'a – Outer Lalande System
Beta Section

Abishai smiled as the Driscolls dug into their dolmades, hot pita bread, and cucumber-tomato salad with feta cheese crumbles. He and Crinea had engaged in a spirited discussion over the spices in the dolmades filling. He finally bowed to her ancestral knowledge and had to admit the result was delicious. Seeing the Driscoll family back together was a spark of joy in the grim current circumstances.

Alexander Driscoll was enjoying his first day free of Medical. He wasn't cleared to put any weight on his legs, but zipped along on his powered mobility chair like the natural pilot he was. Crinea had finally been delivered to the *Nai'a* the previous day by shuttle. In total, the *Nai'a* hosted five local families. All of them were belt miners and known to one another. Unfortunately, two of the families were missing members killed in the initial battle. Abishai didn't like to think about the role the *Nai'a* played in their deaths. He knew the captain had no way to know about the hijacked ships, but it still wracked him with guilt.

He'd met the widow of one of the victims. When he tried to apologize, she'd grabbed him by the hands and made him look into her eyes. "Don't you dare blame yourself for what happened to us!" she said fiercely. "The rebels are responsible for Raul's death. They hijacked our ship, separated us, and forced us into the middle of a battle. You had to defend your ship or more people would have died. You delivered a measure of justice to those terrorists. Don't quit now, we need your help to rid our system of the vermin."

Abishai shook his head at the memory. She was right. He needed to stop dwelling on what couldn't be changed, and help where he could.

***

Captain Brelling smiled at her dinner companion, willing her tense muscles to relax one at a time. She wanted to set aside the weight of command for a small space and enjoy the company. Rolland smiled back. He was still much as she remembered, with a few of his rougher edges worn smooth by time and experience. His frank, admiring gaze still made her heart skip a beat. "Tell me a little of what you've been doing since we parted ways," she said, wanting to hear his voice.

"I stayed in the Lalande System Security Force with stints in the crown guard from time to time. My career stalled out at colonel for a decade or so and I took a leave of absence to go prospecting. I added a profitable sideline gathering intelligence for system security. It's a good thing I did, because I'm a lousy prospector. I knocked around the system getting into and out of scrapes until the current Bancroft's father talked me into mentoring Wallace through his own early years with the security forces. I went back to 'prospecting' for a time before Himself called me back into active service for a third time, then made me his envoy. Since he's responsible for putting us back together, I've decided to forgive him. What about you, Anne?"

Her heart warmed at the sound of her given name on his lips. "My path was a bit simpler," she answered. "I worked my way up to first officer, and eventually captain, through several crossings. The most adventure I had after we met was some rowdy shore leave. Since the sabotage started on the Tau Ceti run, however, my life's become more interesting. I've got a fantastic crew, and we've been through it together over the last two crossings."

Rolland nodded. "Your crew is terrifyingly competent, at least to anyone who opposes you. You picked up several highly skilled pilots in Tau

Ceti. Rest assured someone will try to hire them away before you leave this system. The Bancroft will also make generous offers to your people. He'll need the talent for our own long boat program."

Anne's mouth quirked. "He's welcome to try, anyone is. We always have some crew turnover, and adventurous souls like the challenge of a wide-open system like Lalande. There's plenty of opportunity here, assuming Wallace can stabilize the political situation."

"I think Himself has some news for you on that front. I apologize for talking shop on what's supposed to be a dinner date."

"I'll forgive you this once," Anne answered. "Tell me what you remember from our last visit to Lalande." Their food arrived, a deluxe dinner for two with nine different traditional Chinese dishes to share. Soon the two were lost in conversation and good company.

***

With everyone comfortably stuffed, even Abishai and Mishael, the two families relaxed together. "I'm not sure how we can repay your kindness," said Crinea, with her arm around her daughter on the couch. "I'm just grateful to be a whole family again. We wrestled with bringing Anthea along on this trip, but we didn't want to be away from her for a year. I didn't anticipate a civil war breaking out." She looked at her husband, Alexander.

"I didn't see it coming either," he said. "The last thing I expected from a security force corvette was an order to heave to. The *Suncatcher* was unarmed until the rebels got their hands on her. We couldn't do anything but cooperate if we wanted to live. We're part, or were part, of a mining collective prospecting the outer asteroid belt. We operated six prospecting ships like the *Suncatcher* based on a processing mothership, the *Amphitrite*. The rebels turned her into a missile platform. I understand The Bancroft's fleet destroyed her before she could launch. Sluice Chute Enterprises is basically gone now, along with our life savings. We'll be alright, though." He smiled at his wife and daughter. "By the time we make New Dawn orbit,

I'll be healed up and ready to find a job. Dr. Kalei, did good work on me." He nodded at Kalei sitting on the other side of Anthea.

Kalei smiled, "We aim to please. By the way, Brin is cleared for visitors. Can Anthea come see him in the morning? I know it would cheer him up."

"We'll all come see him," said Crinea. "He and Anthea are old pals. How is he doing?"

"Much better now that his parents are here," Kalei answered. "The Bancroft's forces held them for a few days while they sorted out who was who among the survivors. His arm is healing well, in spite of my rush job, but he was feeling very alone for a while."

"I know how he felt," said Anthea. "After the *Suncatcher* got hit, I didn't know if Dad was alive or where Mom was, and then this giant person pokes his head in the galley." She pointed at Mishael.

"My ear drums are still ringing from that encounter," said Mishael with a suppressed grin. "I don't know who was more surprised."

"Definitely me!" answered Anthea. "I was expecting Roach. I can't say how happy I was when I saw him with a good set of bruises, and webbed to the bulkhead like a spider's dinner. What are they going to do with him?"

"He'll stay in our brig until we get to New Dawn, then he'll probably face a trial," said Abishai. "Hal Renfro told me we're carrying a dozen prisoners for The Bancroft. He's been helping The Bancroft's people with the interrogations. When you're ready, he'll want to get a statement from each of you."

Anthea's eyes got big. "Is he going to interrogate us?"

Abishai laughed. "No, no, Hal is a friendly guy to people like you. It's the criminals he intimidates, I mean interrogates."

"Both!" said Mishael. "I've seen him in action."

"He'll probably want to take your statements together so you'll be as comfortable as possible," continued Abishai. "He'll even do it right here in our quarters if you would prefer."

Anthea nodded enthusiastically. "Is Mr. Renfro a real live detective? I've always wanted to meet one."

"He is," answered Abishai. "He was a professional investigator on Terra and helped the Tau Ceti authorities break the Restoration's organization there. He's a detective now with our Ship Security force."

"Wow! I can't wait to meet him!" Anthea's parents exchanged amused looks. "I've read the entire Ginny Geronimo Girl Detective series."

"I'm sure Hal will enjoy meeting you too," said Abishai. "He has a daughter named Belle, about Kalei's age."

"That's right," said Kalei. "Belle is a Ship Security officer too, but she specializes in cybersecurity like her mother. You two will get along great!"

The two families continued to chat congenially until Anthea and Abishai both started to yawn. They bid each other good night, and the Driscolls departed for their nearby quarters.

***

Wallace the Third's mood was considerably better on his second visit to the *Nai'a* the next morning. He and Rolland met with Captain Brelling, Lisandra Redding, and the *Nai'a's* first officer in the captain's small conference room. "I've good news on several fronts," he began. "First, my people, by that I mean the citizens of Lalande, are systematically dismantling the rebellion. We spread the news of what the Restoration rebels did on New Dawn, and the tide of public opinion turned completely against them. Everyone is taking precautions and informing my government of rebel sightings. They haven't a safe haven in the system. By the time we get to New Dawn orbit, the rebellion will be in tatters. My own forces retook the long-range coms array yesterday.

"My sister, Siobhan, heads the exchequer. Your pledge of credit brought two major interstellar banks to the table with loan offers. We're at least solvent now. We were hanging by a financial thread, but you've thrown us a steel cable. I pledge on my honor, Lalande will not forget the friendship of the *Nai'a* while I live and breathe." The Bancroft pounded his fist on the table and his eyes burned fiercely. "What you've done should burn the last remnants of resentment toward the free trade syndicate from our system."

Captain Brelling gave him a firm nod of acknowledgment. "It's my fondest wish to restore a good relationship between us, not the least because it will help wreck the Restoration's plans. Tau Ceti was the opening salvo, but I believe Lalande is the lynchpin of their strategy. Speaking of the Restoration, we have some information you'll find useful. Lisandra, if you would?"

Lisandra Redding slid a data chip across the table to The Bancroft. "Your Highness, this contains the last three years of Benjamin Yates' bank transactions. I've flagged everything I found suspicious, but someone more familiar with your local financial systems will know better than I. I suggest you wait on tipping your hand until we have a near real-time connection with your financial data network. If you'll trust me to work with your investigators and give me access, I can help them turn this start into a financial map of the Restoration's activities over the last several years."

The Bancroft's eyes narrowed. "Do you consent to full monitoring of your activities?"

"I insist on it," Lisandra answered flatly. "In fact, I prefer to advise while your people take the necessary actions using the tools I provide."

Wallace sighed. "Siobhan won't like this, but it would be criminal of me to waste the opportunity. Fortunately, my emergency powers allow me to authorize what would normally be an illegal intrusion. How did you get Yates' personal records? I'm still surprised you managed to break the encryption on a PCOM."

Lisandra grimaced. "I'll spare you the gory details, but it involved convincing the PCOM that Yates was still alive. I'm glad Dr. Rensaleer isn't squeamish. Encryption is only as good as the security on the decryption protocols. Yates wasn't nearly as careful there as he should have been. The chip contains the decryption protocols and a full image of the PCOM data storage for your people to pick apart. The com logs should be especially interesting.”

Rolland’s eyes lit up and he had to restrain himself from reaching for the chip in The Bancroft’s hands. “Aye, those should be especially useful,” the envoy said. “We only have an incomplete picture of rebel organization. The com records will go a long way toward filling it in.”

Captain Brelling furrowed her brow, fingers drumming lightly on the table. “I’m as pleased with all the good news as you are, Wallace,” she said. “I must caution you, though. From my own hard experience, these people have back up plans to their back up plans. If you really have them on the run, I suggest you keep them that way and be ready for a sucker punch from the least expected vector.”

“The advantage we have now is an angry populace on our side,” answered Wallace. “Since they’ve shown their true colors, most of the people working for them have turned. They’ll have a hard time hiding anything from us. The rebel leadership is concentrated on the Pollux habitat, hereditary home of the Withers clan. They’ll find out we have them pinpointed before my forces are in place to go after them. They might stand and fight or make a run for a bolt hole somewhere in the system. I need access to your prisoners from Tau Ceti. At least one of them will know where the fallback position is. The Withers family is neck deep in this, just as they were part of the conspiracy against the *Nai’a* when you were last in Lalande.”

“I have no problem handing them over to you,” said the captain. “We always intended to give you the evidence of their crimes and let your justice system sort them out. We’ll just need twenty-four hours to put the prisoners through the cold sleep recovery protocol.”

“Rolland will coordinate interrogation and formal extradition with your Ship Security people,” Wallace answered. “My fleet will stay with you all the way to New Dawn orbit. By then I should have the ships I need to secure the New Dawn habitats and go after Pollux. Also, expect a delivery of capital ship missiles. We tracked them down easily based on your tactical data. I assume you'll be able to reuse them."

Commander Hartley nodded. "They can be refueled," he said. "It will be good to have a reload on hand again."

"The missiles you have in those external mounts are going to make people twitchy, but I'm inclined to allow you to leave them in place until we've cleaned the rebels out," Wallace said. "You aren't going to use them in the Sol system, are you?"

Captain Brelling shook her head. "Not on your tintype," she answered. "If we start slinging missiles around in Sol, we've already lost to the Restoration. The courts would hammer us. The same is true for them, though. We should be safe enough, physically. The battle there will be fought in the political arena and courts. We'll keep a couple of sting ships well out of sight, but we'll accept a reasonable offer for the missiles and remaining fighters once we're safely on our way."

"I'll take them off your hands," said Wallace. "I want to incorporate the reusability feature in our own missiles."

***

Brin was sitting up when Kalei, Anthea, and Mishael entered his room in Medical. His mother was in a chair beside the bed and quickly got up with a smile. "See," she said to Brin, "I told you visitors would start popping in."

"Hey Ant!" Brin said with a wide grin. "Where did you get that crazy ship suit?" Other than being a little pale and the cast on his arm, he looked to be in good shape.

"From your doctor, silly," answered Anthea with a mock scowl, "and don't call me 'Ant'. I'm not an insect. Where did you get the fur rug?" she crossed over to his side. The pile of gray and cream fur next to Brin raised its head, opened one bleary eye to survey the room full of people and bleeked.

"That's Lionel, one of our ship cats," said Mishael. "Remember, I promised to introduce you when we were on the *Suncatcher*?" Lionel, stood, arched, yawned mightily, then head bumped Brin under the chin. Brin laughed and gave his fur some long strokes, earning a rumbling purr.

"Wow!" said Anthea. She leaned forward and Lionel touched noses delicately with her. Anthea laughed at the tickle. "You said he scared you to death in a dark corridor, but he seems like a sweetheart."

"Oh, Lionel is very polite with new people," answered Mishael. "Once he gets to know you, though, watch out. His favorite game is trip the human."

Brin's mother nodded. "Lionel has been keeping Brin company since he came out of anesthesia. I was surprised Dr. Rensaleer allowed it, but I'm glad he had some company before we were reunited."

Lionel settled down next to Brin again and rolled on his back for a belly rub, basking in the attention from two young humans.

***

Two days later, Nicholas Withers, AKA Gerald Minnick, sat in the familiar metal chair of the Ship Security interrogation room, listening attentively as Rolland gave him a sanitized version of the current situation. Hal Renfro, sleeves rolled up past his enormous biceps, leaned casually against the bulkhead. Withers still felt weak and unsteady from nearly twenty years in cold sleep, but he had no problem following Rolland's narrative. "We're certain your organization, and your family, have a hideaway in the system," Rolland finished. "We want the location." He let the words hang in the air while he gauged Withers' reaction. So far, he had kept things neutral, offering neither threats nor incentives.

"You're recording?" asked Withers calmly.

Rolland nodded.

"There are five fallback positions. Which ones they use will depend on the system's planetary alignment." Withers proceeded to give the locations, capabilities and entry codes for all five bolt holes. "My family and the

Restoration may have added more in the sixty years I've been gone," he finished. "Those are the ones I know about."

"I have to ask," said Rolland. "Why are you giving us the information?"

Withers looked down at the table. "I'm not sure myself." He looked up again. "There's more if you'd like to hear it." Rolland nodded and Hal put a cup of water and a small bowl of apple slices in front of Withers. He took a drink and started to talk. Two hours later, he ran out of energy and information. Hal and another Ship Security officer escorted him back to his cell in the brig.

Hal took Rolland to his office still shaking his head. "That didn't go anything like I expected. I wonder what happened to the thoroughly nasty person who nearly killed everyone on this ship?" he asked rhetorically. "He didn't even ask for a deal. I know it's Withers, but his combative attitude is completely gone!"

"Maybe he found a conscience while he was in cold sleep," answered Rolland. "Based on what you told me and the outrageous demands of the other Restoration agents, I wasn't expecting cooperation either. I'll happily take full advantage, though. When he's rested, we'll see if he's willing to continue. Between what he told us and the 'Commodore' Yates com logs, we're already light years ahead of where I thought we'd be. We have enough to move on the fallback facilities and give the Restoration leadership no place to go. Himself will be pleased."

"Withers could be playing us."

Rolland nodded acknowledgment, then pointed to a marked location on a three-dimensional representation of the system. "We can check this facility to verify his information one way or the other. We're diverting a patrol craft now. They'll be there in about twelve hours. It's on the opposite side of the system from Pollux habitat. We shouldn't tip our hand."

Four hours later, Pete Worsley stepped into Withers' cell carrying a brown paper bag and bemused expression. Withers looked up from his bunk, a slightly battered paper copy of the Bible in his hands. "You haven't changed a bit in twenty years, Pete," he said. "Do you have cookies in there?" He gestured at the bag." Pete nodded. Withers toed the button to unfold a small table and stool from the deck in front of him. "Have a seat and share them with me if you will."

"You've changed in twenty years, Gerald," said Pete, sitting down on the stool and taking two cookies out of the bag. He laid napkins out and set a cookie on each. "You've never invited me to sit down. Even your face looks different, younger I think."

Withers laughed out loud, a sound that had a disused croak to it. "Pete," he said, "please call me Nicholas. Gerald was a lie that I'm done with."

"You don't know how glad I am to hear it," answered Pete. "Can you tell me what happened?"

"I went into the cold sleep can thinking about everything I'd done to other people to put myself in this position," Withers answered. "I suspect I spent twenty years in my dreams pondering what a waste it was. All those years I spent hating the Long Boat Free Trade Syndicate in general and Captain Brelling in particular. What did I accomplish with all my anger? I made people miserable, poisoned their minds with fear, and enjoyed it because it fed my hate and let me feel superior. I was raised to hate, and I turned it into an art form.

"When I woke up, I felt lost and unfocused, but light as a feather. I tried to figure out what was missing. It took me a while, but when I saw that hulking ship security officer, Renfro, I realized I didn't hate him and everyone around me like I had before. The hate was gone, and with it, my reason for going on, but also the crushing weight I've lived with most of my life. I didn't realize what a burden my hate was until I laid it down." Withers finally looked up at Pete Worsley. His eyes were haunted.

Pete cleared his throat, trying to find his own voice. "I know you don't think so, but you're close to redemption, Nicholas. You've been convinced of your own sin. I hope you know you can't make up for it, and you don't need to. To have God's forgiveness, you just need to repent and ask Jesus to save you."

"I know," answered Nicholas. "I did read the book of John and other passages you pointed me to. I just can't bring myself to believe I deserve to be forgiven."

"None of us deserve God's mercy, but he extends it to all who will receive it anyway," said Pete. "I'm glad you're cooperating with the investigators. You may save some lives, and it will probably reduce the consequences of what you've done. I encourage you to keep cooperating, but nothing you do is going to erase your sin. There's an ancient gospel song that says 'If you tarry till you're better, you will never come at all'. You'll never be better if you don't believe and call on God for salvation."

Nicholas Withers buried his face in his hands for a moment. At last, he looked up and said, "I'll think about it."

"I'll be praying for you," said Pete. He leaned back and took a bite of his cookie. "This is a good batch. Don't let yours dry out."

Nicholas picked his cookie up and bit into it, chewing appreciatively. "I used to dream about these when we were headed to Tau Ceti. I hated your guts, but I loved your cookies. I still don't know why you bother with me."

"I wondered many times myself," Pete answered. "You were a hard case, Nicholas, but God can soften the hardest heart. Maybe the cookies helped. I need to go, but I'll be back." He rose and put his hand on Nicholas' shoulder. "Think on the things we talked about." Nicholas twitched a bit at his touch, but nodded.

***

"Withers turned??" said Captain Brelling incredulously.

Hal Renfro nodded. He and Rolland were meeting with The Bancroft and the captain in her conference room. "I wouldn't have believed it if I hadn't seen it with my own eyes," he said. "What's more, I think he's sincere. We'll know if his information is good when the patrol ship gets to the coordinates he gave us."

"What did you offer him?" asked the captain looking at The Bancroft.

"I didn't authorize any kind of a deal," he said, holding his hands up defensively.

"We didn't offer him anything," said Rolland. "He just asked if we were recording and started spouting information. I can probably get more out of him once he's rested. I didn't want to exhaust him that soon out of cold sleep."

"Show me the recording," said the captain flatly, skepticism written all over her features. She watched the first five minutes then signaled Hal to turn it off. "I'll be spaced without a vac suit," she muttered. "It's hard to believe that's the same person."

"We may have Pete Worsley to thank for Withers' change of heart," said Hal. "He wouldn't take credit, though."

"No, Pete wouldn't," mused the captain. "He always gives God the glory, but I remember he used to visit Withers a couple of times a week when we had him in the brig at hard labor. If that change isn't a miracle, though, I don't know what is." She shook her head. "What do we have in addition to the locations of their hideouts?"

Roland leaned forward, "We have the names of the top leadership of the Restoration here in Lalande. They are the driving force behind the rebellion. Also, a good description of three Restoration operatives from Sol. Withers thinks at least one of them returned to Sol. He gave us what amounts to an organizational chart of the Restoration in Lalande at the time he left. The com logs we got from Yates helped confirm his information and fill in some changes and gaps. I won't be certain until we confirm the hideout, but everything indicates he's been straight with us."

The captain looked at The Bancroft. "Do you have the forces to secure the hideouts and take on Pollux habitat?"

Wallace the Third shook his head. "I'm kicking around ideas with my people on how to approach this. If they know we've eliminated the possibility of retreat, they'll probably fort up in Pollux. I'd happily leave them there to rot, but there are eight hundred thousand people on the habitat. Most of them have little to no part in the rebellion. I don't want them in the middle of a battle, and we know the Restoration will gladly use them as leverage."

"What if you had a battalion of powered-armor equipped militia and a platoon of commandos to add to the mix?" the captain asked.

"Your people will fight with us?" queried The Bancroft.

"I'll have to ask for volunteers and I want assurances on how you'll deploy them, but I know my people will want to help defeat the Restoration."

Wallace rubbed his jaw, "I'm loath to turn down that much combat power. Trained troops and powered armor are both rare outside the System Security Force. We're stretched too thin in several critical spots as it is. We'll need to be careful. The rebels are bought and paid for by interests in the Sol system, but they would jump on a chance to claim we're using foreign troops. Troops of the Long Boat Free Trade Syndicate loose in the system would be an effective rallying cry."

"I agree we need to be careful," said Rolland. "If we need to dig the Restoration leadership out of Pollux habitat, though, it will be a lot easier with the *Nai'a's* militia and commandos. I've seen these people train. They know their business better than anyone but full-time professional military, better than some professional units I could name."

"Until we figure out which way the Restoration will jump, we'll have to plan for contingencies," said Wallace. "Thank you for the offer, Anne. I hope we don't have to take you up on it. We'll keep your people in the loop and include them in our planning. I doubt the hard-core members of the Restoration will surrender, and I don't want them to bunker up in Pollux habitat. We'll leave them an escape option and hope they take it."

***

The next day Rolland and Hal Renfro spent four productive hours with Nicholas Withers. The patrol vessel had confirmed his information on the hideout. "Your father is likely one of the leaders of the Restoration, Rolland said. "From what we've told you, which way do you think he'll jump?"

Withers shook his head, "I can't even guess. I never saw my father after he was put in prison for attempting to poison the *Nai'a* with a bio agent. I was three at the time, so I barely remember him. My uncle Lewis picked up the reins, as I've told you. Lewis won't surrender. He might run, if he's convinced the rebellion is doomed."

Rolland leaned back and considered the man. "What do you want out of this, Withers? I can't promise anything. You'll have to face the Lalande justice system to account for your actions. You *have* been helpful, though. I can at least speak to the judge."

"I don't want anything," Nicholas replied with a troubled expression. "I'm not looking for a deal. I'll serve whatever sentence I'm given. It won't be enough." Rolland looked at Hal, who just gave a slight shrug.

Chapter 23 – Follow the Money

March 19th, AD 3208
Bancroft Station – New Dawn Orbit
Lalande System Security Forces Headquarters

Commander Kevin Hartley's eyebrows went up when he saw the obvious battle scars in the entrance foyer of the Lalande System Security Force headquarters. The captain had decided to send him and Mr. Barboa to this meeting with The Bancroft while she remained aboard the *Nai'a*.

Rolland Dunleavy escorted them. "Things got a bit lively when the rebellion kicked off," he said. "We've had higher priorities than cosmetic repairs in the meantime."

The guard on duty checked Mr. Barboa's and Hartley's virtual credentials, then sent a temporary authorization code to their PCOMs and waived them through.

"I can imagine," the *Nai'a's* first officer replied. "Did they have people inside the headquarters?"

"Three," answered Rolland, "but our security measures limited the damage. The frontal assault was a surprise, but thanks to the sacrifice of the entrance guards, we trapped them in the foyer and mopped them up." The trio passed through two more security checkpoints before arriving at a meeting room sized for forty, but containing only The Bancroft and two crown guards.

Once greetings were exchanged, Rolland Dunleavy activated a holographic depiction of the Lalande system. "Pollux Habitat is here, at the L1 point of the third planet, Yotun. The two closest Restoration bolt holes are one on Yotun's third moon and another in the outer asteroid belt. According to Nicholas Withers, either has the capacity to hide the leadership cadre for decades. We can't approach them without tipping our hand. The one we investigated opened up to the codes Nicholas Withers provided, but it also transmitted a coded signal. We don't think it got through our jamming. It's an impressive installation, a 3-kilometer asteroid honeycombed with tunnels including a sizable interior hanger. From the outside, it looks like a dead rock, but it carries a current corporation mining claim transceiver that warns off visitors.

"The rebellion isn't over, but we believe we've destroyed or captured most of their ships. The intelligence from our people continues to roll in and we have a much better picture of what's going on. Some of their remaining ships were detected on course for Pollux Habitat. We're coming to the end game, but we still don't know if the leadership will run, or fight. We would prefer they run, but it will only happen if they think it's their best chance. I'm afraid they'll use the population of Pollux Habitat as a shield."

"I canna let that happen," said The Bancroft. "We need a way to convince them to run, but I'm out of ideas." As he finished, Lisandra Redding entered the room escorted by a tall red-headed woman who bore a passing resemblance to Wallace the Third. "Siobhan!" he exclaimed warmly, rising to give her a hug. "I dinna expect you to have results this soon."

His sister smiled wryly. "I didn't expect Lisandra, here, to shred the security of our financial system and several banks this quickly either. I did, however, think you should know the results as soon as possible. Lisandra, would you give them the high level?"

"Certainly," the hacker answered, taking a seat. "Most of the data we've uncovered will be more useful to Captain Brelling in her investigation of the Restoration when we return to Sol. Several Sol mega-corps are neck deep in the Restoration, and we have the evidence to directly implicate them now. For your purposes, we have the record of every payment made by those corporations to the Restoration leadership here in Lalande. In the process, they violated a score or two of banking laws trying to cover their tracks."

"The resulting fines should go a long way toward getting the exchequer out of the red," said Siobhan. "Please continue."

"Based on the money trail and other intelligence," said Lisandra, "the fallback base in the outer asteroid belt is the largest and best equipped. We found a schematic and it appears to be a hollowed-out asteroid you could hide the *Nai'a* in." Commander Hartley and Rolland exchanged glances.

"That's where they'll run then," declared The Bancroft. "We just need to give them the right push."

"If you'll authorize it under your emergency powers," said Siobhan, "I can freeze the money in every account they've used across the system, open or clandestine. They'll have other resources, but that should put a serious crimp in their ability to pay for anything. They won't even be able to pay the workers on Pollux Habitat."

Rolland nodded. "If we combine freezing their assets with a leak about a fleet move on Pollux, we stand a good chance of flushing them out."

"The money trail also leads to several informants here on Bancroft Station," said Lisandra. "If you let the information leak to two or three of them, I'm sure it will end up where you want it."

"It's a question of timing," said Rolland. "Do we want to engage them in a fleet action, or take them once they reach the hideout?"

Mr. Barboa looked thoughtful. "You had a number of innocent civilians caught up in your last space battle. Also, you would have a hard time surprising them in space. You're going to lose ships if you make it a fleet action. It won't be fun fighting on their territory, but the cost in ships and lives will probably be lower if you storm the hideout instead. It depends on how robust their defenses are. If you can get good intelligence on those, I lean toward taking the hideout soon after they arrive. You want to trap them with their ships inside the asteroid. I doubt they have well trained troops, or the kinds of weapons we have."

Wallace nodded, "I agree. We aren't aware of any fighting forces in Lalande with the training and capabilities of System Security, or your militia. The founding families are allowed a small personal guard force, but mercenary forces and powered armor are outlawed. I'm sure they have powered armor and heavy weapons, but the knowledge to use them effectively is another matter. If, as we expect, they hide their ships inside the asteroid, it will be a real opportunity to wrap them up in a neat package."

"We need them to believe they've made it clean away," said Rolland. "They won't use active sensors if they're trying to stay hidden. We can get our people in close before they know we're coming."

"Lisandra and I need to get back to untangling the financial web," said Siobhan rising. She and the hacker left the others to their planning.

***

Abishai and Shanyah helped each other into their armor while the rest of their militia platoon did the same. "I wonder what's on the captain's mind," he said. "She's never gathered the entire militia together in full battle rattle."

"I don't know," she answered, "but I suspect it's got to do with the civil war here in Lalande. I doubt anyone would be foolish enough to attack the ship here in New Dawn orbit." They finished their checks, hoisted their weapons and followed the rest of the platoon to Cooper Green.

Captain Brelling surveyed the militia battalion drawn up in neat ranks on the green with a mixture of pride and trepidation. The commando platoon's flat black armor contrasted neatly with the gleaming white ranks of militia. She accepted the battalion commander's salute, then had them all stand at ease. "You're probably wondering why I called you all here today." Her opening sally elicited obligatory chuckles from the troops, then her expression grew serious. "I can't go into details, but the heart of it is this. The Bancroft and his people need our help. If things work out, there will be an opportunity to crush the Restoration leadership and remaining combat power in this system. Our part will likely include assaulting an enemy hideout. I'm confident that both your training and weapons are superior to the people you'd be facing. That doesn't mean the mission won't be dangerous. The enemy will be motivated and making a last stand. You know first-hand the kind of evil the Restoration represents. I told The Bancroft we would only send volunteers. I want you to take a day to think about it, go through the information you'll be receiving shortly and make your decisions. We need to give you time to rehearse and train. I'll meet with the volunteers here in twenty-four hours."

In the end, one pregnant militiawoman, who would have been disqualified anyway, bowed out. The rest of the battalion and all of the commandos volunteered.

***

I never thought we'd be training for an assault," said Abishai, "but this is one mission I'm definitely up for." He and Shanyah were both exhausted from their latest combat rehearsal. They trekked wearily back to their quarters together to get cleaned up.

"I'm with you," said Shanyah. "I wish Kalei wasn't the battalion surgeon, but it would be hypocritical of me to ask her not to go."

"Ditto for Mishael," Abishai answered. "I know he'll try to find a way to be in the thick of it, boat bay officer or not."

"They don't have it in them to stand by while others go into danger. I suppose we should be proud of them, but a big part of me wants to wrap both of them up in cotton and stuff them in a closet until this is over."

"I don't think their Mama could feel any other way," answered Abishai. "I'm worried about Quester too. Since he joined the commandos, his schemes get wilder by the day."

"You don't know the half of it," Shanyah answered. "I've been helping modify the sting ships for the assault."

"One of Quester's ideas?" asked Abishai.

Shanyah nodded. "Sometimes I think he's completely off his rocker. This is one of those times. He's taken to the commandos like a fish to water, and the feeling is mutual. They couldn't have someone faster than their best outside the organization, so they adopted him."

"He's not the only one," said Abishai. "The platoon's core is still former Great Prospects cadre, but they had a number of gaps to fill when we left Tau Ceti and more when we stood up the sting ship squadron. Grady joined up a few years ago. Roan and Paulene weren't thrilled, but Quester took him under his wing and says he's done well."

"Those two make quite a pair," Shanyah answered. "I think they're on the Chief of Boat's permanent watch list."

"Reversing the plus-velocity ring and coating it with coconut oil will do that," replied Abishai. "The results were a lot more fun to witness than experience."

"I hope their plan for the sting ships works," said Shanyah. "If it doesn't, we're in for a tunnel-by-tunnel fight. We both know how hard a defending force can make that kind of slog."

"At least we'll be together," said Abishai. Shanyah had been promoted to platoon leader in the militia with Abishai as her heavy weapons squad leader.

"Just remember," said Shanyah, "you have a job to do. Your priority is to your squad, not me. Also, you'll follow my orders or face the consequences."

Abishai held up both hands in defense. "We've had this discussion before. I'll do my duty."

"Yes, but I know how that brain of yours is hard-wired to protect me. Most of the time it's a comfort, but in combat it's a complication. Remember, I can take care of myself."

"I have the lumps to prove it," Abishai rejoined.

"Don't tempt me to haul you to the dojo and give you another demonstration," said Shanyah darkly.

"You'll have to catch me first!" Abishai summoned the energy to dash down the corridor, only to catch a toe on a gray and cream streak that darted between his feet from a side passageway. Abishai yelped, turned a complete somersault in the air and landed heavily on his tush. "I'll get you back, furball!" he yelled at Lionel's nonchalantly retreating figure. He looked behind him to where Shanyah was laughing so hard she had to lean on the bulkhead to keep from falling down. He gave her his best glare as he wearily pulled himself to his feet.

***

When first officer, Commander Kevin Hartley and Rolland Dunleavy returned to the *Nai'a*, they sat down with Captain Brelling to brief her on the planning for Operation Mop Bucket. "Who came up with that name?" asked the captain.

Kevin looked sheepish. "Guilty," he said. "I meant it as a joke but everyone picked it up and, of course, gave me full credit." Captain Brelling snorted and made a little come-ahead motion with her hand. "You know the basic plan. Our sting ships and troops are equipped and ready. We load everything out on a mini-carrier disguised as the refining ship *Smelt It*, over the next twenty-four hours. Lalande System Security Force assault shuttles are already aboard. Mr. Barboa will be our liaison to The Bancroft, who insists on commanding the mission. Rimon Barkscale commands the militia battalion. Mr. Barboa says he can stay out of Rimon's business, we'll see. Palamar O'Clair commands the commando platoon, and Julian Garrity commands the sting ship squadron. Together, they represent our best chance of forcing an entry the militia can exploit."

"As soon as the mini-carrier is on the way," put in Rolland, "we'll seed the intelligence about an attack on Pollux Habitat to three of the Restoration's operatives on Bancroft Station. We think we know how they communicate with the leadership, but their reaction should confirm our suspicions. After that, we wait and see if the enemy cooperates."

"Have you uncovered any intelligence about their combat capabilities?" asked the captain. "I want our people to know what they're up against."

"We know they have three remote control ambulatory gun platforms," said the first officer. "The twenty-centimeter rail gun main armament of those is a problem even for our powered armor. Taking them out will be a priority. Our best analysis says they'll have limited powered armor, but a number of remote laser turrets. We have an invoice for several hundred. What they don't have is troops trained to fight against a boarding action. We probably have four times the number of combat veterans they do, just in the militia. We're counting on them being motivated and eager, but we can do it the hard way if we have to. The Bancroft's Own is contributing a platoon of shock troops. Add it all up and we should enjoy a significant advantage in combat power. We'll need it to take prepared defenses."

"Mr. Barboa and Rimon are both happy with the combat rehearsals," the first officer continued. "We've always trained for counter-attacks, so assault training wasn't as big a stretch for the militia as I feared."

"You still think this craziness with the commandos will work?" asked the captain.

"I do," Hartley answered. "At the very least, it will sow confusion with our enemy, which is always a good thing."

***

The Driscolls saw Abishai, Shanyah, Kalci and Mishael off the next day. "I wish I could go," said Alexander. "This is our system and our problem."

Abishai gave him a thump on the shoulder, "I know you're willing, but you still need to rehab those legs and we have all the pilots we need. We also have our own good reasons to want the Restoration taken down in Lalande."

Anthea looked up at Mishael, then impulsively ran over to give him a hug. "Be careful," she said, then hugged Kalei, giving her the same admonishment.

"We will," answered Kalei, tousling Anthea's wild curls. "You keep Lionel in line for us and make sure Brin gets to physical therapy." Lionel was busy stropping everyone's legs and getting in the way.

Anthea nodded solemnly, "I'll say extra prayers for all of you."

The Bonaparte' family picked up their bags and headed for the aft boat bay.

Chapter 24 – Hastings Pudding

March 24th, AD 3208
Lalande System Outer Asteroid Belt
Mini Carrier Smelt It Flight Deck

Quester checked Grady's commando suit and combat load out, then stood straight while Grady checked him over. The commando suits were optimized for speed and stealth. Power-assisted movement made a trained commando lightning fast. The exterior's active camouflage could mimic any background, making the commandos nearly invisible when not moving. The ablative armor could shrug off small arms fire for a time, but didn't have the survivability of a full set of powered armor.

Smelt It's flight deck buzzed with activity around them as all twelve sting ships and a battalion's worth of assault shuttles readied for launch. Shanyah trotted across the deck to her platoon's shuttle, her armor's boot clanging on the steel deck. She couldn't resist helping Mishael and his crew with the sting ship preparations, but it was time to check on her platoon. She accepted an armored hand up from Abishai at the top of the ramp, clipped her personal weapon into an overhead rack, and webbed into a seat. She checked her tactical display and found everyone present, showing green on combat readiness. "Any issues?" she asked Abishai, who was her acting platoon sergeant.

"All Ship Rats present and accounted for," answered Abishai. The entire platoon had adopted Quester's rat-face artwork for their helmets. "All systems go, for once. I think the impending combat focused everyone's attention on proper maintenance."

"It has that effect," answered Shanyah. "Now we wait and see if the can opener works."

Grady gave Quester a thumbs-up, not trusting his voice with the pre-combat jitters coursing through his system. Quester cocked his head, then slapped him on the shoulder. "Buck up Grady, we've pulled crazier stunts than this," he said.

Grady squinted at him. "Not by much. I hope these space jockeys don't forget what they're carrying and turn us into paste." He eyed the sting ship with scant favor.

"If nothing else," answered Quester, "we make a fine bomb-load." With the assistance of Mishael and the sting ship's crew chief, they locked themselves to temporary frames mounted to hardpoints on either side of the space fighter. The pilots weren't thrilled with giving up a third of their firepower, or being turned into glorified shuttles, but they understood the mission. With a lot of skill, and a bit of luck, the space-black sting ships would deliver their human cargo without being detected.

The asteroid harboring the leadership of the Restoration appeared to be one more dead rock in the asteroid belt. Only the unnatural rotation of the mountain-sized boulder indicated a human presence. As long as the enemy didn't use active scanners, they had a good chance of getting in undetected.

On the bridge of *Smelt It*, The Bancroft watched the launch countdown timer on the tactical display and tried to exude confidence. Captain Gleeze was a proven veteran, and Wallace wisely chose not to joggle his elbow in the tense moment. The tactical officer gave a verbal countdown as the timer approached zero. "Sting ship launch in five, four, three, two, one, launch." Twelve hatches released and *Smelt It*'s rotation flipped twelve sting ships into the void. Using cold gas thruster packs, the pilots formed up and set course for their asteroid target. "Sting ship squadron on course. Intercept in twenty minutes," the tactical officer intoned.

After a few minutes, Captain Gleeze turned to The Bancroft. "No reaction from the asteroid, sir. Shuttle launch at ten minutes as planned?"

"Aye, Captain, as long as the enemy continues to cooperate, we'll stick to the schedule. Launch shuttles on the least-time trajectory."

The Restoration's leadership had abandoned Pollux Habitat in unseemly haste soon after the leaked information about a planned assault reached them. An assortment of ten ships left within a few hours of one another, initially headed in any direction not on course to the asteroid. Wallace was betting they had gone dark and ended up here at their hideout in the outer belt. *Smelt It* was on a registered course as close to the asteroid as they dared get and still seem to be on legitimate business.

Mr. Barboa hovered in the background; hands clenched behind his back. He knew Rimon Barkscale was up to the task of commanding the militia battalion, but he still longed to be with the troops he had trained up from nothing. At the ten-minute mark *Smelt It* began launching pairs of assault shuttles toward the asteroid in sequence until they were all on a carefully aligned ballistic trajectory toward the asteroid.

***

Abishai felt a clunk, and his stomach tried to climb into his throat as their shuttle dropped into freefall with the velocity imparted by the ship's spin. The shuttle pilot used a few tiny puffs of gas to align them with the direction of flight. He made the tactical plot available to the troops in back. To Abishai, the shuttle icons looked like a double-string of pearls pointed at their objective. Ahead of them, a cluster of green icons marked the position of the sting ships coasting toward the asteroid as well. He said a silent prayer for Quester, Grady, and the rest of the commandos. He reached over and gave his wife's gauntleted hand a squeeze which she returned. Butterflies danced a Texas two-step in his gut, and he tried to relax. He closed his eyes and let "Come Thou Fount of Every Blessing" roll through his mind to calm his nerves.

***

Quester and Grady dealt with their own nervous butterflies as they approached the target. Julian Garrity skillfully guided the sting ship toward the drop point. "Good luck, you two!" he said over their hard-wired com-link. "Drop in five...four...three...two...one...drop!" Garrity released them from the ship mounts, and they floated onward toward the asteroid. Quester's heads-up display overlayed a virtual reality on the surface of the asteroid. He quickly identified a possible access point and used a few measured pulses of his commando suit's thrusters to alter his trajectory toward what was supposed to be a maintenance tunnel hatch. All around this end of the football-shaped asteroid, the other eleven commando teams were vectoring toward their own targets of opportunity. According to the schematics Lalande Security Force intelligence acquired, the camouflaged entrance to the ship hangar was at this end of the asteroid. It was time to open the way for the shuttles.

Quester and Grady landed on either side of the hatch and quickly drove anchors into the asteroid's rocky surface. The big rock's rotation tried to fling them into space, but cables from the anchors to their suits held them steady. They peeled back the camouflage covering hiding the hatch, leaving it attached on one side to hinge open. There were no outside controls, so Quester powered up the hacking device he and Lisandra Redding had put together. He activated the door knocker program and waited while it probed the electromagnetic spectrum and analyzed the local networks. Grady readied an explosive charge in case the subtle approach failed. Within a minute, Lisandra's program co-opted the carrier signal for the hideout's sensors and went to work. From now on, the sensors would show empty space, regardless of any detected signal. Sooner or later, someone would notice the lack of returns, but for a precious few minutes, the shuttles would remain undetected even if the defenders turned on their active sensors. Simultaneously, the lockpick program wormed its way into the maintenance fault detection network, eventually gaining enough control to open every hatch on the commandos' target list. Quester left the hacking package and its small transceiver attached to the exterior of the hatch. After closing the hatch, he found a data port to plug a small accompanying unit into. Across the aft end of the asteroid, eleven other commando teams slipped inside the rock and raced toward their objectives.

***

Back on *Smelt It*, Lisandra Redding and the ship's coms officer worked through the faint signal from the hacking package to pull essential data from the sensor and maintenance nets. Lisandra smiled a small satisfied smile as she penetrated the controller program for the hangar door.

***

The Hangar Control Officer on the asteroid was having a good yawn and stretch in his chair when the warning klaxon for the main hangar door began blaring and a red strobe flashed. He jumped up and was reaching for the emergency shut down breaker when a section of the bulkhead seemed to detach itself. An armored fist knocked him off his feet. He shook his head blearily, but offered no resistance as his wrists and ankles were bound.

***

The final few minutes of approach for the shuttles seemed like an eternity. Every crew expected the asteroid's defensive weapons to open fire at any moment. Instead, what appeared to be the rocky face of the aft end of the asteroid irised open, showing a massive hangar currently occupied by a dozen ships. "We're going in. Brace for acceleration!" the pilot of Abishai's assault shuttle ordered over the combat net. The assault shuttles made a coordinated dash across the remaining gap, finding deck space well short of the ships to touch down.

***

Lewis Withers ran down the short corridor from his quarters to Asteroid Central Control in response to the klaxon blaring a continual alert. He entered the chaotic space in a rush and nearly bowled over Colonel Blenheim, the defense force commander. "What in the misaligned planets is going on?" he demanded.

"I'm assessing that now," replied Blenheim calmly. "The main hangar is open and under assault. I've lost contact with my people there and have to assume they've been taken down. I've ordered Lieutenant Colonel Geary to get a reaction force together and draw the powered armor from the armory."

"How did they get inside the main hangar?" Withers asked.

"Through the door," Colonel Blenheim answered. "They hacked our networks and infiltrated through the aft maintenance tunnels. Phillips is trying to root them out of our systems now." He nodded at a young man typing furiously away at a virtual keyboard while figures danced across his display. "I expect the enemy to advance to the main cavern through one of the large cargo tunnels. We'll have the reaction force meet them and push them back to the hangar. I'll send the rest of our troops down the other two cargo tunnels to help defeat them there. They can't have a large force with all the deployments we're certain of."

"Do it!" spat Withers. "I'd like to know who ratted us out, but that's immaterial now. We'll have to hope they don't disable the ships. If I know Wallace, he'll have a fleet on the way. We'll need to get to the ships, scatter, and rendezvous at the backup location."

Blenheim glanced at him. "You'd better suit up, sir," he said. "We're going to have to fight our way to the ships." He turned back to his tactical display and barked more orders to his subordinates.

***

Abishai and Shanyah waited with their platoon nearly two hundred meters into the arrow-straight cargo tunnel. Fifty meters ahead, an armored door blocked their advance, taking up the entire twenty-meter width of the tunnel. If their schematics were correct, a second armored door another fifty meters past this one opened into the main cavern. There had been surprisingly little resistance in the hangar occupying the aft end of the asteroid. The commandos had secured the maintenance and refueling facilities, quickly taking down the few armed crew members that offered resistance. The militia helped gather the rest and put them under guard in a dead-end parts storage tunnel. The hangar and the tunnel were both unpressurized. The double doors would allow an airlock configuration for future pressurization of the main cavern, but according to their information, only the living spaces under the floor of the cavern were currently aired up.

"I do hate it when the enemy is late to the dance floor," Shanyah said.

"Tell me again why we agreed to be the bait in this trap," said Abishai.

"Because the Ship Rats are the best in the battalion at conducting an orderly retreat," she answered. Just then their acoustic sensors indicated the far door was opening. "Shields up!" Shanyah ordered over the tactical net. The platoon adjusted their disposable ablative armor shields and hunkered down. "Blow it!" she ordered the platoon sapper, kneeling behind Abishai and his shield. A brilliant flash lit up the tunnel, and a shockwave propagated through the rock at their feet. The door fell toward the advancing enemy troops, causing a few seconds of confusion, then a hail of fire descended on the platoon. Shanyah's platoon held their fire as if taken by surprise then got off a few erratic bursts at the advancing enemy. "You know the drill, Ship Rats, advance to the rear by fire teams and give them enough tungsten to keep their heads down." As she finished speaking a crew-served rail gun slug tore through the top of Abishai's shield, clipping her armored shoulder and knocking her backward and down. Before she could move, Abishai picked her up, slung her over his shoulder and moved swiftly back down the tunnel. Shanyah used the opportunity to unclip the ten-millimeter multimode rifle from her armored back. She aimed in the enemy's general direction and send a mix of smoke and EMP rounds into their ranks over the top of Abishai's shield.

"If you had picked me up like this to cross the threshold on our wedding night, you'd have been in trouble," she said to Abishai, continuing to fire. The rest of the platoon was alternately firing at the enemy force and swiftly retreating down the tunnel.

"Just trying to keep up appearances," said Abishai. "If they think we have wounded it will encourage them to keep after us." An enemy grenade landed short, peppering their shields with shrapnel.

"They're a bit too encouraged for my taste," said Shanyah as a flechette round pinged off her helmet.

The platoon quickly reached the hangar end of the tunnel. They'd blown the armored doors on their way in and now used the rubble for cover to make a stand, discarding their used-up shields. Shanyah checked her tactical display, nodding with satisfaction. She hunkered down behind a thick section of steel door and joined the platoon in pouring harassing fire into the oncoming enemy. The concentrated fire caused the Restoration forces to pause their advance and take what cover they could find.

Lieutenant Colonel Geary peered through the smoke trying to assess the attackers' position. "One more push and we've got them!" he encouraged his troops. "Armor section to the front and take that position out!" When the enemy fire suddenly slackened, he switched to the command net. "Send Bravo and Charlie force into the hangar, sir, we've got them on the run." As he cleared the hangar door close behind his powered armor section, he saw the enemy troops retreating and putting the Restoration ships between them. "Move out, move out!" he shouted. "Don't damage our ships. Let's clean these amateurs out of our hangar!" His troops joined with Bravo and Charlie force emerging from the other tunnels. Together they rushed to finish off the attackers.

***

The Restoration's cyber specialist finally cleared the weapons and sensor nets of attacking programs and nodded to the weapons officer in central command. "You can fire up the active sensors and weapons now."

The weapons officer quickly sent the commands to uncover his suite of sensor, missile, and laser installations. His tactical plot slowly populated as the sensors came online. He had just registered the presence of several small vessels in close to the asteroid when the twelve sting ships opened fire.

Before he could acquire a single targeting solution, every radar on the asteroid was turned to slag. He switched to infrared, gritting his teeth as the ships wove a dance of destruction above the asteroid, taking out his weapons one by one.

"What are those things?" demanded Lewis Withers.

"Some sort of space fighter, sir. I wouldn't be surprised if they delivered the first invaders. They seem to know the location of every weapon we've got." He managed to get a shot off with one of his laser batteries but badly missed the swift little ship he had targeted. The next second, he lost the feed from the battery. He leaned back in his seat shaking his head in disgust. "We're down to two optical sensors and no weapons, sir. The only thing useful I can tell you is the big mining ship we saw changed course. It will be here in a few hours."

Withers did his best to remain calm. "How are our troops doing?" he asked.

"They're pushing the enemy hard," said Colonel Blenheim. "They should have control of the hangar shortly."

***

Shanyah had the platoon slow their retreat slightly to allow the Restoration forces to see them running, then sprinted for the cover of the assault shuttles. She checked her status display. Several of her troops showed damaged armor, and there were a few minor injuries, but everyone made it to the fallback position.

Three company's worth of Restoration troops, led by twelve soldiers in powered armor, cleared their space ships and charged across the gap toward the combat shuttles. As the last few troops crossed into the open space, a swarm of one-hundred combat centipedes shot from hiding places all over the hangar. At the same time a dozen assault shuttle auto cannons spoke as one, smashing into the line of powered armor, reducing the formation's main combat power to useless junk. The centipedes needed only seconds to surround the remaining Restoration troops. The twelve autocannon turrets fired once more, this time into the floor of the hangar, throwing up chunks of asteroid between the troops and the shuttles.

"THROW DOWN YOUR WEAPONS NOW!!" Rimon Barkscale's voice over-rode the enemy's combat net.

The *Nai'a's* militia battalion, now sporting garish helmet decorations on their powered armor, rushed the sides and rear of the enemy formation from concealment. Faced with overwhelming odds, most of the survivors dropped their weapons.

At the rear of the formation, Lieutenant Colonel Geary raised his auto-carbine and fired at the nearest militia trooper. He managed to get a single round off, missing his target, before four centipedes shot forward and swarmed over him. There was a high-pitched scream then an audible pop as the centipedes cracked his armor and discharged their high voltage capacitors. Geary dropped like a puppet with the strings cut, the mass of centipedes bearing him to the rocky floor of the hangar. The Restoration troops still holding weapons quickly tossed them aside and raised their hands.

***

"That tears it," spat Lewis Withers as Geary's data feed went black. "They suckered us in. That was an entire battalion of powered armor. We never had a chance, but we can still make them pay. What have you got left, Colonel?"

"The people in this room, sir. We threw everything we had into the assault. I suggest you try to contact the commander of the assault force and negotiate a surrender. We can't fight them with the civilian staff and the leadership's families."

"What about remote-control mobile gun platforms?"

"The technician team is still putting them together, but without supporting troops, they're of limited value."

"They can take down powered armor, can't they?" Withers asked.

"Yes," the colonel answered, "but those are trained assault troops, we'll only get one chance. I don't have anything else to fight them with. From a military perspective, this is over."

The communications officer looked up at Withers. "Sir, I've got an incoming call. They asked for you specifically."

"Put it on the screen," Withers ground out.

The image of The Bancroft filled the monitor a second later. "Lewis Withers, you're accused of high treason and murder," he declared flatly. "I have one offer. If you surrender now, I'll take the death penalty off the table for you and everyone else on the asteroid. If anyone resists, I've authorized deadly force and I will ask the courts to impose capital punishment for anyone complicit in the death of Lalande citizens. This is being broadcast across your public communications system. If anyone decides to resist, I suggest you convince them otherwise. We control your ships and the space around this asteroid. There's no need for further bloodshed."

"I'll not surrender to the likes of you, Wallace!" Withers spat. "Wherever you got those troops, we'll wash the rocks of this asteroid with their blood!" Withers had just finished his declaration when he felt something cold and hard pressed against his temple. The click of the safety on Colonel Blenheim's sidearm was preternaturally loud next to his right ear.

"On second thought, Your Highness," said the Colonel, "we'll be accepting your offer. I'll spread the word and make sure Mr. Withers and the rest don't try anything foolish."

"Aye, you do that, 'Colonel' Blenheim," answered The Bancroft. "Gather everyone in your central dining facility. We'll have people there shortly."

***

Abishai applied a tourniquet to the leg of one of the Restoration's powered armor soldiers. His armor's med suite was dealing with the shock and keeping him from bleeding out, but he needed medical attention. *Nai'a* militia combat medics moved among the wounded, stabilizing the worst and doing what they could for lighter injuries.

Kalei had a field surgery set up in the back of an assault shuttle. She and her team had already filled the litters of one shuttle converted to carry wounded and sent it back to *Smelt It*. She was now frantically working to save the life of a soldier hit in the neck by autocannon shrapnel. Only half the powered armor troops had survived the autocannon barrage, all with severe injuries. The majority of the other wounded were victims of shrapnel and ricochets.

Shanyah's platoon stood guard duty on the captured enemy in the vacuum of the hangar. In small groups, they passed them through an airlock into the aired-up maintenance tunnels where they were divested of their armor and parked in an empty storage space by another platoon. Thanks to a textbook withdrawal under fire and the toughness of their powered armor suits, her troops were relatively unscathed. Clearing the rest of the asteroid would fall to other militia units with a full load-out of ammunition.

***

Four hours later, The Bancroft's people and *Nai'a* militia were in control of the entire asteroid except the armory. A couple of the hardcore Restoration leaders were hunkered down with the technicians operating the mobile gun platforms. The only entrance to the armory was in the main cavern with an unobstructed field of fire in all directions. The gun platforms were operating behind hasty revetments. Several attempts at taking them out from long distance had largely resulted in the gun platforms proving they outranged the militia's armament. They'd also proven to be disturbingly accurate at long range, even with the Coriolis effect cause by the asteroid's spin. A commando team was pinned down two-hundred meters in front of one revetment in a shallow depression.

Rimon Barkscale's brows furrowed as he considered the situation from behind a row a heavy excavation equipment a kilometer and a half away. "Quester and Grady, stay put!" he transmitted as another twenty-millimeter railgun round chewed up the cavern floor just beyond their position. He admired their courage, but there was no way they'd get close enough to use a satchel charge without getting turned into hamburger. The commando's other weapons were useless against what amounted to a three-legged unmanned tank. The gun platforms carried twin seven-millimeter anti-personnel gatlings in addition to the twenty-millimeter main armament.

"Do we have communications with the holdouts in the armory?" he asked his battalion executive officer.

"No, but Mr. Barboa is on the command net asking for you."

Rimon switched his com feed. "I hope you've had a flash of brilliance, Mr. Barboa, because I'm not seeing any good solutions. If we rush those platforms, we'll lose a lot of people."

"No flashes of brilliance," answered Mr. Barboa. "Just a bit of advice. Be patient, your weapons are designed for close quarters ship-board fighting. The people you're up against aren't professionals. Let them stew for a while and they'll do something stupid. While you're waiting for them to get antsy, see what surprises your troops can cook up for them if they rush your position.

"The gun platforms have a weakness. When they run, their leg joints are exposed. If you take away their mobility, the problem gets easier to solve. Remember, we can wait them out. Both the armory and their hard suits have limited environmental endurance. Let them make the first mistake."

"Thanks, Mr. Barboa," Rimon answered. "We'll see what we can come up with for a proper greeting if they come calling."

He turned to his XO. "Spread the word. We're going to wait and see if they come to us. We need some ideas on how to take them out if they rush our position. The leg joints are vulnerable. Also, we need to figure out how to protect Quester and Grady." His XO nodded and strode away to confer with the company commanders.

***

It took six hours for the holdouts to make their move. On Rimon's remote video feed the gun platforms looked like armored aliens taking great gliding leaps in an evasive pattern. He growled deep in his throat when the lead platform fired a long Gatling gun burst into Quester and Grady's position. He checked their status but the telemetry connection was down. He shook his head and focused on the enemy's rapid approach. When they hit three-hundred meters out, the line of excavators and haulers sheltering his people split in two, trundling in opposite directions. The gun platforms hesitated, and a cloud of anti-armor grenades arced toward each of them from behind the heavy equipment. The platforms surged forward again, and their gatlings attempted to sweep the grenades away. By sheer numbers a few got through, firing their shaped charges into the platforms. The platform's armor shrugged the attack off and they kept coming, one toward the left column of vehicles and two toward the right. They fired their twenty-millimeter rail guns as they came, riddling the excavators and haulers until they ground to a halt.

Rimon switched his tactical feed to his fourth back up remote to get eyes-on the gun platforms. What he saw told him the timing wouldn't get any better. "Execute!" he sent over the tactical net. The battalion's remaining combat centipede remotes swarmed forward from under the ruined vehicles, heading straight for the gun platforms just a hundred meters away. All three platforms opened up with their gatlings, rising to maximum height to shoot down into the swarm. As they attempted to chew through the centipedes, Rimon and the rest of the militia rose up from trenches and poured fire with everything they had into the legs of all three mechs for exactly one half second, then dropped back into cover. The hail of flechettes, armor piercing slugs from multi-mode rifles and anti-armor grenades knocked all three mechs off their feet with mobility kills, but the weapons were still active. A few surviving centipedes continued their attack runs, and one managed to deliver an EMP strong enough to knock out the rail gun on the closest platform.

Rimon sent the positions of each platform via the tactical net, designating them Alpha, Bravo and Charlie. "Anti-armor grenade salvo on alpha, on my mark, three...two...one...mark." Grenades arced up from the trenches. Once again, the platforms' gatlings spoke, taking out half the salvo. The remaining grenades were enough to reduce alpha platform to wreckage. Two more salvos silenced Bravo and Charlie. "Alpha Company, you have point," Rimon ordered. Forward at combat intervals." The battalion rose from their trenches and loped forward toward the armory bunker.

Rimon followed Alpha Company closely with his command team. They were just a few hundred meters from the objective when a pile of loose rubble seemed to rise from the cavern floor. Rimon nearly jumped out of his skin, but checked his fire as Quester and Grady shook the loose sand and rocks from their commando suits. They staggered toward the command team. "Status, Quester?" Rimon sent. His tactical display showed them again, both amber.

"Battered, but we'll live," Quester answered. "We slow-crawled to where we could cover ourselves with rubble from the previous shots, then went EMCON silent when they made their move. They missed us, but not by much."

"You took three years off my life turning your telemetry off, but I'm not complaining about the results," growled Rimon. "Get yourselves to the aid station." He loped off after Alpha company, command staff in tow. By the time he caught up, Alpha company sappers had blown the armory hatch off its hinges. Three hard-suited figures with their hands up came staggering out of the armory through the dust. They only made it a few meters before a hail of fire from an overhead turret inside the doorway knocked them to the cavern floor. Immediate fire from Alpha company's heavy weapons soon silenced the turret, and a squad moved forward under covering fire. They sent a fusillade of flash-bang grenades into the bunker then moved by fire teams into the interior. Within a few minutes, the squad leader gave the all-clear.

Rimon entered the bunker to find his troops applying emergency patches to the hard suits of two figures pinned to the floor. He strode over to one, noting the pained look on the man's face behind the visor and failing to dredge up any sympathy. "Stabilize them and turn them over to the system authorities."

The squad leader looked up, "Yes sir! This one was trying to rig a grenade trap but only managed to blow his own hand off. Thanks be for incompetent enemies."

Rimon left the bunker then put in a call to The Bancroft. His heads-up display showed the monarch in an unfamiliar room bustling with people. "We've cleared the armory, Your Highness. We have two wounded enemy and three killed by their own people."

"Well done!" replied Wallace. "We've turned their gymnasium into a field hospital and morgue. Send the prisoners and bodies there. What about your people?"

"All accounted for," answered Rimon. "We're transporting a few wounded troops back to the hangar. We took a lot of shrapnel damage but our armor held up well."

"I followed the fight with the gun platforms," said The Bancroft. "I'm grateful beyond words that the price wasn't higher."

"If they had enabled the AIs on those platforms, it would have been higher," answered Rimon. I knew humans were driving the guns when they hesitated. An AI would have processed the movement of the heavy equipment and attacked instantly."

"Your battalion's job here is done," said Wallace. "You can shuttle to *Smelt It* when you're ready, but I'd like to confer with you here if you have time. I'm set up in their main dining facility."

"Aye sir," answered Rimon. "My executive officer can take over here. I'll be there shortly."

***

The dining facility was still bustling when Rimon arrived, escorted by two of his armored troops. The living space passages weren't sized for troops in powered armor, but they managed to squeeze their way through. Mr. Barboa greeted him and led him to a corner where The Bancroft had his command post set up. The Bancroft returned his salute and motioned to a pile of sandwiches on the table between them. "Help yourself," he said. "These are from the *Nai'a's* mess crew."

Rimon closed his visor then unsealed and removed his helmet. He picked up a sandwich, took a large bite and chewed thoughtfully, "Hmm, pastrami with muenster cheese, honey mustard, mayo, and thin-sliced pickle on rye. These are Abishai's pickles, the crunch is unmistakable. This sure beats combat concentrates."

"Aye," answered The Bancroft. "I noticed the pickles. You people eat uncommonly well. What's Abishai's secret?"

"No secret, though he keeps a few when it comes to recipes," said Rimon. "These are fermented in brine instead of canned in vinegar. The cucumbers don't get cooked by the canning process so they stay super crunchy. It's just like Abishai to donate a batch to the mess for this operation. I'm sure you didn't ask me here to talk about pickles, though."

"Just so," answered Wallace wrinkling his brow. "I need a caretaker crew for this asteroid. I don't want to leave it undefended, and there are some repairs needed. I don't have the people to do it and can't spare troops. I conferred with Captain Bielling. She said I could ask you for volunteers if you feel comfortable with it. Can you leave a platoon or two here for the next month?"

Rimon rubbed his stubbly jaw. "I'm inclined to make it a company so they have their internal support structure in place. You'd also have more people to assist the repair crew. I'm not going to order anyone to do it, but I'm reasonably sure I'll get volunteers."

"To encourage your volunteers, the stay-behinds will get a double stake in this facility. I'm turning it over to my sister who'll convert the operation into a government supervised corporation. It's well positioned to become a shipyard for our own long boat program. Everyone on the *Nai'a* will get a stake since you helped us take it from the Restoration. We'll get them back to you before the *Nai'a* leaves the system."

"I may stay behind myself!" Rimon laughed. "I'm sure we'll get your volunteers."

"Relay my thanks to your combat medical team. They saved a lot of lives. These people are rebels, but they're also Lalande citizens. On that subject, I need to have a talk with the chief culprit." The Bancroft slapped Rimon on his armored shoulder and strode off with four crown guards clearing his path. Rimon grabbed another sandwich. Eating with powered armored gauntlets was one of the first skills he had mastered in the suit. The only one in the militia battalion better at it was Abishai.

***

Shanyah walked through her platoon, helping with minor repairs here and there. He soldiers had commandeered a workshop in the pressurized tunnels off the main hangar to rest and recuperate while they waited for a ride back to *Smelt It*. She was pleased and relieved that both her people and their equipment had come through the day as well as they had. She said another prayer of thanks while moving to the next trooper. A few minutes later she received a PCOM alert with a message from Rimon, relaying The Bancroft's offer and instructing militia platoon leaders to survey their people for volunteers. She conferred briefly with Abishai, who bellowed "AT EASE!" to get everyone's attention.

The low chatter immediately stopped, and Shanyah hopped onto a workbench so she could see everyone. "Listen up, Ship Rats! I'm sure most of you have seen all of this asteroid you want to, but The Bancroft made us a generous offer." She proceeded to lay out the details. "You need to make a decision and register your preference by PCOM. I have a meeting with the battalion commander in 15 minutes. Get it done by then."

All but a few of the militia members eventually volunteered for a temporary assignment to the asteroid. Rimon decided to leave an ad hoc company, pulling no more than one platoon from each of the *Nai'a's* habitat sections. He made sure the stay-behinds had plenty of people with technical skills to help with repairs.

***

The Bancroft swept into the cleared office they were using for on interrogation room and looked Lewis Withers up and down coldly where he was secured to a metal chair. "You've cost this system in the blood of my people and I've no sympathy for you, or your ilk," he stated flatly. "I want to know everything about the Restoration, and how it corrupted this system, so I'll offer one more time to spare your life. Tell us what you know and my prosecutors won't ask the courts for the death penalty. Refuse, and I'll demand it."

"You can take your offer and choke on it!" spat Withers.

"I thought that's how you'd feel," answered The Bancroft, nodding. He motioned to one of his investigators who placed a holo projector on the table between the two men. Shortly a video of Lewis' nephew Nicholas talking to Rolland Dunleavy began to play. As the man he considered a son matter-of-factly laid out the Restoration's organization and goals, Lewis Withers slowly wilted in his chair.

Chapter 25 – New Beginnings and Old Ties

April 4th, AD 3208
Lalande System, New Dawn Orbit
Long Boat Nai'a Boat Bay

Jarman Lal ushered the Driscolls into the *Nai'a's* pinnace, barely able to keep a grin off his face. "What's this all about?" asked Anthea for the dozenth time, exasperation clear in her expression and tone.

"Patience," said Jarman. "You remind me of my sister. She couldn't stand suspense either." Anthea's parents both smiled. They had no better idea than Anthea why they were here. Alexander Driscoll took the copilot seat while his wife and Anthea strapped into jump seats at the back of the cockpit. Once the boat bay officer cycled the atmosphere and gave them a green light, Jarman expertly eased the pinnace out of the boat bay. New Dawn floated, big and beautiful, off the port side, blue seas and white clouds a testament to the planet's potential. Lalande's ruddy light gave the planet a dream-like rose tint.

"We've seen New Dawn before," said Anthea. "I hope this isn't a sight-seeing trip." Jarman just lifted one eyebrow at her then swung the pinnace around toward the *Nai'a's* bow. Midway down the ten-kilometer length of the gleaming long boat, a silver speck hung in space. As they approached, the speck resolved into a very familiar shape. "The *Suncatcher*!" shouted Anthea, unbuckling so she could get a better view.

"Well," said Jarman, "a reasonable approximation, anyway. You've got a new cockpit with an upgraded navcomp and the drive section is from the Plucky Penguin. Nils Sinterman left you the ship in his will. Your hab section is the same, though, and you'll find most of the possessions you left behind still there. We cleaned out the mess Roach and his partner left."

Anthea impulsively grabbed Jarman by the neck and kissed him on the cheek, then hugged her mother and father in turn. All three Driscolls were misty-eyed as Jarman skillfully brought the pinnace alongside the *Suncatcher* and initiated the docking sequence. Once the airlock telltale turned green, Jarman unstrapped. "Let's go inspect your ship!" he said.

Anthea led them out of the airlock and soon they heard her exclaiming as she reclaimed her personal treasures from the sleeping cabin she had been sharing with her father. She exclaimed again when she saw her own newly painted and decorated cabin.

"I don't know how to thank you," said Alexander to Jarman. "I also don't know how we're going to pay for this." His wife was in the cockpit busily scrolling through the menu of the new navcomp.

"Your share of the prize money easily covered the parts and materials," Jarman answered. "You'll find you have a nice stake left over to get you started on whatever you want to do next."

"What about the labor?"

"Donated by the crew of the *Nai'a*," said Jarman. "We don't get the chance to work on ships like yours much. For me, it was a chance to relive a happy part of my youth. When we're done here, we have a meeting with Captain Brelling. She has a proposal for your shakedown cruise with the new *Suncatcher*."

A few hours later, Captain Brelling welcomed Alexander and Crinea Driscoll to her day cabin, serving them coffee and Kouign-Aman pastries at a small table. She kept the conversation light until they were past the finger-licking stage, then she set her cup down and leaned back. "I'm very much enjoying your company, but I should get to the reason I asked you to join me. I don't know you as well as I would like, but I trust Shanyah and Abishai's judgment and they vouch for you.

"I'll start by saying you don't owe us anything. In reality we feel an obligation toward you because you got caught between us and the Restoration. We need someone to replace the Long Boat Free Trade Syndicate Buoy destroyed by the Restoration. I would like to hire you and your ship to do the job. The buoy's location needs to be kept secret, so we'll be placing a great deal of trust in you if you decide to take the job. I would normally use my own crew and lease a ship, but we don't have time to wait and the geometry doesn't work. The Bancroft is well on his way to cleaning the system up, but there's still an element of danger. The Restoration may still have operatives out there who would try to stop you. We'll pay full insurance and double the normal cargo rates for the run. Are you interested?"

Crinea and Alexander exchanged a long look. "You may not think we owe you anything," Crinea stated, "but we *are* thankful for all you and your crew have done for us. We also have a score to settle with the Restoration, though, and this job will make a nice down payment. We'd do it for free, but we'll take your generous offer and, hopefully, get our small mining collective back on its feet. Losing the *Amphitrite* was a big hit, but there's going to be a strong demand for refined metals from The Bancroft's long boat program. We and the other families think we can make a go of it."

"I'm sure you can," said the captain, nodding. "The Bancroft intends to auction off all the seized assets of the Restoration. The funds will be used to pay reparations to victims of the rebellion, including you. This is separate from the prize money coming out of the battle you were in. You may find an opportunity to pick up a replacement for your refining ship at a reasonable cost through the auctions and get a bump in your bank account. Before you go, our CEO will have one of his people sit down with you and go over the contract. You'll be doing a great service for the trade syndicate. We won't forget it. I'll make sure the local office puts your mining collective on its list of preferred local sources."

***

A crisply liveried host escorted Rolland Dunleavy and Anne Brelling to a secluded private table and informed them of Chef Forti's evening's special. "I'd avoid the clams, if I were you." Rolland said after he left. "I had them once and they had the consistency of elastic bands. Everything else is excellent."

"Thanks for the warning," answered Anne. "I wasn't tempted by the special. Ever since you told me about their tacos al pastor, I've been dreaming about trying them." She perused the menu. "There's a little something for all tastes here."

"The story goes that the original Chef Forti had Mexican, Italian, Irish, and Argentinean ancestors. He decided to feature an eclectic menu with those and other influences, focusing on authenticity. It's a formula that's worked well for several centuries. This restaurant predates the ascendance of Uriah Bancroft. I doubt even the Restoration would have messed with Chef Forti's."

Anne grinned. "I won't ask what this meal will cost, but I'm glad you're footing the bill."

An excellent dinner was followed by equally good coffee and crumbly jam-filled alfajores. Rolland closed his eyes and sighed. "It's been too long since I had a meal like that."

"I've never had a meal like that," replied Anne. "It's definitely been too long coming. It's too bad we didn't get a chance to come here during my first stop in the system."

"I wouldn't have been able to afford it," Rolland answered, smiling wistfully, then his expression grew serious. "I know we agreed not to talk shop, but I need to tell you what The Bancroft asked me to do today. He wants to appoint me as a temporary ambassador to the Sol system and send me with the *Nai'a* to back you in the inevitable conflict with the Restoration." He watched Anne's expression carefully to gauge her reaction.

Anne considered his statement for a few moments. "I'll need all the help I can get," she said. "Tau Ceti's representative should already be in system when we arrive. It will be a battle fought in the political arena. Did you accept?"

"I told him I needed to think about it. He wasn't too happy, but Himself needs his will thwarted occasionally to foster his remaining shred of humility. I'm one of the few people who can get away with it. You've managed to take him down several notches, and I thank you for it." Rolland seemed to gather himself then looked her in the eye. "I have an offer for you I should have made a long time ago. I let duty and circumstances stop me. Now, duty and circumstances allow me to correct my mistake. Will you marry me, Anne Brelling?"

An icy shock went through Anne. She felt her emotions vacillate wildly from hope-fulfilled joy to abject fear and back again. She realized her mouth was hanging open and closed it with a snap. Rolland was watching her with a healthy dose of trepidation in his own expression. Decades as captain of the *Nai'a* had prepared her for anything but this. Rolland's eyes grew wider and wider as she struggled to organize her thoughts. "But...I can't just...," suddenly she realized this was what she wanted more than anything and she was acting like a giddy schoolgirl. "What am I saying? YES!" Rolland smiled brightly as she slid over to him and kissed him soundly. "Oh!" Anne said, wiping her eyes. "You nearly did me in. I've been hoping, praying we could somehow make something work, at the same time not daring to hope too much."

Rolland fished a small box out of a jacket pocket and handed it to her. "I hope I got your size right. It took some seriously underhanded spy work to get it." Anne opened the box to see a gold ring with an oval stone striated in shades of deep and light green. She slipped it on her finger and held it up to look at it. "It's New Dawn malachite," said Rolland. "What do you think?"

"It's beautiful and fits just right," Anne replied, resting her head on his shoulder. "This time I'm not letting you get away."

***

Commander Hartley's face turned a whiter shade of pale. Processing Captain Brelling's twin bombshells was going to take him a minute or two.

"You'll have to stand for election to make it official," said the captain, "but with my support, the CEO's, and the Chief Alder's, I think you'll pass muster with the crew. We all have confidence you'll make a fine captain, Kevin. You can get a little practice in as acting CO while I'm on my short honeymoon, then we'll hold the change of command and make it official before we break orbit for Sol."

"Couldn't this wait until we finish the Sol run?" the first officer asked. "I'm not sure I'm ready."

"I sympathize with you," said the captain. "I felt the same way. The captain's seat shouldn't feel too comfortable for anyone, but you know the crew as well as I do, possibly better. They'll have your back and I know you'll have theirs.

"There are three main reasons I can't wait on passing command to you. First, I'm the captain who took the *Nai'a* into a sovereign system armed to the teeth. I'll have to answer for that, but more to the point, the *Nai'a* can *not* be seen as a threat entering Sol. We'll be able to sell the story better if I'm not at the helm. Second, I need the time and space away from being captain to prepare a strategy for the Long Boat Free Trade Syndicate to deal with the Restoration's backers in the Sol system. My duties for the syndicate now take precedence over my duties as a captain. I can do one or the other well, but not both. The third reason, I admit, is selfish. I'm going to be a new bride in a few days and I want to spoil Rolland as much as possible instead of being married to a ten-kilometer ship."

Kevin nodded slowly. "Forgive me, but it still comes as a shock. I'll need a day or two to fully get my mind around the idea of being captain, much less seeing you married."

"It's been a shock to my system also," Captain Brelling admitted. "The pieces are falling into place, though, and I think this is the right path for our ship and the syndicate. We've still got some cleanup left to do with the local office and the investigative team before I hand you the reins.

Chapter 26 – Lancing the Boil

April 5th, AD 3208
Lalande System, New Dawn Orbit
Long Boat Nai'a Captain's Conference Room

Captain Brelling observed her guests carefully as they settled into seats around her conference table. Lillian Quarterman, the local syndicate office chief, was an unknown to her. According to her file, she was a Lalande citizen who had worked her way up to her current position. The well-dressed brunette returned the captain's gaze frankly, earning a small nod of acknowledgment. Chord Olley, the syndicate's investigation team lead, she knew in passing from her last visit to Sol. The chunky man seemed competent enough, but he looked distinctly uncomfortable.

"I'm glad you finally decided to meet with us, Captain," Lillian began. "I know you've been busy, but I would think you'd want a full briefing from the local office and the investigative team as soon as you reached orbit. I would have been glad to host you at our offices, as I communicated several times."

"Yes," said the captain, tapping a stylus lightly on the table. "I apologize for putting you off. The local situation, as you know, is still unstable. It's improved though, and I have enough of my people back on board to be more confident of our security. What I'm not confident of is your security." Both of her guests looked indignant, but she held up a hand to forestall their protests. "The Restoration knows how to infiltrate an organization. They infiltrated my crew, the home office in Sol, the syndicate office in Tau Ccti, your office, Lillian, and your investigative team, Chord."

"I suppose you have proof of this?" Lillian asked archly.

In response Captain Brelling nodded to Lisandra Redding. The hacker turned cybersecurity officer activated the room's display and brought up the record of several substantial financial transactions with names of the recipients highlighted. "Do you recognize any of those names?" the captain asked.

Lillian's eyes went wide as she ran down the list; Chord just shook his head in disgust. "When the trail ran cold here," he said, "I had a lot of suspicions, but nothing to go on. Now I know why. A third of my team is on the Restoration payroll. They made sure we didn't find anything incriminating. I should have suspected."

"They aren't on the Restoration payroll any longer," said Captain Brelling. "Lalande law enforcement is picking the people on this list up as we speak. The local office employees will face The Bancroft's justice system. The members of the syndicate investigation team will be coming back to Sol with us. Their consequences will depend on their level of cooperation. Lillian, you have some holes to fill. I suggest you do it quickly so we can assist you in vetting your new hires."

Lillian nodded; her expression still sour. "I'm surprised you're not firing me. I can't believe how riddled with moles my office is."

"There's no indication you're guilty of anything worse than Chord or I," said the captain. "You trusted people you shouldn't have. Let's all try to learn our lesson and be wiser for it. I arranged for replacement of the trade syndicate buoy and reprogrammed the security protocols and positioning of the others. I'm fairly certain your office was the source of the leak that allowed the Restoration to take one of them out. Before we leave the system, we'll update your office on the new measures, but I want you to get your house in order first." Lillian relaxed a little, but was clearly embarrassed.

"My team's orders are to return with you to Sol if the situation here in Lalande is sufficiently resolved," stated Chord. "I'm not certain it is, and I need your advice."

"Kevin will give you a full update to get you both up to speed. I'm confident we can leave the pursuit of what's left of the Restoration in Lalande to The Bancroft. In a few weeks we'll have our militia all back on board and Hubble will have our cargo and passengers for Sol sorted. Kevin will stand for election as captain of the *Nai'a* in a few days, and I'm getting married. Chord, I'm going to need you and your team to help me sort through the data that Lisandra and the Bancroft's investigators give us. By the time we get to Sol, we need to have an iron-clad case for prosecuting the Restoration and its supporters in the home system. It's going to be a monumental task."

A few hours later, Chord and Lillian were on their way back to the local office, Commander Hartley was reviewing resumes, and the captain was left alone with Lisandra Redding. "Lisandra, you need to make a choice," said the captain. "For a number of selfish reasons, I hope you stay with us, but you're still a wanted person in the Sol system. I'll do whatever I can, but I don't know if we can protect you from the consequences of your past life. You might be better off staying here with your family."

Lisandra chuckled wryly, "The things I'm best at seem to make me persona non grata in every system we visit. Are you sure The Bancroft would let me stay?"

"If I twist his arm he will. He owes me, and he owes you. If he can't see that, I'm willing to open his eyes for him."

"Belle is an adult and can make her own decisions now," replied Lisandra. "I love that girl so much I don't know what I'd do without her, though. She, Hal, and I all see the *Nai'a* as home. I don't think we'll jump ship to avoid what Sol may have in store for me. Also, I've been thinking about some ways I might make amends. I can't do that from Lalande."

The captain nodded, "It's your decision, but Kevin and I will both be very glad if you stay. My investigation will benefit, and the ship will definitely fare better in the lively cyber environment back in Sol. I won't ask you to do anything in the Sol system but defend and protect the ship from cyber-attacks."

"There's another reason I should stick with the ship," said Lisandra, her brow furrowing. "You know Pete Worsley, Greer Kensing, and I are monitoring Mr. Literal's self-programming and maintenance. He's the most proactive artificial intelligence I've ever worked with. We all agree he's well short of classically defined sentience, but he's making steady progress in that direction. There have been some really bad incidents with AIs 'waking up'. I want to help Greer shepherd him along so we don't have an event like that. I'm confident in Mr. Literal's core priorities and fail-safes, but we still need to keep a close watch on his growing capabilities. The real problems are usually caused by conflicting priorities, kind of like a human being."

Captain Brelling chuckled. "Yes, and humans aren't particularly programmable."

Chapter 27 – Fresh Start

April 20th, AD 3208
Lalande System, New Dawn Orbit
Bancroft Habitat, State Chapel

Anne Brelling (she could now think of herself as Anne, instead of "The Captain") stared down the central aisle of Lalande's state chapel, hardly able to believe the number of people crammed into the space. Rolland Dunleavy, in his full-dress uniform, stood waiting at the end of the aisle with a wide grin on his face. It seemed Rolland was a much more important and beloved figure in Lalande than he had admitted. The citizens and The Bancroft weren't allowing one of their favorite sons to get married and leave without a proper sendoff. The ceremony was being broadcast across the system. So much for the quiet, private affair they had both talked about. Her crew had been just as bad, insisting on contributing to the big to-do. She squared her shoulders and started down the aisle with Pete Worsley, wearing a tuxedo she hadn't even known he owned, keeping her steady. She'd faced down a lot worse than a church full of people; surely she could get through a wedding ceremony without fainting. The strains of a Welsh hymn accompanied her firm steps.

***

Captain Hartley (the rank still felt strange only two days into command) sat in the captain's chair on the bridge and contemplated the many things needing his attention. He had been surprised to win the election for captain handily, even though he was the only one put forward. The only votes not cast for him were a handful of write-ins for Pete Worsley. Ex-Captain Brelling, and now merely Long Boat Free Trade Syndicate Ambassador

Brelling, told him her election had gone exactly the same way. Apparently, there was an unofficial underground campaign to get Pete in the captain's seat. Pete would have refused the honor in any case, but the movement wouldn't die.

Now, Anne Brelling and her new husband were taking a brief honeymoon in one of the New Dawn dome cities with an ocean view. The ball was firmly in Captain Kevin Hartley's court. He reviewed the passenger and cargo manifests on his personal monitor. As expected, they had enough cold sleep passengers to outnumber the crew. Yuna Ashworth, he knew, was hovering like a mother hen over the operation, but her former assistant, Patrick, was now the cold sleep director. Between the two of them and their team, he knew they would get all the passengers safely tucked into their vaults.

Hubble Spearsley had done his usual masterful job of squeezing every bit of profit he could out the crossing and setting them up for a good payday in Sol. Lalande produced a good deal of unique artwork and digital entertainment, as well as a number of rare earth elements uncommon in the Sol system. Hubble already had a deal in place to sell all the sting ships and capital ship missiles to the Lalande System Security Force. They would hand those off to a system security collier at heliopause. Despite a generous crew share payout for the trip, or perhaps because of it, a higher than usual percentage of the crew had decided to stay in Lalande. The system was even more wide open with opportunities than Tau Ceti for those with a financial stake to get them started. The Bancroft had also poached as many people as he could manage to help jumpstart his own long boat construction program.

The local syndicate office had pitched in with a will to help the recruiting effort for replacements. Their efforts had yielded what looked like a good crop of new crewmembers. Getting everyone settled in and integrated with the crew was going to be the most important part of the first few years of this crossing. Fortunately, he had Chief of Boat Oswald and

Chief Alder Persephone Belotic still in place to spearhead the effort. One of the bigger holes in the organization was chief engineer. Owen Halsey was now the director of the Lalande Long Boat Building Program. Captain Hartley couldn't blame him for taking the opportunity, but breaking in a newly promoted captain, first officer, and chief engineer was asking a lot of a long boat crew.

Before he left for his new job, Owen had supervised installation of the re-formed ice shield. Despite the beating the double-thick shield had taken in the crossing and battle, it still had plenty of mass to provide water for a standard thickness shield and surplus H2O to sell to the locals. His new command felt both exhilarating and daunting. He only prayed he could live up to the responsibility.

***

Abishai looked over the long table groaning under the weight of food set out for the farewell celebration. He was going to miss the Driscolls, especially Anthea. The other mining families were good people too. It was time for them all to get back to work, but not without a good send-off. Shanyah sidled up beside him and took his arm. "No sampling!" she warned.

"The thought never crossed my mind!" protested Abishai.

"I'll settle for the food not crossing your lips!" Shanyah answered. "Let's go talk to the Driscolls and get your thoughts off poaching." They walked over to where Anthea and Brin were mutually admiring two bouncy, grey-striped balls of fluff vainly trying to pin down Lionel's tail. Their parents smiled with amusement while Lionel did his best to look bored with it all. The kittens were cuter than words could tell and genetically close enough to Lionel to be young cousins.

"Are you sure they'll be good rodent control?" asked Alexander Driscoll. "They don't come across as alpha hunter types." The kittens paid no attention, content with their wrestling match with Lionel and petting from Anthea and Brin.

"They'll grow into it," said Abishai. "Lionel is sudden death on the hunt and females are usually even better than males. You have one of each, so you should be set."

"They'll live on our new processing mothership, the *Amphitrite* II," said Alexander. "The kids will get to spoil them by turns and they can beat the stuffing out of each other when they aren't chasing mice.

"Your captain was right about the auction - we were able to pick up a bulk-hauler cheap and fit her out for ore processing. She has a nifty hab-ring that spins up to .5G, so we can keep our muscle tone up and cook, even when she's holding station. There's room for hydroponics too. We'll be able to plant some of the seeds from the vault you gave us, and use the rest for trade and gifts."

"I almost envy you the start of your new enterprise and the challenges ahead," said Abishai, "but I could have done without the challenges we've faced lately. All the best to you and your family, we'll miss you."

"We'll miss you too," said Alexander. "I hope the *Nai'a* comes back through here somewhere down the line. I hear that plate of ham puffs calling me. Is it time to eat?"

"It's always time to eat!" Abishai replied with a grin. "I'll say thanks and we can get started."

After the meal, Shanya sat with Kalei, an arm around her shoulders. "You had to deal with the results of the violence on the asteroid. How are you doing?" she asked.

"Mostly okay, she answered, "getting back to patients like Brin and Alexander helps,". "I'll be happy to never have that kind of pressure on me again. I lost three patients on the operating table in the space of an hour. I can still see their faces. Dr. Rensaleer says no one could have saved them, but I still feel like I should have."

"You did save over a dozen others," her mother said. "Keep that in mind. This isn't a burden you should carry alone. Talk to me, talk to your father, talk to other militia members. Everyone is carrying their own load of guilt and grief after the fight, but we have each other."

"Mishael didn't participate in the fighting. At least he doesn't have the kinds of images the rest of us will carry."

"He helped with your patients when they got to the *Smelt It*. He does have memories to deal with, and the guilt of not participating in the combat. Lord willing, we'll get out of this system and on our way to Sol without any more need for the militia to suit up. What we did helped free this system of an evil organization. We can be thankful we didn't pay a bigger price."

"You're right," said Kalei. "I should talk to Mishael. We used to share everything with each other, and I miss that. It will be good for both of us."

***

Three days later Captain Hartley, Rolland Dunleavy, and Anne Brelling sat down with The Bancroft and his sister in his private chambers. "I've no wish to see you gone so soon," Wallace said after greeting them, "but I know you have business in Sol and no reason to sit idle here in Lalande. The Restoration is either dead, in custody, or on the run. They shouldn't give you any trouble on the way out of the system. I understand, however, why you'll keep the sting ships and missiles until you're well away.

"We owe you much. I can promise as long as I'm alive and in The Bancroft's chair, Lalande will be a free trading system and a friend to the Long Boat Free Trade Syndicate. Rolland carries my authority with him, for what it's worth in the Sol system. We'll back you one hundred percent against the Restoration."

"Thank you, Wallace," said Anne Brelling. "Tau Ceti pledged the same. I believe we have enough evidence to get the powers that be in Sol to come down hard on those involved. I'm grateful you've allowed us to bring Nicholas Withers along. He has firsthand knowledge of what the organization looked like when we left Sol and is willing to testify. In person testimony will carry a lot more weight than a deposition."

"Aye, the man's crimes were against your crew and ship anyway. You're welcome to him if you can stand to keep him around. His Uncle's trial starts tomorrow. I'm keeping clear of any hint of pressure on the judiciary, but we have the evidence to convict him of murder, high treason, and multiple crimes against the state."

Siobhan arched an eyebrow at him, and he nodded. "We've straightened out most of our government finances and secured a stable funding stream for the long boat project," she said. "The current emergency finally unified parliament on our need for expanded trade and connection to other systems. It's always been in the best interests of all parties to expand the economy, but sometimes it takes a shock to move people off the status quo. Your financial data on long boat profitability helped seal the deal."

Captain Hartley nodded. "I don't envy you the complications of a three-house parliament. I'm glad they saw reason. I hate to give up all our firepower, but Ambassador Brelling is right. We'll win or lose our fight with the Restoration in Sol's political chambers and court rooms. Sol Space Patrol isn't an organization anyone wants to cross swords with. I don't expect the kinds of attacks we survived here and in Tau Ceti."

"I'm pleased with the results of our cooperation, Wallace," said Anne Brelling. "Especially the gift of my co-ambassador." She gave Rolland's hand a squeeze. "I'll trust you and Lillian Quarterman to keep the cooperative momentum going forward here in Lalande. Our task is to pull the Restoration's teeth in Sol without burning every bit of good will the Long Boat Free Trade Syndicate has built up over the centuries."

Epilogue

April 27th, AD 3208
Lalande System, New Dawn Orbit
Long Boat Nai'a, Brig

Jarman Lal paused in the Ship Security corridor leading to the brig. He took stock of his mental state. He thought for the hundredth time he should have refused this meeting, but shook his head and continued on, his face a mask. He passed through the outer security door and found Abishai chatting with Pete Worsley and the guard. "What are you two doing here?" he asked with a scowl, then took a deep breath. "Sorry, I'm not in the best mood, and I'm not even sure I want to be here."

Abishai clapped him on the shoulder. "I thought you would feel that way, so I'm here for moral support if you want it."

Jarman looked thoughtful, then nodded. "As long as you acknowledge I could face him alone if I needed to."

"You wouldn't have shown up if you couldn't," said Abishai reasonably. He gestured down the corridor leading to the cells. "Shall we?"

The two made their way down the corridor and the guard unlocked the door to Nicholas Withers' cell. They entered, Jarman first. Nicholas was standing behind the small table next to his bunk. Jarman took in the figure of a man who was too much a reflection of himself, tall and spare with close-cropped dark hair. No wonder Nicholas had chosen to pass himself off as Jarman using a sophisticated facial mask. The only thing missing was a perpetual scowl. Somewhere along the way, they had both left that behind.

"Please, come in and have a seat," Withers said, gesturing to the pop-up stools across from him. He wiped his hands on his brig ship suit and sat down on his bunk. Nicholas looked nervous and Jarman felt his own spike of unwanted adrenaline as he remembered their last encounter. He forced himself to take the two steps needed to make it to right-hand stool and sat down.

Nicholas visibly gathered himself then looked Jarman in the eye. "I requested this meeting to ask for something I don't deserve. I'm sorry for using the Panic on you and forcing you to harm your ship. I have no excuse and I can't make up in any way for what I did. You have no reason to forgive me, but that's what I'm asking."

"Forgive you?" asked Jarman incredulously. "Do you have any idea what it's like being turned into someone's sock puppet? To experience fear so overpowering you can't even move? To be forced put people you care about in mortal danger? FORGIVE YOU!!??" Jarman's face grew redder and redder as he sputtered to a stop. Nicholas flinched with every question but held his gaze. Abishai put his hand on Jarman's shoulder.

"No," Nicholas' quiet answer came after a short pause. "I don't know what any of those things is like, but I know I caused them for you, and Abishai, and several other members of the crew. I said I don't deserve to be forgiven, and I believe that. What I have a hard time believing, is several people, including Abishai, have forgiven me."

Jarman looked up at Abishai. "Really?"

Abishai nodded solemnly. "Really, I told him I would forgive him for hitting me with a dose of Panic if he would forgive me for throwing him face-first into a bulkhead and breaking his neck."

Nicholas grimaced. "He had every reason to make me eat that bulkhead, so I don't think he needed me to forgive him, but I do."

"Why?" asked Jarman shaking his head. "Why are you even doing this?"

"Pete Worsley suggested it," Nicholas answered. "He said I might understand God's grace better if I see an example of grace in those that choose to forgive me. He also said it would be hard for me to ask, and even harder for my victims to forgive me, but I owe it to them to give them a chance. They...you, will be better off if you don't have to carry around a burning hatred for me the rest of your lives, even if I deserve every bit of it. It's a paltry recompense for what I've done, but the only one I can offer."

"I have crewmates that jump when they see me because of what you did while wearing my face," said Jarman, his countenance still red. "I had to rehash some of the worst moments of my life repeatedly with this gorilla." He jerked his thumb at Abishai. "Just to get to the point where I could function reliably again. What I want to do is punch you in the face."

Nicholas just nodded.

Jarman took a deep breath and blew it out. "One positive thing did come out of that experience," he continued. "I offloaded a huge load of my own anger I'd been carrying around. I had all but put you out of my mind before I got the invitation to come see you. How many of the others have you talked to?"

"Most of them," said Nicholas. "A few sent notes that they'd long since forgiven me and moved on."

"I would've thought I was in that category, but I just proved I'm not," said Jarman. "What kind of reaction did you get out the others?

"Some, like you, needed to vent," answered Nicholas. "Others were curious about my change in attitude. I can imagine why. I was an angry, self-absorbed, nasty person."

"What changed your mind? I know it wasn't a dose of Panic."

"Pete's kindness did. He had every reason to hate me and leave me to years of isolation in the brig. Instead, he refused to give up on me. He visited at least once a week and tried to encourage me. That was my last thought before going into cold sleep in Tau Ceti. What makes a person choose kindness instead of revenge? I know now, it's Pete's relationship with God. It isn't humanly possible, at least not for me."

Jarman nodded. "My story is more parallel to yours than I want to admit. Abishai, here, showed me kindness when I did everything in my power to antagonize him. It helped pull me out of a dangerous downward spiral. I know you've helped us with information about the Restoration. You can't undo what you've done, but I'll be grateful if you help us again when we get to Sol."

"I will," said Nicholas simply.

Jarman considered him for a few moments. "You have my forgiveness," he said, finally. "It isn't worth much, but you have it." Nicholas nodded again.

Abishai leaned forward. "I'm glad you've been willing to face the people you harmed and ask them to forgive you," he told Nicholas. "I'm sure Pete told you, there's someone else whose forgiveness you really need. Have you asked God?"

Nicholas looked bleak. "I don't think I can. I know I need to, but I don't deserve salvation."

"Of course you don't," said Abishai. "None of us does, God's grace, by definition, is undeserved. It's freely available to all, though, regardless of what you've done. I believe you've repented. You just need to call on the Lord in faith for salvation. I know you've read them before, but look again at John 6:37 and Romans 10:13. He's waiting for you."

Nicholas turned away. "I'll read the verses," he mumbled.

Abishai gestured to Jarman. They left the cell and the one-time saboteur to his contemplation. "Do you think he'll get there?" asked Jarman in the corridor.

"If he'll just realize he doesn't need to be worthy," answered Abishai, "I think he will. You did, after all." He clapped Jarman on the shoulder.

***

Captain Hartley reviewed his status display and nodded in satisfaction at the even rows of green. "Sensors, confirm that our course is clear of local shipping," he said.

"Aye, Captain, we have a clear departure vector."

"Coms, get me New Dawn space control," Hartley ordered.

"Aye sir, you have a live channel."

"New Dawn space control, this is the long boat *Nai'a*, requesting departure clearance."

"*Nai'a*, you have a clear lane on your registered course," came the reply. "Departure clearance granted. Safe travels!"

"It's time to go," said Captain Hartley. "Helm, you have the course and call. Engage when ready."

"Aye, Captain," replied Chief Nance. "Engines all ahead one quarter in three...two...one...engaged."

The mighty long boat *Nai'a* slid slowly out of New Dawn orbit, escorted by an honor guard of Lalande System Security ships and pointed her bow toward home.

THE END

Thank you for reading Long Boat Diplomacy! I sincerely hope you enjoyed the story. The adventures of the *Nai'a* and her crew will continue in the next book, Long Boat Homecoming. I plan to release that story in the Fall of 2025. For the latest in the Long Boat universe, visit the Long Boat Space Fans Facebook page. I'd love to hear what you think of the books, and you might find a free back story or two on your favorite characters.

Warm Regards,

Matthew H. Ambrose

About the Author:

Matthew H. Ambrose grew up devouring books and traveling to far places in his imagination. He has been a wrestler, runner, singer, soldier, husband, father, gardener, teacher, and now author (not counting hobbies). He happily resides with his wife in Huntsville, Alabama, home of the Space and Rocket Center and one of the oldest disc golf courses in the world.

www.ingramcontent.com/pod-product-compliance
Lightning Source LLC
Chambersburg PA
CBHW071245300726

48975CB00002B/550